I0614179

SARTOR

Other YA Books by Sherwood Smith

SARTOR

SHERWOOD SMITH

BOOK VIEW CAFE

BOOK VIEW CAFÉ

SARTOR
Copyright © 2012, 2025 Sherwood Smith

Book View Café Second Edition May 27, 2025
ISBN: 978-1-61138-374-4

All Rights Reserved.
This book is a work of fiction. All characters, names, locations, and events portrayed in this book are fictional or used in an imaginary manner to entertain, and any resemblance to any real people, situations, or incidents is purely coincidental.

Cover design: allenaribookcovers.etsy.com

Book View Café
304 S. Jones Blvd.
Suite #2906
Las Vegas NV 89107

www.bookviewcafe.com

PART ONE

PART ONE

ONE

"The problem with being a princess," Lilah Selenna grumped to her artist friend, Bren, "is that it sounds like more fun than it really is."

Bren shrugged, his short, skinny body expressing his complete indifference. As far as he was concerned, all royalty and nobility were evil, though he admitted that Lilah's brother Peitar, the new king, was about as good a king as you could get—if you had to have a king. But then Peitar had grown up like a normal person. He hadn't been coddled like a noble before he went and let the revolutionaries make him into a king.

Lilah went on as if Bren had urged her. "You would think it's fun to always be first going in and out of a room, but while you're walking in front of everybody, you notice how this noble girl is staring at the splotch on your skirt where you accidentally dropped a peach, or those counts are whispering about the way your hair sticks up because you forgot to brush it after you climbed down from the tree."

Lilah flicked her fingers through her short, wiry, rust-colored hair, cut during the revolution a few months past, when Lilah had disguised herself as the palace kitchen's spit boy.

Bren had shared those days of disguises and desperate actions, but he wouldn't be a prince if someone begged him. No use in saying it, so he just laughed. At least, he comforted himself, Lilah was still the same as she'd been all that terrible summer—good company, funny, equally ready for a desperate risk or a game.

"It's all this talk about duty," she went on, gazing on the peaceful lake without seeing it—while Bren fingered his chalks, trying to figure out how to capture the subtleties of those blue shades. "But I don't have any duties yet. Not while Peitar is trying to patch up the government, and the city."

"And so?" Bren asked, fingering a slate gray. Not quite. Some ripples were the gray-blue of clouds about to dump rain…

"And so it's time to keep my promise," Lilah said. "To visit the Unnamed."

"Ah-h-h-h-h." Bren let out a knowing sigh. "Then why aren't you doing it, O your great and mighty majesty? You can't be afraid that Peitar will rant and storm like an evil king at you."

"My title is 'my highness'—"

"Ha, ha, you're shorter than I am!"

"—by an ant's width. And Peitar's is 'your majesty.'" She scowled at her bare toes. Maybe it would be easier if Peitar did rant and storm. If he ranted and stormed, she could rant right back, and call him unfair, but if he was kind and sensible while counting up the perfectly reasonable reasons why she couldn't go up to the Delfina Valley to visit the Unnamed, how to answer *that?*

Maybe it was time to stop worrying about it, and go do it. She was a princess. She had a bedroom in the palace to prove it! Didn't being a princess mean you got your way at least once in a while?

She rose to her feet. Bren returned to his sketch of the lake below the palace wall as Lilah walked into the palace, ducking around parties of carpenters, joiners, and other people busy repairing the last of summer's damage.

Where would she find Peitar? Not in the public rooms, for he did crown business right after breakfast until his lunch (if he ate one). It was late in the day. He'd either be in the private interview room or his new study, which was next to the palace library. He never seemed to take time to relax. If he was not required to entertain someone, he even took his meals in that study so that he could continue working.

Lilah fumed. Peitar worked *all the time.*

The heavy, oily odor of paint made Lilah hold her nose

as she dodged around the gilders and artists painting panels.

Peitar was not in the interview room, which smelled like wet plaster as two artisans fashioned twined leaves up one of the pilasters. She poked her head into the dining room. Empty, except for the table with its white linen cloth and the gold-edged porcelain plates she'd had to stack during her time as a kitchen boy.

Lilah ran down the marble hall to the library. She dashed through the quiet room, pausing at the closed door to the annex. Uh oh. That had to mean Peitar was inside. Studying. Again.

Lilah opened the door, looked in, and there he was, only he wasn't studying. He'd fallen asleep, his head down on his crossed arms, which were cradled around an old book.

She stared. Sometimes she felt like *she* was the nineteen-year-old and *he* was twelve.

"Peitar," she exclaimed. "Don't you *ever* rest?"

Peitar's head jerked up, and they stared at one another, both startled.

Peitar blinked the sleep out of his eyes and kept his retort behind shut lips. Lilah was a child. She had never wanted to be part of government, even as decoration. Even if she wanted to, how could he unload half his responsibilities onto her—responsibilities she was unaware of?

"Lilah," Peitar began.

"I need to keep my promise to You-Know-Who," she said quickly. "*Please* don't tell me all the reasons why I can't."

She watched anxiously for the averted face of refusal, the narrowed gaze that would mean he was doing exactly what she hoped he wouldn't. Instead, she was amazed when Peitar's expression blanked. Then color tinged his thin cheeks.

"To visit You-Know-Who," she said, to be extra clear, because sometimes Peitar might look at you, but his mind would be far beyond the stars.

And it was dangerous to name her. It was even dangerous to say her nickname, Atan. For You-Know-Who was none other than Yustnesveas Landis, the last of the Landis family who had ruled Sartor, the oldest country since humans had come to the world. She, Lilah sometimes thought, was a *real* princess.

Not many things could make a revolution seem small, but Sartor and its problems was one of those things. There were spells so powerful that saying certain names could somehow draw the sinister attention of Norsunder. Atan's name was one of those.

Peitar often looked vague, as if his mind was in another world entirely, especially after being woken up. But Lilah had all his attention now.

She could not define the expression in his dark eyes, except that it was anything but vague. She began babbling. "You told me yourself how important it is to keep promises to friends, and we're friends, me and the Unnamed, and I did make that promise to go and report how the revolution ended. Not that uh, the person of whom we speak would not know already, because of, um, the other person who teaches the Unnamed. They know more than I do, I'm sure. And it's not like those promises you have to keep, though I do, but I also want to, because, you know, we're friends—"

Peitar raised a hand.

Lilah stopped talking so fast her teeth clicked.

Peitar's smile was brief and a little crooked. "We both made a friend," he said. "But you are fortunate in being able to visit. I am not."

He regretted the words as soon as they were out, then reflected that Lilah's mind would go straight to duty. As his ought to!

She gawked at him, honest and bewildered. "But you're the *king*. You can do *anything you want*."

"Not quite. You'll remember our uncle ended up with a revolting populace because enough people didn't like what he was doing." Peitar tried to be honest, for truth was important to him. But there were times when it was better to choose possible truths; nevertheless, he shifted his gaze away from Lilah's wide, innocent gaze and began to straighten his books, a task that seemed to absorb all his attention. Finally he spoke. "You should probably go very soon, before the snows close the mountains in." Then he gave her a real smile, more like the brother she knew. "How long was I asleep? I'd better warn you, Aunt Tislah showed up for another visit. She has her neighbor's great-niece in tow."

Lilah jumped indignantly. "Another would-be queen?

She might be very nice, but I am *not* going to sit by while Aunt Tislah tries to kill us with disgusting matchmaking."

"Death by flirtation?" Peitar murmured.

"Bren and I will make certain there is *no* threat of romance to ruin dinner." She made a gag face. "Let me see if I can tear him away from drawing." She ran out.

The number of former revolutionaries roaming around looking for trouble had considerably lessened, in part due to Peitar's new rule that roaming gangs who did not seem to have work would have work found for them, and there was plenty of cleaning and rebuilding to be done, at guild-set wages. Overseen by the guilds.

Still, he sent an escort with Lilah to Diannah Wood, as everyone knew that the place was uncanny. It was a peaceful journey, though not boring. Too much memory of danger and shared laughter to keep the threat at bay; Lilah recognized places they had hidden, or camped. She wished any of her friends had wanted to come, but they were all busy doing the things they had longed to do, once the threat was over.

The forest guardians saw her safely to the southern border, which was where Diannah Wood crowded up against the mountains. Here was another memory, the four of them wary and worried that the spells wouldn't work.

She climbed a grassy ridge until she could see over the treetops of the forest, and then made the magical sign. She breathed deeply as her body tingled, then lightened in that extraordinary way, so that she felt as light as a cloud — and then she took that glorious first jump, straight into the air.

How she adored flying!

As Peitar had warned, many of the familiar sky-touching peaks now wore blue-white mantles gleaming in the sun. The ancient flight magic kept her warm as she sped up and up over the vast mountain ranges. She veered as much as the spell permitted, swooping high over cliffs and skimming the tops of whispering pines until the spell drew her inexorably into the Valley of Delfina, which long ago had been a hidden retreat for mages. She gazed down at the deep blue waters of the lake, around which cottages had been built on plateaus and cliff ledges.

She glanced toward family's old home as she drifted down to the tree-secluded dwelling tucked against the side of a wooded slope, until she landed lightly. The moment the flying-magic relinquished her, the cold wind of impending winter closed in with unforgiving chill and she shivered, glad of her sturdy cotton-wool robe.

It was so strange to be back. There was no sign here of all the drastic changes that had taken place just a few days' travel to the north. Even stranger was the fact that she had a friend like... At least she could *think* her name, right here, ten paces in front of the cottage where she'd been hidden for fifteen years: Atan. That much protection the mage Tsauderei had been able to extend.

Lilah shivered again. She, ordinary Lilah, a princess for barely two months, friends with the last descendant of the famous, powerful Landis family who had ruled Sartor for nearly four thousand years! Four *thousand* years — since the time when Old Sartor had been destroyed and human life nearly eradicated by the mages of Norsunder. Who knows? Maybe the Landis family had even existed *before* those mysterious days!

There were no royal parents now. There was no royal Sartoran court, or retainers, or heralds. There was no Sartor, for it had vanished behind that horrible enchantment beyond the western mountains for nearly a hundred years.

Lilah's life had seemed pretty exciting until she thought about that. She laughed at herself, gave her best robe a tug, tried to flatten down her thatch of hair, then wondered why she was fussing. Atan's princess wardrobe had seemed to consist of cast-off clothes belonging to some old hermit mage.

And while Lilah marched up the path toward the Hermit's Cottage hidden among the tall trees, Atan was thinking how delightful it was to have a visitor.

She turned from the little window to face the elderly mage, her guide and tutor. "Lilah is back!" Then she laughed. "And of course you knew that."

Tsauderei's mouth twisted. "Of course. Nobody gets into the Valley without my knowing. Or out." His bristly white brows twitched upward.

Atan's cheeks burned. Tsauderei had cautioned her many times against the risk of flying to the border and staring down into the cloud-shrouded, blighted land that lay below.

But Sartor was *hers*. There could be no peace for her until Sartor was free — or she died trying to make it so.

Her nursemaid-guardian, Gehlei, had flown over to the main village to buy fresh food. Gehlei hated it when Atan talked about Sartor and the enchantment, so the time to bring it up was now, with Gehlei away.

Though she'd meant to come around to it gradually, Atan blurted, "I think it's time to make my try."

"Yes," Tsauderei answered.

Atan gazed in shock at the mage's lined, sardonic face. Her carefully-thought-out arguments vanished like smoke.

And that was when Lilah knocked on the door.

Atan got up to open it, though she wished she could freeze time, the way poor Sartor was frozen, until she could get all her questions answered. Why was Tsauderei suddenly giving in, after forbidding her ever since she could remember?

But she knew he'd speak only when he was ready, so she pulled open the door and smiled. "Lilah! Enter! Tsauderei is here."

Lilah stepped down inside the homely cottage, beaming at the old sorcerer sitting near the fire. Ruddy light gleamed along the old man's braided white hair and long beard, and glinted in the diamond drop hanging from one ear.

Lilah turned to Atan, her tilted eyes wide with her anxiety to explain. "I know I promised to come back as soon as the revolution ended, and I wanted to! Oh, you can't *think* how much. But I didn't want to leave Peitar, and then it seemed he was so busy, and I—"

Atan sank down onto a hassock, her hands tightly clasped, her long, bony face serious. "Oh, Lilah, Tsauderei told me about Peitar being chased about, and then captured, and then put on trial. Of course you stayed. It has only been a few weeks! I didn't think to see you again for a year, but I am very glad you came."

"Ugh." Lilah flinched. "That trial and, worse, he was almost executed—it was exactly as nasty as you think. But it's over. And I like to keep my promises. Especially a fun one, like coming back to this valley and seeing you."

Lilah stole a doubtful glance at Atan, who was tall for fifteen. The Sartoran princess was a plain girl, except for those round, protuberant dark blue eyes with the droopy lower lid, recognizable as a Landis family characteristic in far too many books and royal portrait galleries. Atan was also a mage, and so well read, and *smart*. And she understood why Lilah hadn't come, so why did she look so tense?

Atan studied Lilah at the same moment, glad to see her again, but wishing she had come at another time. *Any* other time.

Atan said, "I'm glad you're here. Because another day, and you might have arrived too late." She spoke the words, but she heard them from far away, as if someone else said them. She was a bit giddy with the awareness that she'd made her decision. When Lilah only looked puzzled, Atan dared a glance at Tsauderei. "Did you understand me? I think I must leave as soon as possible."

And Tsauderei said again, "Yes."

Lilah's eyes were round as an owl's, though less from surprise than the joy of actually coming at the right time. She had always felt that anything Atan or Tsauderei did was important. But she'd been sure that her visits were between important moments. And yet everything having to do with Sartor had world importance. Even if Sartor's only living princess stood there in old, mended clothes, with a dash of bread flour on her cheek.

Lilah said slowly, "You're not talking about going visiting. But..." She pointed westward, in the direction of enchanted Sartor. *"There?"*

Atan gazed at her sympathetically. Lilah's foxy face had reddened with excitement under her scattering of freckles. "It's time to go and free my kingdom." And, in a low voice, "I have to try."

Tsauderei sighed. "Yes, the time has come, since you are still determined."

"Wait." Lilah hopped from one foot to the other, waving her hands, her palms out. "Wait. Where's the army? Where are the mages? One thing I learned during that mess of a revolution is that one person can't just sort of *take over* a kingdom—not unless you want disaster. And in Sarendan, we didn't have Norsunder and its dark magic spells holding us, it was only my Uncle Dirty-Hands and his army, and that was bad enough!"

Tsauderei wheezed a laugh. "Ah, Lilah! I have missed your forthright perspective. You're entirely correct. But what Atan is doing is not in the nature of replacing a monarch. She is determined to disenchant a kingdom that has no monarch."

"But — but — *Norsunder!*"

Tsauderei sat back. "Tell her why it must be now, Atan."

Surprised by this unforeseen turn, Atan spoke to Lilah, but she was watching her tutor. "What do you know about Norsunder, Lilah?"

Lilah recoiled at the evil word actually said out loud. "Um. It's a word you don't say in polite company, first of all. Everybody says that evil people like to go to Norsunder and live forever, but they also take people sometimes, against their will."

Atan said, "I don't think anyone lives *forever*, but it's true that Norsunder exists outside time, and that the Old Sartorans who first made it several thousand years ago are apparently still there."

Once again she sent a glance Tsauderei's way. Again he did not speak.

Atan sighed. Ah, this discussion was yet another lesson, or a test, or — as had been increasingly common — both. "We can't go into Sartor with mages or armies, because anything like that will certainly attract Norsunder's notice. Again."

Lilah gave a small nod, and as Atan paused to organize her words, Lilah tried to quell the hunger rumbles in her stomach. She'd expected warm food after her long (and wonderful) flight over the mountains — food and fun talk, like summer. But Atan and Tsauderei looked serious, so serious they'd forgotten about meals.

This was what it was like, to be at important moments. It had certainly been so when Peitar stopped dreaming and started acting — and he'd never remembered meals. That had been Lilah's responsibility. Maybe she was going to have a chance to do the job for Atan?

She folded her arms across her middle as Atan went on, "Sartor is bound in a sort of dream-existence, the season a kind of eternal verge-of-winter because it was late autumn when the spells were cast."

Atan sent a questioning glance at Tsauderei, who gave a slow nod of approval.

"The commander currently in charge of guarding

Sartor from any rescuers is also in charge of Norsunder's temporal base down south," Atan went on.

Tsauderei spoke at last. "His name is Granon Zydes. He's currently in the midst of internal strife, because of a recent defeat he suffered in Bereth Ferian, which was also enchanted, and is now free."

"Bereth Ferian?" Lilah shrugged. "Never heard of it."

"Old center of magic and learning. Almost as old as Sartor, though its history has changed a lot more. But it's way, way north, as far north as we are south."

Lilah waved a hand in dismissal. "Well, who cares about a place a million years' journey away?"

Tsauderei's lips twitched, and Atan got that bubbly feeling in her middle that could turn into laughter, but she didn't laugh. Lilah did not have her head stuffed with knowledge, but young as she was, she had experience. Atan had knowledge, and the added advantage of three years, but no experience.

Tsauderei said, "Zydes in essence suffered a demotion. Guarding Sartor, which has been nearly unreachable for a few years short of a century, is not exactly a post with advancement potential."

Atan gave a nod; she knew that, but Tsauderei had been speaking to Lilah.

"He seldom ventures out from the base himself. What little we know about the Norsundrian base's internal affairs has only come recently, when Savar, a very old colleague of mine, emerged suddenly from his fastness in Shendoral — Lilah, do you recognize the name?"

Lilah had often looked at old maps of Sartor when she was studying the language. She gave a proud nod. "Big woodland in the center of the kingdom of Sartor. There are stories about it being full of magic."

"Correct. Norsunder's enchantment has no effect there. But it is isolated. Norsunder laid lethal spells around it in an effort to keep anyone from coming or going. Savar managed to break those wards long enough to come by magic transfer here, to talk to me. He promised to be back, but we have not seen or heard from him since."

Lilah clasped her hands and wrung them, amazed that she was being included in this conversation between two people she'd considered on so lofty a plane that she was like an ant looking up at a pair of oaks. At the same time, she was aware of worry, as if she was about to be towed into waters far too deep. "You're saying that *mages* are in danger as well as armies?"

Atan propped her forearms on her knees, a pose Lilah was used to seeing boys and men use. How Aunt Tislah would scold if she were here! But then, how much of Proper Court Etiquette could Atan have learned, growing up in this valley with only Tsauderei and Gehlei, once a royal guard? "We don't know. We don't even know if he'd been caught in some sort of time binding, for we do know that time, and distance, in Shendoral work strangely."

"You mean, like a day passes for him and a year for us?"

"Nothing so measurable," Tsauderei said. "More like this: if the Loi, the non-human denizens there, want your journey to last an hour, even if you've spent a week there, it comes to pass. Or the other way." To Atan, "Go on. We left off with Granon Zydes, the Norsundrian commander."

Atan pressed her trembling fingers between her knees to hide her hands. She was most definitely being tested, one last time. "In Norsunder, promotion to command is not by merit, but by defeating others. So they are not unified. Not at all. That means he has to be busy watching for treachery, and I hope he hasn't any time for Sartor, because for him, just as for the rest of the world, nothing has happened in Sartor for a century. Which is the moment for someone to slip in, unnoticed."

Lilah's tilted brows swooped upward at a steeper angle. "You're saying Norsunder isn't really as powerful as everyone says?"

Atan turned to Tsauderei.

"Tell her the risks," the old mage said.

"Well, yes they *are* as powerful as everyone says. More, because we can only see their temporal activities. No one ever sees the real authors, called the Host of Lords," Atan explained, wishing she knew when the test would end—and why Tsauderei had initiated it now. Oughtn't there to be final magic lessons? Except she'd prepared for this day her entire life. If she was not ready, or capable, a few hasty tutorials before departure would not save her.

While Atan bowed her head, lost in this reverie, Lilah stared at her in amazement. She couldn't believe Atan was really going into danger all on her own. It was a horrible idea! Except who else was there to go? Tsauderei was too old. He could barely walk any more. And it sounded like this Savar wasn't any fireball of leadership either, even if he was a mage.

"I get what you are saying." Lilah squirmed uncomfortably, uneasily aware that she might sound as if she was insulting the oldest kingdom in the world. But she said it anyway. "Though Norsunder is powerful, you're hoping they're so busy making evil plans for everybody else, including each other, and on the watch for armies and powerful mages, that they won't notice you sneaking in to undo their spells."

When Tsauderei and Atan each nodded, Lilah scratched her head. "I have just one question. No, I have a lot of questions. This one first. About Shendoral and time being..." She rippled her hands in the air. "That's the kind of magic that made it possible for Sartor to be under a spell for a century, but you're not only still alive, but only fifteen? I mean, I remember you saying that you were a baby when you got smuggled out. That would be fifteen years ago, unless you did the Child Spell to halt aging."

Both Tsauderei and Atan denied there had been any such spell.

"And yet, Sartor got conquered and enchanted practically a century ago. How does that work?"

"Gehlei was Atan's guard as well as a nursemaid, you knew that," Tsauderei said, and on Lilah's nod, "Norsunder ordered all the royal children to be assassinated, but Gehlei defeated the assassin sent to kill Atan. Ran with her to the mountains. The spell froze everyone in time just as she reached the border to Sarendan. She and the baby were frozen along with everyone else. But the enchantment has been slowly melting, rather like ice. I found her fifteen years ago, before Norsunder could. Everyone else in Sartor who survived the defeat has not aged a day."

Lilah said. "So, if you sneak in, Norsunder won't notice the enchantment breaking, and everybody hopping up after a hundred years' sleep?"

Tsauderei said, "Atan's entry will break the first part of the time binding. Not all at once. As for Norsunder, the only reason I'm willing to see her go is that Detlev, the Norsundrian commander we fear most, is currently not even in this world. If he turns his eyes this way, then we'll have more trouble than we can handle. No one in my generation has won against him. This is one reason the world is in such trouble."

Atan said, "There's one tower that, like Shendoral, Norsunder can't touch, because the protective magic is far older than the palace itself. The tower's magic was a gift to my first ancestors. It's why Eidervaen—called Ilderven then—was first built where it was." Atan winced. "Ooops. Story mode. I hope I'm not boring you." She looked up, her countenance contrite.

Lilah exclaimed in surprise, "Of course not! Why should you think that?" But as soon as the words were out, she knew why. From the look on Atan's face, she'd obviously been found boring by someone. Maybe several someones.

It was unsettling to see the smart, well-trained Atan looking wry as she said, "Well, if I don't watch out, I start spouting history. I'm full of history, magic learning, and not much else."

Lilah stared at her, and then all the puzzle pieces flew together, like a broken window repaired by magic. Nothing to do—Peitar—Bren—everyone busy but her—Atan not knowing if she was boring or not, which meant she didn't have many friends—friends and responsibilities—

Lilah was no mage, and no warrior, but she was very good at looking after a brother whose head was constantly in the clouds.

Surprising herself at least as much as Atan, Lilah said, "I think I'd better come with you."

TWO

Lilah watched Atan's eyes widen, dreading a burst of laughter, or—worse—a kindly but condescending head-pat and some words meant to be comforting about being too young. She did not expect the sudden, transforming smile that glowed in Atan's countenance before the worry and concern clouded again.

"Think about it," Lilah said quickly—and leaned forward to squish the sickening *what have I done?* feeling inside. "You said that armies can't help. Norsunder would sure notice an army. But not one girl going alone. Why not two, so she doesn't have to be alone?" She turned to the mage. "You're going to be watching out with magic, right?"

"As much as I can," Tsauderei said. "What would your brother have to say to me, if I let this happen?"

Lilah crossed her arms. "We promised not to nag each other. I can do what I want. Anyway, he was younger than I am when he started sneaking around learning about my uncle's bad government."

Tsauderei drummed his gnarled fingers on his knees as his bushy brows knit. When he looked up, he said unexpectedly, "Are you serious about your offer?"

Lilah couldn't hide her surprise that he was actually considering it. But then, he'd let Lilah, Bren, his cousin Deon, and their friend Innon leave the valley and sneak back into Miraleste as spies in the worst part of the revolution, after her uncle had taken back the kingdom.

Only he'd given them a magical protection. Maybe he was going to hand them something similar.

Lilah glanced at Atan's expression of anxious hope, which warmed her; at twelve, Lilah regarded a fifteen-year-old as next thing to an adult, without realizing that three years' difference wasn't much at all. "I am," she stated firmly.

Tsauderei said, "You will pardon me?"

He made a sign, whispered under his breath, and before Lilah's astonished eyes he vanished.

Tsauderei performed the transfer magic with the Destination chamber of the royal palace in Miraleste fixed in his mind.

He did not need Destination images. It was a courtesy. Unless there was emergency — or you were on familiar terms — you did not fix on close proximity to a person and suddenly appear. The Destination chamber was the equivalent of knocking on a door and giving the porter time to answer and announce you.

It also gave him time to prepare for what might be a difficult interview. As the Destination chamber page ran off to report Tsauderei's arrival, the old mage sat down to permit the transfer reaction to fade. He glanced out the window at the city, full of people crawling over roofs laying new tiles, or rebuilding walls. In the other direction, boats sailed peacefully about on the lake. Fall was well along here, blazing with colors, the breezes over the lake cool and extraordinarily clear. He leaned out, barely making the shapes of the distant mountains bordering Sartor, far to the west.

Tsauderei contemplated those mountains, his hands clasped behind his back, until a quick, arrhythmic step behind him brought his attention round.

He was not pleased to see not-quite-twenty-year-old Peitar Selenna looking more like forty, but he knew that every ruined house, burned field, every family with an empty chair, would weigh on Peitar's conscience until it was somehow amended, or healed, if only by time.

One could not alter that any more than one could alter the intense, severe gaze from the thin, high-browed face, the sensitivity of the curved mouth so much like Lilah's—though the two resembled one another very little otherwise—or the air of almost endless compassion that was striking in one so young.

"Lilah is with us in the Valley," Tsauderei said, and pulled from his pocket a small stone. He whispered a word over it, and the air formed a glittering bubble around him and Peitar. "There. We can speak for a short time in safety. I do not wish to rely on circumlocution when we need plain speaking. Lilah wishes to accompany Atan to Sartor, to break the enchantment."

"Sartor." Peitar's lips shaped the word, but no sound emerged.

"We both know how impetuous Lilah is. And how loyal to her friends. I can also see how much it would mean to Atan to have a friend, or I would not be here."

Tsauderei was surprised and unsettled by the intensity of Peitar's reaction, so swift and then so quickly hidden. "If you want me to, I can tie Lilah by the heels. Give her a pleasant time in the Valley."

Peitar crossed to the other window, the lurch in his walk somewhat easier after several weeks of careful healing spells. It was going to take at least a year to restore those mis-healed bones. Peitar would not take the time to rest, which meant his recovery would be the longer. But pain had always been secondary to what he perceived as his duty.

"You are asking, not telling me to keep her home for her own good." Peitar turned to face the mage. "That suggests to me that you would let her to go into Sartor—enchanted Sartor."

"Yes," Tsauderei said. "Though I have misgivings, on the whole I think it might be a good idea. The important word here is enchanted. Those girls would not be challenging an army, as you did here. They would be walking into a land somnolent after ninety-odd years, while Norsunder's gaze is currently elsewhere. And they would go with certain safeguards."

Peitar looked through the window again, and Tsauderei wondered what his face was expressing that he did not want seen. "Is there a chance of success? I mean, does the possibility of success outweigh the quite obvious dangers?"

He hadn't spoken Atan's name. Tsauderei took a step nearer, until he could see Peitar's profile, half-hidden by the long, splendid dark brown hair he'd obviously forgotten to comb and tie back that morning. If Peitar were not so thin, he would be regarded as a very handsome young king, though he apparently was utterly unaware of the fact. Or, it was utterly irrelevant. "I trust so," Tsauderei said.

"You cannot go with them," Peitar observed.

"No. Too many wards against me. If I perform the smallest spell, Norsunder is alerted in both the temporal and non-temporal realms. What you see before you," he said, smiling with irony, "is a worthless old bag of bones who can no longer even heft a sword. Not that I was ever much good, even in my young days. I was adept at gymnastics and running and riding, but I never did learn to bang at people with steel. And magic I can just as well employ from a distance."

"That would be my preference as well." Peitar's profile was tense, his mouth compressed into a line. Yet he was not refusing.

"I believe the two girls will go unnoticed. Atan is determined. A companion would be a good thing for her to have."

Peitar's head lifted when Tsauderei said 'Atan.' It was a tiny gesture. Most would not have seen it. But Tsauderei had made a lifelong study of human nature as well as magic, and he remembered vividly his own ardent youth. And he guessed what Peitar would have kept hidden: that he was suffering the throes of a first, adolescent love.

The impulse to smile ruefully vanished. Any other young man of nineteen was certain to recover as swiftly as he'd fallen, but Peitar wasn't like the usual young man, any more than Atan was like the usual girl of fifteen.

Of course it had happened—he should have foreseen it, all those conversations during the stresses of the summer, history, reading, theories of government. While rain pattered outside and the fire leaped on the grate. Tsauderei should have foreseen it, and yet he would not have taken away those conversations, which two lonely young people had clearly cherished.

Tsauderei fervently hoped that Peitar would

recover, for such a passion could not go anywhere.

Peitar broke into these thoughts. "Wish them both the best. And tell Lilah I'm glad that she is helping in this quest. She does have a knack for being in the right place at the right time, it seems."

"I shall," Tsauderei said, and performed the transfer spell.

When Tsauderei vanished by magic transfer, a puff of displaced air buffeted Lilah's face as the flames in the fireplace snapped and stirred. "Wow! That was weird!"

"Transfer magic," Atan said, wishing she could go to Miraleste, Sarendan's capital, to see the place for herself, and how it was improving. Talk to Peitar again, as they had during summer. Only now he would be too busy, surely.

"Can you do that kind of magic?"

"Yes." Atan smiled. "But I won't be able to do it in Sartor because it's warded against light magic using that spell."

"Light magic. That's the kind that builds, or repairs, or makes things better in the world, right?"

"And dark magic burns or spends magic. Its primary purpose is warfare. Well, more precisely, force. Dark magic spells are very, very hard to break, whereas light magic spells must be renewed."

Lilah nodded. "I remember reading about magic being gone after the Fall of Old Sartor. Though I thought it was mostly legend-talk, because of all that other stuff that the old poems and things said. You know, about how our ancestors had magic without doing spells, and talked to each other in dreams, and yadoo, yadoo, yadoo."

Atan smiled. "Apparently some of it really did happen."

"Huh." Lilah snapped her fingers. "Tsauderei did tell us that they used to control the aging process, before he did the Child Spell for me and Bren and Deon and Innon." She scowled. "Tsauderei said he can lift it whenever we want to begin the change toward grownup, but I don't want that. Ever. If it means ending up like my mother."

Atan bit her lip. "You are talking about romantic love?"

Lilah held her nose and waved a hand. "More like the stench of romantic love."

"Yet you love your brother," Atan said.

"Of course I do!"

"Family love is to be revered, but not the love that begins the family?" Atan asked.

Lilah snorted. "You haven't read my mother's diary. Family love is smart. It's good. You protect each other, and if you argue, well, you don't get angry forever. But romance?" Her face reddened as she said fiercely, "It just makes you *stupid!* Mother loved my uncle. Yuk! I know, but apparently he wasn't so bad when he was young. However, that's nothing to what she turned into when she fell in *looove* with Derek's father. Drip, drip, drip, her whole diary turned from interest in her garden and other people to moaning about *Kepreos this* and *Kepreos that.* Drip? Rivers and *oceans* of tears, *all the time!"* She made a gesture of warding. "Then *he* walks into a snow bank, in spite of having two small boys, and *she* gets herself sick and dies when I was a baby. Romantic love is selfish and *stupid."*

Atan had never seen Lilah so bitter and angry. It was the more unsettling because some of what Lilah said paralleled things she had wondered. *Your parents were ill-matched in everything but love,* Gehlei had said once. *Strange, how powerful love is, and how poisonous when it doesn't balance.* Then she'd frowned, and refused to say more.

Lilah said, "I can't help thinking that, as usual, the adults don't know anything worthwhile, and what's needed are some kids to solve the mess. Like the rest of the Sharadan Brothers. You probably didn't know, but Deon has gone off to find those kid pirates somewhere up north. If you need more people, I know I could get Bren and Innon to come. Or at least Bren. He's got nothing else to do except draw, and he can do that while traveling."

"But the more people we have, the more likely we are to draw attention."

Lilah jumped when a glittery flicker on the edge of her vision resolved into Tsauderei. Displaced air breezed around the little cottage room.

Tsauderei's face was tight with strain. Obviously, transfer magic wasn't easy for mages, either. "Peitar wishes you both success," he said a little hoarsely.

Lilah grinned, and patted the pocket of her robe. "As it happens, I got into the habit of always traveling with my thief tools. But there's one thing I'm missing. So if I don't come back right away, you better get someone to haul me away from the Lure-flowers."

Tsauderei didn't argue, or even remonstrate. He said only, "You have an appropriate container?"

"The spice bags we used all summer. Kept the blossoms from drying out and losing their strength. But Innon actually got 'em. Is there a trick to harvesting them?"

Tsauderei nodded. "Not a trick, just extreme care. Spot the ones you want, make a dive, and begin holding your breath midway down. You have to get the entire flower, because it's the dust in the center of the petals that carries the magic that puts humans into deep sleep."

Lilah said, "All right. Then I'd better get busy."

Atan watched the girl vanish through the door before turning to Tsauderei.

"What is it, Atan? Second thoughts?" the mage asked, recognizing the expression in his student's face. Twelve years of Atan's fifteen, he had been her teacher, a position he never would have chosen for himself, but he had been appointed by the Mage Council.

He knew at a glance that she was suffering ambivalence, and also knew that getting her to express it required prodding. She kept things inside too readily.

Atan let out a short sigh, trying to ease that awful knotted feeling in her middle. "I want Lilah to come with me, and yet I can't help thinking, what if something happens?"

Tsauderei sat back, the fire reflecting twin pinpoints in his dark eyes. "Ah. I am afraid I don't have any comforting advice to offer you, *Princess* Yustnesveas. The moment you step over that border, your innocence ends. You will begin a lifetime of feeling responsibility for others who willingly offer their lives for your cause. It is the pain of being a ruler, one I never want you to stop feeling, because the day you do, you turn into a tyrant."

Atan ran her damp palms down her sides, but that

didn't help the iciness of her fingers.

"I have regretted the necessity of permitting you to go into Sartor alone, ever since the prospect before us evolved into reality. Lilah's offer makes me glad. She's young, but she's smart and practical. She does not have that visionary gift that runs through the Irad family, but it's more than compensated with the Selenna adaptability and good humor. Lilah will be good company for you. She will do her best to make you laugh. Get her to Shendoral, and if there is danger beyond, leave her there. That magic, I feel safe in venturing, being far older than Norsunder's evil, will keep her safe."

Atan ducked her head. "Thank you. I have one last favor to ask."

The old mage lifted a hand.

"I would like you to teach me the non-aging spell."

Tsauderei looked surprised. "Why?"

"It's something I've been thinking about. A lot. And something Lilah said made me realize that I'm not alone in thinking about it. I am not certain I want to be an adult yet. If don't succeed, it's not going to matter, right?"

Tsauderei heaved a sigh. "I gave Lilah and her friends that spell because it won't do any harm for them to delay the onset of adulthood for a time. But you know it doesn't make you immortal. It simply delays your physical maturation."

"I know that," Atan retorted.

Tsauderei fingered the diamond in his earlobe. "Most young folks your age can scarcely wait to be grown up. But then soon enough the adult begins looking back longingly to the untroubled days of youth." He chuckled, then sobered. "Lilah's reasons I understand. She can blame the unhappy portions of her childhood on her mother's failed romance. But you?"

"I just know that I'm not ready to be courted. Until I learn more about how to be around real people, not just people from history books. And above all, I don't want to be distracted by adult matters, until I understand people my age."

"How are you going to learn about such things except by experience?"

Atan sighed. "Maybe it's a bad idea, and maybe I won't do it. Or I might do it for a year or so. But I think ...

I think I want the option."

Tsauderei rubbed his forehead, then sat back. "You know it won't work if you're over the threshold already. Have you begun your female courses?"

"No," Atan said. "But Gehlei told me it should be soon."

"Well, one good thing about light magic is that it is benign," Tsauderei said wryly. "If you are too close to the threshold, then the spell will not hold. Very well. I'll give it to you. And the antidote." He gave her an ironic glance from under bushy brows, and she wondered for the very first time in all their years of studying together if the old mage had ever had a romance in his life. "Perhaps a year or two more of childhood might be an aid for you."

He reached for the inkwell and paper that always lay ready on the low table.

The door opened then, but instead of Lilah, Gehlei entered, a basket of fresh fruits and vegetables on her good arm.

Gehlei took them in, question lifting her gray brows, then she turned away, so that all they could see was her silvery-white braid.

"Here you go," Tsauderei said, setting the pen down beside the ink bottle. "I have one more thing, which I will fetch directly." He made the transfer magic, and vanished.

Atan thought it better to get the worst over before the other two returned. "Gehlei, I am leaving for Sartor's border," she said. "Lilah is here. She will accompany me."

Gehlei turned around. Atan could see how unhappy — how angry — she was.

"I wish I could go to protect you," Gehlei said.

Atan winced. At near fifty, Gehlei had been able to fight off an assassin, though she'd lost the use of one arm. Fifteen years had passed since Tsauderei had found Gehlei and Atan on the border. Gehlei couldn't fight off an assassin anymore.

"You taught me well," Atan said. "I'm bigger than you are now, and I ought to be able to protect myself."

Gehlei dug her fingers into her right shoulder. "If only this thing would heal right! But I suppose if Tsauderei's magic couldn't do it, nothing will." She pressed her lips together. Tears gleamed along her lower lids. "I wish you'd wait."

"I thought it would be later as well," Atan said. "But this entire week — I can't explain it. I just know I have to leave. And the urgency must be more than fancy, because Tsauderei agrees."

"Leaving us old people to sit here and watch you trot down the mountain to danger." Gehlei's voice roughened. She shook her head, used her apron to wipe her eyes, then straightened up. "Well, you'll do your duty, that's plain to see. Your parents both did that. I'll shut up and not make it worse. There'll be two loaves of nut-bread, both fresh. They'll keep for a couple weeks if wrapped tight after every use. And I'll put up a bag of nuts, and some preserved fruit, and a good wedge of Mistress Rhodei's best cheese."

She mounted the ladder to the loft, where Atan had slept since she was two years old. "I'll also fetch down your gown," she said over her shoulder.

"Thank you," Atan called, and then bent to pick up the scrap of paper with Tsauderei's familiar writing, and tucked the paper into a corner of the travel bag that she had been preparing.

Her magic books had to stay behind, as she didn't dare use magic until the end of her quest. She ran her finger along her oldest one, full of her own writing — every spell she'd mastered, and notes on what she'd observed and learned.

A clatter and a thump outside the door and Lilah bounced in, her hair wild, her face relaxed in a funny grin.

"Got 'em," she proclaimed. "Whew! Those Lure blossoms do get to you!" She flopped down onto her hassock. "But a good hard fly in the cold air revived me."

Gehlei reappeared, holding out two garments, one bulky. "You can take my old coat," she said gruffly to Lilah, who thanked her.

Atan packed her one good gown into the knapsack. Her usual clothes — the tunic and trousers that girls wore for riding — would be suitable for travel, but if she succeeded, she knew she would have to look like the Queen of Sartor. As much as she could. The fine white cotton-wool gown, with its violet trim that she had stitched herself, was going to have to do.

After all, it's not like Sartor has fashions anymore.

Tsauderei reappeared in his chair. He held out a ring. His voice was strained as he said, "This ought to give you a little protection, though only in the form of light. I altered the trip-spell, to make it easier. Touch it here, and say *Sartorias-deles*. Easy to remember."

Atan took the ring, looked at the plain band, the milky-white gem in the middle. Light pooled oddly in it, sending a prickle of warning through her mind: she sensed powerful magic here.

Good.

She slid it on her finger. This evidence of the Landis past made her shiver, the skin on the backs of her arms prickling. The ring had been fashioned by dark magic, so it would escape wards. The long-ago ancestor who had made it had led a very adventurous life. What would future generations say about *her* some day? Or would the last of the Landises disappear without her existence ever being known?

"Let us depart," she said to Lilah, doing her best to look confident.

THREE

L ilah had experienced transfer magic twice in her life.
When Atan shifted them from the cottage to a
point inside Sartor's border, Lilah felt that same weird
vertigo, and plumped down on a mossy rock. "Hoo," she
said. "It's like being stuffed through a keyhole then
yanked out again."

Atan smiled in apology. "I know it would have been
nicer to fly, but the flying spell doesn't extend this far,
and we would have had to transfer anyway, unless we
wanted a fearfully walk added. It's going to be long
enough as is."

They were still in mountains, though the great
peaks were mostly behind them to the east. Below to the
west the mountains were more like rocky hills, and
beyond those, a gray haze obscured what once had been
rich farmland.

Lilah glanced back at the sky-high snowy peaks.
"No, I wouldn't want to walk down those. Or up." She
pulled Gehlei's coat more closely about her. "It's cold."

"Tsauderei says that it will not get much colder.
Part of the enchantment."

"Which is about to break," Lilah said.

Atan had obviously scouted the area out at least
once before, for she made her way confidently around
some thick, scrubby bushes to a narrow sheep-trail, and
began trudging downslope.

Lilah hopped and slid behind her, amazed at how

quickly life could change. Well, the revolution had taught her that much. You wake up one morning, your biggest worry how badly your hair holds curl, for which you'd get a fierce scolding, and the next morning finds you in prison, and half the palace in flames.

She thought about her offer, which had not been prompted by talk of magic spells, kings, or history. It was partly that feeling of responsibility but also because Atan had looked so mortified at the idea that someone had once found her dull. Atan had never had a chance to do normal things like play games, or talk about kid interests. Not having been raised for so long in secret by an old mage and an aging guard.

Atan's face was hidden by the hood of her mountain coat, made of undyed sheep wool of mixed gray and brown shades. Good camouflage, Tsauderei had said.

Lilah smoothed her hands down Gehlei's old coat. It was lined with heavy, smooth cotton-linen. The outside was nubbly and rough. It was an odd garment, unlike anything people in Sarendan wore.

She looked up. They had to be inside Sartor by now. And so far, no lightning bolts or evil mages had showed up, spouting nasty spells.

The crunch of their footsteps was the only noise besides the sough of wind from the heights. Why was going downhill easier on everything but your feet, and going uphill was all right for the feet but difficult for everything else? The trail was scarcely visible, very narrow along ledges as they picked their way down into a gulley overshadowed by trees.

"Is there a road?" Lilah finally asked.

"Not yet. I want to avoid any roads until we reach the most westward of the border mountains, which will open into plains. This path will keep us hidden for as long as possible. Beyond that we'll have to follow along the Luyos River. I trust it has growth alongside. When it bends south, we'll go west along one of the smaller rivers—"

Atan stopped, and swung around to face Lilah. Her cheeks were blotchy with red, her brow knit. "Promise me, Lilah," she said in a low, pleading voice. "If I talk too much, if I ramble and meander on too long about history or magic or the past, tell me. Stop me. Don't nod and smile and let me find out later I am the world's biggest sleep herb."

Lilah said, quite truthfully, "I *like* it when you talk about history."

Atan sighed. "Thank you. I didn't believe so, but then—once—I—well, I know I am used to talking to adults like Tsauderei and Gehlei, but the only friend our age that I had was Dawn, and you know she wants to study magic. We never bored each other. You and your brother were the first people I met outside the Valley whom I didn't bore..." She made a comical face, and an attempt at a smile that hurt Lilah with its falsity. "Let's just say I am ignorant of the arts of conversation."

"That's not true. My brother said that you're the first person he ever talked with who made him lose the sense of time passing. And he talks to *everybody*. I thought so, too! What happened?"

Atan looked around, blushed a deeper red, then said in a low, painfully flat voice, "Tsauderei took me to Bereth Ferian. There is a mage school there. I was transferred to a place of protection. You will understand I am not boasting when I say that everyone paid me the greatest attention? Bowing everywhere I turned, the mages stopping to listen if I so much as asked for a glass of water?"

"I know," Lilah said, thinking of the princess behavior she'd been grumping at Bren about. "Everybody is looking at you, and you think it's with great respect..."

"The respect was more curiosity, I think. Though maybe respect for the ancient name of Landis," Atan said wryly as she gripped a sturdy young tree and lowered herself down a slippery bit of trail. "But I wanted so badly to meet people my age. Finally they agreed, if I promised not to tell anyone who I was, and dressed like a common girl from some northern village. You know how I usually dress, though before I traveled, Tsauderei had had a friend obtain a suitable princess gown."

Lilah laughed. "Full of ribbons, no doubt?"

"Not ribbons. Not for a bony beanpole like me. Lace," she said distinctly, twiddling her fingers at her neck and wrists and waist and knees. "Waterfalls of it. Maybe to fill me out some. But I had taken my old clothes along. I slipped them on, borrowed Gehlei's name, called myself a baker's apprentice, and went to look at the ancient artifacts, and..." She shrugged. "I met artisans and students, people my age...." She shrugged sharply, ducking under a ferny branch before she looked back. "The short of it is, I thought I was doing so very well until I chanced to overhear someone asking someone else who the tall clodpole was who wouldn't shut up, and who did she think she was impressing, was there some scribe tutor around looking to hire? At first I didn't think it meant me until someone I thought a new friend else said, "Whoever thought bakers could bore you on every subject *except* bread?"

Lilah winced in sympathy, but as her own friends had said far worse to her face when they were mad at her, she waited for the worst part.

But that was the worst part. Atan's voice trembled as she said, "Erai Yanya—she's a mage—just laughed and said, who cares what others think? But she lives alone in a ruin. Except for her son. Who is a lot like me. Anyway, I told Tsauderei to take me home. And ever since, I've tried to read about how to get on in groups, but you know, the records never talk about that. Even the most detailed records seem to assume everyone already knows."

Lilah bit her lip against exclaiming, *Is that all?* "I think I told you that I was pretty much stuck at home, no friends, until summer. Court didn't count. Everybody was fake in court. That's why I hated it so much. But anyway, during summer, I learned that anybody who says one thing to you and another about you isn't worth listening to." And after a sideways peek at Atan's unhappy profile, she said, "That can't be new, not after all you've read!"

"Falsity and deceit, of course I have read about such. But are they not bound to politics and kingdoms and power? I can understand falsity to Princess Yustnesveas Landis," Atan said dryly. "But why to a baker's apprentice? Unless my false guise had been penetrated. I ought to have thought of that. Lilah, thank you—"

"Wait, wait." Lilah waved her hands, almost tripped over a tree root, and halted. "That person might not have guessed *anything*. People *do* that. For silly reasons. For no reason. And sometimes it isn't the same person, or the same reason." She thought about the arguments, laughter, and ways she'd had to learn to compromise, and got an idea. "Why don't you practice on me? We can trade off. You tell me stories, and I'll help you practice social things. As much as I can. I'm still not very good at etiquette, as my aunts will tell you, but I learned about not boring friends last summer. My fellow Sharadan Brothers didn't hide their feelings."

"Thank you," Atan said.

The trail angled steeply for a time, forcing the girls to pick their way with care. Lilah slipped once or twice, until she figured out how to watch exactly where Atan stepped, and place her foot in the footprint left by Atan's. She was glad she'd worn sturdy shoes with cork soles, rather than thin green-weave slippers.

Lilah was glad to talk, because she was still apprehensive of a Norsundrian lightning strike bringing down the mountainside on them, or at the very least their finding themselves transformed into mushrooms as a result of breaking the mysterious century-old spell. Even if it was only one spell in a pile of them. It was still Norsunder! But as the cloud-obscured sun passed slowly westward, and the girls worked their way steadily downhill, nothing happened.

When Atan stopped at a stream tumbling down from the mountain, Lilah said, "Are we resting? My toes ache from all that downhill walking."

"We can stop for a little." Atan dropped her knapsack, knelt and cupped her hands to drink from the stream.

"For the people. When the enchantment lifts. Will they know a century passed, or will they think it's a day later, and they are in for a big surprise?"

"Tsauderei thinks it's going to be the big surprise." Atan picked up a pair of brightly colored pebbles, turning them over on her palms. "Sartor," she murmured, almost too softly for Lilah to hear. "At last I have come home."

Lilah hid a sigh. To her eyes, the view was about as ugly as anything she'd ever seen—much uglier than

Sarendan's dry, cracked fields during the famine. She gazed into the gray haze that obscured the land to the west until Atan stirred and said, "I want to get below Point Adan by nightfall. I think it'll be less cold if we get off the heights."

Lilah hopped to her feet. "Sure!" Her stomach growled, and she gulped in a breath to hide it. She'd gone hungry a lot during the summer, so she was used to waiting. "I'll take a turn carrying the stuff," she offered. "I may be short but I'm strong, and I carried my own knapsack for most of the summer."

"All right," Atan said, and handed it over. She was already glad that Lilah had come. They started off.

They wound down next to the stream, as Point Adan—the westernmost height—rose above them, an outthrust of ancient rock colored with angled layers, evidence of the violent and desperate wrenching of the land into protective barriers made by long-dead mages in a vain effort to safeguard Sartor against invasion.

Atan had begun to review past lessons on ancient magic when something moved. Something pale, beyond the hedgerow bordering the trail. She stilled, a hand out to halt Lilah.

The girls poised to run, as the pale something obscured by the tangle of leaves resolved into—another girl!

She stepped carefully around the tangle of dusty-green shrubbery, and stopped.

Lilah stared at this wraith of a girl who looked Lilah's age, or younger, her wide blue-gray eyes regarding them with a mixture of apprehension and curiosity that (Atan reflected) was probably a twin to their own faces.

"I'm Merewen," the girl said. "Ah, eh. Merewen Dei."

Atan was too surprised to speak. Another girl? Not just any girl, but perhaps a relative of some kind? Because Atan's mother had been a Dei before her marriage contract.

Lilah was more interested in the girl, who looked blue with cold. Except that she didn't shiver. Lilah studied her from her long braids of wheat-colored hair past the anomaly of a silvery-white woven yeath-fur cloak worn over a plain, dusty summer tunic that came just below her knees. Her feet and arms were bare, the hue of the sky at sunup, sort of a peachy blue, and not at all mottled. Her gray tunic was sashed. Over her shoulder, peeping out from the soft folds of the expensive cloak, she'd slung a knapsack.

"Are you related to my mother, then?" Atan asked.

Merewen's forehead puckered slightly. "I hardly know," she admitted. "You see, I have lived in Savar's house my whole life, but he was not always there." She gave the girls a wistful smile. "All I really know is the woodland. But I learn quickly."

Atan sent a look at Lilah that the latter had no difficulty interpreting: more evidence of how time had warped the people in this kingdom, then she asked, "What brought you here?"

"Savar sent me," Merewen said. "He said you would come, and I was to meet you here — " She pointed up at Point Adan, staring up at it. "He described it just so. I would know you for a Landis at once, and he showed me a portrait. You look very like." Her smile was tentative. "But he did not mention *two* girls." Merewen's brow puckered again as she considered Lilah's short hair and her robe. "You are a girl?"

"Yup. I came along to help." Lilah couldn't help snickering. "I'm Lilah Selenna. I lived as a boy all summer."

"Oh!" Merewen's eyes rounded with surprise.

"Tsauderei told me that there was a mage named Savar who might help." Atan glanced down the road into the shadowy haze. The thick clouds overhead had darkened; the sun was setting.

Merewen ducked her head in a nod. "I am to show you the way back to Shendoral. Though the way is easy enough, following alongside the River Luyos, and no one else is on it." She waved to the west. "But Savar was very serious about my coming to find you. And those in my dreams said you must make your way first to Shendoral alongside the river, where the enchantment is weakest, and from there to the capital, and there you must break the enchantment binding the Loi beyond time. Savar could not do it. Though he was going to try again, I believe." She frowned at her dusty toes. "I don't know, but I think he did not want me there when he tried."

Atan considered all these things, then said, "Shall we get started on our road?"

Merewen and Lilah fell in step on either side.

Presently Atan said, "Merewen. Is it a family name?"

"Yes, my mother's," Merewen replied.

Atan drew in a deep breath, sounding almost as if she'd taken an unexpected blow. "She was *that* Merewen Dei? You too have been beyond time?"

Lilah had no idea who Merewen Dei was, and didn't really care, if she was a grown-up. She did not like the atmosphere, though the road was indeed empty, the dusty farmland around them silent. But she couldn't see very far. The haze was both unpleasant and uncanny. She felt — well, she felt she was being *watched*.

Merewen didn't seem to mind, but then she'd apparently spent her whole life in this atmosphere. A hundred years of life, or just a few? It made Lilah's head hurt to try to figure it out.

Atan had been counting generations outside and inside the enchantment. She said to Merewen, "You could have a claim to the throne," she observed.

Merewen skipped over some rubble. "That's what Savar said. I don't know what it means. Not really. He said that people would expect it of me if you didn't come, or if you were gone."

"Claim to the throne?" Lilah repeated, walking backwards so she could see both girls. "I know the Dei family is famous — I love the writings of Lasva Dei — but aren't they forbidden to sit on thrones, or something? I remember some saying about how they have birthed kings and queens but never wore crowns. So, for one thing, she can't break the spell. Or can she? And uh, speaking of the spell, I guess the first part of the spell really and truly broke?" She glanced around doubtfully.

"Soon as I crossed the border." Atan grinned. "You did! You expected flashes of lightning."

Lilah flung her arms wide. "It makes sense. Big magic ought to make a big noise, or light, or *something*, don't you think?"

"Against Norsunder, invisible and imperceptible is best." Atan looked about warily in the gathering darkness, where brambles and hedgerows made sinister shapes, and trees, so majestic in sunlight, seemed to loom. "Remember what Tsauderei said about winter's melt. The effect is going to be noticed, but the later the better."

Merewen ran her hands up her arms. "I feel different. Though I can scarcely say how, or why."

Atan turned back to her, brow creased. "You did make it all the way east, and you didn't get lost in the binding."

Merewen nodded soberly. "Savar said I would make it if I kept in my mind Point Adan, the mountain of the rising sun. It's because I am part Loi."

Loi—the bird-people, they were sometimes called in historical records. But Atan was hesitant to say that out loud, until she found out if that was something the Loi called themselves.

She drew in another careful breath before saying, "Gehlei—my … governess, told me your mother was thought to have disappeared when her father tried to renege on the treaty, and take the throne in her name, deposing my father. Tsauderei told me she was rumored to have run to Shendoral to take refuge to escape the, the trouble."

Merewen shrugged. "Disgrace. That's what Savar said. My mother's family left the capital in disgrace, but my mother came to Shendoral."

"I don't get it," Lilah said, looking from one to the other.

Merewen seemed undisturbed, but Atan said carefully, "Merewen's grandfather married into the Dei family, and took their name, as required by ancient treaty: any Landis marrying into the Dei family becomes a Dei, relinquishing all claims to the Landis line. That meant he could never come to the throne. Deis who married Landises also had to renounce their names."

"An ancient treaty?" Lilah asked. "Why?"

"Old problems. I thought the Dei family went on to Everon after they were banished."

"They did," Merewen said. "Except for my mother. They didn't know she was in Shendoral. Nobody did. She didn't like being in the middle of disgrace. Dis-grace. Mis-grace. Sounds like she spilled her soup on her clothes, or tripped over her own toes!" She laughed, a delightful sound, reminding Lilah and Atan of birdsong.

"Did she disappear? You said you lived with Savar." Atan asked.

"She's with the Loi," Merewen said. "She chose that form when she mated with the Aroel. She can't be human again."

"Aroel?" Lilah asked. "Is that a leader or a ruler?"

"No," Atan said. "The Loi don't have human hierarchies, Savar said. It's more like the one chosen to take human form long enough to communicate with us." She turned to Merewen. "Then you are the child of human and Loi."

"Is that why you're blue?" Lilah asked.

Merewen nodded, skipping again. "Savar said that I should be able to shift — ah, alter form, but I don't know how, or when. I can't find them, except in dreams," she added, her voice sad.

"Then how did you get separated from them?" Lilah asked.

"They came to the world to try to help, and nearly got caught in the binding. That's what Savar told me. I *did* get caught. I was with my mother, see, and they thought I'd go back when they shifted. But I didn't. Then Savar found me, and so I lived in Shendoral." Merewen's large blue eyes were wistful. "When the dreams are right, they sing to me, my parents. They call me Linet. I like that."

"You will find them when we break that spell," Atan promised.

Merewen's sweet smile altered her whole face in the fading light. Atan discovered the contours of Merewen and of Lilah, too, were blurring. Darkness was closing in.

"Shall we make ourselves a little camp in that grass over there, and rest for the night?" she suggested.

Lilah sighed with relief. "My feet would like that very much. As for my stomach, it would welcome a bite."

The girls turned off the road toward the bank of the river, making their way over dusty long grasses midway between green and brown. The blades felt strange to Atan as she swept them aside. They had been caught for so long midway between summer and autumn. Time's measure really had become meaningless here.

The Luyos flowed fast, a comforting sound to Atan, for water was too strong to be bound. They made their way down to drink the cold water, and then back up onto the grassy bank.

Merewen pulled from her knapsack a long, wrapped bread-shape and said, "The miller's lady made this for me. I ate one coming, and this one is for going back." As she uncovered it, the girls sniffed the welcome smell of ground nuts and spices.

It was a familiar scent, one Atan had smelled every day that Gehlei baked what she'd called winter-bread. It was a Sartoran bread, and here was another loaf, so homely, so unexpected. Sartoran, made by unknown Sartoran hands.

Atan's throat hurt and her eyes stung with a longing she could not define.

FOUR

From a tower window in the Norsunder base south of Sartor's border, Granon Zydes stared down into a torchlit courtyard and watched the diminutive yellow-haired mage Dejain issue some orders to a number of his own scouts, and then pull them together so she could transfer them one by one quickly and efficiently.

His scouts. How he loathed her! He wished she'd died the year before, when Kessler Sonscarna's crazy conquering plan had been smashed. He preferred soul-bound mages. They did what they were told, and didn't think beyond that; they couldn't, as they were effectively dead.

Dejain wanted the base. He knew it as well as she did. He didn't care what she wanted it for — everyone was plotting — but he needed to find out how she planned to take it from him so he could circumvent her, and make her look like a fool while at it.

He wished he could annihilate her, but Detlev had ordered them to cooperate. "I need her expertise for my own plans," he'd said.

You could revile Detlev all you wanted, but you didn't cross him, not unless you liked him smashing your mind inside your skull without even moving from his chair.

"Kessler is being assigned to you as an errand boy," Detlev had said then.

Zydes closed his eyes, memory of his dismay like a

fist to the gut. Young as he was, Kessler Sonscarna caused fear in many, even the toughest. He was both lethal and crazy—the most lethal and the craziest to survive a family known for its vicious insanity. A combination you only wanted in an ally, not in a subordinate who looked at you with unwinking, undisguised hatred.

But Zydes had known better than to complain, not with Detlev smiling that faint smile and gazing at him with those cold, nasty eyes the same gray-green shade as a winter sea, especially when Detlev added in a mild but deliberate drawl that somehow burned with the threat of mid-winter ice, "He will benefit from lessons in obedience."

Zydes turned away from the tower and wandered back to his desk. What had he meant by *that*? No one understood Detlev. Many had tried to take him out, and his reprisals were both imaginative and lasting. Zydes knew better than to tangle with him directly. Better to build a powerbase here in the physical world, whose rules he understood.

So what was Dejain—

He became aware of a soft green glow at the extreme edge of his vision. He whirled around. The scope, a face-sized mirror-like object supported between two metal rods, gleamed.

Zydes crossed the room to stare into the smooth black dish-shaped scry stone. He had several alarm spells keyed onto it. The iridescent sheen over it was definitely green, not red, or blue, or gold. Green. That meant—

He frowned, thinking over his ward and enchantment alarms, which were not written down anywhere—or told to anyone. Green, an unimportant one, set long ago...

Landis.

He stared at that green glow.

That meant a *Landis* had crossed the border?

He'd almost not bothered setting this particular alarm-spell. Only long habit at being thorough (which included warding against ruling families who'd been deposed) had made him set it. The Landises were the most famous ruling family of all, which was why he'd put himself to the needless exertion of setting that spell. Apparently it wasn't so needless after all.

A Landis was alive?

Irritation and fear tightened the back of his neck. Stupid old stories, nothing but myth, meant to scare children and old people. The Landises were only good at endurance, like rats. The truth was, when they'd been attacked they'd shriveled up like paper on fire, and even if one of them had somehow escaped (and there had been rumors) that one could not be at the head of an army now, or this would not be the only alarm —

He wiped his hands down the sides of his tunic. If it was in truth a Landis just over the border, *he was the only one who knew*. Unless Dejain —

He bolted to the window, but of course they were long gone. No, Dejain and the Landis signal could not be connected. She'd had some scheme going for days, and this alarm spell had been wakened recently, sometime between dawn and now, for he'd been out of the office all morning and most of the afternoon.

He cleared his mind and murmured the spell that activated his magical scope, his most powerful invention. Better than a mere scry stone. He waited for the residual magic vertigo to pass, and then looked down into the black curve of the scope's bowl, and whispered the spell that would locate any living Landis.

Dark had fallen, corroborating that the Landis was indeed in Sartor. It was difficult to make out much. He saw three childish shapes rummaging around. Making a campsite. A distinctive landmark silhouetted against the lighter sky beyond them. He was sure he'd once seen it on the — ah. He flicked open his map and ran his fingers around the bowl of mountains that bordered Sartor, touching at each of the old access ways. Point Adan. As one turned to dig in a basket, a long braid swung down. Then she handed the basket to one of the others; was that long hair?

It seemed that the Landis was only a girl, and she'd just that day crossed the eastern border. And had no magic protections — at least, nothing important, nothing that had warded her from location spells, or his spell would not have worked. She was accompanied by a pair of children. Had to be maidservants. Only which was the Landis? The scope was most useful for spying on the fortress's denizens. The farther away it had to reach, the flatter and more distorted the images. One of the three was doing something, and magical light flared briefly. Of course that would be the Landis, probably taught spells by whoever had secreted her.

Though it was true that this girl's presence would break the key to Detlev's century-old enchantment, those spells would take time to dissolve, and Detlev was elsewhere in the world, or out of it. Once Zydes had the girl, he could weave his own spells, with keys only he knew. Even if Detlev returned, *Sartor would belong to Granon Zydes*.

He gazed hungrily into the scope, a plan flowering in his mind. A capital plan. The spells over Sartor could be renewed, but altered by *him*. The people would be *his*. The land would be his. The Landis child, suitably enchanted into an obedient puppet, could be an enormous asset in a world that still heeded the power of the names *Sartor* and *Landis*, and he would accomplish it all himself, before any of the other soul-devouring death's-heads in Norsunder even noticed.

The lure of power was sweeter than anything in the world.

He snapped his fingers and the spell ended, the scope going black. A quick murmur: the alarm spell vanished as well, leaving no trace of evidence.

He was the only one who knew. He began to reorganize the next day so that he could go in pursuit — except then his absence would be noted. And he couldn't transfer out, not without triggering wards —

How many spies did the place have? *Everyone* was a spy for somebody, even if only for themselves.

Time was limited. Therefore he must act with dispatch, but not careless haste.

The first requirement was to get hold of the Landis girl.

He stepped to the door, then hesitated. His best runners had just been transferred out by that scheming Dejain. But there was always Kessler.

He frowned. Advantages: he was quick, unnervingly fast, which was astonishing because he was a Chwahir, who were known for being the worst-trained fighters in the world. He was smart, and so far he did what he was told with speed and efficiency.

Disadvantages: every one of his advantages, for Zydes knew someone that smart and that fast was not going to remain a runner. He was also crazy, so crazy there was no reading him, no using the usual enticements to keep control of him. He seemed impervious to mind-warping spells as well, and worse, he was just beginning to learn magic—though Zydes tried to keep him busy enough with scutwork to permit little time for *that*.

Zydes opened the door and sent one of the guards to fetch Kessler. Zydes had his plans in place by the time the door opened again. Kessler appeared, barely medium height, and so slim that apparently some less observant warriors thought he was feeble. They didn't survive the mistake.

Zydes didn't care about anyone's personal prowess, real or boasted. The jolt he felt every time he saw Kessler was entirely due to those protuberant eyes with the droopy under-lid. Landis eyes, only pale blue, in a black-haired, pale Chwahir face. Long ago the Landises had married with the Sonscarnas of Chwahirsland, and here was evidence, generations later, in *Prince* Kessler Sonscarna, now putatively a runner. Not for long, if he can help it, Zydes reminded himself.

Kessler only saw a silhouette.

He approached the broad desk set squarely before the window, glowglobes behind it, so that its owner was limned in light, rendering him a shadow. It was a trick to intimidate, but Kessler interpreted it as hiding. That meant Zydes was launching some sort of plan.

It also meant that Kessler was about to be ordered to perform the scut work, whatever Zydes either didn't want to do, or did not want to be seen doing himself.

"There are three children who just crossed into Sartor's eastern border. Bring me the one who has a light-making magical aid. I'm minded to try an experiment."

Kessler said nothing. He waited, not reacting, because he knew that Zydes hated not seeing visual clues, and so was likely to break a silence by saying more than he had planned to.

"At once," came the sharp voice.

"The other two children?" Kessler asked.

Zydes waved a hand. "Kill 'em."

There was a need for no witnesses, and in a hurry?

Yet Zydes would not speed his plans along by giving Kessler access to magic transfer? And he wanted one child — one with magic — without naming names?

The conclusion seemed obvious: the impossible was possible. There was a Landis still alive. And like everyone else, Zydes assumed that a Chwahir was too ignorant of any history but their own to be aware of things like the conditions of Sartor's enchantment.

Kessler withdrew, closing the door soundlessly behind him. By dawn he was already mounted, riding beyond the gates to the northeast under a gray, grim sky. He loathed the errand, but he did not mind several days' hard riding. He was alone, and he had time to make his own plans.

The girls woke up, broke camp, and set out.

Lilah was already bored with the countryside, but she enjoyed her companions. Atan she had admired from their first meeting, and the newcomer, Merewen, was so interested in everything that she became interesting. She talked about everything with such delight — the moths flickering around the weird light on Atan's ring when she used it to help them make camp, the sedge, the subtle colors of rocks along the river's edge, and of course, her companions.

But though Merewen chattered about the world around them, she didn't comment on all that she observed, such as Atan's mood growing of abstraction.

Lilah also noticed. They'd begun the journey with Atan and Lilah talking and Merewen sometimes interposing questions, but that had changed to Lilah and Merewen talking, with occasional questions by Atan.

Atan's mood had indeed changed. She'd begun both exhilarated and afraid, but very determined. Now that she was really carrying out her plan, she wasn't sure what would come next. Until now there'd been one goal: learn enough to go to Sartor and break the enchantment.

The lonely road and the absence of living creatures around them had banished the expectation of discovery, attack, or the need to transfer out fast. But nothing beyond that was sure, so she studied the land as closely as the peculiarities of the slowly dissipating spells permitted.

She could not see very far because of the gray haze, and wondered how many villages and farms it concealed. The weather seemed unchanging, a continuously unbroken gray sky that warded the sun by day (there was no rain or even wind) and permitted no stars by night. The eastern mountains had dwindled to a flat purple-brown smear by the end of the first day's walk, though Atan knew they could not have progressed very far.

Even the shortening of the days, so noticeable before they left, meant nothing here. It was light, then — suddenly — it was dark. She could measure progress only by the diminishing food in their knapsacks, for the days blended into one another, so that, unless she concentrated, she lost count.

One morning as they set out for another day's trudge, she became aware of a pause that had grown into silence, and she discovered two questioning faces. Atan said, "Have I been a sorry companion?"

"A quiet one," Merewen said.

"Is there something to worry about?" Lilah asked, looking around.

"I've been thinking about magic. But instead of talking about it, which I know would be boring, how about we hear about something outside of Sartor? Lilah, why don't you tell Merewen the story of the freeing of Sarendan?"

"Yes, yes," Merewen exclaimed, skipping ahead a few steps. "A story! I like stories."

Lilah paused, considering where to begin. She was delighted to be asked, but the reminder brought back some bad memories.

"What are you looking at?" Merewen asked, causing Lilah to turn her way in surprise.

But Merewen was not talking to her. Atan was several paces behind, crouched in the pathway, intent on something in front of her feet. At first Lilah thought Atan was ill. No, she was weeping! Those were tears along her lower eyelids, but the tears did not fall.

Atan sat back on her heels, her coat dragging unnoticed in the old dust. "Time."

She stretched out her hand to touch the wall of dirt and growth alongside the path. Lilah blinked, seeing only dirt, bounded by the tangled roots and branches of the dusty, ancient dark green holloway topped by an ancient hedgerow—a common enough sight back home in Sarendan through certain areas. "Time, and silence." Atan wiped her eyes. "I didn't think it would hurt so much."

Lilah was still puzzled. Atan's intensity caused her to turn slowly in a circle as she pondered the wall of dirt, root, and tangled undergrowth, sheltered by bare branches and twigs. The hard-beaten path really did dip quite low. Very low indeed. As Lilah looked at that perplexing tangle of root and branch—for it was impossible to descry each individual plant—mortared together with the duff of moldering old prickly dark green leaves, her perspective shifted, and she saw what Atan saw: a path stamped flat by untold generations of Sartorans, the hedge marking a boundary a thousand years old. Older. *Much* older.

"How many generations of people passed this way, singing the old songs?" Atan asked, her lips trembling. "The emptiness—the silence—" She stood, her voice rough. "I don't know the songs. No one wrote them down, Tsauderei said, because everyone knew them. Will anyone remember?"

Lilah shifted her gaze from the path's border to Atan, who wiped her eyes again. "It's only been a day for the Sartorans under the enchantment," she said. "You told me so yourself."

"Yes. That's if Norsunder didn't kill them all when my father and mother were killed." Atan wiped her eyes. "But we don't know any of that yet, and I'm borrowing trouble. Sorry. Sorry! Lilah, may we have that story?"

Lilah cleared her throat, wondering if the enchantment was getting to Atan. If she couldn't understand, at least she could divert. "Shall I start with when I met Bren and his cousin Deon?"

"I'd like that."

Merewen's eyes were very blue, gathering and holding the diffuse light. "I like it when people meet. Is it funny? I love funny things."

"Oh, yes, there are some funny bits." Lilah launched

into the tale, dwelling on the humor, and skipping past the terrible things. Her reward was Atan's chuckle, for Lilah had learned from observing her brother how some people took as wounds in the spirit every evidence of war, or cruelty, or destruction.

Atan enjoyed Lilah's style of talking, and the sound of her voice, but she kept having to catch herself up lest her mind drift outward into that haze, wondering who had survived and how many, and when would they waken from their century-long dream? Would they actually be asleep, or perhaps sitting at a loom or worktable, and they'd put down tools, and glance through the window, and blink dusty eyes, wondering how the war was going? Would their cupboards be filled with dust, and their homes with spider webs?

Late in the afternoon, Lilah's sudden chuckle brought her out of anxious imaginings.

"But I do not know the name for baby horses," Merewen pointed out. "Though horses have passed through Shendoral, they don't seem to live there."

"You don't have to know 'em. Bren *does* know the difference between a foal and a colt, you see, as he used to help his brothers in the stable. But his cousin Deon didn't, because she had no interest in horses, so when she said 'clot' instead of 'colt' and Bren pretended to go along—even the outlaws were laughing, but Deon never knew we were joking!"

"Oh," Merewen said, in a tone of interest.

Lilah chuckled again, a pleasant sound, like a spring fall down the rocks behind her old cottage. A good sound to hear in this vast, dead silence.

"And I'm the only one laughing, I see. I guess it's one of those things that's only funny if you were there."

"Perhaps it's not gasp-for-breath funny, but I like hearing about it, because I get a picture of your friends," Atan said.

"Perhaps it is not funny," Merewen observed, with that bird-like air of curiosity. "But I think it interesting, too, this pretending not to know a thing. Then there are all the extra words and names. Like your calling your uncle Dirty-Hands, even though you say his hands were clean when you saw him. Or is that funny to you?" She swung round to face Atan.

Atan found the question funnier than the image, but she hid it. "Nicknames, even circle names, can be like that," she said.

"Circle names?" Merewen repeated.

"I've read that it's a social thing, some might say a court thing, though there are court names as well. Those usually are centered around titles. Tsauderei told me that Sartoran history is a knotwork of hierarchies—who is important, who isn't."

"Our revolution was supposed to make a circle including all humanity inside our border," Lilah said. "But practically as soon as it happened, you got people not wanting this group in, only that group, and so on."

Atan bobbed her head in enthusiastic agreement, then remembered to practice her queenly manners, and straightened her spine. "One of my ancestors wrote, and Tsauderei said it was true, that for some people, circles are only interesting for who they can keep out."

Lilah rolled her eyes. "Are you going to go back to using, uh, your name, soon as you know it's safe?"

Atan sighed. "I've looked forward to that all my life. I even asked Tsauderei to find copies of the official records about the queens who share my name, so I could learn all about them. At least, I know their official lives as recorded by the heralds. Their private writings are probably hidden in the royal city, if it hasn't been destroyed. But that's just it. The girl with my name seems like someone else. Someone who will have to preside, and pass laws and judgments. I think I can be her, but when I'm being me, I am still Atan. Does that make sense?"

"Sure does," Lilah said.

Merewen cocked her head, more birdlike than ever. "No."

Atan laughed. "Are you not Linet to your parents, but Merewen to us? Your parents are a little circle that we cannot be part of." And when Merewen's eyes widened with understanding, Atan looked around. "The day is almost gone. Shall we find a camp before the light goes?"

"Good idea. I can finish the rest tomorrow, if you like," Lilah said, yawning. "My throat's dry—and I don't want to talk about the trial, or being my uncle's prisoner, at night. We're getting to the horrid parts."

"Not at night," Merewen said, glancing around as Lilah led the way off the road to a grassy spot pretty much indistinguishable from previous nights.

Atan sank down, feeling light-headed and unsteady, as if she sat on a hammock. They seemed to have walked and walked yet stayed in one place, and each night they camped under the same dry-looking, scrubby oak.

No. She forced herself to observe differences. The tributary of the Luyos that they had been following bent toward the south. The day before, it had gone straight west. That line of mossy boulders there, they'd seen nothing like that. Looked like the teeth of some great beast. This oak was quite old, and the first night they'd slept under a young, though equally scraggly, ash.

By the time they were done eating, nightfall was upon them, and Lilah curled up to sleep. Atan couldn't sleep, tired as she was. Her eyelids burned, and her feet ached from the days of walking, but those were not the cause of this sense of wrongness just beyond vision and hearing.

For the first time she wished they had the materials to make a campfire, except if there was danger, would that not draw attention? She drew her knees up under her cloak, grinding her chin against the thick-woven cotton-wool over her knees. How nice it would be to bathe, since there was no chance of stepping through any cleaning frames. Though the cold, and the dry dust, did not really make one feel grimy, just...

She lost herself in a daydream about the hot spring not far from the cottage back in the Valley, and memory nearly took her into dreams until a sound brought her awake.

Sound. What? She frowned. A snapping, a crunching, as of old dry grass.

Another living thing, at last? But not a friend. No, not so late, and so furtive. There was no time-candle, and she could not see the stars, but Tsauderei had taught her to sense the last hour of the day, when Norsunder's magic truly was strongest. The renewal of midnight—the beginning of a new day—belonged to the world, magic so old it was probably as old as the world itself. Of course, those who would destroy would have discovered that the weakest time was right before renewal, when the old day was dying.

But that was a diffuse balance of magical strength and weakness, no more discernible than the pull of the moon on the tides, except to mages. Tsauderei had taught her that Norsundrians also acted at that hour because of the effect of darkness and tiredness, their intent to intimidate by fear.

When the sounds resolved into the thud of human and horse steps, she got to her feet and moved a little away from the sleeping girls to pace restlessly.

"Who is there?" she whispered into the cold, still air.

"Are you the Landis?" a voice responded in very accented Sartoran. The voice was male, low, and husky.

She stayed silent, her heartbeat thumping in her ears.

"You will have to come with me," the voice continued. "It's either that or die here."

"Neither." Atan's voice cracked.

She had nothing but the ring Tsauderei had given her.

Though her fingers trembled with the intensity of her fright, she whispered the magical words and held out her fist with the ring pointing in the direction the voice had come, desperation focusing her will. The light lanced out, sudden and shocking as lightning, and nearly as powerful.

The young man gasped and clapped his hands over his eyes. Atan blinked tears from her own eyes, though the light was aimed away from her, as the young man stumbled away in an attempt to escape the light.

"Go away," she yelled. Her fist prickled unbearably. She dropped her hand, shaking it to restore sensation to her fingers, and the light vanished. Darkness closed in. "Go *away*," she shouted into the night.

The horse's hooves galloped off. Frightened into bolting? Or did the man reach it, and he was in retreat?

Atan retraced her steps on trembling legs and sat on her bedroll for the rest of the night, too frightened for sleep.

FIVE

On the far side of Sartor's northwest border mountains, Rel the Traveler entered an old trade-route inn built beside a waterfall.

The swirl of cold outside air caused the curious and the idle to look up, gazes lingering on the tall, broad-shouldered young fellow entering. Youth? Grown man? He was certainly the size of a grown man, in fact, taller and broader than most. The deep-set dark eyes could be those of a man, but the smooth cheeks, contours of chin, the quantity of glossy black hair cut short at his collar, were those of a youth.

In fact, Rel had not yet reached what would be his full height.

A troublemaker? wondered those who distrusted anyone taller than they were.

His clothing was not warlike. He wore plain riding gear, somewhat worn, but not ragged, dusty and not filthy. His expression was thoughtful, for he had been thinking of geography, and how the mage-raised mountains stretching east and west had adapted over the millennia since the losing battle against Norsunder, to be indistinguishable from those made by natural forces.

But habit also made him wary. Aware of the silence caused by his entry, he cast a quick glance around and, seeing no overt threat, proceeded to the counter, his step quiet. No strutting cock he, looking for a fight.

He also had ready coin, causing the innkeeper's

attitude to change to welcome. He gave his name as "Rel, caravan guard by trade," paid for a bed in the dorm and meals for night and morning. Then he sat with his back to the wall, where he ate and drank, ignoring speculative or challenging glances, and occasionally glancing out the dark windows, beyond which the gathering rain-clouds were slowly blotting the stars.

It had been a long ride for Rel, and for the customers, a long workday. After a time he slipped from the others' interest — all except the innkeeper's teenage daughter, who had an eye for a handsome face. And Rel was very handsome, in a style you saw mainly in heroic tapestries and the like: strong, chiseled bones, deep-set eyes, abundant hair with a bit of a wave.

But after two of three unnecessary trips to Rel's table, and only politeness in his manner and absence in those dark eyes, she too gave up with an internal shrug and returned to the pair of snub-nosed, wiry young weavers by the fire who made up for their lack of handsome looks with enthusiastic flirtation.

When Rel observed that people's boundaries of interest had contracted once again to the perimeters of their own tables, he sat back and sipped the hot mulled wine the waitress had offered in place of pie, which was all gone.

He listened to the quiet hum of chatter. The inn's common room was small, so it was easy enough to catch a sense of what occupied people's attention. Local concerns, as far as he could hear: business, weather, who was stepping out with whom, who had cheated whom, and weather again.

Shortly after he'd finished, the rain came, an earnest, slanting downpour that roared on the roof. He trod up the worn stone stairs to the next half-level, set into the mountain cliff, and opened the door first on the left.

The room was round, with one window set facing the waterfall. Four beds framed the room, with a battered old table in the center, bare except for a burning lamp. This being autumn, the bed nearest the window was free; the other three had been claimed. Rel was just as glad. He hated stuffy rooms, and didn't mind cold, as long as he wasn't wet.

He dumped his gear on the empty bed and was about to get out his map for another study when the door opened and three fellows walked in. One was older. The other two were around the same age as Rel.

The oldest gave Rel a furtive glance, which Rel noted. He also noted the relief that lightened the man's face on seeing that Rel was not going to make trouble about being left with the worst bed.

"Brisk night," this man said, coming forward to stand near the floor vent, through which the kitchen fires below sent warm air.

Rel shrugged. "Winter's comin' on," he replied in the same conversational tone.

The two young journey-weavers were obviously brothers—both blond, skinny, with snub noses that betrayed in their ruddiness the consumption of too much winter punch. Their flirtation with the innkeeper's daughter had apparently been cut short. And—yes, they were looking for trouble. It was clear from their expressions that they had decided (maybe hoped) Rel's meek acceptance of the worst bed meant that they could maybe take out their disappointment on him.

"Aye, that was one mighty bright comment," the first brother said, sneering.

"Think you can come up with another?" Brother Two followed his sib's witty jab with a verbal lunge of his own.

Rel hid a sigh. As the brothers shuffled with many side glances to what they considered the commanding positions in the small room, Rel had noted several things: the two might be hotheads but they had no training; the first one was wild-eyed in his belligerence, but the second one's wide eyes and huge pupils betrayed fear underneath his bravado; the old man withdrawing quietly to a corner to fuss with his pack.

Three years ago, Rel would have felt obliged to fight, and he'd despised himself afterwards for the damage he caused foolish people. He'd learned since that brute strength was not always necessary.

"I'll try," Rel said, standing up.

His left hand scratched his head, his right gestured emptily, elbow slightly out as he appeared to stumble against the table. Another step, and *Ow!*, *Whoog!*, his elbow collided with one Brother One's midsection, making breathing into an operation that took intense concentration, and his dropping left hand thumped against Brother Two's nose, causing tears of pain to blind that fellow.

"Oh, pardon! I didn't see — here, want a hand?" In Rel's clumsy efforts to help, somehow Brother Two got his elbow knocked against the table in just the wrong place, sending agony zapping up his arm into his already aching head, and Brother One's shin collided with a chair.

"Here — so sorry, please, I'll have you steady in a trice — "

"No!" Brother One gasped.

"Heegh," Brother Two whuffled.

They retired to sit on their beds, and the older man slid something back into his pack, and sat down, smiling. "Traveling far?"

Rel saw above the smile the speculation in that steady blue gaze, and said, "Around. Pa wants to retire, wants mountains at his back, that being a habit."

"Retire here, in Oneh Kaer?" the man asked with a skeptical air.

Rel gave a shrug. "Nobody's ever heard of it. Sounds just about right to Pa. He said he wants somewhere boring, a place no one ever hears about, with mountains at the back that no one ever crosses. He having a constitutional dislike for waking up to surprises."

"Ah," the man said, nodding. "Come from a military background, do you?"

Rel shrugged again. "Pa spent a life guarding the coast o' Khanerenth against pirates. Me, I like to travel. Usually work as a caravan guard."

Comprehension cleared the old man's brow. Khanerenth — famous for its military school — fighting pirates — border guard — it all added up to training but no trouble.

The still-groaning brothers had also registered the same information, and Rel saw the signs that they had decided to retire honorably from the list.

"Well, you could tell your pa here's the place, then," the man said. "There is the old road up behind town, but no one's been over from it since before my grandfather's day."

"Where's it lead to?" Rel asked.

The old man sighed. "That was once Sartor over there. You've heard of Sartor," he added.

Rel nodded. "Gran used to tell us old stories about it."

"And don't forget 'em." The man shook his head, pain furrowing his brow. "Bad times, we live in. But we all make our way, and never forget the better days."

Rel said, "Anyone ever been over that back road, just to see what's what?"

"Sure. Every generation some hothead has to go, and they never come back. Some sort o' bad magic traps a-layin' for the unwary, I hear," the man said. "But at least whatever's beyond it don't come back over this way. Road's probably grown over long since. Sartor is gone from history, except in memory." He shook his head. "Well, I'm for bed. Long, soggy ride for the coast, come morning, looks like."

"Good night," Rel said.

The brothers were already in bed. Rel leaned over to extinguish the lamp.

The next morning, Merewen sat up, rubbed her eyes, and sighed with relief.

Lilah sat up with a snort. "Something wrong?"

"I had a terrible dream," Merewen exclaimed.

Their voices roused Atan, who blinked tired eyes. "Danger last night." Her voice came out hoarse. She cleared her throat. "I didn't fall asleep until the sun began to rise."

Shocked and dismayed, Lilah and Merewen listened to Atan's story as they walked to the edge of the river.

"A Norsundrian," Lilah whispered, looking fearfully around. "Has to be! Did he threaten you?"

"He wanted to take me away, so he must know who I am. That means someone—Norsunder, I'm sure—knows I'm here, though Tsauderei had hoped that crossing the border on foot as we did would escape their notice, after all this time. Anyway, I used the ring. The light is very powerful. It made my own vision go dark for a time. I think it might have blinded that man, for he took it full in his face. He rode away."

"Then let's put some distance between us and him. We can go faster without any food weighing us down," Lilah said doubtfully, as she watched Merewen's small hands divide the last of the journey bread. "My guess is, Norsunder now knows the spell got broken. Or *a* spell, or whatever it was you said."

"One spell was broken," Atan said. "But the enchantment still binds."

"I thought 'enchantment' was a fancy word for spells." And at Atan's surprise, "Big ones?"

Atan walked quickly, her stale breakfast forgotten in one hand. "An enchantment is more than one spell, bound together for a purpose. The binding spell requires a key to hold it all together. That key can be a time, or a thing, or a person—just about anything."

"Then we broke one spell. What does that actually mean?" Lilah asked, hoping the answer would be, *No more danger.* "Why would they bother with a lot of little spells, anyway?"

Atan considered, then said slowly, "Are you asking about enchantments in general, or this one in specific?"

"Both. I guess," Lilah said, befogged.

Atan gave a tiny nod, more sure of herself now. "An enchantment, as I said, is many little spells bound by one that is called a key. Think of a bundle of sticks. Alone, they are not strong, and their utility is limited. Bound together, they're strong...a better example might be a bridge enchantment. These are common all over the world. There's a spell to protect the wood, a spell to protect the joins of wood to stone, or stone to stone, and so on. Then a spell—the key—that binds them together, keeping the bridge from weakening over time."

"Key, as in a door key?"

"That's the idea, but the key can be anything, as I said. Which is always the problem, because to get the key is part of undoing the enchantment. And keys can be persons, or objects. Stones of various sorts have been used."

"Stones can be pinched," Lilah said.

"Exactly. Keys can be words—"

"Which can be guessed at."

"They can be whistled song," Merewen put in suddenly, hopping over a little lizard scurrying into the underbrush.

"Got it," Lilah said, eyeing the half-buried stone the lizard had emerged from. There was faded lettering etched on it.

"To the specific enchantment over Sartor. And, I'm told, a similar one over Everon, and Wnelder Vee above it, and maybe other places. A spell to establish a boundary, a spell to separate everything in the boundary from its surroundings. A spell to ... do something that takes it out of time, somehow. Tsauderei says that this kind of spell uses truly frightening amounts of dark magic—there is no corresponding spell in light magic. To hold such power takes ferocious skill."

"And a mean spirit," Lilah commented.

"As you say. A bent for cruelty. All this bound to a key—which turns out to be me, as the last Landis."

"That is so creepy. You were just a *baby*."

"But don't you see, it's far more cruel, because I'm not supposed to be alive! The Norsundrians wanted to wipe out my family entirely, and Detlev bound the key to the last of us alive, expecting that to happen right before..." She drew her finger across her throat. "I was supposed to take the enchantment with me in death, cementing it forever. Or until he chose to undo it."

"Eugh, that really is cruel," Lilah exclaimed.

"Oh, it gets worse, because it's said he did the spell in front of my father before he was killed.'

"Even worse!"

"It was calculated to be as cruel as possible." Atan shivered.

Lilah flinched, but persisted in the manner of one who cannot resist picking at a scab, knowing it would hurt, "Did Gehlei see that happen?"

"No—she'd killed the assassin assigned to me, and escaped. Tsauderei showed me a copy of a message sent by a scribe at that last confrontation. No one witnessed the conversation between the king my father and Detlev, though many were watching. The king's face was wet with tears before Detlev went away to complete the spell, and the Norsundrians cut him down. The message got sent—it's scribbled on a page torn from a book—then silence."

Lilah wished she hadn't asked.

Atan, who had grown up with these grim tales, regretted having spoken. "Perhaps we should wait to talk about these things until we are safely in Shendoral. If we are out of journey bread, I trust we will see it before too long."

Merewen smiled tremulously. "We are very near."

"*You* can see it?" Lilah asked, squinting into the distant gray haze that looked to her exactly the same as always.

"No. But I feel it." Merewen laid her hand over her heart. "I feel it is close — maybe today, if we hurry."

"Can you lead us?" Atan asked, hope banishing her tiredness.

Merewen faced west, her eyes closed. "It's all along there." She opened her eyes, her hand pointing to the northwest.

"Then we have to leave the road," Atan said. "Because it seems to be bending to the south."

Fear was a better fuel than the dry remnants of their bread. Ignoring hunger, and then growing thirst, the girls sped through the gently undulating landscape to the west. Late in the day, a black line began to emerge through the smeary gray haze, resolving into sharp definition just as the light faded. From beyond the tangled brambles and dusty hedgerows and occasional copses of autumn-scraggly trees emerged the sky-sweeping green of tall conifers and pine, stippled here and there by the flash of scarlet and gold of just-turned leaves. The brambles gradually gave way to withered blackberry shrubs and sharp-leafed hazel.

The air smelled different. It smelled *green*, Lilah thought. To Atan it smelled like life, and to Merewen it was home.

Kessler recovered his vision with the dawn, and though the headache still lingered, he returned to where he'd left the targets.

There was no sign of prints on the aged, hard ground of the road, which continued to bend southward around Shendoral. He wasted the morning following the road until he came to a shallow valley at the bottom of which the gradual accumulation of dust revealed that no living thing had come this way for uncounted years.

The rest of the afternoon he spent riding back to that last campsite, and then searching the hard ground in widening circles until he discovered three sets of prints along the bottom of a muddy stream-bed. The prints vanished in the tall, scrubby grass, but their northwestward direction was enough to give him a vector.

He knew their destination. He also knew Shendoral's reputation. Were it true, and were his targets to reach the boundary of the purported magic, he would be forced to ignore the second part of Zydes's orders, a matter that left him indifferent: Shendoral's magic was said to visit any violence onto the perpetrator. Kessler did not want to test whether that was truth or myth, so he would ignore the order to kill the servants. But it might make grabbing his target a little more difficult.

He spotted the three silhouetted on a brief rise just as the sun was setting.

Atan heard the approach of his horse's hooves on the otherwise silent air, and croaked, "Run!"

Despite dry mouths, aching legs, and gnawing bellies, the girls ran.

Kessler urged his drooping horse into a steady trot, for it would go no faster. Trees blocked the straight chase; the animal wove its way westward through the increasing growth.

Kessler kept watching for signs of magical boundaries, but there were none. He ducked thorny creepers and nearly invisible twigs as he tried to keep his eyes on the running targets — from the voice in the night, the Landis was a girl, a matter of total indifference. The blinding magic had not permitted him to see which one of the three up ahead possessed the magical object.

It was time for a fast experiment. He pulled one of his throwing knives from a boot top, and, choosing the tallest of the three, he threw. The idea was to wing her, and thus stop all three so he could find the one wearing or carrying a magic artifact; untrained civs usually panicked at the first sight of a weapon or wound and stood around wailing and fussing.

The three veered just as his knife left his hand, disappearing down a sudden incline.

Then his horse stumbled over an unseen root and fell to its knees. Tree branches lashed his face. He reached, touched the horse's sweaty neck, and decided to retrieve his knife and abandon the chase for now. He would rest the animal, and track the three in daylight.

Lilah had been the one to see the fading light glint on the blade in the man's hand as he cocked his wrist for the throw. "Duck," she whispered, and all three dived flat into a thick growth of ferns a heartbeat before the knife thunked in a great tree trunk where they had been.

Wriggling through the ferns, they emerged from the other side and ran until lightning jabbed their sides and their throats burned.

They ran until they realized the galloping they heard was their own heartbeats, and the soft, moist air around them soothed minds as well as tired bodies. They splashed into a running stream, and bent and drank of the sweet, cold water. Then they collapsed on the soft grassy bank, and once their terror had subsided, all three fell straight into exhausted sleep.

SIX

Kessler knew that Norsunder's commanders doubted his hold on sanity. He didn't care. Surviving childhood in the deliberate savagery of the king's fortress in Narad, capital of Chwahirsland, had refined in him the ability to live in the moment, detached from any emotion except anger, which lent strength and speed.

But even that had to be rationed, for he'd seen what uncontrolled rage did to his ancestor's plans. Overweening self-indulgence in a taste for vengeance and cruelty for the sake of cruelty had been the direct cause of the failure of the king's plans. Though his army was the largest in the world, it was also the worst trained — again because the king was suspicious of conspiracy, especially from his family. There could be no thinker, no leader, but him. And that's why all the Sonscarnas were dead, except for Kessler's doddering uncle Prince Kwenz, no threat to anyone, and Kessler, who alone had escaped.

He had learned self-control, learned it so well his mind was like a series of locked vaults behind which little but darkness could be descried, even in Norsunder, a realm where mind raids were both common and unheralded.

Here in Shendoral, he sensed the blanketing protection of ancient magic that denied outside access to his mind. He also knew that the magic in Zydes's scope was not able to penetrate the border of the woodland.

For a brief time, he was free.

But it would be brief. He had no illusions about that.

He let the horse range among the sweet grasses of Shendoral, and he himself sat on a riverbank to indulge in the luxury of solitary magic studies while not being spied upon.

When night fell, he'd resume his duties. As long as he reappeared at the Base with the Landis girl as ordered, Zydes would not be interested in an exact accounting of his time.

While he sat down with his back to a tree and the morning's ration of hard biscuit and cheese in his hand, an hour's brisk walk northwards the three girls roused at last from sleep.

Lilah woke first, looking up at first with non-comprehension and then with pleasure through a ceiling of interlaced broad leaves to blue sky beyond. Blue sky! The pure blue of a cool autumn morning. And below it, crimson, amber, gold, yellow, rust, and myriad shades in-between delighted eyes that had been looking for a seeming eternity on indistinct gray-grown haze.

"Oh," she breathed.

Merewen hugged herself, knowing that she was home. Surely danger could not follow them in Shendoral! "Savar's house is not far," she cried. "There we can find hot food, and bathe, and rest."

"There are seasons here?" Lilah asked. "I thought time didn't work right."

"We do have seasons, and I have grown from very small to what I am now," Merewen answered, gesturing down herself to her bare feet. "So time is... time. But not the same in all parts of the forest, so Savar said."

All day the girls walked toward the northeast bulge of the woodland, where Shendoral ridged the gentle valley that led down to the Arveas Lake. They stopped only to eat. Blackberry bushes grew wild here, as did grapevines, and they found gleanings of nuts everywhere. The berries were not the strange, withered ones they'd found on the periphery of Shendoral. These were sweet and good, evidence of clean rain and the march of seasons. Munching these foods staved off hunger, but they all looked forward to the good soup that Merewen promised would be waiting.

Hunger, leftover tiredness, and memory of the

chase of the night before kept them from talking much. Speed was necessary, they felt — Lilah out of anticipation, Atan out of the sense of urgency that had driven her since she woke up weeks before and knew that she had to leave the Valley. And Merewen rushed along with the joy one feels at arriving home after a long trip. A favorite dell, here a mossy stone bridge, the carved patterns on the sides worn into blurs over the past thousand years, there a path—

"Just ahead," she cried at last, when the filtered greenish-gold light was beginning to slant toward afternoon. "Down this hill, past all those great redwoods."

Atan forced herself to hurry, though her feet ached and her neck felt tight. Here, at last, was a glimpse of the *real* Sartor. Wild scents assailed her, scents that she had never in her life smelled, or at least could not identify, except somehow, she must have remembered, because it smelled like *home*. She breathed in the mossy bark, the duff underfoot, the tangled vines and shrubs, and the great forest trees, her spirit winging between anguish and joy.

"There," Merewen cried. "Beyond the trees. We should see the chimney in half a breath. Come, come!" She ran, and Lilah stumped after her, imagining a hot bath and a table full of hot food.

In fact, she was thinking so hard about them — trying to decide which she wanted first — that she did not see Merewen stop, and consequently she almost ran into her back. She stumbled to a halt beside Merewen, who gazed, her eyes wide and dark with horror, her mouth open, at a square of flattened soil.

"It's not here," Merewen whispered.

Atan joined on her other side.

All three stared at the bare ground, through which tiny blades of grass could be seen springing up.

"The house. It's gone," Merewen said, louder, as though testing the truth of it. "It must have caught fire?"

Lilah frowned, staring around. "There wasn't any fire. I know what burned houses look like. Ours at home got burned in a riot. They don't just disappear, and no harm to the things growing next to the walls. What could have happened?"

"Magic," Atan said. "I can't tell you what kind."

Sorrow and grief bent Merewen until she sank to her knees in the dirt. Lilah hunched her shoulders up, her hands sliding into her pockets to close around her thief tools. Only how would those defend her against magic?

Atan looked eastward. *Do you know, Tsauderei?*

Of course there was no answer. She was in charge, as she'd always wanted to be. Had studied since her earliest memories to be—and here were two faces turned toward her, one smeared with tears, the other pale and tense.

"The house is gone, but that does not necessarily mean that Savar is gone as well. He might even have bound it in some spell, if he had something important inside," she said.

Merewen drew in a ragged breath. "Yes." She gulped. "That's right! We must hope to find him anon."

Atan nodded, relieved and worried. "Shall we camp, then find something to eat? We'll keep watch, as well. And tomorrow we'll plan our trip to the tower."

Merewen wiped her eyes. "There's a hot spring not far, and I can see if any of our kitchen garden is left. I saw the grove where the cow lived, but I fear she is gone, too. Perhaps Heron the wood-gatherer has her."

"How about later for that?" Lilah asked. "Did you say there was a hot spring?" She scratched her head, gritty from sleeping on dusty ground for so many nights.

Atan exclaimed. "Oh, that does sound good. I think I'll go into it, clothes and all. I'm one giant itch."

"Me too!" Lilah laughed.

With only a few wistful glances back, Merewen led them down mossy banks to the pool where hot water boiled up in great bubbles. It was fed by a small stream, tumbling down rocks. Dense ferns grew all around and leafy trees above, forming a kind of shelter.

Pausing long enough only to throw off shoes and cloaks (and for Lilah to bundle her thief tools under her cloak), Atan and Lilah waded in. The water at first was shockingly cold, but as they swam toward the bubbling end, eddies and swirls of warm water—sometimes hot—fizzed around them. It was exhilarating, leeching away their tiredness. Laughing, Lilah sent a wave of water sloshing over Atan, who swung her arm down and smacked up a hefty splash right back.

The water fight lasted until Merewen returned, her tunic laden with apples, three kinds of grapes, and several tubers. Atan and Lilah climbed out, exclaiming over how heavy their soggy clothes felt, and they flopped on the grass at the hot-spring end, where warm air that smelled of minerals wafted over them.

They sat and ate, and then stretched out to dry — utterly unaware that their voices, ringing through the trees, had acted as a beacon for Kessler, who had abandoned his initial plan to wait for nightfall when a bow twanged, and an arrow hit grassy bank a finger's breadth from his hand.

He turned in the direction the arrow had come. No one in sight. More importantly, no sign of numbers.

He moved away as he considered the arrow. The close correlation between the twang and the impact indicated someone not very strong, possibly another child. The arrow was a warning — possible proof of the myth about violence reacting back on the perpetrator in Shendoral. Even the wolves (it was said) ate windfall.

He, unlike many in Norsunder, did not scorn children for being children. He himself had been very small when he escaped Chwahirsland, and he recollected every detail of what he'd done.

He got up, whistled to the horse, saddled it, and rode in a slow circle, seeking the unknown archer. He respected the fact that he found no sign whatsoever; eventually he circled back to his three targets, two shod, one barefoot. Laughter rang through the trees. He noted their position, but kept at a prudent distance.

While Kessler waited for the cloak of darkness, Rel the Traveler had boarded his horse with the village smith and trudged up the weed-choked, overgrown mountain trail that had once been a mountain road.

He was alone. He did not want to risk the horse in case he was wrong, for he meant to test the strength of generations of rumor about Sartor, the oldest kingdom, the heart of the world. When he was a boy and lay in a grassy field in faraway Tser Mearsies, reading in one of his foster-father's old books about how Sartoran travelers

used to carry a handful of home soil in their pockets when
they had to leave, he'd decided one day to see Sartor for
himself.

After doing as much reading as he could, and
asking indirect questions along the route, he'd selected
Oneh Kaer as the least famed route to Sartor. It was stated
in all the books, and repeated at harbor and trade city,
that Norsunder guarded all the old roads into Sartor. But
garrisons left tracks in traffic and supply, and there was
no reference to any outpost or watchtower in rough,
bandit-infested Oneh Kaer.

The border was supposed to be half a day's march
from Waterdown Village. He would know he had
reached the border when he crossed beneath an ancient
stone archway with the words *Sartor hails thee, traveler*
carved down each side, for the oldest version of Sartoran
did not flow across the page, but vertically. The ancient
scrolls called taerans from before Sartor's Fall, rare now,
unrolled right to left, with neat lines written from top
edge to bottom.

The rain slowed Rel's progress, sometimes forcing
him to find shelter until the worst was over, but late in
the afternoon it cleared, and mellow golden light bathed
the last of his trail with light.

He slogged through ankle-deep mud, his breath
clouding at each step.

When at last he reached the archway, he nearly
passed beneath it without realizing what it was, for it was
almost completely grown over. But the unnaturally even
shape of the twining starliss made him pause and look
closer at the archway of stone, green with moss, almost
hidden by a tangle of ferns and berry bushes.

Through the archway he could see a path and
greenery.

He tossed a rock through.

No blasts of withering fire — no sparks. Nothing.

He pulled his knife, and extended it...

Nothing.

His hand.

Nothing.

His heart beat in his ears. He drew in a deep breath,
and — stepped through.

Again, nothing.

He looked around.

The road ahead was curiously clear, and even more curious, it was dry. Weirder, the backs of the stone arches were clean stone. All the moss and vine growth was on the Oneh Kaer side of the ancient gate.

The eeriness of the scene prickled the hairs on the back of his neck. He looked around again, expecting anything from some powerful mage to a host of armed warriors to bodies lying about, un-Disappeared by kin or conquerors.

Nothing.

He looked up. Gray clouds covered the sky in both directions.

Shaking his head, he began the long walk down the road, until darkness forced him to camp.

By the time Rel had found a rocky shelter and enough dry brushwood to make a fire, the girls far to the south in Shendoral were also preparing to sleep.

Atan's and Lilah's clothes and hair had sun-dried, Lilah restoring her thief tools securely in her pocket. Over a supper of raw carrots and fresh-picked grapes, the two discussed the necessity of dividing the night into watches. They agreed that poor Merewen should sleep. Not only was she dealing with her feelings about her guardian, but fair's fair: she'd found the food.

Lilah insisted on taking the first watch. "You stayed up that first night the man threatened us, so you need to catch up on sleep," she repeated.

Atan was too tired to argue. She finally gave in, saying as she slipped off her ring, "Then you must take this." And she explained in a few swift, low-voiced words how it worked.

She pillowed her head on the silky long grasses, smiling up at the trees as night birds called and chuckled. Three breaths, and she was asleep.

Lilah settled comfortably into a crook made by great tree-roots, her head against the trunk. She looked up through the treetops at the stars gleaming with faint color beyond the forest canopy.

Twice she almost dozed off, and jerked upright

guiltily. The stars had barely moved — it was still much too early. After the second time, she wondered if she ought to walk around, except her face was chilly, and she did not want to unwrap from her coat-cocoon.

Then a twig snapped not far away. Her heart thumped, sleepiness gone. She thrust her hand out, muttered the spell, and the ring blasted eye-searing light in that direction.

Lilah squinted, but saw nothing. She clapped a hand over the ring so she could regain her night vision, but a heartbeat later a hand slid over her mouth, and something sharp and cold pricked just below her jawline. She froze, afraid to make a sound.

This was the reaction Kessler had counted on — as far as he could think. Pain throbbed through his head, for he'd come straight from an encounter with one of the forest denizens. He'd struck the brat, smashing him against a tree, and the magic promptly smashed him back, driving him to his knees. Rumor, for once, did not lie. But he was used to pain. He got up and trod the last few steps to where the girls were sleeping. He stepped on a twig, averted his gaze against the expected shock of light, then grabbed the Landis girl and stuck a knife under her chin, counting on her forgetting about the magical echo effect. Sure enough, she forgot. He took her to his horse, bound and gagged her, and tossed her up onto the saddle for the ride south to Norsunder's base.

SEVEN

A tan woke up to the light murmur of voices. Birds? She opened her eyes, and found a circle of round faces looking down at her.

She sat up. "Who?" she croaked, dry-voiced.

Merewen was already awake. "They live here. I wonder if Savar knew." Her forehead puckered sadly, as Atan began taking in details. The crowd was her age or younger. Lilah was not among them

"Savar?" That was said by a sturdy boy with nut brown skin and a head of curly brown hair. "You know Savar?"

"I lived with Savar." Merewen clasped her hands. "But his house is gone, and so is he. Have you seen him?"

Four heads shook.

"Not since he brought the little one," a red-haired boy mumbled.

Quick looks sidled around.

"During winter," a girl said, and then turned her dark gaze Atan's way.

The forest-dwellers were dressed in worn, carefully mended clothes, but they were clean and did not look starved. And they all spoke Sartoran, though with a different accent than the one Tsauderei had taught her, and was used elsewhere in the world.

"Who are you?" the girl asked. The awkward lines of her gown suggested an adult's dress adapted to fit a skinny girl of maybe thirteen or fourteen. Her dark braids swung down, two neat, shining lines, to her fingertips.

Atan got to her feet and self-consciously dusted herself off, noticing distractedly that she was taller than the others, and possibly older than all but two or three of them as they looked back at her with expressions varying from wary and curious to worried.

"My mother called me Atan, and so I was raised," she said, but then she remembered that she was in Shendoral, where no dark magic would penetrate. She drew in a deep breath and stated, "My name is Yustnesveas Landis."

There. She'd said it out loud.

No lightning bolts crackled out of the sky, no temblors opened the ground to swallow them. But her own name... it felt like someone else's.

All four looked quite startled, and the girl said in a tentative voice, "Landis? Descended from — ?"

For the first time outside the cottage in the Valley, Atan said, "The king and queen."

"Savar did say the youngest of *them* might live," the dark-haired boy whispered.

The others regarded her with puzzlement and disbelief. Before anyone could speak, a groan startled them all.

The girl with the long braids was first to break and run. Everyone else followed down the banks, across the stream in heedless splashes, and up again. Halting beside a tree, Atan stared down in blank-minded amazement at a white-haired boy who sat up slowly, carefully fingering the back of his head.

That fine drift of blue-white hair, the pale skin, the taloned finger-ends... Atan was seeing her first morvende.

Eyes so light a brown they looked amber glanced up at her, then narrowed in a wince. The girl with the braids bent. "Let me see."

The white head turned, and Atan caught sight of blood-matted hair. Her stomach lurched.

"Ouch!" the morvende boy yelped. "Ooh. It was that black-haired man."

"*Told* you to get the rest of us," the stocky boy said. Then he snorted. "Trying to be a champion, eh, Hinder?"

The morvende sat up, wincing against a mountain-sized headache. "No! I was following him, as we decided. But next thing I knew he'd vanished, and then he came up behind me—"

"And you got clobbered," the girl finished.

Atan said, "A youngish man with black hair? Blue eyes?"

Four heads nodded, and everyone else looked grim. "That's the one," the girl said.

"There's no sign of him now," the redhead put in. "We looked. Since dawn."

Atan frowned uneasily, peering across the stream at the girls' campsite. No sign of Lilah. She remembered that man's demand, and fear squeezed her heart in her chest. She was reluctant to give voice to that fear, so she said, "Merewen, did Lilah tell you where she was going?"

"I did not see her when I wakened," Merewen said.

"That is odd. I would not think it like her to wander off, but then we were all so tired, she might not have wanted to disturb us. Oh, how I wish she'd woken me up for my watch," Atan declared.

The forest-dwellers scarcely listened. They were not at all interested in the missing girl. Their attention was solely on Atan, as the braid girl whispered to Hinder.

"Yustnesveas Landis?" Hinder repeated, then glanced around furtively.

Atan gave him a distracted glance. "Yes?" She peered intently into the woods, turning in a slow circle in hopes of spotting Lilah's rusty-red hair.

Hinder sighed. "Well, then, Savar was right, wasn't he?"

"And Norsunder knows it," the brown boy added, with a dire frown. "That man had to be from them."

"Of course Savar was right," Merewen said wistfully.

The girl with the braids put the horrible thought into words, saying, "He was stalking. I will venture a guess that he made off with your friend."

"He was after me," Atan admitted, sick with guilt. "I have to go after her." Fine start to reclaiming her kingdom from Norsunder, losing the first person who offered to help her.

Even if Atan had not been anxiously looking around and around as if hope and will could restore

Lilah, she would not have recognized in the furtive glances and nudges of the forest-dwellers the progress from question to decision.

Merewen was no better at interpreting these cues, and so, when the braid girl said, "We can talk about it at our place," Merewen asked, "But what if Lilah is exploring? We don't want her to come back and find us gone."

"We patrol all the time," the stocky boy said. "We'll pass the word. If anyone sees her, we'll bring her. Dorea?" He tipped his head toward a tall, skinny girl, who ran off, vanishing almost immediately among the leafy greens.

Atan sighed. She knew she was not likely to find Lilah by running around, screaming her name. And what if that man was lurking about? "I was going to call her name —"

And several voices said, "Don't!"

"We don't know if there is more than one enemy," the braid girl said. "We would rather not all be carried off, if there is a force of them."

Hinder said, "Pouldi, help me up. My head's swimming faster than a whirlpool. We'll retreat to the hideout, where we can plan in safety."

Safety? Atan cast a look at Merewen's hopeful face and thought bitterly, I can't lose this one, too. "Safety, that I can agree to. Then we will plan."

Happy, relieved smiles all around.

The braid girl introduced herself as Nirsandeas, or Sana for short. She walked at Atan's left, her bow strung, and the stocky boy — Pouldi — on the right. Atan was kept in the middle. They each carried bows, and Atan saw in the contours of their arms in those soft, old clothes that Sana and Pouldi knew how to shoot. And they knew the price they'd pay if they shot a Norsundrian in order to kill, just to protect her.

That sick feeling gripped her insides, as if events had wrenched free of her control, and tumbled down an increasingly wild river.

The redhead introduced himself as Brick — no surprise there — then gave her a rambling account of their lives in Shendoral, much punctuated by comments from the others. Only the fourth one, a weedy boy with long black hair, stayed quiet, but he was walking behind, hand on a deadly-looking dirk stuck sidewise through a worn blackweave belt, as he looked back and forth, back and forth. Atan discovered by and bye that his name was Mendaen.

"...and the first thing I really remember is meeting all the others, and Savar telling me to stay with them, and I'd be safe, but never to go outside Shendoral's boundaries, or I'd forget again," Brick said.

"You don't know who your family is?" Atan asked.

"I don't," Brick said with a shy smile. "But others do. You'll hear Lir — some of them bla — talk on about who is related to who, right down to their great-great-great-great grandparents. But those are the ones with titles and so forth. I think Savar just found me somewhere."

"How did Savar find you?"

"I don't know. He just did."

"One at a time?"

"The others just appeared, and he would always say, 'Here is a new one, children. Be very careful when you go beyond the bridge, for time works differently all over the forest.'"

"You don't know how long you've been here?" Atan asked.

The others exchanged glances. Some shrugged.

The tall teen boy said, "Here's what I noticed. Savar never remembered any of our names when he would turn up with a new one."

They sped along old pathways through dells, gentle vales, and over little stone bridges that were very old indeed. But every step that took her farther away from Lilah and the danger that had been meant for her seemed to weigh down her heart the more.

They stopped only once to drink from a stream, though everyone was hungry. From the few comments the others made, Atan gathered that the teenage orphans patrolled regularly through Shendoral, looking for anyone out of place — either others like themselves, or the occasional enemies that rode through.

"Norsunder people used to come in a lot, mostly to be away from what happens outside," Sana said as they resumed their walk.

"But they don't like it here, because they can't kill

anything," Brick added. He chortled. "And even the woods don't like 'em. I heard tell of branches falling on them, and vines tripping them, and things like that. Some of them ride round and round in a big circle. Leastways, they always seem happy enough to get out and ride south again."

"But they haven't been through in ages and ages," Sana said. "At least, until that one yesterday."

Atan wondered exactly what 'ages and ages' meant. It could be that in this forest, 'ages' were meaningless in measure.

The light slanted through the tall trees in golden shafts when at last Hinder paused, whistled a liquid series of notes. A similar whistle echoed faintly through the trees. The forest-dwellers began to run. Merewen, who had listened without speaking, ran lightly after, and Atan pounded next to Mendaen.

Over a last bridge—the brush of magic tingled along her nerves, and inside her head—and onto a grassy dell that was surrounded by leafy green trees, and huge-trunked redwoods that towered high above the others. Winter was not anywhere near this place, which glowed the bright green of spring.

She scarcely had time to register this strangeness before she found herself surrounded by a crowd. A few looked like they were her age, but most were younger.

Brick said, "In *here*, it will be safe to talk."

Hinder—still rubbing his head—stepped up onto a boulder and said, "A descendant of the king and queen did indeed live, and we have her now! Here is Yustnesveas Landis!"

A shout rang through the trees, breaking into swift chatter. Atan tried to follow the conversations, and caught scraps of words. "Man from Norsunder—another girl, got taken, we think—followed for two days, and ran out of food—didn't expect the patrol to last so long—knew Savar—house missing—" and last, "When I saw Savar last, he said that one of Them truly existed." Brick extended a hand toward Atan, and she discovered everyone looking at her, then back at Brick as he said, "And if that person came, we would have to protect the person all the way to Eidervaen and the tower."

Merewen listened with a pensive expression.

"Eidervaen," a dark-haired boy whispered. "I think—I think I remember it. A little."

"Me, too," someone else said, again hidden in the crowd. "Me, too."

"But we can't go north." That was a new voice— another morvende.

This one was a girl, who looked much Hinder's age, though she was thin as a twig and moved in a curious, drifting manner, like a leaf in the wind. She tended to look at you from the sides of her eyes, her expression less humorous and more intense than Hinder's. Her eyes were pale blue, her white hair wispy as cobwebs. "The magic still lies strong northward, for we tested it mere days ago. I almost got lost, but when I didn't come back, Averseas came after me." She pointed at an older girl.

"Sin!" Hinder exclaimed.

Sin shrugged. "It wasn't on purpose, Hin." But she looked down at the ground.

Hinder sighed. "What was it?"

The morvende girl lifted her face. "I saw someone. I really did. I thought whoever it was needed a rescue— was trying to reach us. There was no chance to go back and get a whole group together."

Silence fell, broken only by heedless birds high in the trees. Hinder touched the back of his head and winced. "I felt the same way about not getting the others when I followed that fellow, and I think the only reason why I'm not dead is because he knew what would happen if he killed me. Well, what's done is done. Sin, you were right. We have to be careful. But it could be that the spell is breaking up in pockets, just like the Loi magic makes places like this." He waved around at the springtime dell.

"I take it time does not change here?" Atan asked.

Sin and Brick shook their heads.

"But it's not like Norsunder's spells. We get day and night, and rain, and water, but otherwise it's always spring. We don't get older here. And the Norsunder people have never found us. This dell seems to be warded against adults," Hinder added.

"That would explain why Savar brought us here and let us go," Pouldi explained, waving his hand. "But he never crossed the bridge."

Before Atan could ask any more questions, a whisper ran through the crowd, sounding a little like a sough of wind in the treetops, and children parted as someone very small made her way forward.

Atan stared down in amazement at a self-possessed child of about six, who was dressed in an odd assortment of castoffs much too large for her. Blonde-streaked brown hair hung down her back, and grave brown eyes looked up at her, protuberant brown eyes with a rim of white below the iris.

"Irza says you are my first circle cousin," this child commented.

"I don't know. I hope I am. I would love to have a cousin in any circle," Atan said, sincerity ringing in her voice. "Who are you?"

"Julian," said the child. She stared up at this new cousin who smiled so kindly, a real smile, like Hinder's, only even nicer. The sunlight shone just behind her head, striking drifting hairs with gold. "Cousin," she breathed, shivering with a new, warm feeling inside.

A new teen girl stepped forward with the air of one who had the right of way. She had a cloud of curling light hair and a prepossessing gaze. She was the most well-groomed of them all, though her clothes were patched and ragged like everyone else's. But they were neat, the patches edged with embroidery to hide them. "I am Irzaveas Ianth of the third circle of Star Chamber and of the duchy of Yostavos. I have watched over Julian. She is daughter to Julian-Sartora Dei, the queen's sister — your mother's sister." Irzaveas's voice slowed to a testing tone.

Atan was not yet ready to deal with the complexities of Irza's tone. In her mind she repeated the words: *your mother's sister*. Julian was not a Landis, then, even though she had the eyes; two had not escaped Detlev's vicious enchantment. The Dei family, so famous (some records said infamous) had intermarried with the Landises several times in past generations.

Atan squashed the impulse to ask what had happened to her aunt. Julian might not know, and the answer in any case could not be a happy one. She held out her hand. "Call me Atan, Julian. That was my mother's heart-name for me."

Irzaveas lifted her chin, then brought it down. "In

my turn, I beg you will call me Irza, which is my circle-name."

Atan had practiced her speech about circle-names and court-names and the like so many times she felt the words shaping her lips, but always before, she'd imagined speaking to friendly faces, each wanting to share her idea of the circle of humanity.

There was no sign of that friendliness in Irza's face. The smile was there on the lips, but not in her cheeks, or her direct gaze. Irza's chin was lifted, her head tilted. Challenge.

And here were small, warm fingers clutching her hand. Julian smiled up into Atan's face. "I'm so glad you came," she said.

Perhaps it was better to save the speech. "I'm so glad to meet you," Atan said to Julian, and then to Irza and the others, "All of you. But right now, I wish to rescue Lilah," she said firmly. She had almost said the word 'command' but what if they did not obey? There was no sign yet that they would obey her. Cherish her because of her name, yes. Listen to her, possibly. Definitely respect her rank. But actually follow her commands?

No one answered. No one moved as the older teens sidled glances at each other.

Merewen got to her feet and ran back across the bridge, vanishing among the trees. No one tried to stop her. Atan wondered what would happen if she did the same, then saw Brick and Sana looking uneasy, and both stepped toward the bridge, standing firmly to block it.

"We feel sorry for your friend," Hinder said earnestly. He looked apologetic, as did Brick and Pouldi and Sana.

"But *you* cannot go chasing after a Norsundrian, not if you are the last Landis," Irza stated. She did not look sorry at all. "*We* know our duty. Our patrollers will be on the watch for the enemy and your friend. But your place is here, and our place is to guard you and keep you safe for the kingdom." The words, that tone, stung. But they were right. Atan had to think of everybody, did she not?

"We'll make a celebration," Hinder suggested, and Sin cheered, looking around and making surreptitious hand motions.

"We have a swing," Julian announced proudly. Shall I show you?"

Others quickly joined it, the younger children with enthusiasm. They liked celebrations.

Atan sighed. She now had before her a horrible dilemma: if she resisted, her very first conflict would be with her own people.

She agreed outwardly, but resolved inwardly to find a way to get a message to Tsauderei—that is, if he was not already watching. Yes! Tsauderei must be watching the borders of Norsunder, as he had for years. Surely he would see Lilah. And he'd be able to act. Because even if she caught up with that knife-throwing man, what else could she really do? *He* certainly wasn't going to obey a command from Sartor's last queen. But Tsauderei had been tangling with them all his long life.

She smiled at Julian. "Show me your swing," she said.

EIGHT

An arm strong as a steel band clamped round Lilah's middle, making it impossible to move. Her wrists hurt, but when she tried to raise her hands to pull at the knot with her teeth, her assailant dropped the reins long enough to clip the side of her head, and she stilled. She next tried to work her tongue and teeth against cotton-tasting gag, but it was too tight, her jaw ached, and her head began to pang. She had to give up.

Thus began a frightening ride through the night.

Time crawled in a dreary swing between awareness of cold, and dust, and endless road, and a nightmarish doze. Her head would drop forward until the horse's gait broke rhythm and she'd jolt awake, her neck throbbing, to discover that *this* part of the nightmare was in fact real.

A dull gray dawn gradually pushed the shadows back while Lilah dozed again. When the horse paused at a stream to drink, Lilah roused into wakefulness, flinching at invisible needle prickling through her muscles. Day had arrived.

The horse was dark brown, its mane snaggled after days of travel, its sides dusty. Whoever had grabbed her clearly didn't have another mount waiting somewhere — like with friends. So he was alone. They were entirely alone, and had been all night, so why was she still gagged?

Indignation mixed with fear and aches. Who was this villain, anyway? She twisted her head to peek up behind her, and caught sight of a young man's face. He looked a little older than Peitar, but younger than Uncle Dirty-Hands, the horrible, awful, disgusting former king of Sarendan, Darian Irad.

This man had short, curly black hair and light blue eyes. His eyes were shaped like Atan's. That gave her a really nasty jolt. Was it *possible* that Norsunder had managed to twist one of Atan's relatives and send him after her? Except why had he grabbed Lilah instead?

She winced. Her head hurt, her mouth felt dry as the dusty trail, and her neck ached. She tried to ease that rock-like grip round her middle, only to feel the arm tighten. The reins snapped against her ear, stinging smartly. "Sit still," he snapped in flat-accented Sartoran.

Lilah yelped behind the gag.

"I suppose," the man said, "you are hungry and thirsty. We'll stop at sundown. Until then, you'll live." His voice was slightly husky, almost more whisper than voice.

It was creepy because there wasn't any expression at all in it, except for the sarcasm in the last two words. Was this man, maybe, one of those ones who were killed and sent back alive again, their souls taken by the authors of Norsunder? The idea of it made her quake inside.

The dreary, plodding ride made the day seem the longest she had ever endured. It was broken only by stops for the animal to drink as the hidden sun made its slow way across the sky behind those thick clouds. Still no sign of anyone. And yet she was still gagged. Indignation built into frustration and simmering anger, words of protest piling up behind that gag.

They finally stopped on the banks of a tributary to the Ilder River. The man dismounted, pulled Lilah off, plunked her down onto a flat rock hanging over the rushing water. "Sit. Don't move."

She sat, fingering uselessly at the tight-bound gag, too tired and achy and light-headed to run—she could always try, but she knew she wouldn't get far. And her ear still stung a bit, making her wary of what would happen if she did run and he caught up.

The man took care of the horse, leading it to drink a few paces away, then rubbing it down thoroughly. He finished by putting a feedbag around its head.

While the animal lipped and snuffled its way through its dinner, the man dug out another sack from his saddlebags, and pulled out one of the hard-crusted breads that looked a lot like what the warriors at home in Sarendan ate, when they couldn't get anything else. Supposedly the inside stayed soft—though that depended on how old the bread was.

He tore the bread in half, cut crumbly cheese, and tossed her share onto her lap. To that he added a few grapes that he'd obviously picked while riding through Shendoral.

The sight of the grapes reminded her of Shendoral. A cramp of anguish tightened her insides, but she was glad to have them.

With a sudden yank he pulled off the gag, ripping out a few strands of her hair with it. Then he did something to that tight knot at her wrists, and the rope fell away.

"Eat up," he said as she rubbed her sore wrists. She was puzzled by his leaning out over the water, until she saw him trail the gag in it to wash it clean. A tidy assailant. Weirdly, she almost laughed, but she was too scared, too mad—and too thirsty.

Lilah looked at river, her tongue dryer than the dust around her feet. She carefully folded her food into her dusty robe, holding it in place as she knelt on the bank to drink.

The water was so cold it made her teeth ache, but it tasted good, and felt good on the wrist of the hand she used to scoop it up. She drank until she gasped for air, then sat with her back to a stone and tackled her food.

He was already done with his share. As she chewed the bread (yes, it was just as dry and tough as she'd feared), he washed his hands and his knife, sheathed that, and then sat down, staring at her.

"Landis is your family, that much I know. What's your given name?" he asked.

Lilah squeaked in her home tongue, "You mean Atan's?" And almost choked on a bit of cheese.

"What?" he repeated in Sartoran, eyes narrowed.

Of course her first instinct was to exclaim that he was a blockhead, and that he had the wrong person. She wasn't Yustnesveas Landis! She was Lilah Selenna of

Sarendan!

But she hesitated, and stared down at the crumbs in her lap as her fingers toyed with her last grape.

And here began a furious inward battle.

She could tell him who she was, of course. And then what? He'd probably kill her on the spot and ride all the way back—and get Atan, and condemn all of Sartor forever.

The backs of her arms prickled with chill and her insides churned as she struggled mentally. Not even the night before her brother's trial had been this terrible, for that time it was not her own life in jeopardy, but her brother's—and there had been no agonizing decision before her. Just the sickening waiting.

Either she spoke up now, probably ending up dead, and definitely endangering Atan. And everyone else who depended on her breaking the waiting spells.

Or... what? Go on, pretend she was Atan? And then what? Probably get killed! But so far it hadn't happened. That meant someone wanted Atan alive. If she could fool them long enough for Atan to free Sartor—wouldn't that be a good thing? Yes, for Sartor. But what about her?

She was already in trouble—how could it get worse? Oh, she knew it could always get worse. She'd seen plenty of how worse things could get during the revolution.

In difficult situations she'd always asked herself what Peitar would do. She could see so clearly her brother's austere face, the ardent ring of conviction in his voice at the trial. His life had been forfeit, but he'd spoken up for the sake of others, because he'd thought it was the only chance he had to speak and be heard.

If he could do it, could she do less? And with bleak wryness—not humor, she was too afraid for that—she realized the decision had been made.

And so she opened her eyes, and though her stomach by now was roiling and boiling with fear, she popped that last grape in her mouth, and sighed inwardly, then said, "The name is Yustnesveas Landis." She couldn't quite lie.

"You're done," the man said. "Turn around."

"What?" She blinked, confused.

The man yanked her wrists behind her and tied

them in a way that did not cut off her circulation, but she could not wriggle loose or reach the knots. Too late she remembered the Lure in her pocket. *Why* hadn't she pulled it out, thrown the petals at him, and when he fell over into the deep sleep caused by the Valley flowers, escaped?

Because of the headache, and tiredness, and him thinking I'm Atan, that's why. Still, she scolded herself as her ankles were bound. Stupid stupid stupid!

"Two nights and two days I've spent running after you," the man said as he tired the long end of the rope around his own wrist. "I want some sleep, and this way I am sure to get it. If you make any noise, you'll get the gag as well."

So saying, he pulled her coat around her so she turned into a giant worm, and then pushed her so she landed flat in the dust. She curled onto her side so her hands wouldn't hurt quite as much. She turtled her head into the collar of Gehlei's thick coat. At least it pillowed her head a little against the hard ground.

Sounds were loud and distinct: the crunch of boot heels in the gravel, the snap and rustle of a trail blanket that he spread on the flat stone, the thud of the horse's hooves. The endless rush, rush, rush of water over stone.

About the time she fell asleep, up in Shendoral to the northeast, Hinder faltered in the middle of a song, touched the back of his head, then slid into a faint.

NINE

The next morning, while Hinder lay safely in Shendoral's springtime glade, recovering — and far to the south Kessler forced himself to saddle the horse, untie his pris-oner, and begin the long ride to the Norsunder Base — Atan tried to learn the names of Savar's rescuees. She listened to as much of their stories as they wished to tell. She was polite, attentive, and courteous, but not forth-coming.

"She's angry with us for not letting her search for her friend," Hinder said to his cousin as they stood in line for pan bread one morning.

"So what?" Sinder responded with a shrug. "The patrols are looking. Could she really do any better?"

"I don't know, Sin. You've known her as long as I have."

"Exactly, Hin." Sinder clapped her cousin on his bony shoulder, and tapped her talons against her bowl. "If she were trained for scouting, if she were an expert with weapons, if her magic skills could penetrated Norsunder's spells, I'd say, let her do what she wants. But she's not even forest-trained." The cousins observed Atan climbing carefully down the rope ladder from the tree platform they'd given her.

Sinder picked up her bread in one hand, her bow in the other, and ran off to join the morning patrol. Hinder sighed, knowing that his cousin wouldn't think about Atan's reflective gaze, her sad smile. Sin wasn't interested in people the way she could crouch at the side of a pond and watch the flutter and flex of a duck's feet, or stare up at the slow pattern of leafy boughs swaying in a wind. He let her go, picked up his own bread and, hearing the familiar triple-beat melodies of a swing song, ducked under a low branch and ran to the smaller clearing beneath the girls' tree, where they'd discovered an old platform swing.

Tall Atan stood with her eyes closed, surrounded by smaller figures. The only time Hinder had seen her smile was when she swung, though he could see from her stiff stance and her tight grip on the bar that she still was getting used to the motion. The older forest-dwellers had agreed that there'd be no circle over the bar until Atan was ready.

There was a space on one side. He jammed the last of his bread in his mouth and hopped on.

Several days passed, rain moving in.

The forest-dwellers stayed in great tree-platforms that the dawnsingers had constructed centuries ago. Atan lay in her snug hammock at the end of each day, listening to the patter of rain on green leaves, and fighting against that anxious helplessness that underlay everything she did, said, or thought. Every day that ended without news of Lilah was another day of personal failure; the only escape was this new thing she'd read about, but no book could possibly describe the pleasure of the plain old Sartoran swing. Sometimes she counted the arcs, hoping that each would bring her closer to news of Lilah.

As for Lilah, each day saw her further south.

Lilah had decided to keep on pretending to be Atan, but how to escape? She could use her Lure, make Kessler sleep, but what if the horse also went to sleep? She wasn't sure how far the power of the blossoms reached, or what its effect on animals was. What if it threw her off, or ran toward the Norsunder Base? How would she know, as she had no idea which direction to go in? The sky was always gray, and the landscape steadily more dusty and rocky, with no landmarks at all to guide by.

It would be better to bide her time. She suspected

that she would only get to use the Lure once. It had better be when escape was a clear way out.

Kessler had no use for Yustnesveas Landis. Being a mage-trained princess, she'd either prate a lot of gibberish about good and evil, or else she'd mouth out defiant lies. His intention was to get this demeaning assignment done with as fast as possible, and carry on with his plans—but he must first deliver a live prisoner who was reasonably in her wits.

At the same time, he respected the abilities of the young. There was not only his own experience, but his defeat in '33 had been initiated by a pair of girls even younger than this Landis.

On finishing her ration the next morning, she asked, "Are we going to the Norsunder Base?" he answered "Yes."

Then she blurted out, "Are you really dead?"

None of his astonishment at that question showed on his face. When he saw the incipient terror in her slanted gaze, he lied. "Yes. Killed by a brat your age. I exist only for revenge."

That last part was true enough—and his reward was a shocked silence, which was scarcely broken for the remainder of the journey.

Now Lilah was too afraid to attempt to use her Lure. What could possibly work against the walking dead whose souls were owned by Norsunder's distant creators? She was afraid that the magic keeping him alive would also keep him from falling into Lure sleep— though she wasn't sure, because he did seem to need regular sleep, though far less than she did.

She was even afraid to use that ring again, which obviously hadn't worked, or she wouldn't be here. In fact, she didn't even like looking at it, she discovered when she examined the milky gem. Its soft glow rippled slightly, as if water ebbed across its surface or just under. When she stared at it, she felt a nasty sensation, as if the ring sucked light right out of her eyes.

When Kessler led the horse to water, she pulled the ring from her finger and slid it into her robe's secret pocket next to the Lure, her heart slamming against her ribs. What if he asked for it? Did he even remember it? The ring was Atan's, not hers, and she didn't want to lose it, uncanny as it was.

Better to wait, keep her tools secret, and use them on those she knew were still, well, *human*. This Norsundrian didn't really act human. He talked in that flat soft voice, never looked around, never showed any kind of emotion — even anger.

The rain caught up with them when they reached some barren mountains. Great fire-blackened cliffs rose on either side, obviously blasted by magic. Beyond the ridge of mountains jutted a massive fortress. It had to be the Norsunder Base. They had run out of journey food, and even Kessler's canteen was empty. Though she could orient by heading away from that thing, how long would she last without food or water? Not long, she suspected, her eyes stinging with tears as she feared she'd waited too long.

But she still had her tools. She would not give up yet.

Zydes stood on one of the western towers, watching a field exercise through a glass, though he was far more aware of Detlev standing at his left than of the warriors skirmishing on the dusty plains.

Dejain stood beyond, busily plying a field glass, the hypocrite. Zydes knew she detested the noise, stink, and squalor of battle even more than he did.

And he was right. That is, mostly right. She swept her glass over the converging forces, most of whom thought they were wargaming, trying to find by some sign which unit had been given the kill order. She always watched the beginning of an exercise in order to descry, if she could, who had the kill order. Sometimes they betrayed their triumph by subtle signs, sometimes obvious — and sometimes not at all. Then she'd watch the others for reactions to the realization that they had become targets. Or trophies. Or warnings.

Keeping the glass aimed toward the plain, she flicked a quick sideways glance.

Detlev stood with his hands behind his back, his attention downward, in appearance an ordinary man brown of hair. He did not use a glass. She wondered if he made any sense of the chaos of blades, dashing horses, milling infantry, and dust obscuring everything. Probably. Though he gave no sign, one wing of cavalry wheeled, streaming toward a flank. She knew he had somehow sent an order mentally. It was so sudden, and there had been no trumpet call or waving of banners from any of the captains below.

An intense spasm of envy and longing tightened her insides. *How* she would love to have that power! She indulged herself with a daydream: her first target would be that slab-faced fool standing at Detlev's right...

While she enjoyed her fantasy, Zydes was thinking much the same thing about her. But underneath his desire to crush Dejain's life out — slowly, slowly — he was anxious about time.

He'd ordered the field exercise mostly to divert focus from Kessler, who, he had seen in the scope just that morning, would arrive within the day from the other direction. But the exercise had somehow been noised beyond the physical realm, and Detlev had shown up, unannounced as always, with Dejain mincing sycophantically at his heels.

Zydes gripped his glass, wishing he had her skinny neck between his hands. After exhaustive investigation he had discovered that she'd not only managed to keep herself free from the disaster of Kessler's astonishing plans in '33, though she had been his ally, but she'd managed to twine his *own* magic in her machinations, causing his defeat in Bereth Ferian. She was therefore responsible for him being stuck in this dusty hole far from anywhere interesting.

Well, he'd pay her in like coin — as soon as he had that Landis safely locked up. Before anyone could discover who she was.

He plied his glass, trying not to shift from one foot to the other.

Dejain observed the signs of his impatience and laughed inwardly. He was obviously up to something. Oh yes. She'd find out what.

He, like these military fools below, all thought they were on the rise to power. But she'd learned that those with real power in Norsunder tolerated mages like Zydes so that they would handle logistics. Probably the only

mage, outside of Detlev and of course *Them*—the Host of
Lords, to whom Detlev answered—that held power was
the vicious old mage Vatiora, who rarely emerged from
Norsunder. Her deeds had bloodied the pages of
countless histories several centuries back, and though
she'd escaped death only by hiding out in Norsunder, she
made Kessler look sane and mild by comparison, her only
weakness a pettiness equal to her bloodlust. She was
ruled by whim, and put the same no-limits effort into
spite as she did into vast plans.

Outside of people like Vatiora, who seemed to live
for cruelty and bloodshed, most allied with Norsunder in
order to indulge a taste for war, or for spying—but never
for logistics, the necessary third component for war.

Zydes was the perfect quartermaster, and he didn't
even know it.

Both Zydes and Dejain were startled when Detlev
turned away from the battlement. The field exercise had
scarcely begun. What now?

Detlev's gaze flicked Zydes's way. Zydes braced
himself inwardly; he was considerably taller, but
somehow you never thought of Detlev as shorter. He
forced himself to meet that gaze, felt the expected pain
strike through temples to the backs of his eyes, and then
Detlev said, "Marigor is slow, and he doesn't seem to
understand that heavy cavalry can break a line, not just
protect the foot's back. I suggest a protracted maneuver."

Zydes nodded.

Detlev smiled slightly. "You don't want them
getting lazy, either foot or mounted."

Without waiting for an answer, he lifted his hands
and transferred out.

Zydes became aware of the sweat on his brow, but
he wasn't going to wipe it with that smirking Dejain
there.

"Quite edifying," she said.

Apart from the sudden, vicious desire to smash his
glass across her face—of course he controlled that—
Zydes did not react. Then, as the rage ebbed a little, he
recognized that tone, an attempt to emulate Detlev.

She'd failed. He laughed, not bothering this time to
hide it.

She transferred out. He cursed her, then worried at

Detlev's parting remark. What did he mean? Did he know about Zydes's forming plans for Sartor? He *couldn't* know. Could he?

Zydes forced himself not to hurry down to his rooms, but he was blind to anything else besides his agonized questions until he reached the relative safety of his warded lair. There he cautiously performed the oblique ward he'd set up to track Detlev.

It still worked. And, better, Detlev was again off-world.

Letting his breath trickle out, Zydes prepared for Kessler's arrival.

Lilah's eyes were gritty with dust, and ached from the long ride and the parched air, when they reached an outpost. Kessler did not permit them to stop long enough for a drink of water. He left the exhausted horse and demanded two more. Lilah got to ride alone, but he held the reins to her horse.

It was nearly impossible to see where the gray-covered sky began and the rocky, broken land ended, except for a weird line somewhere in the distance. It seemed to waver beyond the fortress.

Lilah couldn't make out what it was, but Kessler stilled, then made one of his sudden moves. *Snap!* His reins slapped against the rump of the Lilah's mount, and it leaped forward, nearly casting her off its back.

The animals raced down the road as the light began to fade — and that line got closer as the lines of the fortress sharpened.

Exhausted, hungry, desperate with thirst, Lilah wondered if she had somehow been taken into Norsunder's realm beyond death, for the light faded so slowly, making her feel blind, and they rode and rode and rode.

How her head throbbed! And her butt ached, and her lungs from the dust, and her lips were dry. Kessler had dwindled to a sinister shadow on her left, his gray tunic-jacket blending with the landscape.

But then, just as the last of the light faded, the fortress loomed over them. Torchlight high on the battlements glowed, red and wicked. The dust was worse than ever; a cold wind had arisen from where the last pale gray gleamed on the horizon, bringing gouts of dust, and an ugly hot-metal smell that made her shoulders hunch and her neck-hairs prickle.

Gradually she became aware that the sound she heard, a low, thundering noise, was not just her aching head. Just before they rounded a massive stone tower, she glanced to the side and saw a vast line of bobbing torches.

An army! An invasion?

Fear made her look to Kessler, though she wondered why. He was certainly not going to save her from anything. The orange light of the torches overhead illumined the angry jut of his chin and his narrowed eyes. It was almost a human expression, but not a pleasant one. They galloped up a ramp and into a stable yard, from the smell. Only then did they stop.

"Dismount and come along."

Lilah blinked wearily. Kessler was standing at her stirrup. She managed to slide out of the saddle and fell right onto the stones. A strong hand yanked her up by the arm. She stumbled against the horse's heaving sides. The animal's hair was slick with sweat, and bits of foam had splashed over its withers. The smell stung her nose — not unpleasant, just sharp. Anything was better than dust.

The hand yanked her again, as the thunder grew louder. Her feet fumbled beneath her. Pangs shot up her arm into her head as Kessler thrust her through a torchlit archway.

Stable hands dashed out for the horses. Lilah's last glimpse of the courtyard was two grim faces glancing after them before the animals were led away. They'd arrived just ahead of a big army, it seemed. Not invading, but returning.

Up stairs. Down a long corridor. The air was stuffy and smelled of old stone. The world seemed to have turned into darkness and dust.

She sneezed three times as Kessler rapped on a thick wooden door. He pushed her into a room. Blinking tears from her eyes, she stumbled, then looked up at a huge man dressed in Norsunder gray and black, who glowered at her, twin gleams of red torchlight briefly reflecting in his dark eyes. He stood behind a great dark-wood desk.

Zydes was quite pleased with what he saw. This fox-faced scrub of a child was as unlike the tall, strong, farseeing Landises of legend as was humanly possible. She didn't have the ugly gooseberry eyes common to the Landises, which were so well-known he'd hoped to be able to brandish her (when he was ready), letting her face serve as proof of who she was. But not all of them had those eyes. This girl's father hadn't, from all accounts. He hoped she was as stupid as she looked.

"To business," he began, but a rap at the door interrupted him.

The door opened. A tall fellow came in, bearing papers. Lilah tried to blink away the bleary rings round the lamps on the desk and the torches outside the windows. The hulking form of the newcomer blocked the man behind the desk.

That meant he couldn't see her. A heartbeat's chance. She took it.

She sprang through the open door just before it shut, and dashed madly down the hall — where? Where?

She'd forgotten Kessler, who had retired out of the reach of the lamplight to lean against the wall. The world revolved slowly, for he, too, was exhausted. He had been reflecting with regret on the days when Dejain's magic had enabled him to work straight through nights without ever having to sleep. Except after the spell had worn off — causing a stupid sleep-haze for weeks — he'd understood that she had done him no favor, that clear thought had disintegrated with imperceptible slowness, leaving him with the distortion of dream-image overlaying reality.

He was startled when the brat whirled and bolted. He caught up in five steps.

Once again those five steel bands clamped onto Lilah's arm, just before she was about to launch herself down a stairway. She was suspended in the air, arms and legs extended useless as a lifted turtle's, and then her vision whirled and her feet landed with a painful thump on the flagged flooring.

Kessler's fingers shifted to the scruff of her neck, almost choking her, and back to that office they marched. In the doorway he paused, and she glanced up, bracing for violence, glaring past her overlong bangs.

"You need a haircut," he remarked, and then thrust her back inside.

The messenger was gone. Zydes drummed his fingers on the desk.

He said to Lilah, "Don't waste my time again." And with a glance at Kessler, who had released the neck of Lilah's dust-caked robe and retreated to his place at the wall, "At least not while I have my hound who is so quick on the fetch."

Lilah stared. The tall one smirked, a very unpleasant expression in that glaring lamplight. Kessler's face — as usual — did not change.

"Where is your magical aid, young Landis?" the man asked, holding out his hand.

Magic aid? Magic aid?

Her bewilderment was plain. Zydes sighed. Was she really so stupid? Better so, perhaps. "You used magic against Kessler."

Lilah tried to lick her lips, but her tongue felt dusty. Her voice came out like a frog's croak. "It was a magic ring that makes light. But I lost it when he grabbed me." Her heart thumped again at the lie.

Zydes looked at her grubby robe in disgust and disappointment. He was too disinterested to bother searching the brat. A magic ring that only emitted light: that matched what he'd seen. Useless to him. But it also meant the brat was no mage.

He snapped his fingers at Kessler. "Put her in the far room, and lock the door. She's too sleep-sodden to hear one word in five. We'll begin again in the morning."

Out they went again, Kessler's hand on Lilah's collar. He pushed her into a plain room with a single window. She turned around. "Who is that villain?" she asked, her mind now weirdly numb after all the frights.

"Zydes," said Kessler. And with that faint almost-humor, "He likes subordination. You had better stay with 'sir.'"

He slammed the door and locked it.

Lilah slapped her pocket, wherein resided her thief tools, including her lock pick. She'd been well-trained during the revolution, and could tell from the sound that these locks were old indeed — old and crude.

Why would they bother with new locks? Once one

got out, where would one go? "But I have to try," she whispered, becoming aware of the steady sounds of horses and iron-reinforced boot heels on stone. She moved to the window and looked out. The window gave onto a complicated angle of tower curves and buttresses, thence to a narrow concourse below.

What seemed to be an entire army marched under her tired eyes. Streams of warriors passed below, some mounted, most not. Numbers of them bore wounds, evidenced by cloth wrapped around arms, and comrades carrying those who had difficulty walking.

Her mind wheeled purposeless, like a bird caught in vicious crosswinds, until she was startled out of fugue by a vaguely familiar outline, and a familiar walk in the midst of that countless horde: a slim man of medium height in the middle of a row of three, dark hair pulled back, the wary walk of the life-trained warrior —

The man's head lifted at the last moment, and Lilah stared down into a face she had known her entire life.

Then he was gone, leaving her to stumble to the single wooden chair and sink down, terror having scattered all her wits. Everything was gone except one inescapable fact: she had seen her uncle, Darian Irad, former king of Sarendan.

And he had seen her.

TEN

The first live creatures that Rel encountered were horses.

Trained horses, wandering about in a small herd. At first they were skittish, but they stayed close to him, and after a half day of steady walking, he was able to make friends with one. They had no saddles, and their hooves were new-shod. That was odd, but because there were no people around to ask, he mounted the one that nudged his shoulder expectantly. The rest of the herd followed.

He'd learned to ride bareback when he was so small that he'd had to climb onto a fence to scramble onto horses' backs. As a teen, it had been a matter of challenge among his friends to be able to vault to horseback. He took a moment to rub that spot on the animal's spine where the shoulders joined, and when the horse licked its lips, he pressed his palm lightly and leaped up.

The animal walked a couple of steps, getting used to Rel's size, then tossed its head. He nudged with his knees—and sure enough, the horse obediently began to trot.

Shifting from horse to horse, he rode down the great mage-made mountains, wondering what it had been like to live through such a spectacular cataclysm. Purple-gray haze obscured the horizons, masking the lowlands.

No one stopped him, neither friend nor enemy. Most noticeable was the silence. Not even the trill of birds broke the profound hush. To find Sartor silent, after reading of its endless music, was more sinister to Rel than anything he had seen so far.

Not that he saw anything threatening. It was as if the entire kingdom were empty. The haze was never quite like fog—he never passed through it. It seemed to recede into the middle distance, like a mirage on a sunbaked road, and the sky remained obscured beyond a thick layer of cloud.

Occasionally he passed villages and, as he proceeded southward, towns. On the borders of each he'd feel as if someone had stuffed his head with that haze. Once he tried forcing his way past. The animals became restive, and his own mind slipped into a strange sort of dream-state. He retained enough of a sense of alarm to turn away, without knowing that he was escaping the whirlpools and eddies of magic that still bound the inhabited areas.

He did not try any villages or towns again. Instead, he stayed on the south road until he reached the great city of Eidervaen. Ancient as it was, it was built on the ruins of an even more ancient city, legendary Ilderven, made before the terrible mage-war that had raised that ring of mountains to the north and far to the east, like the rim of a bowl round the kingdom.

A bowl that had not been able to keep the enemy out.

Nothing prevented him from riding into the city. The streets were entirely empty. All Rel heard were the clopping steps of the horses.

The strange gray haze swirled around various buildings, muting them. Rel kept riding, veering not at all, as the street widened, becoming a great concourse lined with old silver-leafed argan trees.

The upper arches, spires and towers of a palace soared above the rooftops. Central to the palace gleamed the white-stoned tower that was reputed to go all the way back in time when humans had first come to this world. That tower reminded him of another castle he knew of on the other side of the world, raised to a cloud city above a mountain. Until now he'd thought that white castle the only one of its kind.

He kept his gaze on that tower, and rode steadily.

When he neared the palace, again the horses began

to get skittish. Rel dismounted and walked alone, for no one was in sight. He thought back and back, of old histories he'd read in the house of his foster-father, and ancient ballads. Voices seemed to whisper in a tricky wind; cold air that smelled of ice made him flex his hands and hunch inside his cloak.

He stayed on his path, unable to look away from that tower. He had no plan, nothing but unvoiced intent. His mind filled with images from dreams, his and those of the records he'd read, the voices mixing and whispering in liminal space.

He sat down at last on the steps of a terrace at the entrance to the great palace, wondering what it was he was supposed to do here.

He did not notice when the light faded. And then rose. And faded again, for he was now beyond hunger and thirst, and such things as the passing of days no longer carried meaning.

Norsundrians in the military and magical branches seldom bothered with children. No one wanted to be cumbered with the unending physical care of the very young, and the sort of people who chose Norsunder were seldom domestic in inclination or talent.

If you needed recruits, it was far simpler to pinch them at an age old enough so that daily care was not much more than that of a horse, but young enough so that you could exert your will to make them into what you wanted.

The sight of a child (boy? girl? who cared!) up in Zydes's lair, reported by some stable hands, caused some surprise. It was duly corroborated later when the quartermaster was told by Kessler to issue the smallest uniform they had ready. The only reaction was some laughter—finally Zydes found someone to impress—or some speculation on what plots he was concocting now.

Before Lilah saw Zydes next she got to walk through a cleaning frame, feeling a brief sense of relief as magic separated grime and dust and sweat from her skin and hair and teeth. But the air smelled so stale and flat and dusty, she didn't enjoy it long.

Her gown, ruined by the journey, was exchanged for long black trousers, a heavy linen shirt, and a sturdy black winter tunic-jacket, for they didn't have any of the gray ones small enough. The tunic had inner pockets, she discovered. She ignored those, and unpicked tiny places in the hem of sleeves and jacket to stash Atan's ring and her thief tools, plus the Lure. That way, if Zydes changed his mind about the ring and wanted to search her pockets, he'd find them empty. When she walked out, she looked like the youngest of the night-riding scouts or messengers.

Kessler was waiting. He said, "Don't try another bolt."

"I won't," she squeaked, her throat tight with worry. Did the dead also read minds? "Are you a long-dead Landis?" she asked.

He laughed, and she flinched at the mockery. "No," he said. "My ancestral line crossed yours centuries ago. Why?"

She almost said, *Because your eyes look like Atan's,* but managed to remember her guise. A thrill of fear made her desperate. "I—I don't know. Something Zydes said."

He had clearly lost interest. "Come along. You'll mess down this way."

"With all those warriors I heard last night?" She was almost breathless with relief at the close call.

"No. This end is command and support staff. Zydes," he added in his soft, expressionless voice, "is the current commander."

"Oh." She heard the faint emphasis on *current*. Her neck-hairs prickled again.

They walked to a plain room of stone and high windows that looked out at gray sky. Sounds of weapons and shouts drifted in from an unseen court, a rhythm that called up unexpected memories from early childhood, when she heard her uncle's guard drilling at the royal palace. She felt the same dread, intensified by her wondering if her Uncle Dirty-Hands had told anyone his niece was here, and what would happen when he did.

Lilah tried not to worry as she was shown where to get her food. She plunked her plate down at a table where no one else sat. Kessler left her alone.

The food was plain: fresh-baked bread, cheese, limp

greens obviously brought in from somewhere a long ways away, because there were certainly no gardens here, and broiled chicken. She was hungry, so she ate it all, and was pressing her thumb over the crumbs in order to munch those, too, when Kessler returned.

He jerked his thumb and out they went through another door.

"That way is the garrison," he said. "The cavalry is housed over the stables. The foot in the far wing. Except for new recruits, which are the greatest number. New recruits from elsewhere in the world are transferred down here for training, and they are housed underground in our wing."

"New recruits," she repeated.

"Seldom volunteers," Kessler replied with that sardonic edge to his flat voice. "Frequently what they must learn is not skills so much as obedience. This way for Zydes's rooms."

That meant the 'new recruits' were prisoners.

The effect of the word was like an inner blow, because she knew as soon as he spoke, she *knew* that Uncle Darian was a prisoner. How he'd loathed the thought of Norsunder in the old days! His entire life he'd been preparing to defend Sarendan *against* Norsunder. And whatever else you could say about him—nothing nice, of course—he had been no liar.

A prisoner. Why, that meant—

That meant—

She sighed, wrestling with duty and desire, until the Zydes's voice interrupted her thoughts. He spoke over her head at Kessler. "I want a report from the scouts Dejain sidetracked."

Kessler left without speaking.

Zydes frowned down at Lilah. "Where did you lose that magical ring?"

"In Shendoral, when that man grabbed me."

Zydes turned his eyes upward in disgust. "A pity Kessler did not possess the wit to take it from you at the outset. Never mind. I can make better myself. So. You can either be enchanted so that your will is entirely subsumed under my whim, or else you will give me your pledge of obedience by choice. The latter I prefer, because I can then teach you magic, and you will, if you are quick and sensible, find yourself in a position of power in your kingdom. More than you would ever have had while you were under the thumb of some prating mage like Evend of Bereth Ferian or that old cripple Tsauderei."

Lilah chewed her lip. "You mean an oath of loyalty?"

Zydes laughed. It was a harsh sound that hurt her ears. "If you like, though your pledge is bound by a magical ward. Don't waste my time gassing about light magic sentiment such as loyalty — there is no such thing. There is only obedience." He smiled slightly. The lines in his face made it a smirk. "If you speak the pledge, rather than I, the power is the greater. But the reward is that you will have complete freedom within the boundaries I set, which will be the entire fortress. For the initial part of your learning will be as a messenger, an observer, and then as a...scout, shall we say."

A spy, she thought, with sour dislike. Spying on his underlings, and everyone will hate me for it. Including him. Just like that disgusting Kalaeb during Uncle Dirty-Hands' time.

He spoke a spell. She couldn't hear the words — the sound of his voice blurred — but her teeth tingled, and her nails prickled as if she'd scratched them down granite. The air smelled metallic, as if lightning were about to strike.

Panic made her ears ring. How would she get out of it?

Zydes paused, and switched to Sartoran.

"Yustnesveas Landis. Give me your pledge to abide by my commands, within the set boundaries. You must be precise," he added, waving his hand for her to speak.

Atan.

Lilah took in a shaky breath. "I swear that as long as I am Yustnesveas Landis that I will abide by your commands, within the set boundaries."

She looked at him, trying to hide her anxiety. Was he fooled?

Yes, he was fooled. Her pledge was more wordy than he'd expected, but he attributed that to light magic pomposity. They set great store by their oaths and ceremonies and rituals. All nonsense, of course, and yet he was quite clever to bind the spell to her own words.

Let that fool Dejain try to figure that out, and alter it!

Lilah heard more of those blurry words, then a snap. Her head felt brief pressure, which dissipated almost immediately: she was too ignorant of the ways of magic to know that the ward had failed.

And Zydes was concentrating too hard on hiding the reaction of casting heavy magic to detect a failed ward. He sat down behind his desk, and when the head-pang and corresponding nausea eased, he contemplated his new student.

She certainly had given in quickly. Was it stupidity? Cowardice? She was young, and weak, as all light magic people were. That was evidenced in how easily she'd been caught.

Still, intimidation was a cheap safeguard. "You are either unexpectedly practical, or else futilely devious." His voice was slightly hoarse—as if he'd run up several flights of stairs. "It had better not be the latter."

Lilah tried not to let her own voice quake. "Just for information, if I did try to run off, would some magic come out and strike me dead?"

"Oh no." Zydes smirked. "That would not leave time for regret, would it?"

She heard the threat, but it was just another of so many. She thought instead about how making magic spells had had some sort of nasty effect on him, even though he was trying to hide it. Dark magic: greater power: harder to perform; more of a cost. Just as Atan had said.

He got up, crossed the room, and pointed at a round mirror thing on a side table. Time to give her some incentive for obedience. "Now. Your first lesson. If you are diligent, I will teach you the command spell, and you can amuse yourself spying on your kingdom from here — except within the Loi boundaries, but there is nothing of interest for us there. I call this my scope..."

That same morning, many days' travel to the northeast, Tsauderei sat in his little house high in the magic-protected Valley of Delfina, staring out the windows onto the drifting snow.

The Valley was beautiful during all seasons, the deep glacier-carved lake reflecting the silvery gray sky, against which snow etched itself as if by a master hand. But Tsauderei was in no mood for aesthetics.

His brooding thoughts were interrupted by the internal tingle of an alert: someone had crossed the border. With the ease of many years' practice he performed an adjunct spell, and knew from the resultant echo of magic that the newcomers came by light magic transfer.

He sat back in his chair, and before long the flicker and wind of transfer magic deposited two figures on the upper level of his one-room cottage. The upper level functioned as a Destination.

He had time to survey his guests while they recovered from what had obviously been a very long transfer indeed. Evend, his old friend from their early days at Bereth Ferian's Mage Guild, looked terrible. He, like Tsauderei, had been dressy in the arrogance of their youth, his beard braided with ribbon, his robes edged with embroidery. Now his beard lay against his robes in disarray. His hair, white with gray streaks, was shorn close in back.

They were once young, handsome, and powerful, he reflected as Evend's deeply lined eyes slowly regained their focus. Now only the power remained, and they had learned how little of worth it was.

The second guest had recovered first, as the young will do. Resilient, their lives and hopes ahead, youth always recovered first—except from acts of injustice.

Tsauderei liked the look of this boy. A year or two younger than Atan, perhaps, light haired, light coloring and eyes, a serious face with vaguely familiar features—

Ah. Vithya-Vadnais. Was this Erai-Yanya's child, then? Strange, that she'd had a boy. The Vithya-Vadnais mages had been women for generations, a long line of mother-daughter.

"Tsauderei," Evend said hoarsely.

"Come. Sit. I get about with difficulty these years, so please overlook my lack of manners," Tsauderei said to the youngster.

Evend and the boy came down to the circle of chairs before the window. Evend looked out, his deep-set eyes narrowed. "Spring has come again," he said, and despite the wheeze in his voice, Tsauderei heard the timbre of satisfaction, of triumph. Like Sartor and Everon, Bereth Ferian had been bound beyond time for many, many years, until just last year.

Evend dropped into a chair, and said, "This is Irtur Vithya-Vadnais. I have adopted him as my heir."

Tsauderei said all the right things to boy and man, though sadness suffused him. Evend was already foreseeing his own end.

Irtur politely thanked him for the congratulations. Tsauderei liked his voice, a quiet voice, with clear enunciation, and a straightforward assessment to his gaze. Irtur was an observer.

It seemed that Evend was not yet ready to state his business. "Is the Unnamed still contemplating a crossing?" Evend made a gesture toward the west.

"She's gone," Tsauderei said.

The lines in Evend's long face deepened. "You permitted her to go?"

"It was her choice." Tsauderei sat back. "We have had this discussion at least twice."

Evend shook his head, and sighed. "I did not believe you would act."

"I did not act. I stood aside. The timing is not good, I know you will say, but we will never have better: the enchantment is definitely starting to erode. Any time Detlev could notice, and renew it, which would mean waiting another century — or two, or ten. And yes, Norsunder is still a threat, but at least Detlev's gone; Erai Yanya probably told you that Lilith the Guardian reported he's causing trouble on one or other of our sister worlds. It was time."

Evend scowled, as the boy Irtur looked at his hands, wishing he'd been permitted to go with Yustnesveas. But Evend never would have allowed it.

Tsauderei's thoughts seemed to parallel the boy's. "We're going to have to get used to stepping aside and letting the young take the risks, you know," he said, smiling. "You said it yourself, last spring, hard on Zydes's defeat. Once it was us taking their risks, and we were not all that much older than your youngster here."

"I said that this was no longer our world, the one

we watched over all our lives," Evend said slowly. "I spoke perhaps out of defeat, out of the shock of discovery of the changes that had taken place while I was hiding beyond time."

Tsauderei said with deliberate emphasis, "Sartor has faded from world consciousness. Everon is also a dream, as is Wnelder Vee. Imar is mired in pettiness. Colend is ruled by a madman."

In other words: there are no more world leaders who know magic. It's down to you and me, my friend. And this boy's mother, whose magical knowledge is great, but who respects magic-wary kings by withdrawing from the political world.

Evend passed his hand before his face, and pressed his fingertips into his brow. "And those remaining allies have walled themselves off in isolation," Evend said. "But we're still bound by our old oaths."

"When you start telling me things we both know, you're about to ask me something we both also know I'm going to—question." *Hate*, Tsauderei once would have said. But Evend had taken more damage while Detlev's prisoner than Tsauderei had at first surmised. More, even, than Evend seemed aware. "Let's jump right to that part, shall we?"

"I believe that Norsunder's defeat last year was too easy. I know Detlev is going to come back. Himself, this time. He won't send one of his minions. I can face that prospect and prepare for it, if I know that I have in some way secured our future."

Tsauderei watched the boy drop his head forward and look down at his hands.

"I want you to ward Irtur against what happened to me. Until he is an adult," he added with haste, avoiding Tsauderei's gaze.

Tsauderei thought: *I was right. I do hate it.* But he was the stronger in knowledge of defensive magic.

He said, "Leave the boy here. We will discuss it."

Evend looked from one to the other, then bowed his head. The etiquette that deplored this type of magic was so ingrained that he would not argue, though Tsauderei could see the anxiety goading the once-tranquil Evend. "You will keep me apprised of the Unnamed's progress?" Evend asked.

"I will," Tsauderei said. Now was not the time to report the discovery he'd made.

Evend transferred out, leaving Tsauderei and Irtur studying one another. Tsauderei took in that high, thoughtful brow, the question in the quirk of the boy's light brows, and said, "Do you know what Evend is asking?"

They spoke in the quaint, archaic form of Sartoran that had been maintained without much alteration (mostly due to the age of the books that they all grew up studying) since the days when the northern and southern mage schools had allied.

"I think so," Irtur said. "He wants some kind of spell that will protect me if Norsunder comes again to Bereth Ferian."

"Do you know what it means?" Tsauderei asked.

Irtur's lips parted and his gaze lifted to the horizon. "It means—to Evend—that he need never worry about my safety. That I can spend my time learning magic, and not defense."

"It means that you, unlike the people about you, will never have to think about danger. If it came, you would instantly be transferred to safety. It is very powerful magic, very involved magic. It takes time, strength, and concentration, but I know how to do it, and I don't think Norsunder could break it, at least not currently." He sat back. "It also goes directly against the vows we made when we were confirmed masters at the mage school in Bereth Ferian. It is deemed inappropriate for us to protect ourselves when that kind of magic cannot be extended to those we are supposed to be serving. But you have taken no vows."

Irtur looked out the window at the falling snow. "We are almost finished with winter, where we live," he murmured. "It is strange, transferring so far."

Tsauderei lifted a hand then dropped it.

Irtur faced him. "I know Evend wants me to be safe." His lips pressed into a line.

To give the boy a chance to master the conflict of emotions he couldn't quite hide, Tsauderei said easily, "Evend's magic was always focused toward land interface. He is the best there is at the subtle intricacies of weather protection, quake easement, and the flow of water."

Irtur jerked his head in a nod. "He's training me to learn the same magic, along with translation of old records. Especially from the Venn."

"All of which call for tremendous patience, but you know that. Did he tell you that, at least in the old days, you would have been required to live as a hermit somewhere outside of reach of humans, for at least ten years, just watching the seasons change as you did your translation work? Perhaps what you have not yet perceived is that Evend's studies select for — and perhaps develop — a type of horizon-to-horizon awareness of the changing seasons, the interconnection of natural forces, that often precludes knowledge of human interaction."

Irtur's eyes rounded. "You know what happened to my mother."

Tsauderei recognized in himself an echo of old anger, and older fear. "Erai Yanya has shared her history with me. She was the only survivor of that particular attack, was she not?"

"Because she had one of those wards on her," he said. "It — it makes a difference. You can be alone, if you like, and study whatever you want, because you don't have to worry. It was she who rescued Evend from Detlev's enchantment. And kept him hidden." Irtur turned that desperate gaze outside again. The snow continued to fall, white, neutral. Indifferent. "And you live with mages, away from your family and friends, so you won't get drawn into politics at home. I've been reading all the records and reasons. I listen to the older people talk —"

"And?" Tsauderei prompted.

"And you cease to worry about people," Irtur offered in a tentative voice. "In the same way that you would if you lived among them, and shared their dangers. That's why the vow, isn't it?"

"This is why we agreed never to perform that ward upon ourselves," Tsauderei stated. And, lest the boy think him accusing Evend even indirectly, he added, "Evend never thought to ward himself. Not even after Bereth Ferian's defeat. He wants to protect you, and thereby protect the future."

"But if I'm not strong enough to protect myself,

what good will I be?" Irtur asked. He ran his thumb absently along the carving on the chair arm, then said in a quick voice, "You know the enchantment over Bereth Ferian was broken by two boys and a girl. It was the girl who knew the magic. Younger than I am. No wards on *them*. They came all the way north from some tiny little kingdom no one has ever heard of—"

"Mearsies Heili." Tsauderei smiled. "I've done some research since Evend told me about them. That enchantment had been marred by Norsundrian mages undercutting one another. The key was practically thrown in their laps because one mage wanted the other to suffer defeat."

"It's true, but I still want to meet them," Irtur said. "I want to find out how they did it. And why. What makes them the way they are."

"That's a good goal," Tsauderei said.

Irtur said, "Was there a ward on the Unnamed?"

"No. She refused to have it," Tsauderei said. "Also: she could not have entered the kingdom with that ward on her, for there are Norsundrian wards against that type of magic all along the border. Dark magic is very good at defense," he added. "You have to remember that. Its purpose is control, not protection."

Irtur frowned. "So she went under those Norsundrian wards with no protection at all, only her wits?"

"I gave her a ring that had belonged to one of her ancestors. It has limited use," Tsauderei said. "It also has a tracer ward on it, one that will go undetected by the Norsundrians." *And the ring is now at the Norsunder base.*

Irtur said, "I don't want any wards on me. I never did, but I have not been able to convince Evend." He drew in a breath. "If those people my age from tiny, insignificant Mearsies Heili can do what they've done without being warded, or hidden away for their own safety, so can I." He gave Tsauderei a tense smile. "I don't think I'm strong enough yet to hold the transport spell all the way to Bereth Ferian. Would you please send me home?"

"You will not be warded?"

"No. I will tell Evend why."

"Very well," Tsauderei said. "I expect we'll see

more of one another by and bye. You can tell Evend that I approve his choice of heir." He smiled, and as the boy's face turned scarlet, Tsauderei quickly transferred him.

When the reaction had dissipated, he closed his eyes, whispered another spell, and — as he expected — found that the ring had not moved.

His gamble had been wrong, and Atan was at the Norsunder Base. But she was alive, for the ring conveyed a heartbeat.

He turned his gaze back to the window, and the soft and steady snowfall beyond. He had chosen not to add yet another burden to Evend's load. This watch he would have to suffer alone.

ELEVEN

Lilah's skin prickled with terror sweat. She wished she could claw off that sturdy woolen tunic, but of course she did not dare, for it was black, and as she ghosted down the silent hallway from her room to Zydes's, she hoped that the black clothing would keep her from being easily seen.

In one hand she gripped her lock pick, and in the other, her thief tools. Outside Zydes's office door, she paused long enough to send fearful glances in both directions.

Lilah had left the office after her first long interview with Zydes, realizing that she had to escape before he started experimenting with spells on her, or she might not be able to. She walked away knowing two things: that she had to get away *right now*, but before she could escape, she had to get rid of that scope thing, because otherwise he'd find her wherever she ran.

The torchlit halls were empty, the ruddy light beating on the stone, making shadows leap and quiver.

She listened at the door.

Kessler had said that Zydes would be gone for most the night — a supply run all the way to the other side of the world — but she listened just in case.

Nothing.

She fingered her lock pick. Wiped her sweating palm. Gripped the lock pick again, eased it into the old lock, pressed the mechanisms into line, and pulled the latch.

Click!

Gratitude flooded through her for all those weeks of practice over the summer. She shouldered the door open, slipped inside, and then eased the door shut again. Her insides gripped painfully as she tiptoed over to the table where that horrible scope thing rested. All day, while Zydes had blabbered on and on about military stuff, she'd considered how to break it.

Lilah approached fearfully, bracing against some kind of terrible protective spell. Nothing happened. She bent close, staring down at the round black shiny disc supported between the thin metal rods. She did not dare touch it until she was ready to smash it. She was convinced she'd only get one try before some nasty magic came right back at her.

She didn't want to touch the thing. Better to use some piece of furniture from Zydes's room.

But when she peered close, the cold, sickening sense of failure pooled inside her when she saw that it wasn't made of darkened glass after all. It was heavy, solid, metal. Metal wouldn't smash.

Now what? As she stared at it, no, *into* it, the blackness seemed to tug at her mind. She turned away quickly.

That horrible feeling was instantly familiar. The ring!

The ring did that same thing to your mind, except it made light.

Was it possible that light and dark could mix each other up somehow?

She'd learned last year, when she and the other Sharadan Brothers were striving against Uncle Dirty-Hands's forces, that if she was already in danger, to keep on trying until she either succeeded — or someone stopped her.

She forced her trembling fingers to pull the ring free, then jammed it onto her thumb. She whispered the words Atan had taught her, and aimed the ring at the scope.

Light blazed from the ring straight into the shiny metal disc — and did not reflect! Her scalp crawled as the light was entirely *swallowed* into the blackness.

The ring grew warm on her finger, then hot, but she gritted her teeth and held it there, for the metal of the scope was also glowing, and it smelled hot—like a blacksmith's shop when the forge was being used. She held the ring steady, ignoring the pain of heat as red light ringed round the edges of the scope.

Hotter... hotter... tears ran down her face, and her arm shook with the effort it took to hold it still, as pain licked up her muscles and bones and jabbed right into her eyes—

—and the metal disc exploded into weirdly glowing shards that winked out of existence, leaving white ash to drift down to the floor.

She jumped back, not wanting even that to touch her, then flung the ring down onto the floor and cradled her arm against her middle for an agonizing time. When the throbbing had died down from red heat to a sharp pang, she blinked teary eyes at the two curving rods, now holding up nothing, and then finally forced herself to look down at her hand, expecting to see it sickeningly charred.

But astonishment turned to shock when she saw her skin unbroken—not even pink. Yet pain still sang up her nerves in throbbing waves.

She wiggled her fingers. They worked, though the pain intensified briefly. But as she flexed her fingers, the pain receded, leaving only the ache of memory.

And a ruined scope.

It was time to leave.

She forced her shaky fingers to pick up the now-cold ring, stuck it back into her pocket, and ran to the door. There she paused, enduring the last inward struggle: Uncle Dirty-Hands.

She even knew where he was. After Zydes had released her earlier that day, Kessler had sent her to execute some of the errands that Zydes stuck on him, after explaining how the castle was laid out, and the rules for passing from one wing to another.

And so, while delivering a bunch of messages, she discovered where the new "recruits" were housed, and who guarded them. She'd glimpsed her uncle in a line of men leaving a barracks for one of the practice yards. Had he seen her? If so, he certainly hadn't shown any sign. No telling what he thought, either.

She *hated* her uncle, the more because he and Peitar looked so much alike. In her mind, he was no better than Norsunder, but Peitar did not agree. It would be so easy to just leave her uncle here, where (she argued with herself) he belonged. But he didn't belong. She knew it, or there would be no argument.

And if she didn't do something, she could never go home again. Because there would be no facing Peitar.

That decided her.

She slipped out, closed the door, and ran down the hall toward the stairway to the lower level where the recruits were housed. Before she got to the last turning, she reached again into her pocket for the little bag of Lure flowers. It had been many days, but she knew that as long as the bag stayed tightly closed so the flowers did not dry out, they would stay potent.

She untied the knot at the mouth of the bag. A faint whiff escaped, smelling overwhelmingly sweet and enticing. And with such powerful effect! The faint whiff seemed to brush her mind with soft cobwebs, obscuring thought, emotion, almost obscuring consciousness. She staggered, then crushed the bag closed again, jamming it down inside her pocket.

Holding her breath, she walked a few steps. Breathed out. Sucked in a deep breath. Her head cleared as she rounded the corner.

Two bored-looking guards looked up and gripped their weapons. When they recognized her, they relaxed a little.

"What now?" one of them asked her.

She sucked in a deep breath as she walked up to them, then she silently pulled open the bag and held it out. They both bent to see what she was offering.

When the men gasped and swayed, she ran around the corner again, with the bag crushed closed. Dizziness twinkled darkly at the edges of her vision as the two guards thudded to the ground, followed by the clatter of their fallen weapons.

She whooped in another lungful of air and ran back to where the guards both slumped, then pulled the edge of her coat over her nose and breathed as little as possible as she hopped over them and let herself through the iron-reinforced door. There she threw back her head and gasped in a deep breath, grateful for the flat, stale, stone-scented but flower-free air.

She ran down the empty hall, past locked barracks rooms from which came the low murmur of voices, until she reached the door at the very end. She used her tool on the old-fashioned lock—for the men inside were locked in at night—and cried in her home language, "Hold your breath, Uncle Dirty-Hands!" then opened the door and tossed the entire bag of Lure inside.

Thud! Thud! Exclamation – thud!

She opened the door to find her uncle standing just on the other side. Reflexive terror almost made her slam it shut again, but in the instant she wavered he got out and pulled the door shut, then let out his breath in a long, shuddering sigh.

"The last time I smelled that odor I woke up to discover that I'd lost a kingdom," he murmured, his eyes closed.

Lilah stared up at him, heart-sickened. How could she have forgotten that? It was *she* who'd used the Lure on her uncle and his commanders, just before Peitar and his people had arrived. That had brought the revolution to an abrupt close. *The easiest way to shipwreck a government is to capture the leaders*, Atan had told her, and she'd done just that.

She stared doubtfully up at him, wondering if he wanted revenge. He was watching her, his familiar blue eyes both cold and amused, two expressions she'd always hated.

"Well?" he asked, brows raised. "It's your move."

She groped toward the door, still staring up at him. "I—I need to get the Lure back. In case. Then we can escape."

His expression changed. "Do it, then."

Nothing about the past, about Sarendan, or kingship. Or revenge.

She was so frightened, it was easier to follow commands than to think of her next actions. She snorted in a lungful of air, opened the door, scooped up the withered flowers, and then ran out, stuffing them into their bag.

She and her uncle ran down the hall. She pounded

ten, twenty steps, her vision twinkling. She gasped for air. Again she caught a faint whiff of sweet flower scent, feeling the inside of her head going foggy, but fear and the stale, dry air of the next corridor banished the weird cottony sense.

"Guards?" her uncle asked as they ran up the corridor toward the entrance.

"Sleeping," she said, patting her pocket. And she turned to go, but he stood there, looking down at her, the torchlight from the corner highlighting the sharp bones in his face, emphasizing his bleak expression.

His question took her completely by surprise. "Why are you here?"

"I got pinched," she said, numb with too many reactions coming too fast. "That nasty villain Zydes has this thingie that spies on the land—used to, anyway. I hope. Well, um, anyhow, he sent that Kessler to pinch Atan, and they thought she was me—"

"Never mind," he said. "You've told me enough." He glanced along the halls, then said, "We will exchange histories later. Do you have any weapons?"

"No. Just my thief tools. You know, when we were the Sharadan Brothers." She jerked her thumb toward a passing door.

"Effective." He gave her an ironic smile. "But I think we'll require steel as well." He gestured for her to follow.

And the rest of the escape was under his direction.

Lilah complied, relief easing her fear just enough to keep her from the nausea and trembling that had plagued her so far. Once upon a time her uncle's quickness to decision, his cold, dispassionate military attitude had contributed to her dislike of him, but she discovered that it was welcome now. At least he seemed to know what he was doing, she reflected as she pounded along behind him. More than she did, anyway.

When they reached the outer access to the command wing, he stopped, asked her to get the sleepweeds out, and she threw it when she was told. Listened to the thud of falling guards. Retrieved it when he said it was safe, as he relieved the guards of weapons.

Then they ran again, Lilah wondering worriedly, *Why are we back here? Is he lost?* Her uncle seemed to be looking for something—or for someone. He ran fast, and

Lilah pounded along behind, doing her best to catch up when he paused at corners to listen and then to look.

After three or four of these pauses she heard someone walking, and dug her hand in her pocket, but Uncle Darian put out a hand to stay her, and hefted the sword and knife he'd taken from the first pair of snoring guards.

"This one has to die," he murmured.

"But—" she squeaked. "But!"

Her uncle gave her a strained look. "I can't save the others, but at least I can spare them serving as entertainment when he is in the mood for blood." He jerked his chin toward the approaching footsteps.

And what if you lose? Lilah wanted to say, but it was already too late. She already knew the answer: her uncle would not kill someone who'd been dropped into sleep by Lure. Even his worst enemy, and maybe this Norsundrian was, would be given the chance to fight for his life.

She gritted her teeth and stayed silent, too terrified to do anything but press herself flat against the wall as a big, brawny Norsundrian tromped around the corner. Lilah caught a brief glimpse of a habitually mean face that turned into an ugly sneer when the man saw Darian Irad, who was so much shorter and lighter in build.

The Norsundrian pulled his weapons, and the fight began.

The hallway was about as wide as two men could stretch out their arms. Plenty wide, until you are stuck within range of sharp-edged steel arcing and swinging, and then it becomes close and confining. Trying to watch the fight made Lilah dizzy, but at least it did not last long—that is, she thought so afterward. At the time, it seemed to go on forever, until Darian Irad disarmed the larger man with a fast stroke of the sword, and then with his other hand ripped the knife across the man's neck.

Lilah flinched away, though not before she saw a dark stream jet out from the cut throat, and there was nothing to prevent her from hearing the terrible gargling sounds of the man dying.

"This way," her uncle said, and ran. She fled at his heels, terror singing in her ears.

At the stable, he stood back and waved for her to

put the stable guards to sleep. Her hands shook terribly, and she almost dropped the Lure, but she managed to do her job while her uncle leaned against the wall, breathing hard, the knife still dark-smeared.

When the guards were asleep, they slipped into the stable.

"Get the headstalls and reins while I clean this weapon and saddle us up." He pointed with that bloodstained knife.

She turned away, fighting nausea again, and made it to the long row of bridles and headstalls and blackweave reins before she bent over, retching dryly as she whispered the Waste Spell. Dizzy and miserable, she straightened up, forced herself to get what she'd been sent to get

When she got back, it was to find that he had saddled both horses and found a second sword, one of those heavy ones the cavalry warriors used, and now he was waiting. He took the bridles and finished that job in silence.

Then he looked around. No one. He said in an undertone, "We are both dressed in uniform. Since no alarm has been raised, there's a chance we'll be able to ride out unmolested. But you have to look as if you have business to attend to. And do not speak. If they address us, you leave the talking to me. Understand?"

Lilah jerked her head in a nod.

They mounted up, rode through the empty court and out the gates, under the eyes of the marching sentries.

Surges of terror wrung Lilah's insides at the way her uncle glanced back at the walls, but he said nothing, and she heard no pursuit, no noises of alarm.

No one stopped them as they rode out into the darkness. Lilah began to believe in the escape only when the torchlit crenellations smeared into a red-glowing blur behind them.

Neither of them was aware of Kessler standing on the highest tower, looking down at their receding figures and laughing soundlessly as their hoof beats diminished rapidly into the distance.

TWELVE

The expected summons came not long after sunup.

Kessler was waiting at Zydes's office when the latter arrived, as he wanted the pleasure of observing his commander's process of discovery. Before he opened the office door, Zydes's face revealed the pallor and tension lines of residual magic reaction. He had to have been off somewhere, planting magic traps for someone. Probable Dejain.

Good.

"Where's that Landis brat?" Zydes snapped as he let himself into the office. Kessler followed, watching obliquely, but Zydes did not move toward the scope. He didn't even turn in that direction; his intent seemed to be on the papers accumulated on the desk. "If she's still sleeping, yank her out by the ear. I'll not tolerate laziness."

Kessler lingered as long as he could without causing comment. Zydes sat down, scowling as he read the top report. With an inward shrug, Kessler left.

He went through all the motions, just as if he'd expected to find the Landis brat in the end chamber. He unlocked the door, surveyed the empty bed, the barren stone corners of the room, shut the door, locked it again, and returned to the office. He could tell instantly that Zydes hadn't moved—he was halfway through his stack of secret reports. He couldn't have looked at the side table yet.

"She's not there," Kessler said.

Zydes neatly set a paper on a third pile as he said irritably, "Well, go get her, then, fool."

Kessler took his time. He walked down to the mess and looked about with the air of a diligent searcher. He examined hallways where a child might conceivably have loitered, and the practice court, and even the stable yard before he returned to the tower.

Zydes had nearly finished his reading, and had divided the reports into four piles. He kept Kessler waiting, as usual, thereby wasting more time in his attempt at intimidation while Kessler enjoyed his anticipation.

At last Zydes deposited the last paper on a pile, tidied each of the four meticulously, then looked up impatiently. Kessler wanted to laugh—he still hadn't looked at the scope.

"I did not find her in the mess, or in this wing, or the stable. Did you send her elsewhere?"

"I didn't send her anywhere," Zydes snarled. Then he rose, and at last turned toward the scope, a gesture so habitual Kessler suspected Zydes was unaware how revealing it was.

His reaction was better than Kessler could have hoped.

His face drained of what color it had. It really was a blanch, the exact expression, or as near as the living might get, to the look on someone's face whose guts have just been ripped open by a blade. Kessler let himself glance at the table, and he mimed a look of surprise when he saw that the scope was gone, its support rods curved around empty space.

Zydes stared at that empty space, his eyes distended, as though the force of angry disbelief could remake what had obviously been turned to ash. Then he actually walked all the way around the side table, his mouth gaping like a beached fish.

Kessler counted three breaths. Four.

Zydes swung about. Kessler waited. It took no mind-reading abilities to follow the chain of his thoughts here: accusation. Then realization that Kessler could not possibly have entered the chamber, because there were heavy wards against him crossing the threshold without

Zydes being present. And Zydes thought he knew no magic. Then he'd remember the wards he'd put in place against Detlev, Dejain, and a half-dozen other mages who did know enough magic —

"Who did this?" It was scarcely a whisper, but Kessler heard it. Then, "Get out!"

Kessler left, and executed all his errands, moving without haste, or furtiveness, because he knew that at some point magic would be tracking him.

One of his stops was to the quartermaster, to pick up supply reports. While the man assembled his papers Kessler wandered along the shelves near the transport square, where new commodities were always offloaded against the incoming magical transfer of more.

Most of what he saw was foodstuffs: barrels of rice, bushels of oats, and crates and crates of various greens that would be transported by magic. But at the other end were rolls of heavy gray wool — the same kind he had ordered some years before, when he'd had to equip an army. This wool was the kind that made the best riding cloak that could be besorcelled against wet.

Invasion. Sartor? Probably. Zydes still had not told anyone that Detlev's time-bindings had been released.

"Here you go."

Kessler picked up the papers and left.

The signal came for the guard to change. This was also the signal for the midday meal for those on the day watch. Kessler retreated to his room to wait.

Mentally he had been tracking Zydes's likely movements. He would, by now, have found out that one of the recruits was also gone — Darian Irad, former king of Sarendan, no less. And that the two recruit-wing sentries had been rendered unconscious by unknown means, as well as the recruits in Irad's barracks room, and the command wing guards at the barracks entryway, and stable guards; that Jaskuil, the command wing rover — a notorious informer with an insatiable taste for floggings — was dead, his throat slit. That the two roving patrols whose entire purpose was to question anyone walking about had been sidetracked, one to the prison, the other to the south wall. That two mounts were missing, that two figures, a scout and a guide, had been seen riding out on the north road.

A scout and a guide? Who had issued orders to pass them?

The order traced back to Jaskuil.

Written? No, spoken. By whom?

No one could remember... during the relay of general orders at the watch change?

Whence had come the warning that sent the two roving patrols on futile investigations? The relay of spoken orders again would lead back to Jaskuil.

Kessler knew that his speculations were correct because there was no summons. He did not waste any time thinking about what might happen if someone did manage to place him along the escapees' trail, clearing the way for them without their knowing it. The most interesting part of the day was the destruction of the scope, which he had not expected the brat to be capable of. (And from the long silence, it was clear that Zydes still had not put the missing brat and the destroyed scope together. He was futilely investigating his rival mages.)

The scope's destruction changed Kessler's plans. He sat back, watching through the north window. There were now two possibilities: either Zydes revealed who his "messenger" was, in which case he'd be sending half the mounted after her — or else he'd want to keep her identity secret, in which case —

A bang on his door. "Summons."

Zydes was pacing back and forth. "The brat is definitely missing. How could she have learned enough of our magic to break my ward?" He flung out a hand in the direction of the side table. "More important, could she possibly be the one who destroyed the scope? Even Dejain couldn't get at it, and she's tried. Four times during the last half a year, at least." He smirked, but his expression immediately soured. "It *couldn't* have been that soul-sucking brat!"

Kessler remained silent.

A hand smashed on the desk. "It gets worse. She made a detour, it seems, and managed to spring Irad of Sarendan. That has to mean he's offered the Landis brat his army to help her retake Sartor. If they make it over the Sarendan border —"

Kessler had come to the same conclusion. It made tactical sense. Moreover, everyone in the world, on both sides, would know that Sartor's time binding was broken.

Kessler said, his voice devoid of any hint of interest, "I thought Irad was deposed."

A searching look from dark-pouched, yellowed eyes. "Yes. But the puling cripple they replaced him with apparently can't even lift a blade. My guess is, if Irad shows up in Sarendan again, especially with the Landis girl at his side, and he whistles, his entire army will come running. Especially if they think they can measure blades against us. That's what he'd been training them for, right?"

Kessler did not answer.

Another look. Another angry, impotent gesture. Then unwilling speech, as if forced out: "You. Take as many as you think necessary, and bring them back before they reach Sarendan."

Kessler left, issued the orders to detach squads he'd long since chosen against just such an opportunity, and saw to the supplies and to the selection of the extra mounts himself. Within a short time, they were riding east toward Sarendan.

And there was no scope to follow their movements.

Kessler held no ill-will toward either the Landis girl or Irad. When she'd begun asking her clumsy questions about the recruits, it had been obvious that she was contemplating a run, but he hadn't thought she'd have the guts to actually try. She'd surprised him considerably when she'd not only appeared, but let herself into Zydes's office with commendable speed, and then emerged again, trailing the stink of burning metal, and proceeding straight down to recruit territory. Again a surprise, when she reappeared with Irad of Sarendan.

Kessler had enjoyed deflecting the worst of their obstacles; covert action was in some ways more demanding and more complex than assault. Irad's killing of Jaskuil—not at all surprising—had even provided a convenient source for all the false orders.

The Landis girl definitely lived up to the standards of her ancestors. Not even Detlev could have surmised that the stupid front she presented to the world hid not only formidable magic skills—dark magic, yet—but also the ability to execute a clever move like springing the former king of Sarendan—against whom Kessler had, a couple of years ago, looked forward to taking the field himself. Irad, who had been betrayed into recruitment in much the same fashion Kessler had, evoked enough sympathy that, had Zydes released their names and sent the regulars after them, Kessler would have wished they'd manage to stay at large, if only to frustrate Zydes.

But now they had been handed to Kessler, and so they were transformed from objects of interest into weapons to be used against Zydes and Dejain.

He would give them no more consideration than the archer gives the arrow that will accomplish the kill.

A flight of squeaking bats wheeled through the thick, still night air and vanished with a whisper of wings into the peaks above.

"Oh, can't we rest?" Lilah cried, unable to endure any more riding or walking, especially without water or food.

The sun had only begun to smear the eastern clouds with grayish light. Her uncle turned her way, but she could not see his expression.

"It was too easy," he said. "We have to keep on the move." He gestured. "The horses need water, anyway."

"So do we," she muttered.

There was no answer.

Too easy? Too EASY?

Lilah was much too tired — and afraid of her uncle — to wail, but she wanted desperately to yowl and howl and stamp her feet. If a horrible night like the one they'd just endured was too easy, what would he consider tough?

But she neither yowled nor stamped, for she needed every bit of her failing strength to plonk one foot in front of the other. Uncle Dirty-Hands held the reins of both horses, for Lilah couldn't even do that anymore. The animals' hooves thudded behind her, their heads drooping, their sweaty sides shuddering.

"Rain coming," her uncle said.

Water. The thought revived her just enough for her to be able to lift her head and look skyward. Indeed, the flat gray clouds she'd gotten used to had given way to the lowering, ragged-edged blue-gray of moisture-laden thunderheads. Two cold splats landed on her face, and drops chuffed into the aged dust of the hill trail.

Her uncle had insisted they leave the road right before dawn, which had slowed them even more. Lilah had obeyed, beyond questioning, though the sight of the trail upward into the hills on either side of the road had compounded her misery.

She dropped her head, and a cold buffet of wind nearly knocked her off her feet. "Please, Uncle Dirty-Hands, can't we stop? Just a little?"

"Rain will obliterate our trail," he said. "I think we can look for shelter now, at least until the storm passes."

Shelter. Her eyes were too bleary for looking around for hidey-holes. She followed, sticking her tongue out in hopes of water. Two or three drops had finally fallen onto it (though they didn't make much difference) by the time he said, "Here."

Two gigantic slabs of striated rock had fallen sideways long ago in some unimaginable tremor, forming a kind of rock tent. It was large enough for both horses, as well as the two of them.

Lilah flung herself down onto the gathered dust along one side, grateful to stop moving at last. But she was too thirsty to sleep.

Her uncle unslung one sword from across his back, and the other from his belt, set them down, and dropped the knife on top. Then he set to work unsaddling and caring for the horses. She saw that he'd managed to pack food for them in the saddlebags, the same feedbags full of pressed squares of oat-and-hay that Kessler had used for the horses on the road south. She felt a faint flare of hope that was swiftly extinguished when she reflected that stable supplies were unlikely to provide stuff for people.

Presently he came back and sat on a rock opposite Lilah. In the sky, a long mutter of thunder prefaced a sudden downpour of slanting, hissing rain. The air swiftly chilled, and rivulets of dust-laden brown liquid ran into their shelter.

Lilah pulled her feet aside. "I don't know why you said this escape was too easy," she said fretfully.

"It was too easy to get out of the fortress," her uncle replied.

Lilah's mouth dropped open.

He shook his head. "We will have to ascribe it to internal politics, short of any further enlightenment."

Lilah groaned. Tired as she was, and hungry, and thirsty, and frightened, she felt as if she swam in deep water very far from shore. What did he mean? Oh, who cared what he meant. They were out, and he hadn't abandoned her, or said he was going to murder her in revenge for the revolution. That was all that mattered now.

She looked out at the brown water slopping along the insides of the biggest slab of rock. "Do we have to drink that?"

"Wait. It'll run clear after a time."

Lilah sighed.

Her uncle transferred his gaze to her. "How came you there?" He added wryly, "The invasion of Sarendan was, I thought, postponed against some evolving trouble to the north. But ground-level rumor is often untrustworthy no matter what side one is on."

Lilah hesitated. Then she said uneasily, "Maybe I ought to ask how *you* got there?"

"Whom do you expect me to betray?" he retorted. But at the expression of unfeigned misery in her face, exaggerated by her evident exhaustion, he relented, and said, "My own betrayal was affected by Kalaeb Flendar, in a mistaken attempt to bargain himself into a position of influence. Commander Benoni suspected what had happened and took the time-honored way out. I was too slow."

Lilah realized only belatedly what the dry voice meant by *time-honored way*: suicide. Sickened, she said, "Then Peitar was right."

"He foresaw that, did he?"

"Well, not in so many words. But he was afraid you might run into some kind of trouble after you went away. He really wanted you to let Tsauderei send you by magic to somewhere safe."

"What else did your clairvoyant brother predict on my behalf?"

His sarcasm had always stung, but he'd never, in all her experience, talked about himself. Ever. She fought back through memory and retrieved one of Peitar's many incomprehensible utterances. "He said he hoped you were watching him from a distance, because it would keep him honest."

She peeked her uncle's way to see if that confused him as much as it did her, but his brow cleared, and his eyes narrowed in a kind of ironic humor. He understood. That was so strange.

Outside their little space, the rain roared down, a stream having carved itself in the trail they'd made.

"It is a cause for regret," he said presently, "that your brother and I are not likely to speak again this side of death."

"Oh, Uncle Dirty-Hands, don't say things like that." Her shoulders hunched right up to her ears.

"I will refrain from voicing bleak prognostications," he said with even more pronounced irony than before, "if you will favor me with my name, and not that lamentable soubriquet."

"Lament — oh! Dirty-Ha — urble. I — it's just — "

"Habit. So I apprehended during my brief perusal of your, ah, chronicle."

Her stomach churned with embarrassment when she thought back to all the insults she'd written into the diary that she'd kept during the revolution. At the end, her uncle had had the diary for a short time. Words of self-justification formed, but she didn't voice them. After all, he'd already lost everything. And anyway, he didn't sound angry or even accusing. Just sort of amused.

A humorous Uncle Dirty-Hands — Uncle Darian, that is — was infinitely preferable to an angry one, especially when they were penned up here, with who knew how many Norsundrians chasing after them, and a long way to go until they reached some sort of safety.

Bringing her thoughts back to his original question.

"I went into Sartor with...someone I can't name, because there are magic spells if she's mentioned." As her uncle's brows twitched upward, she said in a whisper — as if that would fool any lurking magic — "She's the last of that family. That rules Sartor. Kept hidden."

Gratified by her uncle's evident surprise, Lilah went on with a little more confidence. "See, the Norsundrians don't know she's alive. Or they didn't. They think she's me. I'm her. Anyway, she broke the time-spell over

Sartor, and is on her way to sweep out the rest of their rotten magic. At least, I hope she is. She was when I got pinched in her place, by that horrible man with the black hair. Is he really dead? He said he was."

"If he was Kessler Sonscarna, Zydes's runner, he probably told you that for his own entertainment. How did you come to be selected for this quest?"

"Well, I offered. And *She* was glad of my company," she added defensively. "Anyway, we didn't know that disgusting villain Zydes had this magic scope thing that let him see anywhere within the enchanted borders, and he found us, but I don't think he knew which of us was which, because they grabbed me, like I said. Well, he tried to put a spell on me, only it didn't work because it was bound on her name. I wonder if it will suddenly pounce on her and work if she ever gets stuck in that fortress?" Lilah frowned. "Well, the mages can worry about that, and I hope it never comes to pass, because —"

Darian Irad raised a hand, and Lilah stuttered to a stop.

He said, "Permit me to restate. Zydes and those under his command believe that you are a descendant of the Landis family?"

"Yes."

"And Zydes can see anywhere with this magic object."

"Not anymore," Lilah said, and for the first time, she grinned, though her lips cracked painfully. "I used Atan's ring and smashed it. Right before I came to get you out." She patted her pocket where the ring resided. "Hurt like crazy, too, but it was worth it."

"Well done," he said.

It was the first praise she'd ever heard from him.

"So they will misunderstand your liberating me — for which I neglected to thank you, by the way."

Lilah's face burned again. She said, "Peitar would expect me to do what I did. But what's that about misunderstanding?"

"They will be expecting us to ride straight east. If nothing else, you — as this missing princess — could throw yourself on Peitar's mercy. But I am as sure as I can be of anything that Zydes will expect me to foreswear myself and raise Sarendan's army for an invasion of Sartor."

"Oh. Um, is that bad, or good?"

"As it happens, I chose the northern route as the flattest and therefore the fastest. I'd expected us to cut for the east today, and run along Sartor's southern border."

"But now?"

"He will send Kessler, who, I am told, cannot be outrun when he's on the hunt. We will not test the truth of that boast. We'll remain on the northern road, straight into Sartor."

THIRTEEN

Zydes—furious, worried, beset by the endless compli-
cations of a troublesome command—tried to win
enough free time to perform a complicated series of
spells. They were especially vicious, a summoning
against the will, which was correspondingly harsh on the
magician casting them, but he was desperate.

By the third day, he was in fact desperate enough to
extend the magic almost until he was consumed by it, and
yet the spells did not work: Yustnesveas Landis was not
yanked by magic transfer into his warded office.

He slumped back behind his desk, dazed and exhausted, defeat—loss of control—gnawing at his vitals,
for it was not just that girl's obviously superior magic that
baffled him, but with the scope gone he could not spy
upon Kessler, still out on the chase.

Kessler had nearly reached the border. His respect for
Irad and the Landis girl had intensified as the chase
lengthened, for he drove his handpicked warriors to the
limits of their endurance, with only the briefest pauses for
food and water when they changed mounts at relay
outposts along the east road.

His detachment exerted themselves quite beyond
any effort they might have made for Zydes, for they had
all heard murmured stories about Kessler in action. The
likelihood of the rumors being true had been

demonstrated in his performance with sword or knife during practices, not long after he had first arrived. And when he won, there was no tap, no strike with the flat of the blade. He broke bones, ripped flesh, just short of the kill, never with any word of anger or even any change of expression.

So they kept complaints to themselves, brutal as the journey was—each step of which he was sharing. No one wanted the kiss of steel for answer.

Though Zydes couldn't see him, he wasn't free of observers. Dejain had chanced to return to the fortress in time to witness his fast departure. She made it her business to transfer to each of the replay outposts after him, and once she determined the direction of the chase, she returned to the fortress to sift rumors for the object. According to gossip, Zydes had had some mysterious boy as a prisoner—or recruit—who had vanished with no less a prisoner—or recruit—than Darian Irad.

She nearly made the same mistake that Zydes did: assume that Kessler Sonscarna on the hunt finished the business. But she had built a career on the expert sifting of talk from the lowly, the people everyone in power ignored. A mention of fresh horse droppings to the north and speculation about what idiotic plans Zydes might be hatching in Sartor, when everyone knew what happened to you there, sent her exploring.

She would have to act fast.

The larger reach any spell has, the more difficult it is to place. But she took the time to set a warning tracer beyond the last northern outpost, extending into the hills on one side and into the cracked, waterless plains in the other.

Then she went about her business.

Not three days later, the warning tracer pinged its blue flower in her mind, and she dropped everything to transfer to a suitable observation Destination, already chosen.

When the transfer reaction wore off, she spotted a Norsundrian riding with a red-haired scout northward. Again, she nearly returned, but she remembered the red-haired boy Zydes had had for a short time as a runner. Already sent on errands without training? That was unusual.

More unusual was the fact that the two traveled parallel to the road. She watched the horses plod northward toward Sartor and its time binding, which would effectively place them beyond tracing. They *had* to be Darian Irad, former king of Sarendan, and the mystery boy. Irad was worthless, except in a military sense. From all reports, he was almost, if not quite, as volatile as Kessler. But that brat? Zydes had wanted this unnamed boy, so there was some mystery here, all right.

There was still time before they crossed into Sartor. Good thing? No one knew they were there except Dejain! Bad thing? Capturing them herself meant magic, and that much magic always left traces. She would have to make certain that Zydes was busy with something else before she could act.

She transferred back to the fortress.

Tsauderei, high up in the Valley, had maintained his ceaseless watch on the movement of the ring.

He had rejoiced when it moved away from the fortress, and he had scarcely slept since. When they reached the territory before the border of Sartor, he waited until nightfall and transferred, using the ring as Destination.

Lilah and her uncle found shelter along a riverbed on the other side, and once he'd cared for the animals as best he could, they lay down to sleep. But the soft sound of footsteps in the gravel and a gasp caused Darian Irad, trained from childhood to be wary, to whirl up from his blanket bedroll, steel in either hand.

Tsauderei raised his hands and lowered himself carefully onto a nearby rock, palms up. The last fading light gleamed with ruddy color on a few short strands of hair on the small figure lying nearby. He exclaimed softly, "Lilah?"

Poor Lilah was so tired she didn't even stir.

Irad's eyes narrowed. "Tsauderei?"

"Yes."

They'd met very seldom. Both were thinking of the last time, just after Darian Irad lost his throne to his nephew, through Lilah's use of her magical flowers.

"One of you has a magic ring I gave to a young magic student of mine," Tsauderei said in a tone that invited response.

"Lilah has it. I'm taking her north into Sartor. They are searching east for us," Darian Irad said. He added with sardonic humor, "They also believe she is —"

"Don't say the name," Tsauderei cut in quickly. "There are spells waiting to catch the unwary."

Darian Irad hated magic. But he respected its reach.

"Ah." Tsauderei winced against the unforgiving unevenness of the rock, which did his withered haunches and ancient joints no good at all, and said, "The time-bindings on Sartor have been broken. There's more to be done to free the kingdom, but it cannot be completed until the person of whom we speak gets safely to her capital. I don't know why Zydes isn't chasing you, or her now, but I suspect that will change sooner than later."

Darian Irad said, "I know nothing about magic battles, as you are aware. Can the populace be raised to defend themselves?"

"I don't know," Tsauderei admitted. "I don't know how the time-binding spells are diminishing, or where. But yes, if the populace were to be raised, that would be an advantage to her, perhaps."

Irad said nothing.

Tsauderei waited, and when the pause had become a silence, he said, "I could transfer you to the border of Shendoral, if you like. That is a vast woodland in the center of the kingdom in which Norsunder cannot perform magic. Lilah can rejoin Atan. And you'd be that much farther removed from our friends to the south."

Irad's ironic expression was just discernible in the fading light. "No demands?"

Tsauderei spread his hands. "You ought to know by now that direct interference is not one of my habits. You made an agreement with Peitar, which you seem to be keeping. I will not interfere with you anywhere outside of Sarendan's border."

A nod.

Tsauderei said, "Then we'd better act fast."

Darian Irad roused Lilah, who barely had time to rub her eyes and look around before magic took hold of her and her uncle.

When Dejain transferred back to put her plans in place, it was to find her quarry gone.

That had to mean somebody more powerful than she was entering the game. Sometimes silence was more deadly than overt threats and posturing of the sort that Zydes favored. It meant that someone was waiting for the right moment to strike.

She retired to consider and to observe.

FOURTEEN

Atan swung down from her sleeping platform, handed herself down two branches, her feet only touching the vine-ladder twice, and then dropped onto the grass. When she'd first arrived, it had taken time, effort, and all her concentration to get up and down again. Now it was easy.

As soon as she appeared, voices clamored for her attention.

"Arlas is not doing her share—"

"They're accusing us of being lazy ristos again—"

"Atan, I need to talk to you. Just you and me."

Atan had learned the etiquette of the dawnsinger sleeping platforms. When you were up, you were away—as if in a locked room—unless you specifically invited someone up. But when you came down, then that meant you were ready for company.

She looked around at the faces—some angry, some sulky. Hinder looked worried.

"Hinder, is something wrong?" she asked, remembering that he'd volunteered for the last forest sweep. In fact, wasn't he supposed to be back in two days?

Hinder ducked his head in a nod, his wispy white hair falling forward to hide his face. Atan was still trying to make sense of where she fit in this crowd, but she knew one thing: when Hinder spoke, it never was a personal demand, it was always about something that had to do with the forest-dwellers as a group, or Shendoral.

She moved toward the rock in the center of the clearing, which she'd come to understand as the group's speaking place. Since her arrival, a few had treated it like it was her throne.

She felt ridiculous, sitting on a rock with others at her feet, faces upturned expectantly. But they all did it, so that indicated a social pattern. She'd read about social patterns. She'd talked about them with Tsauderei. She understood that humans acted in patterns. But she didn't feel a part of this pattern, that is, she felt like she was enacting a role. It was neither natural or custom for her.

As she walked, she observed the others. Irza, as usual, fell in behind Atan as one who had the right. It had nothing to do with friendship, and everything with the patterns of rank.

On the other side of the clearing, Rip and the Poisoners—the four boys and two girls who did food-preparation—sang, a cheery song. Atan suspected the melody was old, half-remembered, because the forest-dwellers had made up their own words:

"Stir! Stir! Stir! The spoon goes in a blur, stir stir!

Chop! Chop! Chop! Off the leaves with a lop, chop chop!"

Rip and the Poisoners paid no attention to the etiquette of the rock.

Hinder wriggled his toe talons through the grass at each step. How he loved sunside and all its growing things! They grew things in the morvende caverns—of course—but there was no wind and weather there for the wild beauty of shape, or the tumble of unplanned gardens.

He loved sunside, and his expectations, well, his dread, of the return of the rumored Last Landis had been met, but she wasn't another Irza, even more arrogant and assured of her place at the pinnacle of human hierarchy.

Sin had said earlier, "You tell her." She added with a flickering smile, "Are you sure you don't just like her because she's powerless, and knows it?"

Hinder was sure. Atan was never boring, she knew more history than he did, and, well, liking to help didn't mean you wanted people to be powerless.

He waited until she sat on the rock, then leaned

close. "Your friend who disappeared? I think we've found her," Hinder said, and watched as Atan's sober, slightly worried expression changed.

It was everything he'd hoped for, that change — like sunrise after a night of storms.

Atan never thought about her face. She was only aware of her heart giving a thump against her ribs, then drumming. "Lilah? You found Lilah?"

"I think so. It was your other friend, the one who ran off, who used to live with Savar, who found me —"

"You mean Merewen?"

"That's the one." Hinder held out his hand at approximately Merewen's height. "Blue skin. Came smack on me like a dropped rock as if we saw each other every day. Said she's been all over the eastern end of the forest — I guess she can travel a whole lot faster than we can."

"She's part Loi," Atan said.

"Ah, that would explain not just her speed, but some of the other part."

"Part?" Atan was thoroughly confused.

Hinder sighed. "I'm telling it backwards. Merewen said she'd tried to go after Lilah, but when she got to the border, she said she was drying up like old leaves. She was afraid if she tried to cross into Norsunder's parched lands, she would fly into ash." He cocked his head. "I thought she was being, you know, poetic."

Atan opened her hands. "I don't know her well enough to tell you if she speaks truly or figuratively."

"Ah. She seemed quite sad, and said she'd returned, having failed to help Lilah and failed to find Savar." He hesitated. He came close — so close he could feel the first word shaping his tongue — to saying *Fancy her going off all alone to run a rescue.* It was exactly what the rest of the patrol had said, but he looked at Atan's wide gaze, bright with a suspicious gathering of moisture, and remembered that Atan had wanted to do the very same thing.

She would have, if the group hadn't stopped her.

Why did her smile of happiness hurt? *Because she thought she was our prisoner.*

He cleared his throat, fingered the scab on his scalp, and continued as naturally as he could, "They're way down the south end of Shendoral, which you'd expect, I guess, coming from the direction of the Norsunder base." He waved his hand behind him. "They look like two Norsunder riders, I mean, one our age and one man. The man is dressed like a Norsunder warrior, and the other one like those spies that sneak around at night—you know, all in black. I waited for daylight so I could get a better look at 'em." His tone changed to uncertainty.

"And?"

"Well, the scout could be a girl or a boy, I can't tell. Red hair, like you said, and tilted eyes, but that's not so unusual among sunsiders. No robe, though. Black uniform. The man is somewhat like the one that brained me—not tall, lean—but he doesn't have curly, short black hair. This one's got long brown hair." Hinder's thin, taloned morvende fingers wiggled downward, indicating waves. "Blue eyes. The one I followed I was mostly behind and so I never got all that clear a look at his face, but I do remember he had blue eyes. Those were the last thing I saw before he hit me. And this one also has blue eyes. I saw 'em clear as anything when they made a campfire. So you might want to be sure."

He paused, rubbing his chin again.

Atan said, "Take me to them! Or is there something else?"

"Only that they were talking in another language. Not Norsunder's tongue, which has some familiar words, but another, with different familiarities. In the middle of it, I heard the little one say what sounded like 'Uncle Darian'. Or would have been in Sartoran."

The name obviously meant nothing to Hinder, whose historical perspective stopped at Sartor's border a century ago, but Atan drew in her breath. It couldn't be Darian Irad—could it?

Of course it could. Atan remembered having asked Tsauderei once what Darian Irad looked like, to which the mage had replied that he would not say this in any of the family's hearing, but except for the Selenna tilt to the eyes, Peitar Selenna could be Darian Irad's son, so strong was the resemblance.

And she had a clear memory of Peitar Selenna: not quite full grown, slender in build, and long, waving brown hair.

If that was indeed Darian Irad in that uniform, had the deposed king of Sarendan known for his cold-bloodedness gone over to Norsunder? Why would he have Lilah with him? Tsauderei had never named the former king as an evil man, just driven. And Peitar Selenna had said last summer that his uncle hated Norsunder.

Atan dug her thumbnail into the lichen growing across the rock on the south side. If the "scout" was Lilah, there was at least a chance that Darian Irad had helped her escape. Only why would he come into Sartor?

Stupid question. What better prospect for a deposed king than another kingdom that needed, above anything else, either a mage—or a military leader?

She looked up at Hinder, who waited for her to answer, his happy smile fading to question. In the background, the singing voices rose and fell once more, then broke into laughter, and then chatter, the succession of sounds reminding her of the waterfall splashing down onto the rocks and into a sunlit pool.

Tsauderei had said that she would spend the rest of her life compromising between burdensome choices.

"What bothers me most," she said slowly, "is that Merewen wasn't sure that the scout was Lilah."

"She saw them last night. Then *whish*." Hinder waved a hand through the air. "She ran to find us."

"Is anyone watching them now?" she asked, pressing her forearms across her middle, which was tight with worry.

"Sin and Pouldi."

"Good." She let out her breath. "Take me to them."

Darian Irad woke up from the first long, unbroken sleep he'd had in half a year at least.

Shendoral Woodland was unlike any forest in Sarendan, even the ancient and tricksy Diannah, though some types of growth and scents were familiar. The light filtering down through sky-scraping trees in moisture-laden shafts, the constant rustle of wind-stirred foliage, took him back to childhood, when his father had still been alive to protect him from the worst of his grandfather's inimical focus. In those days, camping with the cadets at Obrin's military training ground, and exploring the palace's secret passageways with his sister Rana, and later, running the forested hills above the military school in Khanerenth, had been the happiest times of his life.

It seemed appropriate that his present surroundings should hearken back to childhood, for his mood was much the same. In those days, every dawn had brought the light of promise: anticipation of mastering the wherewithal for change, and the prospect of at last using what he'd learned. One day, if he lived, he would be king, and when he was, life would be different. Better.

But it hadn't become better. His plans for improvement had stretched on and on into the future, leaving him striving for years to ready for war with Norsunder, after the sighting of Norsundrian scouting missions all during '33 — a fact that the civilians didn't believe when he'd raised taxes again in order to support the force he knew he'd need.

Scouting missions, he'd discovered since his summary recruitment, had been sent by Kessler Sonscarna, who indeed had been planning an invasion. But events had prevented them both from meeting in battle.

Meanwhile, during those endless nights in the barren stone of Norsunder's fortress barracks, breathing in the atmosphere of fear, and force, and intent that had nothing whatsoever to do with moral authority, he had faced the bleak truth: he had failed as a king, and though one could trace the reasoning behind every single decision, the end result was the same. Failure. Only separation from the bindings of power — and of expectation — granted one the space to contemplate the slow distortion of perspective that had brought him to face his own people in revolt.

He had failed as a king, but Sarendan would not founder, for Peitar Selenna would not compound generations of error.

Peitar comprehended the exigencies of power, all right. Otherwise he wouldn't have sat there quite alone and unarmed when Darian was waking up after that dose of Lilah's magical flowers, at the very end.

They both were aware that it would take Darian
about two heartbeats to kill Peitar. They both knew that
Peitar's strength lay in the willing and loyal crowd
beyond the door. And so they'd walked out together,
Darian to exile, and Peitar to the throne that Darian
couldn't keep.

Darian got to his feet and set about refreshing the
campfire that had kept him and his scruffy young niece
warm during the night. The horses were not far, their
heads down over a small stream. He bent to drink water,
clear, cold, and tasting a little of wood. Refreshing. Only
hunger remained, but that was no great matter. Very
soon he would be sitting alone on the bank of a stream,
catching a trout or two.

Lilah woke a little while later, rubbed her eyes, and
breathed in. It was true! They were out of Norsunder's
horrible land! She scooted closer to the fire, for the
morning was chill. The bite of winter was in the air.

Then she looked around, her mouth open, her
freckled face round and expressive with wonder and joy.
"Shendoral," she breathed.

"We'll just make certain of that," Darian said.

"I'm sure it's Shendoral," she said. "It looked, and
smelled, just like this. All we have to do is find Atan!"

She sat back, eyeing him in an uncertain manner
that had become familiar. She'd rescued him not for her
own protection, he had discovered, but because she had
thought it right. Even so, she clearly did not trust him. He
had made no effort to change that. In his experience, trust
resulted from experience, not persuasion.

"If you recognize this place," he said, "it will suffice.
I believe I will take my leave of you now."

Lilah said tentatively, "Now? But aren't you going
to wait till we find Atan?" In her worried gaze he saw the
direction of her thoughts: she was afraid for her friend,
the last Landis, kept hidden by Tsauderei all these years.

Darian hid the wash of bitterness. He would have
kept her safe, had he known of her existence. But he
hadn't been offered the option.

"No," he said, and whistled to his mount.

As he began to saddle the horse, Lilah hovered at
his side, looking up, and down, and sideways. Then she
scrubbed her grubby fingers over her dirty face and

blinked up him.

"If — if you have a long way to go, why don't you take both horses? Atan didn't have one, so I probably won't need that one."

He nodded and made that one ready as well. She followed him, chewing on her chapped lips.

Finally she said, "Are you sure you'll be — well, all right?"

He hesitated, wondering if it would be possible to make her see how very sweet was the prospect of real freedom. But he didn't think she would comprehend. Probably no one could, no one who had not been born yoked to a position of power and its endless obligations, and then had lost not only that but the ability to make the simplest choices. Going from king to Norsundrian "recruit" certainly caused one to reflect upon the significance of autonomy.

"Yes," he said.

When he'd tested the last saddle girth and slid the bigger saber home into the saddle sheath, he turned around, and this time saw decision in her face. "So," she said. "No more fox hunts, Uncle Darian?"

Laughter was another long-forgotten luxury. "No more fox hunts, Lilah."

He mounted up, and set out at an easy pace toward the northeast.

PART TWO

ONE

The long fall of notes from a warbler high in the tree above rippled through Atan's dream.

She woke slowly, the jumble of dream-images mixing with sounds from below and above. The sweet, or shrill, or sharp sounds of forest birds and birds of the meadows, of the lakes, and of the mountains, complemented the chatter of young voices.

Birds.

She wondered if some of these birds had found their way out of the disintegrating time-binding.

Her first instinct was to ask Tsauderei, from lifetime habit. She could picture his old, sardonic face, and his rusty voice when he'd told her to contemplate the fact that magic-training for a prospective ruler was at best a slapdash affair. Far better that the heir had a sibling or cousin or friend who was trusted, who could spend the required ten or twenty years living in the wilds, doing nothing but listening to the land — and another who could spend ten or twenty years working a craft, and listening and learning how people interacted. Only when mages know the balance of nature could they master the great magic. Kings in training wanted shortcuts, because the day was only so long, and the exigencies of learning to rule always came first.

Atan knew she was ignorant. She could read and

read and read, until I spend enough candles for a family of twenty, and her eyes burned, and yet she was ignorant about ruling, for all she'd had were histories to read. No experience in anything but magic.

Sunlight—warm, golden—flickered across her eyelids, dappled by leaves rustling in the morning breeze. Urgency, then memory brought back the evening before: Lilah, back among them!

She still didn't know what to make of that. They'd traveled most of the day through the forest, to find Lilah alone, walking alongside a stream. She'd looked up, and smiled, and greeted everyone as though she'd only been gone since breakfast. As if there had been no Norsunder, except there she was in those black clothes, her face tired with those terrible circles under her eyes.

She'd answered questions with a shrug and grimace, no words. Then said, "Tell me about the hideout."

Atan had found herself talking, no, babbling, to fill the silence as they all walked back to the hideout. She'd walked the silent Lilah around the clearing, explained the two morvende tree platforms, pointed out the girls' tree, then taking Lilah to the swing. Lilah had stared at that, her lips parted, her gaze so strange that Atan had instinctively waved off the others.

She and Lilah stepped alone onto the swing. Lilah said in a creaky voice utterly unlike her own, "I heard of these. But never. Saw one."

Atan said, "Put your hands on this bar. Lean back while I lean forward. Brick and Pouldi and Sana all swing it all the way up and over the bar, but I haven't dared yet..." She found herself babbling again, as they swung back and forth, back and forth, Lilah's breathing more ragged. Then Atan made the mistake of singing one of the simpler swing songs, the one that reminded her of Larksong.

Lilah's face had gone a nasty shade of yellow-white, and gulping, bone-shaking sobs racked her so badly she couldn't talk. She crouched down with her head on her knees, her arms tightly wrapped around her legs, heedless of the sway of the platform, and wept.

Atan grimaced, hating the memory of her own helplessness, the sick sense of guilt that this was her fault, and she could not fix it. Some queen of ancient lineage, couldn't even assuage the grief of her first friend!

A pretty voice broke into her thoughts, shaping words with haughty precision and studied musicality. "...well *I* would think that the Sarendan princess would wake up today, unless she plans to sleep until Norsunder is defeated. Oh! I did not see that you had returned! Good morning, Princess Merewen."

It was the *tone* that Atan could not define, except that she did not like it — and she immediately scolded herself for thinking such a thing.

Then came Merewen's soft reply: "Good morning, Irza."

Merewen was back? Time to get up.

Atan opened her eyes, and rolled onto her elbows to peer over the platform's edge, relieved and surprised to see Merewen's golden hair gleaming in the mellow sunlight directly below her. Merewen and Julian sat next to one another, each with a lapful of daisies and white starliss and tiny lavender bee-blossoms, Julian watching with her characteristic solemn gaze as Merewen's clever fingers twined the flowers together.

Merewen shook her hair back and glanced up, question in her face.

Atan cast a quick look behind her at Lilah, who was, not surprisingly, still slumbering. Her eyes no longer looked so dark underneath, and her coloring had returned to normal during the night.

Atan looked down at the ring on her finger, twisting it around. It had seemed neutral, when Tsauderei gave it to her. An artifact of history, possibly useful. After having pieced together from Lilah's halting words what it had accomplished in the Norsunder base, she regarded it differently: the ring now carried mute threat. A powerful symbol of the violence of once-living ancestors.

Atan sent one last glance at Lilah's peaceful face. She'd cried herself out, then pulled off the ring and surrendered it, then followed Atan to the platform, where she'd wrapped herself up in the quilt Atan pointed out, and lay down with her face turned away. Atan had climbed down to leave her in peace, finding the customarily loquacious Hinder and Pouldi waiting below in compassionate silence, and Sin in narrow-eyed wariness.

Atan hoped Lilah would wake up wanting to talk. She would not pester Lilah. She had made a vow. But she wanted — very badly — to know what Darian Irad was going to do in Sartor. Not that she could stop him. But not to know — it was like turning your back on a lightning storm.

She worked a brush through her long brown hair and braided it quickly. Then she descended, careful not to make a sound.

Merewen and Julian both looked up, and smiled a welcome. Atan sniffed: fresh pan-biscuits, smeared with the tart berry jam that Rip and his Poisoners made so well.

As she passed by the girls, Merewen looked her way. So, too, did Julian, her gaze unnervingly watchful in that small, round face.

Tsauderei had told Atan that her education was far beyond what most princes and princesses got. But when they weren't reading, they were learning how to deal with real people, and here she felt her own lack every single day.

She listened to the happy chatter of the Poisoners. Rip, whose nickname came from the initials of "Rest in Peace" was a big, cheery half-morvende. His hands did not end in the morvende talons, but he had pale coloring and a shock of blue-white hair. It was his cheery habit of experimenting with food that had earned him his nickname.

With him worked Hannla, the oldest one in the group, Atan had recently discovered, though Hannla was very small and slight and didn't look sixteen. Hannla's mother had run a pleasure house in Eidervaen.

There had been no pleasure house or anything like it in tiny Delfina Valley, where Atan had stayed hidden. Hannla had explained cheerfully, "Oh, downstairs is where families come, for the food is always the very best, and there is always music, and entertainment. The grownups might go upstairs, but everybody young stayed down below, and at *our* house, we were always getting up plays."

"Plays?" Atan had asked. "I thought people went to the theater to see those."

"They did. But if they wanted to act themselves, or

sometimes to make one up, they came to *us*." Hannla impatiently pushed back an unruly strand of her thick, curly hair.

Plays! Music! Dancing! Wonderful foods from all other the world! This was what Norsunder had either destroyed or froze beyond time. It made Atan wild with longing, and regret, and anger.

But Hannla was cheerful and friendly. It was she who knew how to cook so well, how to find spices (and grow more), and to sew small, exquisite stitches—when they were able to get sewing materials.

Atan walked across the grass to join them.

"Good morning," Hannla said, her ruddy brown curls bouncing on her back as she whirled around. "Here's your share, fresh out of the pan."

"Thanks," Atan said.

"How is Lilah?" Hannla asked, glancing back at Atan's tree.

"Sleeping still."

Hannla pursed her lips. "Was it very bad?"

"Bad enough, I gather," Atan said.

Hannla gave a quick nod and returned to kneading dough, as Rip waved his stirring spoon at two of his helpers, who were wrestling on the ground, and told them to get to work before he dumped soup on them.

Atan bit into her biscuit. Crunchy on the outside, soft and warm in the middle, it was a miracle of tastiness in these surroundings. So much unspoken ability—and promise—and potential strife—all symbolized here in this little brown piece of food.

When she looked up, Merewen was there, her wide sky-colored eyes alert, her head canted in mute question.

"You have news?" Atan asked. The words "of Savar" stayed unspoken because Merewen did not seem happy. She hadn't gone along to meet Lilah, but had run off in the other direction.

"Last night I went seeking," Merewen said in her soft voice. "And I found something new that I think is important. In some of the little villages, and even some towns, I saw lights. Hin and Sin told me that the villages are always dark, and when you go near them, you find yourself drawn into dreams. But I didn't feel that at the small villages I spied from the forest's edge. Only the large town. And I went quickly away."

"Then the magic must be stronger where there are more people," Atan said. "I guess that would make sense: it must have taken greater magic to bind the enchantment in villages, towns, and cities."

"Yes, but there's another thing I saw, and that by accident." Merewen frowned. "I don't know if everyone can see it, for it isn't quite like seeing this way." She bent, picked up a leaf, and held it up so that sunlight glowed round its edges. "Some things I see—this way." She touched her forehead, her eyes closed. "And this." She touched her heart. "I don't know that I can explain how, or why."

"It's all right," Atan said. "Explain it as you can."

"Over those villages, the ones with lights at night, there was also a kind of glow, but I felt it more than I saw it. It felt like here, when we cross the bridge." Again, she touched her forehead.

"Magic," Atan breathed. "I wonder—I wonder if that is where we will begin to find allies."

Merewen nodded. "The lights in the houses mean the people are no longer dreaming, doesn't it? I didn't leave the forest's edge, or talk to anyone. I was too afraid."

"I think we need to find out," Atan said. Her heart thumped again. "Before Norsunder does."

Some days' journey upriver to the northwest Rel was still sitting on the steps of the great palace, lost in memory-dream. He sat there peacefully until a sudden clap on his shoulder smashed through the dreams.

"Wake up. Wake up," a male voice commanded.

Rel fought his way to consciousness. It was not a quick fight. It took the space of several breaths, while his body protested any sudden movements. His joints twinged and his neck zinged him with a pang as he twisted his head to see who'd struck him.

A man ran lightly down the steps, visible only from the back: medium height, light of build, long brown hair tied back, dark clothes.

"Hey." Rel was surprised to discover how much

effort that took.

The man paused and glanced back, blue eyes wary and curious.

"What?" Rel asked. His mouth was dry, his tongue awkward. All he could manage was that one word.

Before he could frame another, the man pointed. "Go south," he said, in accented Sartoran. "Norsunder is going to find out this kingdom is waking up, and the Landis princess is going to need allies." Without waiting for an answer, the man leaped down the steps and strode away.

Landis—Rel knew *that* name. Every child in the world had at least heard that name. But history taught that they had all died.

Rel forced himself to his feet, and that act broke the last of the magic hold. He started moving, at first feeling like he was trying to run in water. He walked into a spacious street and saw others still sitting here and there, staring into space.

Magic. Bad magic. Rel kept walking in hopes of finding the man who'd wakened him, for his mind filled with questions, but after a time he gave up. Thirst and hunger clamored much too fiercely, and his knees trembled. He stopped at a fountain to drink, and then sat down on the rim to stare in bemusement at the water shooting up, falling into the pool, and draining away somewhere. Surely that fountain had not run for over a hundred years.

He shook his head, then dug in his pack for something to eat.

Darian Irad hastened his way through Eidervaen, trying to rouse every single person he encountered. Many dropped back into the weird torpor from which he briefly brought them. Others got up and moved about, looking lost and disoriented.

He never halted long. This wasn't his kingdom, nor was it his war. His single-minded focus, his hatred of Norsunder, and the unconscious mental resistance he'd built up to the pervasive atmosphere of defeat and despair in the Norsunder base, kept the weakening magic from taking hold of him.

And so he kept going, hoping that a leader would emerge from the groggy, bewildered people he found. He kept going straight north, without knowing that the strange magic of Shendoral had transferred him several days' journey to the very northwestern edge of the forest, a few days' journey from the capital.

He rode along the Ilder river, encountering dwellings wherein people sat as they'd been magic-bound for over a century, the pots and pans in their kitchens dry with ancient dust, yet meager supplies from that last war-ravaged harvest still stored in larders, cellars, and cupboards. Two days he traveled, finding loose horses ready for a fast gallop, and untouched haystacks, and the occasional smoke-blackened ruins of war from which the fires had long since cooled. In some places the old war was strangely immediate, in others, long past.

Once he stopped to share a supper with people who had apparently just woken on their own, and who, still perplexed and dream-mazed, had fixed a meal, and were slowly rediscovering their attachment to the material world. The questions they asked him were straight-forward, but few of them could he answer.

At the end of this strange meal Darian picked up an apple that had been laid in the cellar just before his grand-father's birth, during a war that that grandfather had grown up hearing about, and whose ferocity had shaped the Irad line through the three succeeding generations.

He rode across Sartor, waking up every person he encountered, until he reached the border at last and thence into a new life.

Lilah woke up loving the forest foliage overhead, and the sounds of forest-dweller talking and singing. By the end of that day, she'd joined the bigger ones in circle swinging, which meant going over the bar. The thrill of motion, almost of terror, made her scream with laughter.

I could stay here forever, she exulted at the end of the first night. And when she woke again in the morning to the same leaves.

The third day, she began to pay attention to the

regular patterns of the forest-dwellers, specifically the training the older ones put themselves through every morning.

"Here's how you string a bow." Hinder showed Lilah the oiled snapvine string, then demonstrated how to hook it to the other end of the bow. "You draw your arrow back like this." He made it look easy.

Lilah blew her breath out. She was determined to never be a victim again. She gritted her teeth, yanked the arrow back — and let go.

The arrow shot backward.

"Whoop!"

"Ulp!"

She whirled around, horrified as a bunch of forest-dwellers scrambled out of the way. *Chuff!* Her arrow flumped ignominiously on the grass.

"Never mind," Hinder said over his shoulder as he ran to retrieve the arrow. "Your pull wasn't hard enough to do much besides give someone a good poke. And when we started, we were just as bad." He took the bow from her hands. "Watch. Carefully."

This time Hinder explained everything he was doing with his hands and arms. Lilah, standing back, noticed that his entire body moved. It looked as if he drew his strength from his wide-planted feet as he nocked an arrow, aimed, adjusting for the rising western breeze, and then let fly. *Zoing!* The arrow smacked dead center into the target he and his friends had made from straw and some old cloth, painted with circles.

Lilah tried a couple more times, and on the last one actually managed to send an arrow in the general direction of the target, though it fell far short and quite a bit to the right.

By then, several others had gathered around, and they all complimented her with friendly and generous cheers.

"Better than I," Brick declared. "Why, when I first began to shoot, everyone ran to stand in front of the target, figuring that was the only safe place!"

Lilah laughed with the rest, pretending it was funny. She didn't want them to see how useless she felt. She still had her thief tools, but sometimes there weren't any locks to pick, or villains to send off to sleep with Lure flowers — if the flowers had any potency left. Hinder and Sana and Sin and Mendaen and all these others looked so, so *effortless* with their excellent shots.

Lilah said, "I want to watch. Then I'll take a turn." She moved to the side as the others commenced practice.

Atan appeared next to her. "Lilah, are you all right? Do you need more rest?" she asked.

Her gaze was friendly and steady, but the shape of her eyes was a nasty reminder of Kessler's flat stare. Lilah had avoided Atan the past couple of days, but she knew it wasn't fair. Atan was a friend, and she couldn't help sharing an ancestor with that horrible Kessler Sonscarna.

She said, "I'm all right."

Atan looked away, then back again, her shoulders tight, her chin jutting. "Lilah, I'm so sorry I didn't come after you."

"He would have killed you. Or me, once he found out I wasn't you."

Atan shook her head. "I still feel..." Another, harder head shake. "They said I had an obligation to stay. I felt I had an obligation to you."

Lilah's skin prickled. She hated seeing Atan look so unhappy. "I think this is what my brother talked about, how horrid you feel when you're king and have two choices that are completely opposite."

"Peitar talked about that? What did he say?"

"He told me what Tsauderei said. Didn't Tsauderei tell you?"

Atan's lips twitched, almost a smile. "Is it the 'delegate' talk?"

"That was it! You delegate whichever choice you can, and do the other one. Well, when I got out with my uncle's help, then Tsauderei came. And Merewen and Hinder were looking for me. I mean, I know you didn't send my uncle, but in a way the others were kind of delegated. Weren't they?"

Atan rubbed her fingers up her sleeve two or three times, then said, "If you don't feel I failed you, then I'll accept that."

"You *didn't*," Lilah said. "I never thought you were supposed to chase that evil stinker Kessler. It would only have got us both into trouble."

Atan smiled, at least her mouth did, but her

forehead was still puckered with concern. She lifted a hand toward the others. "You want to learn the bow?"

Lilah sighed. "I figure it'll only be ten years before I can actually touch the target. Did they teach you anything while I was gone?"

"Sinder showed me a little," Atan said. "But like you, I need practice."

Everyone paired off to work with swords or knives, some with both. Lilah and Atan didn't join. They sat on the scattering of boulders bordering the clearing and watched the tall, black-haired Mendaen, who was by far the best.

"He told me that his family were palace guards," Atan said to Lilah. "He's been trying to teach them defense, but a couple of the others insist on only learning the art of dueling."

"Courtiers," Lilah guessed, and Atan brought her chin down in a slow nod.

Lilah knew what that meant: snobs. There were maybe forty forest-dwellers here overall. Everybody dressed in ragged old clothes. But even so, there were still snobs. It seemed there was no getting away from snobs, even in Sartor.

It was easy enough to pick out the nobles. Several forest-dwellers had somehow managed to find, or bring with them, big, heavy sabers, fancy light rapiers of the sort that nobles used to wear every day at court the generation or so before, one or two curved cavalry swords, used only by the biggest, and they used them with two hands. The only thing that these weapons had in common was their old-fashioned design.

The nobles stayed to themselves, in their midst a vaguely familiar girl with blonde braids. Lilah remembered her from the night before, asking Atan in a precise, insistent voice, "Did someone say that she wasn't born a princess? Of course, it's merely Sarendan..."

'Merely.' Lilah's stomach surged with disgust.

Atan lowered her voice. "Lilah, you can go home if you like. I think I can work a transfer from here."

Lilah wondered if Atan didn't want her anymore because she'd managed to get herself pinched. And here she'd just arrived, to find the most amazing hideout ever. No adults, just kids her age, and it looked like they had fun all the time! "If you don't need me, I'll go back. I don't want to cause any more trouble," she forced herself to say.

Atan frowned, made uneasy by the way Lilah looked down, and mumbled instead of her usual brisk, happy speech. What did it mean? "Lilah, I asked only because you've already been through a lot on my behalf. Please be plain. I'm having so much trouble understanding..." She swooped her hand through the air. "The differences between what is said and what is *meant*."

Lilah whooshed her breath out. "I hoped it was just that, and not because I was fathead enough to get caught. I promise I won't cause any trouble, I'll be careful—"

"As if we're all experienced warriors?" Atan countered, relieved. "Lilah, you're not to blame for anything. Nobody thinks it. I believe I can claim that much, at least."

Relief flooded through Lilah. "Well, count me in."

"Thank you." Atan drew in a breath. "The truth is, I need your perspective terribly. Though I've read so much about irony and hidden meanings, I don't know how to hear it. And I don't know how to ... to see intent not expressed in words." She sighed. "When you talk, your actions fit your tone. When Peitar talked, it was the same. And with Tsauderei—if he wanted me to know what he was thinking. With Merewen it mostly fits, but I don't think she's trying to hide anything. It's more that her Loi side is difficult to understand. With Hinder and Sin Mendaen, Brick and Hannla and Sana, everything fits together. But some—"

Lilah watched the blonde girl, who stood with her head erect, her wrists straight as she whipped the rapier through the air to clash against her opponent's blade. "I think I know what you mean."

Clang-g-g! At the other end of the clearing, two Poisoners began a mock battle with a battered wooden practice sword against a cauldron ladle, chins so elevated the two almost tipped backward, their movements prissy. Atan looked puzzled, but Lilah understood the mimicry at once.

Rip stuck out a foot. The one with the ladle stumbled and fell with a splat, which caused a wrestling match. Lilah sent a quick look at the nobles. They were paying Rip and the Poisoners no heed.

Lilah snickered, and Atan was glad to see her laughing. As Lilah watched the Poisoners clowning, Atan let her gaze wander until it was caught by a tight group talking earnestly on the other side of the clearing, who flicked looks her way. She'd better find out why.

Lilah didn't notice her going. She watched the Poisoners until Hinder sauntered up, wringing his hand. He hopped up on Lilah's rock to sit next to her, wiggling his bare toes. Lilah bent to look more closely at his toe talons.

Hinder said, "No, I don't know why we morvende have talons. I guess for digging."

"I wasn't going to ask such a nosy question," Lilah said, though she felt foolish, because she certainly had been thinking it.

Hinder grinned. "Really? Well then, you're the first. Soon's I came sunside and found my way here, they all asked us. The little ones right away, the older ones in roundabout ways. Said they'd heard of morvende, but never seen any of us."

"Probably everybody's *heard* of morvende." Lilah shook her head. "It's just that we weren't sure you really existed anymore, over in Sarendan. That Norsunder had managed to get all of you, along with Sartor, and Everon, and all the great kingdoms of the old stories."

"Not many of our kind have been in those old geliaths that far east, not for centuries and centuries," Hinder said. "Norsundrians *have* found some geliaths. And..." He made a swiping gesture, his talons ripping through the air. "Nobody comes out alive."

"Ugh. So 'geliath,' is that what morvende call their caves?"

"More like cave communities. I always wanted to hear about the sun and about weather, and life on the surface, and so I came up once I was past eight. And got caught here."

Lilah had heard stories about the morvende — how they taught Sartorans their style of music thousands of years ago, how they were half-human. How they lived in fantastic caverns full of rare, singing jewels. She was too embarrassed to ask directly, so she said, "I guess morvende can just leave?"

He shrugged. "Of course. Why not? A few of us like going sunside, that much I remember. Many go right back home." He shrugged again. "Wherever they come from, people tend to stick to what they're used to, mostly. That's what my grandmother told Sin and me, before she taught us the accesses."

"Those accesses," she said. "Are they obvious?"

Hinder grinned. "No. And we don't show 'em, not without permission. We agree to that, which is why they don't let us out until we're at least eight. See, it takes only one Norsundrian to find out, and then—" Another ripple through the air, then he flicked one talon against the black sleeve of her tunic. "Do you want to get rid of those duds?"

Lilah glanced down in vague surprise and remembered her Norsundrian scout's uniform. She looked up. "I hated it at first, but then I got used to it. It's comfortable and warm. Do I have to? My robe is lost."

Hinder shrugged. "If you don't mind, nobody else should, either. It's just, if you wanted new, we'd have to get busy finding others with extras and making 'em over, which takes time, and unless I miss my guess, Atan is not going to be keeping us here much longer."

His chin lifted, and Lilah stared across the clearing to where her tall friend stood with four or five others. Lilah's nerves jolted. This was why they'd come, not to live in a forest with other kids, and swing and play and learn Sartoran songs, but to get rid of that enchantment.

Atan beckoned, and Hinder grinned. "I was right," he said, pursed his lips, and startled Lilah by giving the clear, sharp whistle of a night bird.

Lilah gazed in amazement as everybody scrambled into a big mass, which sorted itself into eight groups of five. Only Hinder, Lilah, and Atan remained where they were.

Hinder jumped off the rock and crossed his arms. "Rather slow."

Groans and scornful cries echoed through the trees in response.

From the other side of the clearing, Brick hooted like an owl.

The group scattered, some ducking behind trees

and others flattening behind shrubs, orienting on Brick, who called, "I see your shadow, Hannla. And who's laughing?"

"We should be better than that," Sinder called, her voice clear and challenging. "Because practice is over. We're going to leave." She drifted into the clearing, her head tipped to one side as she regarded Atan expectantly.

Atan bent her head and walked toward the center rock. Lilah recognized that teeth-gritted determination. *It's happening already.*

She made herself meet all those gazing eyes and take in the expressions of question, wariness, and skepticism. The ones that hurt the most were those of hope.

She drew in a breath, her body vibrating like one of those snapvine bowstrings. History changes with a word, a step. You read it, and you're comfortable, expecting something to happen. But when *you* are the one doing it... "The time has come for me to leave Shendoral, and go to Eidervaen to find the last bindings. And destroy them."

Irza spoke up. "What is *our* part?"

"Whatever you want it to be," Atan said, feeling how every word she spoke laid down life paths for all forty — paths that could be short, a violent sending out of life and the world. *I'm trying to free Sartor. They have to choose if they want to come with me.* It was the only way to make the burden bearable. "Merewen discovered that the magic over the villages nearest here is breaking up. That means people are waking from the enchantment, and we might be able to find allies against Norsunder. But it also means that Norsunder is going to notice that the enchantment is gone, if they haven't already. I must be swift in finishing the end of their spells before they come in force."

"*We* must be swift, and guard and guide you," Irza stated.

Again the cheer, only louder.

"Our parents led. Now we have to," Irza added, bolstered by the approval. She straightened up, head high. "What is the plan?"

This is it. Atan took a deep breath.

"This is our last night here," she said. "Anyone who wishes to go with me and raise allies on the way to Eidervaen, we leave tomorrow."

TWO

Night.
In Shendoral's springtime glade, the forest-dwellers' faces were colorless blobs in the soft moonlight. Lilah tried to fit herself into the mood of expectation, of celebration. She wanted to stay, to play. To help Atan. She never wanted to see any Norsundrian again, ever, ever, *ever*.

Atan's turmoil was so intense it was almost painful. Was it like this, then, so far in the past, when her ancestors and the morvende had found one another after the long recovery from the Fall?

Moonlight glowed silver on Hinder's wild hair as he climbed the rock and put an arrow to his bow. Sin brought a tiny candle flame and held it to the shiny string bound around the arrowhead, which flared and burned blue.

A sigh of satisfaction ran through the forest-dwellers around Lilah, like the soughing of branches in the wind.

Hinder drew the bow, aimed high, high, and *spang!*

The burning arrow kissed the moon before descending to land square in the center of the fire pit prepared by the Poisoners earlier. Smoke, a whoosh, and flames licked at tiny dry branches. Cheers rose from the circle of watchful, orange-lit faces as the fire took hold.

Rip gave an infectious chuckle on Lilah's right. Firelight glowed on his broad, pale face and his cheerful smile. "I invented that stuff on the arrowhead," he said.

"Never flames out, no matter what the wind."

"Tell her how," Hannla added from just beyond, laughing.

"Well, I was trying to make gravy," Rip admitted.

Maybe it was going to be all right. Rip and Hannla don't seem to be worried, and they're not warriors, like Mendaen and Pouldi and even Hinder. Lilah snickered, then crowed as three older boys stood up and began singing a round.

Everybody clapped on the beat, then followed a stream of songs, skits, and more songs, most in the triple-beat chord-shift, counterpoint harmonies peculiar to Sartor. Lilah had heard Sartoran music once or twice at home, and a little more of it during her stay in the Valley of Delfina. It was distinctive and compelling with its counterpoint melodies, its weaving of major chords and minor. But it had not been performed at court for three generations. Sartoran music had dwindled to folk ballads heard along trails or in woods, or sometimes at harvest time during the long hours of work — it had nearly vanished, except in memory. Now it was alive, all around her, like she'd fallen into one of the old histories sitting on the shelves in the library back in Miraleste.

Atan closed her eyes, her throat aching. The melodies — the words — reached ghost-fingers back into her earliest memories, unknotting images, sounds, and their attendant emotions.

The others celebrated so happily. Didn't anyone else feel the pressure of responsibility? Hinder and Sinder capered about as the others sang. Little Julian, so odd, so quiet on Arlas's lap, fingering the daisy wreath on her head. Mendaen's profile was so serious as he sang. Hannla's face upturned as she laughed, sounding like a brook.

If any one of these voices was silenced as a result of her announcing, *We leave tomorrow for Eidervaen*, she knew she would bear the guilt through her entire life.

Dejain paced the tower balcony at the Norsunder base. Except for the crunch of her shoes on stone, silence surrounded her.

She liked it that way, silence except for the subdued hush of her hem over the stones, because she was able to hear the footfalls of anyone approaching.

Like her two suborned scouts, coming now. Supposedly Zydes's most trusted, though only a fool like Zydes could believe you could trust anyone.

The tall one, Wend, said, "We're here."

Short skinny Xoll said nothing, just licked his lips.

Dejain had had a couple of days to watch from a distance. Kessler had reached the border of Sarendan the day Irad and the brat vanished from the border.

She'd risked a transfer to spy on Kessler and his band, who of course were empty-handed; she'd stayed long enough to overhear one of Kessler's scouts returning from the overgrown tangle of a road into Sarendan to report that there were no hoof or footprints anywhere, no broken branches or campfires or even any fruit missing from the wild trees. No one could have used that road for a century.

Kessler had ordered them to return to Norsunder Base.

If they rode hard, they might be back within a day or so, and Dejain needed to get her plans into place before then. Kessler would be very angry, which made him even more impossible to predict.

She had to assume that someone had transferred Irad and that brat straight to Shendoral in order to get them past the time-binding. *If* the time-binding was still in place. That was the only place her magic wouldn't be able to trace them.

The idea that anyone would tamper with Detlev's spells, no matter how old they were, was stunning in its temerity. Not that she'd put it past that idiot Zydes, if he thought he could get away with it. The only reason why he might protect Irad would be to indirectly aid him in reaching his old army. If Sarendan marched over the border to "liberate" Sartor, that would be an excuse to raise a major force.

The recent military exercises, the inflow of supplies, meant that he intended to put a considerable number into the field—soon. He *said* the target was Everon, but everybody lied.

She turned to Wend.

"There is a chance that Zydes has tampered with the time-bindings. I want you to test the truth. You are to find Irad as soon as he emerges from Shendoral."

Wend nodded, thinking that it would probably take Irad more like a month than mere days. Though he didn't believe a lot of the gas the light magic idiots had blabbed about that place (standard scare tactics, he figured); he did believe the place was much larger than the map showed, because both times he'd been detailed to ride through there, it had taken a lot longer than he'd bargained for. *Grim* riding. Overgrown thorns and stickers everywhere, no matter how low you bent, or how carefully you dismounted. If the weather hadn't been both cold and dripping wet, he would have been glad to torch the damn place and laugh while it burned.

Dejain continued. "You know what he looks like? About your height and build, Xoll. Brown hair worn long. Blue eyes. Might still be in recruit uniform, since I doubt he'll find clothing supplies in Shendoral, whatever else might or might not exist there."

She paused, and both men nodded. "Irad will attempt to reach Sarendan, where he will raise his army against us. This is why I do not want him to live past his leaving the border of Shendoral. How you accomplish that death—and when—is of course your own affair. Bring the brat to me."

Xoll licked his lips again, a disgusting sight.

She turned around so she wouldn't have to see his ferret face. Giving him orders to kill was enough to guarantee his cooperation. Zydes too often wanted prisoners who could be questioned, and Xoll liked, very much, playing with his victims. Wend had more brains—and more ambition—and it was for him she'd made the statement about Sarendan's army. In case Zydes (or anyone else for that matter) did manage to find out about this conversation, her reason for wanting Irad dead—the army of Sarendan and the obvious military necessity—would deflect interest in that brat. Whoever he was.

"Take whomever you need, but they must be swift and circumspect," she said. "Just for the sake of thoroughness, you might also put someone in the north, but I don't believe Irad would take so roundabout a route."

They departed as noise reached her from the northeast. Dust, distant steady thunder: hooves. A force, at the gallop. Her heart thumped, though it couldn't possibly be Kessler.

But it was, two days ahead of what she had assumed the outside limit of possibility. That meant he'd forced them to ride through nights.

She drew the hood of her gray cloak well over her head and most of her face so that her silhouette would blend with the stone, and stared down into the torchlit main court. The steaming, blowing horses and the dusty, mud-spattered riders were obviously at the limits of exhaustion.

At the front was Kessler's straight, slight figure. She could not make out any detail of his face, but she knew — oh, how well she knew — how very angry he would be, to return empty-handed from so hard a chase.

She started at a sound. Xoll and Wend were back again, with their chosen minions.

She transferred them to the destinations she had so carefully selected on the Sartor map, and then retreated to safety to wait.

The forest-dwellers shared out a last breakfast, and while the Poisoners packed up the last of their carefully planned meals, everyone except the morvende pulled on all the clothing they had in storage, with the smallest bundled up the warmest.

Atan listened to the chatter. She understood that though the dell was always springtime, everyone had been out in all weathers, and so understood that winter was nigh.

When all was ready and those carrying supplies had hefted their packs, they got into their groups and walked over the bridge and away. Only a few looked back.

Lilah started out walking by Atan, with Merewen on the other side, the way they'd traveled from Sarendan's border to Shendoral. But people kept crowding up to ask Atan this question or that, and Lilah would drop back to make space. Finally she stayed back, looking up at the enormous redwoods and trying to guess their age.

"Having trouble remembering everyone's name, your highness?"

Lilah was surprised to be addressed by the blonde girl who talked like a court snob. Even though her clothes were ragged with many washings, she was careful of them.

"Irza," the girl said, smiling. "Irzaveas Ianth Yostavos, third circle. Your highness."

"Sorry. Were we introduced?" Lilah's face heated, and she wondered if she was supposed to know what *third circle* was. "You don't need to say 'your highness' to me. Lilah will do. The king and princess business is too new, and anyway it really belongs back in Sarendan."

Irza smiled confidently. "A princess," she stated in her precise way, "is a princess anywhere. And it's all right if you forgot my name. It took me the longest time to sort everyone out after what happened to us."

Lilah nodded. "You remember — what happened?" She tried to choose her words carefully.

"I remember the war, yes. I don't want to forget how Norsunder slaughtered my father and neighbors," Irza said, her mouth pressing into a white line. "And I want to remember how I got my sister away by slipping down through the grating into the old tunnel, where we'd once been forbidden to play. But we'd explored anyway, because I wanted to see what the ruins of the ancient city were like — who wouldn't?" She flashed a quick smile. "Especially if it's forbidden."

Lilah laughed. "If all the grownups told me to stay away, I would have explored it first thing."

Irza pointed at a tall, thin girl with long blonde braids who looked about Lilah's own age. She walked hand in hand with little Julian. "There's my sister Arlaseas, but everyone calls her Arlas. Once my younger sister, now my only one." She smiled again and stepped back, with a practiced gesture giving Lilah precedence when they came to a great mossy root in the trail.

Lilah hopped over. Irza stepped over, holding her skirts in the correct manner.

"Who else are you confused about?" she asked. "Do you want the names, or who we are?"

"Who you are?" Lilah repeated, glancing back at the clumps of two and three or four. Three girls sang a round, but one of the voices rose above the others, reminding Lilah of crystal in the sunlight.

"That girl with the good voice," Irza said, nodding over her shoulder. "Sana. She's also quite good as an archer. She had one parent in the king's forces, and the other was some sort of player or performer. I hope," Irza added, "that our new queen will remember her with a royal patent for players, or something appropriate."

Lilah heard a generous tone and saw a smile, but her mind still lurched, as if her foot had stepped on what she thought was solid ground and it turned out to be slippery mud. "Does she want to be a player?"

Irza gave Lilah a fast glance, and Lilah felt the conversational ground shift again. "I don't know. But she's quite good, isn't she?" Again she gave a pretty smile.

"Yes," Lilah said, as from behind, Sana's voice soared faultlessly up a long series of tripled notes in the old ballad style, the sound echoing through the trees.

Irza said, "None of us know who is still going to be found alive. Obviously there must be people still living, for Savar pulled us all from the time-binding. Our new queen will need to make order once again, and we don't know who from the important families has survived. All we are sure of are..." In that same easy, confident voice she named half a dozen of those walking in a cluster with Arlas and Julian.

Clearly Irza was a noble, and wanted Lilah to understand that she was important. Why?

Because I'm now a princess? Lilah wondered. Except no one here had once asked any questions about Sarendan. Not to be mean. They were just too busy thinking about Sartor — and the Sartor they thought about was a hundred years old. Probably, Lilah thought as she and Irza separated again in order to hop from stone to stone over a stream, if any of the older ones thought about who might be on the throne of Sarendan, they would name Lilah's great-great grandmother. Weird!

"Mendaen, there, is son of one of the best army leaders," Irza said, as though continuing a conversation. "Died defending the king."

"What about the morvende, Hinder and his cousin?" Lilah asked.

"Oh, they came of their own desire," Irza said.

"That is not to say that many did not die in the fighting, for there were quite a few who allied with the king and kept their word and didn't vanish into their caves when Norsunder came. But these all chose to come to the surface. Except the boy who does the cooking, but his family had been on the surface for a couple of generations."

"Doing what? Cooking?" Lilah asked, sneaking a sideways look.

Irza's shrug was expressive—and threw Lilah straight back in memory to her snobbish cousins at court in Miraleste, during the bad old days under her uncle. "Probably something of the sort." Irza's little shoulder twitch and faint smile were dismissive. "No star chamber families, no position."

Lilah wanted to ask what "star chamber families" meant, but Irza's tone made it clear enough: they were common.

"Well, maybe that will change," Lilah said, thinking of her own experiences and how her brother had appointed people in positions of responsibility based on merit, and not on family background.

And as soon as she said it, she saw in the quick tightening of Irza's features that this girl did not like this idea.

"Irza?"

Both looked up. Blonde braids swinging, Arlas hopped back down the trail. "She's tired," Irza's sister said in a low voice, nodding at the drooping Julian.

Irza gave a quick nod and looked around in question.

Arlas pointed off to one side to where Atan walked, deep in conversation with Merewen and Sin and a couple others.

Irza smiled at Lilah. "Will you pardon me?"

Lilah nodded and watched as Irza moved with swift, graceful stride to Atan. She couldn't hear the conversation, but she saw Atan look up with a quick gesture, her expression full of concern, even remorse.

Soon the group was settled in a mossy clearing, some seated on a fallen log, eating the cheese-stuffed bread that Rip and his group had prepared. Lilah sat with Hinder, whose friendly smile was the same even if he wasn't being watched. He reminded Lilah of Bren, except not as moody.

Little Julian seemed to be in the charge of Irza and her sister. The Ianth sisters got Julian fed, and then settled on either side of Atan as Julian squatted happily in the dirt, playing some sort of game with twigs that she hopped and skipped about. She was whispering under her breath. Acting out a story with twig people? Lilah grinned, remembering when she used to do exactly the same thing in the garden at her old home in Selenna, before the revolution. She wondered if a Sartoran kid's story would be anything like a Sarendan kid's.

A flicker of color at one side caused her to look up, and Atan said, "Ready to go?"

Lilah nodded.

"Julian?" a voice called.

The solemn-faced little girl tossed her twigs away and hopped to Arlas to taken her hand.

Atan fell in step beside Lilah. The group started down an animal trail that Brick and Sana had picked, walking mostly in twos and threes. After a time, Atan said in a soft voice, "May I put a question to you about etiquette?"

Etiquette? Lilah's lips framed the word.

"Is it still proper etiquette for monarchs to require titles and bowing, and the precedence at all times?"

Lilah said, "It was in my uncle's court." She thought back, then added, "That is, I always saw it done, though he never actually said anything. My father used to get mad if people forgot etiquette, but my uncle didn't. Of course, I don't think anyone forgot, when he was king. He was so very scary." She shrugged, a sort of laugh escaping her—more a nervous sound than one of light-hearted amusement. "He certainly didn't expect me to bow when we got away from the Norsunder base. He only asked me to stop calling him Uncle Dirty-Hands."

"You *didn't* say that." Atan winced.

"Um, yup. Habit. A nasty moment."

"Yes! Your brother requires the protocols of rank, or doesn't?"

"He's never said anything around me, but people just do it, I think." Lilah frowned, trying to recover a memory. "Wait, I was wrong, he did say something. If I can just remember..."

While she sorted through the jumble of memories from summer, Atan said, "Gehlei taught me all the ins and outs of court etiquette."

"Then you can tell me what star chamber families are?"

"Those are families whose lines go back a certain number of centuries. There is apparently a formal hall for certain kinds of gatherings, where representatives of families stand on their star, and get a say in certain kinds of decisions."

"It sounds complicated."

"It is very complicated, because the stars alter according to seasons."

"Wow." Lilah tried to imagine that. It sounded so very... *Sartoran*.

Atan went on. "When Hinder first introduced me to the entire group, and Irza made them all bow, I felt, well, *stupid*, and I said, without thinking, *No protocol*. But — certain reactions from some of them — convinced me that was a mistake, though I'm not certain why. Had I somehow denied my true background or diminished my family in some symbolic way? And so I added, *Not until Eidervaen is free again*, which I guess turned it into a sort of heroic statement instead of me being a coward."

Lilah laughed at the self-deprecating irony in Atan's voice on the word 'heroic'. "That reminds me! I knew there was something. Peitar did say that when we were in the formal rooms that formal etiquette serves to transform an ordinary person into a symbol of the state."

Atan nodded slowly. "Yes, I see that. And also that the symbol must be separated off, in order to enable him — or her — to make decisions that might affect all the others' lives. And to enable those others to accept those decisions and to act upon them."

Lilah sighed and kicked at a pile of withered autumn leaves. "Peitar was going on one night. About that first moment of power. How it's created, when one speaks and the other chooses to act as directed. As usual, I understood about one word in ten. He kept going on about whether or not this power ought to exist, and if it could be sustained without the clank of pikes on the floor, and the march of boots when the guard changes."

"Moral authority versus power," Atan said.

"Tsauderei has talked to me about it since I was small, but I'm beginning to see that what you read about and talk about while sitting with your tutor in a hermit's cottage, and when you're dealing with others — well, let me say this. I wish I could have had more time to talk to your brother! But I guess if he could figure out all these things for himself, so can I."

Lilah flapped her hands. "Besides, he doesn't always make sense. Like when he started mumbling stuff about why and when the guards choose to obey, transferring their implied power to him. So I said, *We all know the answer to that — we lived through it this summer, when no one was in power, and everything was a mess, and no one planted the crops,* and he laughed at me and said, *As always, Lilah, you cut through the illusions and find the truth.* But you know, I *don't* always know the truth, and I'm definitely not always right!"

"But you're practical," Atan said, laughing very softly, so her voice would not carry. "I suspect — little as I know your brother — that he both values and admires that quality in you."

Lilah shrugged, feeling a conflict of emotions: pride, and laughter at her own mistakes. "About that bowing," she said. "I think you were absolutely right. Making the kids bow while wearing rags in the forest seems kind of pompous, if you ask me."

"'Kids'?" Hadn't she heard the word before?

"Us." Lilah smacked her ribs. "Our age. Derek taught us the word, from some adventuring kids from faraway Mearsies Heili. Anyway. Time enough for etiquette, and fancy clothes, and the like, after you kick the villains out of the kingdom. And you know," Lilah added, feeling surer of herself by the moment, "if you do manage to get rid of Norsunder, then people might *want* to do all the old polite forms, because it makes life orderly again. Like they do at home, for my brother."

"I thought of that, too." Atan lifted her chin, glancing ahead.

Lilah gazed in the same direction, and spotted Arlas and Irza on either side of Julian. The sisters held the small girl's hands, swinging her over every rock and root in the path, while Julian laughed in delight, as they sang an old marching ballad in counterpoint.

THREE

Gradually the abrupt shift from the eternal spring of the glade to the winter of the rest of the forest began to trouble Atan and her band.

During the day, while they kept moving, they were fine. But the first night was troublesome, and Merewen was startled when she discovered little Julian's fingers stuffed in her armpits the second morning, her lips bluish. Blue was a good healthy color for a Loi, but not for anyone else, and the sisters were trying to figure out which of them could do without her own scanty warm things when Merewen stooped down and wrapped her yeath-fur cloak around the child.

Julian's color returned to normal almost immediately. Merewen smiled. She'd worn the yeath-fur cloak because her mage guardian had given it to her, but she'd discovered that she didn't really need it. Dressed only in her tunic, Merewen still felt a pleasant sense of coolness, not cold, and so too did the morvende, used as they were to the stone depths never warmed by the sun. As long as they were dry, the morvende did not mind cold. But as the forest thinned and they emerged onto the hills above the River Ilder, the others felt the grip of winter closing around bones and flesh.

That wasn't the only problem. Used as the patrollers were to gleaning for nuts during autumn and fresh berries during spring as they roamed Shendoral, trading work for milled wheat from the miller, they had assumed that scavenging along the road would make their stores last longer.

But the land was barren, ready for winter, and the streams they'd found so far had no mills. There were no other spring glades with fruit growing year-round, much less the vegetable patch that the Poisoners had tended so carefully. Unless they found people who had extra stores, food was going to become scarce.

Bigger than both these problems was that of the riders.

The forest-dweller emerged from the protection of Shendoral just before sunset. As they peered down the road toward a winding river, they saw horseback riders on the other side, between the river and the twinkling lights of their first village.

Arlas was certain they were villagers, Hannla cheerfully pointed out that here was proof Sartor was waking up, and shouldn't they flag down the riders?

"They're searching," Lilah said, remembering the king's patrols of summer. "They're not riding around having fun. They're on a search." She watched the riders as she spoke, appearing and vanishing again beyond the distant hedgerows and fences and the last of the trees. She saw weapons at the saddles, the back-and-forth movement of heads.

"Searching for us?" Atan looked up. "Who even knows we're—oh, yes." Her gaze fell on Lilah's black clothes. "They're looking for me."

Searchers. The whisper worked down the line, quieting everyone. Faces turned Atan's way. She felt those gazes, felt the question behind them.

Brick pointed from behind a broad tree. "Are they Norsundrians? Mendaen, you'd know." He turned his head the other way and beckoned wildly.

Mendaen had supervised the small ones ducking behind a hedgerow. He ran quick and low to join the others. "They wear no one's livery," he said.

From above in the tree, Sindan said softly, "They all wear gray."

"Norsunder," Atan whispered. She glanced at the expectant faces, then said, "Hinder, I think you and the others ought to go back. I will go on alone, because they have to know where I'd be going if they really are searching for me."

"I'm going with you," Lilah said stoutly, though her insides quivered like watery jelly. But she'd seen how those others had almost begun yelling for the horsemen's attention.

"I am, too," Hinder said from behind a tree, so that his white hair would not draw the riders' eyes. Lilah crouched beside Atan, her shoulders hunched to her ears, arms folded across her front.

Merewen was nowhere in sight.

Atan was thinking rapidly. "Since we don't know who they are, let's stay quiet," she suggested. "We might wait until midnight, and then we'll see the magic that Merewen saw, showing us who is free of the enchantment, and who not. If it's safe, maybe we will find allies in the village."

Her suggestion was turned into an order as it passed down the line.

This plan spread down the line, and they clumped up together on top of the highest hill so they could peer at the village, with its golden lights in a few windows.

None of them had any idea that they'd been spotted.

Wend and Xoll, Dejain's trackers, found the footprints of Atan's group in the otherwise undisturbed dust of the road. They eased up until they heard the forest-dwellers' voices clear on the cold air.

"They're sitting on the ridge on the other side of the river, watching the village in the valley," Wend reported to Dejain after they transferred back.

"Why?" Dejain asked.

"One of them said that at midnight they'll perceive some sort of light picking out the domiciles of those breaking out of the time-bindings. They seem to think these people will be potential allies."

"Some sort of light?" Dejain repeated. "Magic. But whose?"

Wend shrugged. "Didn't say. Only that they were waiting to see it."

"None are adults, you say?"

"None."

"How many?"

"Somewhere between three and five tens."

"Irad wasn't with them?"

"No sign of Irad, other than the hoof prints we spotted at the very north end. Might be his, might be someone else's."

It was midnight now. Dejain studied Zydes's best tracker and tried to read the long, ugly face. Ech, he was ugly, and she preferred men to be pretty. This one had a broken nose, scars, a belligerent cast to eyes and forehead, but he was good at his work. He also had to be considered a danger because she didn't—yet—know his weakness.

Xoll, now, standing there licking his lips, his weakness was a craving for catching and playing with prisoners. He loved killing. Give him an order to kill, and he worked for you.

Dejain said, "What does Zydes know?"

Wend's mouth twisted into a sneer. "Nothing. Too busy ranting."

Ah. He didn't deny reporting to Zydes before coming to her. Lesca the head cook had seen Wend coming out of Zydes's office, or Dejain wouldn't have known, but her question didn't seem to worry Wend. "Let me guess," she said. "A new search for Irad?"

"Eastern border. Mountains. And if not, then he wants me to go covert over the mountains and down into Miraleste."

"He won't be there, he's still in Shendoral, hiding out—has to be," Dejain said. "Unless he rode into the time binding."

Wend shrugged.

Inwardly Dejain cursed the clumsiness of having to use these trackers, and having to slink around to hold these private conversations without unwanted witnesses. Magic tracers would be so much neater! But Zydes had a net of wards over the Base, and Sartor's enchantment was still too strong for any other spells to work.

As for the trackers, if only she could find out Wend's ambition, his weakness. His desire.

She pulled her cloak tighter about her. There was no weather—of course—but the cold had intensified. The fangs of winter were about to sink deep into their hides. It made her bones and joints ache. Even her teeth hurt. Twice she'd had to force her hundred-year-old self back to this youthful appearance, but dark magic could not truly rejuvenate.

"Children," she repeated, turning about and staring north. Her thoughts returned to Darian Irad and the brat he'd had in tow. "Find that child, the one Irad had. Bring him back here. Do what you want with the rest."

Xoll uttered his high, keening giggle, a sound like the dying shrieks of a ferret.

"We have to leave," Merewen whispered, breathing hard from her run. "Now."

"What?" Atan whispered back. She looked around. The sky was clear, peaceful with brilliant stars, and below lay the village, apparently asleep. And... was that a silvery glow, above the middle there? No, it was probably her imagination. Midnight was still a while off.

"I went back up the road, and I saw two more of those riders. But they weren't riding. They sneaked up behind that old vine there." She pointed. "And listened to you. Then they went away again, and I followed, and I saw them go out like a candle flame." She snapped her fingers.

"Transfer magic," Atan whispered.

Atan's doubts resolved. "We can't wait around to see magic lights. We have to get to Eidervaen, as fast as we can," she said.

"But—wouldn't allies be good to get?" Hinder pointed to the village.

She shook her head. "Can't be helped. Merewen is right. If the enemy vanished by magic, they can transfer back by magic, and then they could follow us in and kill everyone we lead them to."

Hinder whistled, short and sharp.

Tired, cold forest-dweller scrambled into their groups, some whispering, others looking about fearfully. Hinder motioned them together.

"We're going to cross the Ilder," Hinder said, "and run. Hard, fast, and stay low. No one go up a hill and create a silhouette." That much morvende children, with their white heads, were taught from an early age.

Hinder began to run, followed by the rest in a long

snake.

Mendaen and Sana separated and ran within sight of one another at the back, bows within easy reach. For a time, the long line pounded along in silence. At the bottom of a hill, the stream they followed dumped into the Ilder, and they pattered across an old bridge. On the other side, an old oak grove was discernible in the darkness. Used to forest living for so long, Hinder made straight for it.

Once they were running under the shelter of branches, the children separated, a few teens laughing breathlessly, and a couple attempting to whistle birdcalls. Lilah and Atan spotted Merewen in the midst of one group, silvery moonlight bathing her happy face as they raced across a glade.

They stopped when the wood became dense, and they lost their sense of direction. Occasional cries rang out as the children ran into unseen twigs and branches, which stung faces and arms. The little ones were lagging, a few sobbing quietly.

Atan caught Hinder by the arm. "We'd better stop for the night. But somewhere secluded."

Hinder paused and whistled the *gather!* signal. "Wait here," he said. "I smell water. I'm going to find us a camping spot."

The youngest flung themselves onto the mossy ground, too exhausted to question. The teens whispered, sometimes looking speculatively Atan's way. Lilah watched, uneasy.

When Hinder returned, he gave a soft whistle. Sighs and grunts and muffled moans broke the night's silence as they followed in single file down a gulley into almost complete darkness.

"Hold hands," Sin called softly.

They found themselves in a rock grotto at the base of a waterfall. Above them the cliff was thick with growth; they could no longer see the stars. After everyone got a drink of water, which was good but lip-numbingly cold, they pressed up into a group to rest. The smallest ones dropped immediately into slumber.

Lilah fought yawn after yawn. Her eyes burned, her stomach gnawed with hunger, and her limbs ached, but her mind reeled with memories: Kessler forcing her to ride, the dust, the terrible atmosphere at that fortress.

Atan let out a sigh, so soft it was a trickle of breath just audible above the rush of the waterfall.

Lilah scooted nearer. "What's wrong?"

"Nothing," Atan murmured. "That is, nothing besides the obvious. I know what to do now."

"Which is?" Hinder asked, scooting up on the other side. He was barely visible except as a moon-touched silhouette.

"If Norsunder comes chasing us—and they are almost bound to—then I am going to have to separate off. I have to make my way straight for Eidervaen."

"And so? The rest of the group?" Hinder asked. "What, a decoy?"

Atan said, "Here is how I perceive the situation. Norsunder knows that a Landis lives, so they've surely guessed I'll go as fast as I can for the old tower, to break the rest of their spells. But they won't know the road I'm taking. So if the patrollers lead them hither and yon, it might cause them to spread their search very thin. The little ones can be taken to a village. Why would they worry about the actions of a bunch of children?"

"Target practice," Lilah muttered, but beneath her breath. And, in case she'd been heard, she said, "I'll volunteer for decoy duty." She forced a grin. "I already did it by accident once. They don't know for sure that I'm *not* Atan."

Hinder saw Atan's wince and knew how much she hated Lilah's gallant offer, how badly she still felt. He said, "Why don't we figure it out come morning? Right now everyone should sleep while we've got the chance."

"Yes. Let us do that." Atan sighed.

Lilah thought she hid her own relief, but Atan saw her face ease as she curled up against a thick, spongy plant that felt like moss and smelled like some sort of herb. Once again that sickening sense of responsibility harrowed her soul. She hated the utter unfairness of the fact that her lightest word could and would launch others so high of heart into action that might end their lives.

The scent, not unpleasant, tickled Lilah's nose. She was warm in her sturdy clothes and would have slept, but for the tall outline still discernible against the stone, her head bowed.

"Atan?" she breathed.

"Sorry. Do sleep, if you can."

"Something's wrong."

"No... no. Nothing new."

"Please tell. If you worry, then I worry."

"I apologize, Lilah." Atan's cold fingers pressed Lilah's. "I can't sleep because I see my duty so clearly, but I don't know if I can do it. Is it because I spent my childhood with a mage who insisted on telling me his mistakes? I have always thought, if Tsauderei thinks he's inadequate for the fight against Norsunder, what does that make me?"

"Why did he do that?"

"Because he says we have to learn from our mistakes, not just mourn over them. He says he'd always assumed that Detlev would be a brainless minion, mindlessly acting out his masters' will, but every single encounter Tsauderei lost, and so he was forced to conclude that Detlev did not give up will, or cognizance, or initiative when he surrendered. Only honor and morals. Tsauderei said to me, oh, so many times, *You can be certain that he never suffers remorse after mistakes, and we must be forced to learn at least not to permit our own contrition to paralyze us.*"

Lilah tried to understand, but meaning cascaded past her like the waterfall, eluding her just as water eluded any attempt to force it into shape. Peitar talked like that sometimes.

"...and so I have spent my entire life thinking, *If this happens, then that must happen.* Action, reaction, consequence. That lesson of Tsauderei's has shaped me into what I am now, more than anything else. I see my duty. I just have to be able to find the right path from action to reaction to imagined consequence. I have to figure out what Norsunder will do—and stay ahead. And not let remorse defeat me before they do, if I make a mistake. But can I? Bear it, I mean."

"You will."

Both girls jumped, then recognized the drowsy voice: Hinder.

"You will," he said. "Make it to Eidervaen, I mean. Though I won't tell anyone else, because—well, just because. But you see, Sin and I know where we are."

FOUR

Dejain drew a deep breath.

"This changes everything," she said.

She busied herself with the cup of fresh coffee that she had not wanted, just so she could think.

The cold had intensified, and though she was now settled deep within the fortress in Lesca's warm rooms, her bones felt brittle as winter ice, making thought difficult.

She'd always been careful where her own existence was concerned. When her first non-aging spells had been so disastrously destroyed, the tracer had sent her straight to Norsunder. But Detlev had found her and had re-engendered the spells, restoring her youth, before she could attempt recovery on her own. His magic was exponentially stronger than hers—and he was very seldom overt. It was enough that they both knew she owed her life to him, and he could just as easily take it away without exerting himself.

She sighed. At least he was at a distance, involved in something or other that kept him occupied except for brief and rare visits. She sipped the coffee—disgusting stuff—and frowned at her hostess. "You are certain you heard the word 'Landis.'"

Lesca lay back on her cushions, her smile lazy. "If you wish to believe that I misheard, feel free."

"Of course not," Dejain said. "My question is a measure of my surprise, not at all indicative of disbelief."

She could not afford to make an enemy of Lesca, who knew just about everything going on in the fortress. Lesca might be lazy and love comfort above all things, but she had a quick mind. Dejain did not know what her background was. Obviously she'd been trained as kitchen-steward for huge establishments. Maybe even royal palaces. But she liked it here at the Norsunder base. Being a cook, she was invisible to those who had no interest in anyone of so low a position, and that meant she overheard an astonishing number of conversations. She also knew how to find out about the few she didn't overhear.

Lesca smiled and helped herself to fresh fruit, transferred all the way from the northern hemisphere. "Zydes was quite distinct. *Kessler, find that Landis girl, wherever you have to go. Take anyone you want. But don't fail.*" Lesca tossed a rind into the bowl. "Kessler brought back a red-haired urchin, therefore the urchin is this Landis girl. And then she vanished, leaving Zydes in a pretty panic. Not that the sight is all that pretty."

She laughed, and Dejain smiled, appreciating the image of Zydes in a sweat. "A Landis is alive," she repeated. The astounding news was overlaid by early childhood memory; how the world seemed to have lost its meaning when the news came that Sartor had succumbed to the enemy. And nothing had happened. The sky did not fall. Birds pecked at seeds. Traders came and dangled ribbons before the girls of the village. The seasons changed, and changed again, with blithe indifference to human tragedy. The so-called great and powerful mages of Bereth Ferian did not descend like a singing of angels and do away with the enemy—in fact, they were soon defeated themselves.

She'd been a child, and the lesson she took was that only power was true, in that those with power dictated truth.

So began a lifelong quest for power.

She said, "Then Detlev's spells were not destroyed by Zydes. My only question is, why hasn't Detlev been here before? Surely he had some sort of ward set up to warn him. He'd have to, for spells that powerful."

"Who knows, with him?" Lesca said, shrugging her round, plump shoulders. "Maybe he has been. He's sneaky, that one. You don't know he's there unless he wants you to." She affected a shudder, then languorously threw back her lemon-colored braid.

A Landis, alive. A girl, not a boy.

Dejain tried to recall what that brat had looked like, but her focus had been on Irad, and all she remembered was a type found all over this portion of the continent: ruddy hair and complexion, with foxy features, sturdy build. Not even remotely resembling the Landises whose portraits she'd seen when she was young. Of course, distinctive features did not show up in every single family member, even in the Landises, but really, Kessler had more of that distinctive shape of the eyes than that brat had — and the Sonscarnas and Landises had only had a single marriage alliance that she was aware of, generations ago.

Obviously, the first requirement now was to get hold of the old field reports, and review exactly who had done what, or seen what, at the very end of the Sartor war. But the thought of going into Norsunder, where there was no time, or space, not by any definition that had meaning — and where the Host of Lords could, and did, amuse themselves with rifling one's mind and memories at any time — made her flinch.

Maybe she could send someone.

Magic-warning flickered across her vision. Wend! Signaling for transfer.

She smiled. She'd fixed the transfer spell so he couldn't activate it at his end, which meant that this time she would definitely be the first to hear whatever news he had.

Lesca watched her in growing amusement. Really, she rather liked Dejain. Ambitious, of course — all the mages and rankers were. But she showed no interest in flirtation with anyone at all, and she hadn't displayed any of those lamentable tastes for torture and protracted death that made some of the other would-be commanders so tiresome. She also shared information, which Zydes never did.

She watched the small, pretty face, and saw the inward look. Magic contact, of course. Probably Wend. He was currently running tame for her. Did she even know how badly he wanted revenge against Detlev? No, for the humiliation of Wend's very public demotion after he and the horrible Vatiora lost that tangle with the Venn had taken place up north, and Dejain seemed to confine her interests to the southern hemisphere.

"Thank you for the coffee," Dejain said, rising to shake out her skirts.

Lesca watched the small hands, dainty movements, the swinging blonde curls against the straight, slender back. Dejain's vanity was so very inward, so self-absorbed, that Lesca found her endlessly entertaining.

As Dejain disappeared up the corridor, Lesca laid an inward bet she was bracing for another trip to the tower, where she so trustingly thought she was not overheard, and prepared for a night of rich diversion. All the signs were in place. Wend was plotting, Zydes was plotting, Dejain was plotting, and Kessler prowled around looking crazier than ever. Not as crazy as Vatiora, who might appear at any time.

Now *that* was a frightening thought.

Lesca decided it was time to find a safe vantage from which to watch the confrontation she knew was nigh, as soon as Detlev appeared.

"They're searching," Sin said, sliding down the rock next to her cousin.

"How many?" Atan asked.

"Riding in twos, that much I saw. But the fog is getting heavy."

No one needed to voice the next thought: how many were waiting somewhere just out of sight?

Atan asked, "Thick fog?"

Sin shook her head. "No. Fingers and drifts. But getting worse. I couldn't see the farther hills."

Atan said, "Maybe we should talk about our diversion plan."

Hinder and Sin worked their way round the clumps of damp, filthy forest-dwellers in the grotto where they had been forced to spend the day. Cold, dank air made it thoroughly unpleasant, but that was better than being discovered. The fog intensified the damp chill, but they dared not start a fire.

Sin and Mendaen had posted watchers in the shrubs all night. It had been Kevri, one of Brick's friends, who'd seen the Norsundrian searchers at dawn, riding hard through the woods. She'd scrambled back down to the slowly waking group, and Atan bade them all stay put until the searchers were safely gone.

That had not happened all day; they'd continued to trade off watches.

Mendaen approached, his dark hair lank and damp, and his face blotchy from the damp cold.

"If they haven't gone, it means they've got a perimeter," he said. "An accurate one."

"That being?" Atan asked.

"They'll put a... a line, or a limit, at one end where we were first seen, and for the other end where we're likeliest to be headed. Make a circle. Search methodically within it."

"And the other end is going to be Eidervaen," Atan guessed.

No one argued.

As the day wore on, the fear changed to restlessness in some, boredom in others. Lilah watched Arlas take from her clothing a tight scroll of hoarded paper, a silverpoint drawing crayon, and sketch her sister sitting on a rock in her dirty gown and tangled hair, while Julian slept.

Mendaen worried, checking his weapons and peering upward toward the sky. From above, the grotto was all but invisible, but eventually some Norsundrian was going to press past the shrubs that hid the ancient quake crack that formed their hideaway, and he feared they'd be bottled between enemy searchers.

Atan sat up straighter, trying to ease her aching back. Hinder and Sin had finished their circuit. The group scrunched close to one another. Atan looked at the expectant faces—tired, grubby, but alert—and said, "Here's a plan. I will continue on alone, except perhaps for one or two others, for I am the one drawing danger to you. If the group spreads out, wandering about and pretending to be lost, or caught in the magic, so the Norsundrians have to stop and question everyone, then you have a better chance of escaping notice. If you never mention Shendoral or me, then you should be all right, I hope. And I will go north to Eidervaen."

"Who are the one or two others you would honor with such a trust?" Irza asked.

Lilah looked around, and noticed both Hinder and Sin with bent heads.

"I would leave that to volunteers," Atan stated. "But those volunteers would have to understand that the worst danger is where I go."

"Then we all shall volunteer."

All heads swung Irza's way.

She didn't speak loudly, but her whisper was all the more forceful.

Silence from the group.

"But it's better if I go alone," Atan said.

Irza bowed, but her face was blanched with anger, her fingers shaking. "I know you wish to preserve us from danger, your majesty," she said.

Lilah grimaced into her knees. The tone in that *your majesty* would was a slap in the spirit. She didn't even have to look at Atan to know she felt the sting; Lilah sensed it in the way Atan's body tensed into stillness.

"But in denying us the right to face danger with you, and defend you, you also deny us honor."

There was That Word. Now that it was out, nobody was going to make any sense anymore. Lilah sighed. She'd learned that much over the summer, when adults had slammed one another with accusations about honor with exactly as much heat and passion as a duel with swords. The wounds couldn't be seen, but obviously they sure could be felt.

Yes, Atan looked as if she'd been stabbed. Hinder was red with anger.

Lilah muttered as loudly as she dared, "Nonsense!"

Foosh! She fancied she could feel the wind as all heads snapped to face her.

Lilah struggled to sit up. Her cheeks and neck prickled with the heat of embarrassment, but she wasn't going to back down now. "It's a perfectly good plan. Diversion is something military people do. I learned that much when Sarendan had civil war last summer. Nobody loses honor."

"She is right." Heads snapped again.

That was Sin, who almost never spoke above a soft

murmur — and rarely when more than one person could hear her. But she too had red cheeks and narrowed eyes. "There is no honor lost in leading the enemy away from the monarch." When had all the morvende gathered to her? Suddenly all five of them were there, with cobwebby white hair and taloned fingers. And Rip was with them, his round face unwontedly sober.

"I will not put my own safety above that of the only Landis in the world," Irza stated, her head high. "My parents swore when they first took the Yostavos coronet that they would spend their lives defending their lands and the royal family. I can do no less."

"That's right," Arlas stated, arms crossed.

"It's true of my family as well," young Vian Ryadas proclaimed, his snub nose elevated.

Murmurs came from the others — and not just the nobles.

"We can't divert if no one will go," Pouldi said, scratching his ears.

"Maybe we can divert as a group." That came from Yoread, one of the quiet ones.

Everyone started talking, their eyes wide, their fingers stiff and shoulders tense as they all struggled to keep their emotions to whispers.

Atan listened in dismay, burdened by that constant awareness that every decision she made shaped their future interactions, just as everything she did would be remembered, and told and retold. If they lived. She lifted a hand, and the whispering ceased.

"Then how about this? We divert as a group."

Irza conceded with a regal nod, as one would in court. Lilah watched Hinder send her a long, stony glance, but Irza didn't notice. She was busy whispering to her sister.

Lilah turned toward Atan in time to catch a quick, private grimace Hinder's way that caused Hinder to grin just as quickly.

"We'll manage," the morvende said softly.

Once again the ground had shifted. No, it was more like the world had shifted. Lilah knew that she'd missed an important cue and didn't dare ask, because if Atan was not being obvious, then that meant she didn't want to call attention to whatever-it-was. She felt miserable and stupid, until she noticed Merewen watching with the painful concentration of someone who is trying her very best to make sense of a conversation in a foreign tongue of which she knows a few words.

At least she wasn't the only one

Dejain made her way up to the command tower. When she reached one of the landings with the correct view, she stood on tiptoe to peer out the air-slit. All Zydes's windows were lit, giving off a faintly bluish cast that indicated lots of magic.

She turned away and found herself face to face with Kessler.

She controlled the instinct to recoil, but shock was like a dagger of ice as he stood there blocking her path. Though she had magic and he had no visible weapons, he didn't need any weapons to be a danger. He was too near for her to speak any spell before he could close his hands around her throat.

"Zydes didn't tell anyone the brat is a surviving Landis," she said.

"No."

"The field reports," she said. "From the Sartor attack a hundred years ago. I want to see—"

Another shock: "Hidden," he said, his pale blue gaze as always devoid of any expression.

But he wasn't trying to kill her. "You sought them out?"

"A week ago," Kessler said. "And again. No access."

"Who took them? Where are they?" Dejain considered this new wrinkle as her heart thumped wildly. "Not in the Garden of the Twelve!"

He said, "Do you want to go there to find out?"

Horror gripped her at the idea of entering the center of Norsunder, where *They* had created their own paradise—a place where time and space responded only to the strongest will. And no one's will was as strong as that of the Host of Lords.

Not even Detlev's, who had surrendered to them, four thousand years ago.

"No," she said.

Kessler smiled slightly. "I believe Vatiora has those reports."

"Vatiora?"

But he said nothing more.

Dejain stepped aside, her heartbeat a fast drum of fear — and he walked past, the sound of his footsteps diminishing rapidly.

Dejain shuddered and hurried on her way, hating the distances she had to cover — but she dared not transfer, lest Zydes have mirror-wards against transfer anywhere on her route. He was certainly capable of it.

When she reached the tower, she completed the transfer, and Wend appeared. "Get the rest of my men," he said.

"Not until the plan is complete," she retorted.

He said, "We don't have supplies for a long search. Those brats have gone to ground, and my people need rest and food."

She looked into that ugly face and knew two things: that he would not report in more detail until he had his team, and second, that he was up to something, and she did not know what it was.

Fighting the urge to scream and curse, she began the transfer spells. One by one she brought his people in, until the last had arrived and her head buzzed with magic reaction.

"Fog's come down hard. Like night," Pouldi said, reappearing after a careful, scouting check on his hands and knees.

"And none of the enemy in sight or hearing," Sin added. "I think they went away."

Hinder nodded.

"Then everyone take hands," Atan said. "We're going to leave."

In silence, except for the crunch of footfalls on gravel and the occasional skittering of rocks, they slunk to the surface again, and pushed past the shrubs into a world of soft, cold whiteness.

Hinder's white head, pale skin, and his light-colored tunic made him nearly invisible, though he was only three people in front of Atan. On her right Lilah toiled, her breathing loud after the long upward climb, her small, square hand warm and strong. On her left was Sin, her thin, strong fingers cool and dry to the touch, the talons flexed away from Atan's flesh.

"Stay in line," Sin murmured. "Pass it down."

Atan heard Lilah whisper to whoever was beyond her.

They kept moving.

And while the forest-dwellers snaked slowly up a hill away from the river, Dejain stood on the tower, fighting anger and nausea, her eyes closed — until she heard a shout echo up from the courtyard directly below:

"Now!"

FIVE

A nd she almost missed it.
    She stared down into the torchlit courtyard. In the time it takes for the heart to drum once, she marked the ring of waiting conspirators facing Detlev.

Where did *he* come from?

Wend, Xoll, and a couple of his particular followers had joined with Vatiora, whose hair and clothes still billowed, lifting slightly in the weird, lightning-charged wind that came with long transfers directly from Norsunder.

Dejain took an involuntary step back, but lunged forward. She had to watch, for two things were now clear: that this was an ambush that someone else had planned, and that Detlev was the intended prey.

Vatiora raised her hands, teeth bared in her death's head grin, the torchlight reflecting red and bright in her distended eyes. Dejain sensed the hum of building magic. Her skin roughened, and as the eerie glow of power flickered around Vatiora's hands, Wend and three others closed in together, two from the side and one forward, hands full of steel. Others in the ring circled as backup.

Detlev took a single step, with deceptive slowness, then he moved in a half-circle, his arms a blur. Blink. Three were down, Wend rolling back and forth in helpless agony, Xoll and the other motionless, and only Detlev still standing. The outer ring of fighters faded back.

Detlev raised his head.

Vatiora had inexplicably frozen, her chin up at a strained angle. For a long moment, Dejain looked down into that narrow face, its furrows carved by unmeasured years of insatiable cruelty, twin torches reflecting in the wide, staring eyes, and then Detlev made a gesture, and Vatiora staggered as though released from an invisible hold.

Then she screamed. A horrible, long scream, the sound echoing in ear-flaying agony as her spell mirrored back onto her, and she was consumed by fire. Real fire. Smoke rose. The stench of cooking flesh made Dejain's guts heave and her eyes water, but she dared not look away.

Light shimmered: transfer. Dejain realized belatedly that Zydes had been standing on the edge of that crowd. None of the rest could escape by magic, for they were all military.

Detlev stepped over Xoll, whose neck was obviously broken, and reached down to Wend. The bigger man recoiled, but Detlev took his forearm in a firm grip, put a foot against Wend's ribcage, and yanked.

Wend let out a gasp and then flopped back, limp and sweaty. Dejain had just enough time to realize that she was not witnessing further play with the fallen but resetting of a dislocated shoulder, and then Detlev spoke at last.

"Go get that wrapped up. You might also contemplate, before you decide your next move, the observation that fools can give only foolish advice."

He looked up at two of Wend's lurking people, pointed, and they sprang to haul Wend up and take him off. The rest backed away farther, some glancing down at the smear of soot and grease where Vatiora had stood, the rest sending furtive glances back at Detlev, as one by one they retreated into the barracks. The two dead trackers lay where they had fallen.

"Dejain." Detlev lifted his head and nodded toward the row of windows comprising the command office.

How *could* he have seen her? He had not looked up once. Was it true, then, that he somehow listened to minds even out of his sight?

Dread, anticipation, and reaction made her joints go

watery, as if she really were twenty again, instead of just looking it. For a moment she leaned against the wall, cold as it was, and forced herself to consider that still-smoking smear on the court stones. The wretched smell lingered in her hindbrain, if not in her nostrils, but she made herself acknowledge it. She was much older than most of these people, and most of the time she was aware of how time changed a person's pleasures, goals, outlooks. But the truth was, Detlev made her feel like a gawky adolescent.

What frightened her most was how he could have smoked out that ambush from an entire world away. It wasn't mere trickery, it was eternal vigilance. Habit made one unheeding, Kessler had told her early on in their alliance.

Kessler. Where was he?

She saw no one as she made her way down to the command rooms, though she knew that word had to be ricocheting through the fortress faster than a cross-bolt. Three dead, one wounded. Two had been trained assassins, and Detlev hadn't even used a weapon, nor a spell. Just his hands. He hadn't touched Vatiora, but she'd reacted as though held in some invisible grip. *Mental grip.*

This was more evidence that he was, after all, one of *Them.*

She reached the door. Hesitated.

Heard his voice: "Come in. The wards are gone."

And how long had *that* taken? Zydes had laid wards over the wards; she'd felt them from a distance the one time she had come in this wing without his sanction.

But Detlev stood in the middle of the room, the glowglobes illuminating him from the side. He looked neat and calm in his customary gray tunic and dark trousers, a man just over medium height, maybe in his thirties — but then They controlled the aging process from within. Brown hair, hazel eyes. He never dressed flash, like the Black Knives or some of the other war-branch commanders. In fact, you rarely saw him with a weapon at all. Yet here he was after that ambush, not the least bit sweaty or disheveled.

She stepped in, her tongue working in her dry mouth. Excuses — explanations — denials winged through her mind like the bats on the rocky heights.

Detlev said, "What do you want?"

The bats squeaked and were gone, leaving her brain empty and hollow.

Questions she had expected, but not that one.

Her lips shaped the word: "What?"

Get some control! she commanded herself, and she drew in her breath. Reaching for the motivation behind the question, she said, "I was not part of —"

Detlev lifted a hand. "Everyone is conspiring. Part of the sport. Vatiora's recent gamble was only a feint for someone else, whom I will have to address presently. First I wish to stabilize the problems here. Now I ask you again, what do you want?"

Why don't you just listen to my thoughts? But she didn't voice that retort — nor did she meet that steady gaze as she wondered if the question was a trick. Maybe he expected her to reveal herself by thinking one thing and saying something else. Everybody did that.

"Power," she said. Her inner voice said, *Order.*

"*To win.*" Inside, *And no one, ever, can take me by surprise again.*

Memory flooded her brain, too strong to suppress: the village after the Brotherhood of Blood had sacked it, burning all the houses; the helpless worry caused by rumors of imminent war; seeking magic to learn to defend herself, because she knew she would always be too small for steel, and after her long, arduous search the mage cautioning her that learning magic took years and years, and she would be expected to sit in some cave somewhere, and watch caterpillars turn into butterflies.

Light magic. Sartor had fallen, yet they hadn't changed their ways. That was not power, it was weak, sentimental foolishness. So she had to find her way to the magic of power, of strength...

She blinked away the memory. Detlev was still waiting. She wondered if he'd somehow read her memory, and hatred burned inside her. If he had, there was no way to withstand that. She said, "Is that enough, or do you want specifics?"

"No." As usual, he was utterly unreadable. "As I said, everyone is plotting. So am I. Understand this: I have no interest in anyone's plans, except as they concern me. Then I interfere."

'Interfere.' That was not how she'd characterize what she'd just seen. She recognized how the lack of threat in his choice of words, or in his tone, was so very much more sinister than rants and raves and overt threats could ever be.

She nodded.

"Then I leave you in charge here. Zydes will be back before long. Do what you want with him. Kessler Sonscarna is to take orders from you."

No, he won't. She nearly said it, but managed not to speak. Detlev could place her in command, but she'd have to hold that command herself. He clearly wasn't going to stay around to back her up.

He waited just long enough to see her nod again, and then he was gone. She waited until the brief, wild breeze of displaced air had brushed her face, and then she turned to the door, to see Lesca leaning against it.

Shock rang in her ears. Lesca's lazy smile, her languorous posture, all belied the intensity of the last few moments. It was unsettling.

"Any orders, O commander?" Lesca asked.

Detlev had let her stand there and hear it all? Well, he did say he didn't care—

That could wait. Dejain waved her hand around the room. "Zydes's prison guard decoration does not appeal to me. Can you make this office more comfortable? I had better get Wend's report."

Lesca laughed, made an ironic bow, and then left. Dejain looked in distaste at that huge desk and forbore going through the papers on it. Most of it would be worthless. She might as well save herself the time and throw everything but the garrison status reports into the fire.

Right now she had to establish command, and then get her own information. The fact that Lesca had been eavesdropping, unpleasant as it was, would probably redound to her credit. Of course she could not even remotely match Detlev's little demonstration. But she could make her own presence felt by two things: magic and immediate action.

Using the response adrenaline still firing her nerves, she envisioned Wend's ugly face and transferred to him.

The moment she appeared she said, "Report."

And then used all her strength, all her concentration, to hold herself still and mask the transfer reaction. *Breathe, breathe.* The vertigo began to dissipate. She hoped Wend and the two others hadn't seen it. Wend lay on a bed, his upper half freshly bandaged.

"...no sign of any of the brats. When the fog got so bad we couldn't see our feet, I sent the signal for transfer."

She hadn't heard everything, of course, but she'd heard enough. Her mouth tightened at his last words. Fog? Magical in origin? That meant someone was also running Wend. But that, obviously, was over. She searched her mind for something to say, decided that Detlev's silence was more effective, and so she transferred back to Zydes's old command chamber.

Two transfers so quick in a row gave her a mild headache. She wondered how Detlev could deal with long distance double transfers — then she saw Kessler.

She rushed into speech. "Detlev put me in charge." As if that was a defense!

"Yes." He sounded exactly as flat as always. "What did he say about me?"

"His exact words were, 'Kessler Sonscarna is to take orders from you.'"

As she spoke them, she realized what she'd missed before, the implied threat there. She had no idea what hold Detlev had over Kessler. More important, she had no idea why he didn't put Kessler in charge of this army — or any other — and loose him against the world. He had to know how good he was. Whatever that hold might be, it had kept Kessler running as hound for a fool like Zydes.

She didn't know if the same hold was strong enough to make him take her orders.

"Then what are your orders?" he asked.

She was going to lick her dry lips, was suddenly reminded of Xoll, and suppressed a shudder of disgust. "Our first objective is to recover Sartor. It's going to be a matter for magery or I wouldn't be here, is my reasoning. But we'll also need field backup. You are in charge of that. All I want is the Landis girl, alive if you can. But removed from Sartor. She must not reach Eidervaen. This is why I need to see those field reports, because I must find out exactly what was done at the end of the attack."

Kessler said nothing.

How could she get her own hold over him — maybe make him grateful? "As for Zydes," she said, "you can do what you like with him."

Xoll would have licked his lips in pleasure. Wend — a dozen others — would have grinned and rubbed their hands, or made some similar move. Kessler jerked his head, a slight movement, as though throwing off something. "Waste of time. The Landis girl was last seen heading north toward the capital. It's a short distance, but it's bad terrain, according to the map. Old volcanic area. Caves, cracks in the ground, hidden fissures and chasms. A search is going to require a sizable detachment. And you will have to transfer us all by magic, if you don't want to lose weeks of travel time."

Dejain sat down, knowing that this first night and day were going to tax her strength to the maximum — but if she survived it, she would be able to hold the base. And then start on her plans again, this time with all its resources at her command.

"Get who you need and supply them," she said. "Let me know when you're ready to go."

He left, his quick step diminishing.

Leaving her with a silent room and relief that dealing with him — so far — had been so easy. And as for Zydes, why shouldn't she have some fun, after all? Sword duels were disgusting, but a magic duel was very much to her taste.

"They're back."

Mendaen slid down the muddy hillside and landed next to Atan.

Everyone had to look. Atan didn't try to stop them. She climbed as well. They all knew now to keep their heads from creating a silhouette, and so they peered through scrubby hedges or low plants at the precisely spaced line of horseback riders crossing the hilltops as they searched.

Atan didn't know much about horses — there

weren't any in Delfina Valley — but it didn't take experience to recognize that this was terrible ground for riding, what with all the rocks, and cracks, and screes. But the line of Norsundrians rode fast, wheeling at once when the foremost one raised a hand, and for a brief time the group vanished over a hilltop — to reappear farther on.

Then a nudge from Mendaen, and she peered into the late afternoon sun. Another set of riders crested a hillside in that direction.

Atan scrambled down the hill and waited until most of the group were gathered around.

She turned her gaze to Mendaen. "They have to be searching for us."

He nodded. "They'll be coming back this way soon. Looking for our tracks. And they'll stay in sight of one another as much as they can."

Lilah groaned. "This is bad."

"What we expected, though," Sin murmured.

"At least we had three days."

"One, really," someone in the back retorted.

Lilah scowled, but it was no more than the truth. The sleety rain had come in hard, much too cold and dangerous to travel in, and so they'd spent more time holed up in makeshift caves than actually traveling. And the travel had been slow because of all the mud and puddles. Ugh! And this morning, when they set out, the remaining puddles had been covered over with a thin film of ice.

"Come on," Hinder said. "We're cutting north and east. Now. We can talk as we go."

"We'll leave tracks," Arlas pointed out.

"Can't be helped. But we'll be on rock soon. North and east, and when we reach Terrace Rock, we'll go straight west. That'll put them off our trail for a bit."

No one spoke. They used what strength they had remaining to keep up with the leaders. Merewen listened and watched, trying to grasp the quick exchanges, the ways people expressed themselves through words, through tone, through gestures, and how sometimes all three were at variance in the same person. Lilah and Atan did not seem to mind her listening. Atan would ask, "What do you think is meant by..." And Lilah would try to explain.

Mostly, it appeared, there was some emotion the speaker wished to hide.

Merewen also observed the variations in the slanting striations forming the hills, and the wildly different types of stone. The sky was ever-changing now, as if weather was rediscovering itself. It was not home, like Shendoral, but it was interesting.

She felt magic stirring, sometimes in dizzying whirls that she sensed in some inward way that was not sight, hearing, taste, touch, or smell. Sometimes she felt it in subtle traces as she walked. At a distance pooled great, heavy quagmires of badness, and they weighed on her spirit, as did the friction between some of those around her. She did not know how to solve that last one—she wanted to run when someone was unkind, or felt hurt— but Atan, she'd discovered, sometimes could mend at least the surface hurt with a word or a gesture.

Lilah worried about her brother at home, and about her ability to keep up here. If only the nasties would get close enough so she could fell them with the last of her Lure! Only she didn't know if she'd gotten those petals stuffed back into their bag in time. What if the Lure had completely lost their virtue after all those uses? Euw, she didn't want to find out the hard way!

Sana was busy composing a ballad about their hardships, complete with internal rhymes in the old wanderer mode. The world she'd known had changed forever, but as long as there was music, life was good— despite the cold, and the hunger, and dirt, and the ever-present threat of discovery by the Norsundrians. Her unswerving desire was to go to a music academy, and become a bard or a theater musician. As she walked, she sang under her breath, her gaze on the mud and slush ahead of her ragged shoes, but her mind soaring on a current of song through images from ancient ballads.

Rip and Hannla were also composing a song about their hardships, but this one wasn't meant to last beyond the next time they camped long enough to share a song. Pompous, stiff, and very, very silly, it was meant to make them all laugh.

Mendaen worried. He was sick with anxiety, knowing from the sight of those well-trained riders that this new commander was far more competent than the previous one, and Mendaen feared that his friends wouldn't last in a fight past three breaths. He didn't know whether he ought to die first or last. Gripping, regripping the dagger he'd taken from his dead father's hands, he kept watching Hinder for signals.

Hinder and Sin knew these hills, but only in a general sense. Each time they stopped, one or two of the five morvende scouted ahead for the next segment of trail. They had one fallback — but it would be risky. If they were wrong, it might mean an entire geliath sealed for at least a generation, maybe forever. And exile for them.

Pouldi was hungry. Oh, for some grub!

Arlas stole worried looks at Julian, who was stumbling, though not a peep did she make. Honor, she kept telling herself. Act with honor. If we die, we die with honor. Our names won't die. That's what Irza says, and she knows. She's the one who remembers everything Mama used to say.

The sisters were too tired to sketch one another, but at least they had one portrait each, to rest in the family archives — if the sketches and the archives survived — to the glory of the Ianth family.

Fear, tiredness, resentment, hunger, cold, sometimes panic-sparked giggles, and sometimes panic sparked short, hissing arguments.

The one who stayed quiet was Irza, who kept watching the morvende. Once her mother had dressed for a ball on the eve of the war, but there'd been no sign of fear or threat in the capital, no hint of trouble in her mother's exquisite grooming and straight back. Last, she'd put on the ancient coronet, rude and misshapen gold, that came out so seldom, and it had ruined the beauty of her handmade dress, a froth of white and silver and peach silk blossoms.

Why wear that ugly thing? Irza had asked. It ruins the effect of your gown.

I know, Mama had said. It is not the thing itself that we treasure, but what it means. Everyone who looks upon it will be reminded that the Ianth family has been in Sartor for thousands of years, with illustrious members in Sword, Pen, and Star. Remember the symbols, my child, because they are the magic of the nobility, and without this magic you cannot hold power.

Irza did not have the least interest in going into damp, dark old morvende caves. She did not believe the wondrous stories about mysterious caves full of singing gemstones, each more precious and rare than the last. She thought the whole idea of the morvende culture repellent, but they did carry tremendous prestige. They were a part of Sartor's history, and somehow they managed to have enormous power, though as yet she didn't see how.

But she knew this much: the tradition was, any sunsiders the morvende brought into the geliaths were forever honored, in Sartor — even out in the world. And she was determined that she was going to find out those accesses, even if she had to sneak. Oh, she'd never, ever, *ever* use them — if they all lived — but to let it be known that she was one of the blessed...

And so they endured three long days of steady tramping in horrible weather, over rough terrain, their supplies more scant with each meal.

But they had no experience, so time was against them.

Once there was a close call, when a child's shrill laugh had rung echoing up grate slabs of old granite, but the echoes led the Norsundrians wrong just long enough for Sin to hear their pursuit, and Hinder found a chasm in which to hide the group for the night.

They spent the next half a day crouched in one place, quiet as the stone around them, while at intervals pebbles skittered down, a dry and stinging rain on their heads and shoulders, indicating the night-long search.

But at last Mendaen reported early one morning, "They've closed in around us. By noon they'll have us."

Four white heads turned Hinder's way. He brought his chin down once. Sin also nodded. And so did the younger three: a pact agreed to.

Hinder said, "We've tried not just to go northwest toward Eidervaen, but to be within range of our geliath accesses. Well, we're by one now. Right over the next ridge."

He looked at tired little Julian and the other grimy, exhausted faces, and he couldn't regret the decision. The morvende had all agreed, though they knew the rules: they were to check ahead before bringing Sunsiders down underground. It was the first rule. But the emergency (they all agreed) was greater.

Tough, determined Mendaen was pale, almost greenish, with relief, and Hinder sustained a wash of sympathy. Even if he ended up exiled sunside forever, it would not be so bad, if he could save his friends. "Come on," he said.

They ran.

And so it was they topped a steep cliff just as Kessler and his riders entered the narrow rocky defile below.

Kessler reined in when the little rocks fell on them, and looked up. Atan and her group looked down.

Kessler and his people were tired, too, for they'd had less rest than the forest-dweller had. He lifted a hand to ward the low winter sun that had moments before crowned the southeastern mountains, and surveyed the little group. He saw a black-clad child with ruddy hair, and recognized his Landis. Except who was the tall one next to her with the long brown braids and filthy riding clothes? The morning sun on her face illuminated every feature, including the eyes shaped so much like his, and it glinted on the ring she wore on one grubby hand.

Ah. He had been wrong from the outset. This one was the Landis.

Atan recognized those blue eyes, that black hair. Here was the villain who had threatened her early on their journey, and had grabbed Lilah—and a glance at poor Lilah, who looked as if she'd been stabbed, proved her right.

Kessler said, "You've nowhere to run."

"I know," Atan said, and as she wiped a wind-stirred strand of dirty hair from her face, she glanced covertly behind her, at where Hinder was gesticulating violently from the lee of an outcropping of rock, where the Norsundrians couldn't see him, as Sin and two others struggled with some precariously balanced big stones.

Stall them, Atan guessed.

"Go away and leave us alone," she called.

The Norsundrians laughed and settled back to watch the show.

"Or what?" one of them called, causing a guffaw down their line. "You'll cry us to death?"

Hinder and Sin belly-crawled up and grabbed the

youngest forest-dwellers. They began hauling them backward, as Hannla blocked them from view by walking along the ridge, wailing and shaking her fists.

"Go away! Go away!" Atan shrilled, causing more laughter. "Leave us alone! We never did anything to you!"

Brick and all the Poisoners joined in, howling and bellowing threats and pleadings, as the Norsundrians richly enjoyed protracting the forest-dwellers' fear.

One by one the forest-dweller vanished, until only the teens were left.

"Now," Hinder hissed from behind.

Atan's heartbeat thumped in her ears. During her days in the forest, she'd been catching up on forest-dwellers' slang and gestures. Keeping her gaze on Kessler's watching face she lifted a hand, put her thumb to her nose, and wiggled her fingers skyward.

Then she turned and ran.

From below came the clatter of horses' hooves as the Norsundrians started up the gulley in pursuit.

Atan and the last of her friends scrambled down the back of the ridge in a welter of rubble. Following Hinder, they ducked around some big slabs, and into the darkness beyond.

The morvende did something to some precariously balanced boulders, which teetered, toppled, cracked, clattered, and bounced down the hillside, bringing a train of smaller rocks with them, which in their turn skirled up a popping, spinning cascade of pebbles. By the time the Norsundrians reached the far side of the ridge, they discovered an avalanche, which sent up a choking cloud of dust. Their quarry had vanished, apparently beneath it.

SIX

The world vanished into darkness and the smell of stone.

Atan stretched out her hands. Coughs, sneezes, and muffled cries sounded around her, followed by whimpers of fear, hisses of excitement, shuffling, and blind steps echoing weirdly. The younger children pressed close to one another.

Atan whispered, "Julian?" and a quiet sigh escaped her when a small, cold hand slid into hers.

Then the little hand was tugged away, and Irza whispered, "Julian, stay by me. I'll keep you safe. Your cousin has important things to do." A distracted thought: this had happened before, and not once. Atan had been relieved, as she did not know what to do with small children. But right now no one was doing anything. And she had nothing more important than holding the hand of a small child.

Before she could formulate words, Hinder's voice rose, joyful and clear, "We're home!"

The morvende lived in this darkness? Atan bit her lip. She would be grateful for the rescue. She had to hide her dismay.

Then Sin said, more quietly, "Not yet. Take hands. We still have a ways to go."

Hinder couldn't wait. He ran ahead down the tunnel, right hand out, talons trailing along the wall that guided him downward, distinctive carvings warning him of twists and turns as well as naming byways.

When he came out of the access tunnel, the blue-white glowglobes, and the smells of old stone and pure water made him shiver with longing and familiarity. Though he loved life sunside, now that he was here, the old remembered smells and the beautiful diffused light hurt inside, making him feel that he'd been gone forever.

The soft sough of the wind through the great cavern and the dark tunnels sounded of emptiness, as if it had been a long time since anyone had come this way.

He ran across the floor of the cavern, scarcely heeding the ancient paintings glowing down at him from the high walls, or the old gray of aged clay smoothing the smaller tunnel walls. He'd ruined an access for a generation or two, but at least it wasn't one that people depended on. The carving that had named the access had felt very old, untouched; he wondered when it had last been used.

At the far end lay the dark pool he sought. Sunsiders might have hesitated before that blackness, but he plunged into the warm water, concentrating on his family, and when he came up gasping, glad to be rid of his coating of mud and dust, he found a ring of people waiting.

His attention homed straight to the oldest, a man with long hair braided in the leaf pattern. "Hinder, welcome home."

"Grandfather Lonender," Hinder said in their own tongue, holding out his dripping hands as he sloshed out of the pool. His grandfather clasped him in a damp hug, and Hinder smiled, then sobered as he stepped back. "I have brought sunsiders down. We were chased by Norsundrians, and with us is Atan Landis, daughter of the last king and queen."

The gathered circle exclaimed in soft voices at this news.

"Where are they?"

"Below the fireflower access," Hinder said. "I left Sin with them."

Lonender clasped Hinder on the shoulders reassuringly. "Well then, we must welcome them."

Not just relief but joy brightened Hinder's heart. He would not be exiled from his family, or his home—but more important, his judgment had been deemed good.

"Are we far?" Hinder asked.

"Not at all," Lonender said, smiling. "No need to transfer there and greet our guests dripping wet. We will proceed as we are."

Hinder agreed, hiding his impatience. He wanted to find and greet his mother, yet he felt he should accompany his grandfather.

Lonender saw Hinder's glance toward the inward access, and said, "We will bring them here and prepare a feast. Rejoin us when you have seen your family."

Hinder flashed a happy grin, then raced across the rocky ground, his feet slapping the cool stone. How familiar that was! He dashed up to the dwellings shared by his mother and her sister, to meet them on the rockway down.

"Hinder!" He'd forgotten how musical his mother's voice was. Joy was tempered with guilt—he knew she'd be disappointed that he'd never settled down to be a chamber-singer, and she would try to hide it.

"I'm back, with news," he declared, when everyone had exchanged hugs and kisses.

"Sin?" asked Aunt Adel, as she brushed back Hinder's damp hair.

"She's with the sunsiders we brought."

His mother's amber eyes narrowed, but she smiled and caressed his forehead and cheek with her fingertips.

They smiled at one another again, and he followed them back up to the pretty caves he'd been born in. How small they seemed! But they were snug, and he still loved the bright shades of green that his mother and aunt had chosen for rugs and pillows.

"You were right to have me go sunside in Shendoral, for the binding magic over the rest of the land was still strong," he said. "Here's why I did not come back. I found others my age living in the forest, rescued by a mage called Savar..."

As he talked, he watched their faces. Aunt Adel listened with her eyes narrowed, looking so very much like Sin. His mother smiled wistfully, and at the end, when Aunt Adel excused herself to get him some rice cake and pressed cider, his mother murmured, "So you have not quenched the sun-thirst?"

He shook his head.

She pulled him up against her in a warm, understanding hug. "We are all human," she said, quoting the old, old proverb. "And humans were born under sky and stars."

A soft-footed group of white-haired people appeared. Some were grownups, a thing many had not seen for a very long time, discounting those sinister figures on horseback. Most of Atan's little band fell back in doubt and apprehension.

"Welcome," a woman said in Sartoran. Her voice was clear, a singer's voice, Sana recognized with an inward shiver of joy. "Come and eat, and drink, and rest. There will be time to talk as well."

Irza stared around. The cave really wasn't as awful as she'd supposed—not at all like those they'd been forced to hide in, with fungus all over, and rubble, and spider webs, or stinky animal nests. The air smelled clean and fresh, and she heard the hush of steady wind and the running chuckle of water. Light came from somewhere, though she could not find the source; it almost seemed to be part of the air.

As they walked along a series of accesses, reaching at last a big cavern, an involuntary "Oh!" escaped her when she saw the stylized paintings along the walls. Intricate weavings of bird shapes, painted many colors and edged with the rich glow of gold, fascinated not just Irza, but all those who responded to beauty.

Irza began to understand why morvende had so honored a place in history. She'd seen nothing but a hole when Hinder had gotten them away from those Norsundrians. And though she'd looked back, she'd only seen the light source suddenly cut off, and then she'd heard the roar of falling rock.

But now they were *in*, and she hoped that that meant they would become the Chosen. Or at least Atan would—and if she did, why not those of noble blood? It was not necessary for the descendants of the trades to be Chosen to know the accesses, for they would never become leaders, surely.

Shendoral's children were invited to sit on woven rugs set on the stone near a black pool that was the first uninviting thing Irza'd seen. There seemed to be no equivalent to a high table, a place where nobles took precedence. Irza waited, to see where the others sat. Where would be the center?

Atan hadn't yet sat. She was talking to the old man with the braided hair.

"I'm tired, Irza." Julian tugged fretfully on the hem of Irza's tunic.

"Go, then." Irza shook the child's fingers free, and sighed with relief when Julian flung herself down beside Arlas, who was yawning as she slumped on the blanket next to Sana.

Irza noticed a couple of the others looking her way, so she sat down with care, trying to move with grace and dignity as befitting Ianth House.

Good smells assailed her nostrils. Morvende moved among the children, carrying bowls of something steaming. Servants? She glanced at the old one still talking with Atan.

Irza nodded and smiled her thanks to the two adults that brought her a steaming bowl of golden tea and a plate of some kind of cut fruit and some crunchy cakes, but the girl morvende who came last with a jug, looking to refill the tea dishes, she put out a hand to stop.

"Is that your king?" she asked, indicating the old morvende with Atan.

"We do not have kings," the girl said. Her accent was pretty, reminding Irza of Hinder and Sin when they first arrived at the dell. "He is..." She tipped her head. "It translates only as 'Grandfather.' But this—Grandfather or Grandmother—is how we call our oldest and wisest."

Irza nodded her thanks and then said, as casually as she could, "I suppose you'll need to make a new access? I'm afraid we ruined the one we came in. But you know, everyone here would be willing to dig and help restore it, or to make another."

"It is kind," the girl said. "We give thanks for generous offer." She moved away, stooping to refill cups of everyone who needed more, never asking their status, or giving anyone deference or precedence.

Irza sighed inwardly. She'd have to wait, and

meanwhile, did the morvende have cleaning frames or would they get to bathe?

The bath was offered after everyone had eaten. They were led to a chamber lower down that steamed at one end and had a waterfall at the other, pouring into a shallow pool. Around a corner was another similar. The boys got one, the girls the other.

Atan soon floated gratefully in bubbling water, which churned and fizzed around her like gentle fingers brushing over her skin. Not only the grime of their terrible journey washed away, but the aches in her body as well.

Happy shouts echoed up the rock walls into the dark shadows above. There were no straight angles in these caverns. The rock was not uniform gray, but a rich variety of subtle colors, compressed into sedimentary lines, testament to the violent tectonics of the past, possibly going back to the world's birth.

At last, the others heaved themselves out, looking tired and heavy-limbed as they dressed again in clothes that had been put through cleaning frames. A delightful surprise was the quick zap of warm dry air when they stepped between a pair of old stones, and then soft-voiced, smiling adults offered the children places to rest.

Most accepted and were led away yawning toward a honeycomb of small caves up the side of one vast cavern shelf.

"Oh!" That was Sana, sounding as if she had suddenly stepped in ice. No. Her tone was one of surprise, shock even, but nonetheless pleasure.

And then Atan realized what she'd been hearing: singing. Faint, almost too faint to discern above the soughing of wind over stone, the sound was so beautiful that at first she was not even certain it was voices. They sounded like silver bells.

Then she saw the singers, high in another cavern, facing the other direction. Walls bounced the sound back, blending the voices. Triplets in one chord, then another, echoed from stone to stone, forming a new and more subtle counterpoint, while the melodic line bound it all together in threads of gold—no—of rainbow—no, that wasn't right either—

Atan closed her eyes, trying to comprehend the

beauty, but it sounded and felt, so high... deep... vast, as the melody chased up and up, shifting in chords from somber to joyful. The glory exalted her, so intense that she was not aware of the tears cooling on her cheeks or the ache in her chest from sobs, until the echoes began to fade as singers fell silent one by one, until only a single voice remained. Then that one, too, sang a high note that dwindled into the hush of the wind.

Sana stumbled forward, weeping. Atan started up in concern, then fell back when she saw that it was elation, not sadness, that moved Sana. Atan sank back on her pile of rugs and pillows.

Most of the forest-dwellers had fallen into slumber. Irza sat in the center, Julian asleep between her and an equally somnolent Arlas.

"They said it was a lullaby," Irza said, her face calm, her voice pleasant. "But it was much too beautiful for that."

Atan did not understand Irza. Lilah had been able to help a little when she explained that Irza had courtly manners. Atan had read about courtly manners and how they were supposed to hide real feelings.

"It was," Atan said.

Irza's eyes narrowed. "Everyone seems to be falling asleep, and the little ones certainly need their rest. They are very tired."

Remorse sent a pang through Atan when she glanced at Julian. "I—I keep forgetting. I don't know much about the care of the young," she said contritely.

"Well, I do," Irza said, smiling with confidence. Then she yawned. "I'm tired, so if nothing else is going on..." She lay down and arranged herself neatly.

Atan watched the way she settled herself, almost as if she performed a dance. It was much more than the arrogant expectation that one would always be watched, the center of interest or attention. This was living art, using grace to underscore leadership, more of that symbolic transference.

Atan knew she would have to compromise with the courtly attitudes toward life.

But not right now, she thought tiredly, and lay down near Lilah.

She was too tired to notice that Merewen was

missing.

Atan woke to the sounds of others sitting up, stretching, yawning, and talking as they looked about in sleepy pleasure or wonder. It was so good to be safe and out of the cold, and to know they would not have to walk hungry all through the day.

Julian was happy. She loved the warm cave, the food, and the kind people. She waved at Atan, who smiled back. It was a smile just for her, Julian knew. Not a smile for others to see or a smile put on like clothes, to vanish again when others turned their faces elsewhere, because Atan's smile was still there when the old man with the white hair touched her shoulder and she turned his way.

"If you have rested," Lonender said to Atan. "Perhaps we might meet to exchange views on matters concerning both morvende and sunsiders."

"Yes, let's," Atan agreed.

Lonender led the way to a little chamber above a waterfall.

Lilah saw Atan led away, and wondered if she ought to offer to go along. Those grownups obviously didn't want to talk to her, or she would have been included. And though Atan had relied on her to help understand the other forest-dwellers, morvende were far outside of Lilah's experience. She doubted whether she'd comprehend them any better than Atan.

Hinder appeared, grinning. "Want to look around?"

"Would I!" Lilah exclaimed.

"What would you like to see?"

"Oh, anything." She frowned. "But what about Norsunder, and breaking the spells?"

Hinder's face changed to a kind of rueful wince. "The elders aren't going to let any of us sunside. Those Norsundrians are all over the hills, and just this morning—it's morning now, as it happens—the report came back that they have Eidervaen ringed. Nobody can get in or out."

Lilah whistled. "What are we going to do?"

"Ah, there are ways." He made a vague gesture, then shrugged, and Lilah figured that there were some morvende secrets involved, ones that Hinder wasn't allowed to talk about. "Anyway, those plans are being made. In the meantime, we're supposed to rest and have fun. So?"

"I suppose you'll laugh at me if I ask about the wonderful jewel caves? I can't help what people write in records, you know."

Hinder laughed, but it wasn't mean, or even gloating. "Oh, they're real."

"They are?"

He laughed silently and nodded, his cobwebby hair drifting into his eyes.

"But I take it something nasty will happen if you try to steal the jewels or something?"

Hinder snickered again.

Lilah pretended to fume. She knew he wasn't being a show-off, but she really did hate being ignorant. "Well, how am I supposed to learn the truth of these things? The legends and songs all talk about them."

Hinder fought down the laughter. "Not your fault. Just—I know about the jewel caves. Seen 'em once. There are, I forget, six or seven of them in various places over the world. People do try to get to 'em and steal. And get a big surprise."

"Nasty magic traps! I knew it."

Hinder shook his head, and Lilah watched his silky hair drift. She longed to touch it, but knew better than to ask. "Not traps," he said. "It's just—hmm, I suppose I can take you. But first let's get some of the others. Sana won't come. Nobody's getting her away from those singers. But Pouldi, and Brick, and Vanya, and a couple of the others I know would like to see the really, really old caverns, with the old paintings from before the Fall, and dive off the big warm waterfall—that's where we like swimming best—"

Lilah rubbed her hands. "What are we waiting for?"

SEVEN

The morvende formed a comfortable circle, sitting cross-legged on cushions, their pale fabrics lying in soft folds over their limbs, hands loose in laps or on knees. Atan noticed that everyone could see everyone else, but there was no sense of hierarchy, no person made focus of all eyes. They talked easily, passing small cups of freshly steeped leaf back and forth, and Atan felt the invisible fist somewhere inside her chest unlock its grip, one finger at a time.

She was not in danger. She was not on trial.

As if he sensed that she was ready, Lonender said, quite kindly, "How do we know you are who you claim to be?"

Atan had expected this question. In fact, she had thought about it long into nights when she tried to imagine what her first days in Sartor would be like — assuming she made it that far.

She had expected the question from the orphans of Shendoral, but they had taken her appearance as proof enough, maybe because they were young, too, or maybe because Savar had told them of her after his single meeting with Tsauderei. Maybe it was because of her looks, though those couldn't be trusted as proof of birth. Kessler had been proof of that.

She said, "I can't prove it. In truth, I cannot prove it even to myself, for I have no memories beyond growing up with Gehlei protecting me and Tsauderei teaching me.

It was they who told me who I was, and told me the stories of what happened. It is they you must question for the truth of my identity. Not I."

Sin's mother exchanged looks with two other women, her eyes so pale it was difficult to determine their color, their expression cool and watchful. "We have taught our young ones few of your sunsider manners. Shall we have them bow to you?"

Atan said, frowning, "I wasn't raised to them, but I've read much. Is that your own custom, too?"

The woman rippled her fingers, then flicked them away, a gesture of negation.

"Then no bowing here. The customs of my realm can wait on my success in restoring my kingdom. At that time — Tsauderei counseled me I should — I will comply with expectation. At first, anyway." Atan's hands locked together.

Lonender said, "If they do not accept your authority?"

Atan sighed. "I have thought about that, too. I don't have an answer, beyond the conviction that each day will bring its questions. Challenges. Decisions. But I won't have any throne or name, or anything else that has to be secured by violence, that much I know. Either they have me by their own choice." She swallowed. "Or not."

———

"Here we are." Hinder pointed the way to a tunnel from which dim light touched his white hair with warm highlights, and struck tiny reflective gleams in the strata of the tunnel walls. The two were alone after all, for the other morvende young preferred swimming and fun.

Lilah stopped, wailing in disappointment, "This is *it*? The famous caves, and we ran all the way up that long, long, LONG trail just — " She remembered she was a guest and shut her mouth.

Until she realized Hinder was laughing. She groaned.

"Come on," he said. "Not much farther." He started running again, and Lilah, sweaty in her sturdy black clothes that were made for bitter winter weather — toiled after him, despite the sweat running down her sides and making her neck itchy and hot.

The upward slant of the tunnel was sharp for only another turn, and then leveled out, widening gradually. The light was also stronger, enough to cast subtle shadows that picked out the roughness of the stone walls. Here no one had smoothed the walls with clay or paint or anything else. Perhaps nature had made this tunnel, or perhaps not, but morvende hands had not finished the job as they had everywhere else.

"Here we are," Hinder said, breathless.

Lilah slowed, also panting. The air wasn't heated, it was... it was... *strange.*

They rounded a last corner, and she entered a chamber filled with light, so bright and clear her eyes teared. She sucked in a long, shuddering breath. Hinder stood in the center, hugging his thin, strong arms to himself and gazing upward with a happy smile.

Lilah blinked away her tears and stared. Jewels, indeed! That was her first impression. The walls, the ceiling, even the floor, glimmered and coruscated with brilliant hues, though the floor was smooth, so they were not stepping on the sharp facets that covered the rest of the cave.

Jewels of every color shone with light from within. There were blues so deep and so pure it almost hurt to look at them, more cerulean than a mountain lake on midsummer's day, their centers glowing with a fiery cobalt more celestial than the twilight sky. Then there were the yellows, from the palest shade of cream just turning to butter to a complex peachy gold, and thence to the deep, bright yellow that would shame the daffodils of spring by comparison. The reds varied from crimson, vermillion, and deep rose to the palest blush of pink.

"Oh," she breathed. "Oh."

Hinder chuckled.

Lilah spun around. The light was so strange, so *pure,* like the air, it felt hot and cold at once, and as she stood breathing, she thought she heard, so faint she could not be sure, the endless rise and fall of sweet voices singing. But there were no words, it was a hum, the sound of the stars, if stars sang.

"Oh."

"You see," Hinder said. "Go ahead. Try to take

one."

Lilah put her hands behind her back and shook her head, and for a moment the dreamy singing faded, and she was closed inside her own head, which felt hot and confined and stuffy. "No. I daren't."

"It's all right. You won't turn into a mushroom or anything."

"They look like they are ... on fire."

"Hah! No, they don't burn. At least, not in the way ordinary fire does, but your intentions are not to harm. And they know it."

Lilah walked slowly to one of the walls and reached with tentative fingers to touch a great emerald, its heart glowing the deep, dark green of ancient woodland. The stone was smooth, like a stone should be, not hot or cold, but her bones and teeth vibrated with a hum. This was magic. *Power.*

She dropped her hand and turned away. "Are they, well, *alive*?"

Hinder shrugged. "First you'd have to say what alive is."

"You must know that if you do emerge sunside," Lonender said, "and you are successful in removing the binding spells, that your tasks will have just begun."

"I know." Atan ducked her head in agreement, her throat still tight. "Tsauderei never let a day go by without reminding me of that. Ever since I was very small." She drew in a deep breath. "I know I will be a target for Norsunder, just as my parents were. As my ancestors were. I have much to learn, and I must trust my allies. Perhaps, together we can prevail against Norsunder, because I know I can't alone."

"Then we will cease issuing dire warnings," an older woman spoke from the other side of the circle.

Morvende shifted position, one or two exchanging minute, elusive signs with their fingers, and here and there a soft whisper.

Lonender said, in the Old Sartoran, "Tsauderei is known to us. His name is good."

Atan knew how to translate that: *worthy of trust,*

reliable for truth. "His name is good," she said. "To that I can attest."

"You are young," the old woman spoke again. "But you have learned to listen to wise counsel. What do you know about Norsunder?"

"Little enough," Atan replied. "Again, what I have read in records and what Tsauderei has told me, as well as what Hinder reported to you of our recent encounters. Is there something you can add, so that I might be aware?"

Lonender said, "We have in truth been in hiding this century past, except for the few who desire the sun. The news they bring back matches what you already know, that Norsunder holds some of Sartor's ancient allies, and that others pay tribute either directly or indirectly."

Again came that brief exchange of glances, signs, a breathed word or two, but Atan sensed that some sort of agreement had been made.

The youngest morvende there, a teenage girl with a merry smile, said, "Numbered among your ancestors were those we trusted with the access signs, giving them freedom to come and go among us. I will show you those signs now, if you will have them."

Atan flushed. "I know what that means. And I thank you." Then she thought of what the responsibility meant, and her joy spun away, leaving sick fear. "Perhaps you should wait. I mean, I must go out again, and I know the enemy is waiting. But there is something I must do." Her voice trembled. She stilled it with an effort. "If I succeed. Perhaps then."

Again she noted the stirrings, the sense of signals, but the faces turned to her were kind and understanding, and though Grandfather smiled, there sadness in it. "We honor you for your concern on our behalf. Be at peace. The signs might come to your aid. As for being forced to reveal what we teach you, remember this, for we do, always. The Great Betrayer, who reigns now in the Garden of the Twelve—he was once one of us."

Hinder's mother held out her hand. "We shall begin here, with this region..."

"I think I can hear the morvende talking to Atan," Lilah exclaimed. "Are they all close by?"

Hinder was dancing around the cave, a hopping, spinning dance that looked like fun, but he performed it with his eyes shut, as though he heard music that Lilah could not.

When she spoke, he stopped. "I hate to keep saying what has to sound silly, but *close* and *far* don't mean much here." He hesitated, then shook his head, hard enough to send his silky white hair flying. "What I mean is, they are kind of close, yes, but your hearing is happening because you're thinking about them, not because they're in a cavern nearby."

Lilah shut her eyes and thought about Atan. "Flowers. Rocks. Atan is talking about flowers and rocks, or else I'm dreaming. Urk! I *feel* like I'm in a dream—that if I lie down, I'll sleep for a year!" She threw her arms wide.

Hinder looked at her flushed face and recognized how close he'd come to saying what he must not say. The exhilaration of the jewel cave was turning into that dreamy state that made one want to talk recklessly. "It's time to go." He pointed. "Now comes another thing you will like, the warm pools. And rocks you can dive off!"

Lilah clapped her hands. "Let's run!" She welcomed the idea of a cool dash downward with a pool at the end, after the boiling toil of the upward climb.

They began a race, laughing all the way.

EIGHT

Merewen wandered along a narrow rock bridgeway between two old tunnels, peering down into the immense cavern and admiring the subtle ways the glowglobes at various levels gave light. Up, down, and side to side had never been so interesting. The floor was not even, the walls not straight. She had never thought about it before, but the people who lived on the surface seemed to value symmetry. Here, in the caves underground and in the mountains, there was no such thing, and as a result, no view in any direction was ever boring.

With sorrow she remembered Savar's little house, and though it had been cozy when a fierce blizzard blew, the rest of the time she'd stayed outside as much as possible. She had never liked being closed in. Was that her human side or her Loi side?

In dreams she could sometimes hear the Loi. She knew they were there but a kind of curtain divided her from hearing and seeing them in waking life. No, it was more like fog or smoke. She knew there was something she ought to be doing to reach them, for they tried and tried to reach her through her dreams, but she'd learned that dream images could not be trusted, because when she was awake, nothing worked.

It did not upset her, for she knew she had so very much to learn. More troubling were the occasions when she accidentally slipped inside someone else's dream.

She hadn't discussed that with anyone, not even Atan, who might feel obliged to tell the people whose dreams Merewen accidentally visited. She loved Atan, who 'felt' like clean-running stream water, whose inside—dreams, even—was just the same as her outside. But Atan made herself do what she saw as her duty, including telling people things. Merewen was not certain that some of the things she herself was learning ought to be told.

Down here in the morvende part of the world, she always knew where she was—just as she knew, somehow, that four days had passed since Hinder brought them inside in order to escape the enemy who roamed on the surface searching for them.

Was that the Loi side or the human? She couldn't figure that out either. She had observed that the morvende were not telling the Shendoral children that some of the pools and lakes were full of live beings, and that the water in one pool could transfer you to water in other places. Distance did not mean anything to those water beings, any more than did physical form.

This, like being in dreams, felt like 'privacy.' Merewen had learned about privacy when she and Atan first met the Shendoral group. Some days, the boys wanted to swim in the stream without their clothes on, and on those days, the girls went elsewhere. It was the same when the girls wanted to swim. Atan had told her that was privacy of person. Merewen could understand that concept; your inside and your outside had a boundary between. Clothing was a boundary between your physical self and the world. The boundary around dreams and emotions was harder to define.

She heard voices and glanced below. Ah! Two adult morvende appeared from one of the steeper trails above, leading Irza, her sister, Julian, and a couple of the other ones who thought a lot about ancestors and titles.

Irza wanted to find the secret of the way out. Merewen had heard her say so to her sister when everyone woke up. But Irza seemed to think they were all still under the hill where they'd been found. No one appeared to realize that the bath pool had transferred them a very great distance and they were deep in the mountains. Irza might go up and up and up, but it would take days to make her way to the surface.

Merewen listened. The morvende were not telling her that now, either. "You might get lost," one man was saying. How beautiful their voices were! "We do not wish harm to come to you. It is so easy to lose oneself here, for there is no sense of north and south, not the way you sunsiders orient yourselves on the surface."

"Oh." Irza laughed. "I didn't think! I just explored, because it's so very fascinating. If you could guide us to an intersection with the surface, just so we could orient ourselves. We won't peek! I just want to make sure we are less of a bother..."

There she went again. So often, Irza's inside intent was directly opposite her outside intent. It made Merewen dizzy, as if her eyes saw double. It hurt. But to say out loud that she saw this contrast would be a trespass against privacy. Merewen understood that much.

The voices faded, and Merewen sighed. What ought she to do now?

She closed her eyes—and yes, there was Atan. Strange! She had only to close her eyes and think, and she knew where people were. She could also point to Shendoral, which lay *that* way—and to Eidervaen, where the magic awaited them inside its boundaries...

Merewen popped her eyes open. "I've never seen that before," she whispered.

Atan must know. That much was certain.

She raced back over the narrow stone arch and into the tunnel, then down, down to the water, and in. Beings crowded all around her, full of images and emotions too quick to pick out. They were very much like colored stars—similar to the gems grown in those caves where people could go to be in dreamtime, and hear the beings and be heard by them. *Selenseh Redian*, that was the human name for those jewel caves. Sel-enseh red-yan, the old Sartoran pronunciation. Very, very, *very* old! Merewen knew somehow that those jewel caves had been made by these beings, as a kind of guide for humans to come and communicate—

Merewen climbed out of the water and dashed between the stones with the magic that made you dry. She found Atan alone on one of the ledges with pillows, eating some of the cakes that tasted so good.

"Merewen!" Atan smiled a welcome, and Merewen hugged herself, delighting in how the smile came with light from inside Atan's spirit. "Hungry?"

Merewen discovered that she was.

"I don't know how they get their food," Atan said. "I was just thinking about it. They don't have any sun to grow things, and though I know there are ways to make food by magic, that expends a tremendous amount of magic. Just think of it! You have to hold it all in your mind and do every step through spells, from seed-gathering to growing, and water and sun, and harvest and milling. Much easier to get it the regular way!"

Merewen suspected that the ways distances could be circumvented had to do with food distribution — ah. When she closed her eyes, inside was an image of the plateaus on Sky Island, where surface-living mountain morvende grew things. Then there were caves with the crystal lights above, below which trees grew, stately and as nearly symmetrical is could be, for there was no wind or weather, and all the water flowed from below. And there were other morvende who traded talk as well as goods. But she only smiled and bit into the rice-and-nut cake, and then said, "Is it good, the talking?"

"It's strange," Atan said, her forehead puckered. "There is so little time, and though they've been very nice, I could not but be aware that they were testing me with every single question. Every word. Yet I could feel how they want to trust me — " She paused, thinking, *Just as I want to trust Irza.*

Merewen didn't hear the thought, but she didn't need to. Atan's expression was the same one she often wore when Irza talked.

Atan finished her cake, got to her feet, and dusted off her tunic. "I know they won't mind if I test something with you also, if you don't mind shutting your eyes at the end."

Merewen nodded, enjoying the glee that Atan tried so hard to hide. She would also have her chance to discuss her discovery with Atan, and not have to watch for those who might want to listen.

They ran up one of the narrow tunnels, noting the transition from stone to clay-covered dirt that marked off access-ways. The clay in the old access-ways had slowly dried to a soft gray, but the newer ones were still brownish. It took centuries for the color to alter, Atan had been told.

Centuries. And immeasurable distances. And another language. She had always wanted to see where the morvende lived, but her imagination had fallen far short of reality.

She was both flattered and afraid, because they had chosen to show her not just a local access, but how to read the signs marking any access on the world — and how to activate the magic protections.

She did that when they reached the end. Atan gave Merewen an anxious glance, and Merewen obligingly shut her eyes — though if she *reached* with her inside self, she could see the stylized carving that Atan traced so carefully with her fingers.

Always a narrow crack existed, masked by so limited an illusion that anyone trying to sense magic would have to find the spot and touch it before discovering it, and they were always behind great stones. Then one touched the carving and said the words, and the boundary vanished.

Atan and Merewen stood very still, their skin roughing as cold air flowed from the outside world. There were no sounds and no sense of Norsundrians present.

Atan made the last passes and said the words that enabled them to slip out. They found themselves on a barren hillside. Above, snow clouds covered the pale winter sky. Golden shafts slanted down, and Atan blinked in pleasure.

She turned back, and panic fluttered inside her. She couldn't see the access! But she *knew* the stone. So she knelt, ran her fingers over it, and was reassured when she felt the subtle indentations of the access, right where it should be. "We did it."

"Eidervaen lies that way," Merewen said, pointing. "I found it, inside." She smacked her forehead. "And I know where it is you need to go."

Atan stared at her in amazement. "You do?"

Merewen closed her eyes. "There's magic there, needs to be free. Other magic is already free. I can feel it all around. Some of it is dangerous. Something happened there, while we were below."

"What?"

Merewen sighed. "All I can feel is magic. Like lightning, and not."

"And naught. And naught!" Atan said, and laughed. "Ah, Merewen, we will have to make our try soon." Fear and delight, and excitement and dread, swooped inside her, making her giddy. "But I must make myself ready. Thinkest thou we shall one day be the subject of great ballads?" She had dropped into the old-fashioned Sartoran that some of the morvende had spoken to them. Its quaintness was instantly familiar to Merewen, who had been read to from very old texts by Savar.

"Mayhap," Merewen said, delighted to play with the language she'd heard every day as a small girl, and never since. "I should like me a great ballad with all our names enflowered amid heroic deeds."

"Better that than to be mere examples of woe and sorrow." Atan wrinkled her nose. "Oh, now leave me to ponder. I shall have Sana write it but insist she shall cast it in most proper pompous language, full of praises—"

"Old-word praises," Merewen said happily as they neared the top of the hill. "I myself would be yclept fair and—"

"And fell! Nay, that would be our enemy, sore afraid—"

"Wouldst thou," began Merewen. "Full of dole—"

"Hark! Believeth-me there is yonder a—"

"Flapdoodle," Merewen supplied, remembering one of Rip's favorite insults.

She gripped her elbows, laughing inside—too delighted with their game to note much beyond the fact that they'd discovered another person, but since the tall—*boy? young man?* sitting on a rock at the bottom of the ravine did not raise any sense of alarm in her, her interest was fleeting, and she scrambled through memory, trying to find more words.

Atan had stopped. Her first instinct was danger— she felt horribly exposed, being on the outside again. But she'd come to rely on Merewen's instincts, and Merewen smiled at the boy with no indication of worry or distrust. "Let us step yonder and inquire of him his wherefores and forebyes!" She wondered if she had just encountered her very first Sartoran citizen, outside of the Shendoral orphans.

As she and Merewen picked their way down, the fellow stood up — and up and up. He was the tallest boy Atan had ever met, and she was tall for a girl her age.

He was also older. Not grown, for his hands were larger yet, his wrists bony, and there was no hint of beard on his face; she knew that that started when young men crossed the puberty threshold, once they were full-grown. Though this one must be near, for he was quite tall indeed and broad through chest and shoulder.

He had a long face with strong bones, deep-set dark eyes, an abundance of badly cut waving dark hair, and a generous mouth. An interesting face.

He said, "I'm looking for the Landis princess."

"Why, that is I," Atan exclaimed. She was so surprised that at first she did not register the muted clack and clatter that indicated they were not alone in these hills.

The boy turned his head, his hand out, and then he looked back, his mouth grim. "They did find my trail again. I'm afraid I brought danger on you."

Horse hooves! Pursuit?

Atan looked helplessly at Merewen, who waved her hands and keened, "Take him in! Take him in!"

Atan relied on Merewen's instincts. "There's a morvende tunnel near here." Atan looked around fearfully. "But we daren't use it if they can see us."

For answer, the fellow ran a few steps down the little ravine, cupped his hands, and shouted something in another language.

Then he returned, bent to pick up his pack — and they heard horse hooves clattering on the other side of the hill.

"Fast, fast," Atan whispered as they scrambled back up the trail. They reached the rock, but how to protect the access? She could not betray the morvende — despite the danger!

Merewen said, drawing the fellow's attention away, "Who are you?"

"Rel," he said, and he obligingly kept his gaze averted.

With shaking hands Atan did the magic, the tunnel opened, they slid in, and she made the sign to close the place behind them.

They stood in the narrow tunnel, Rel stooping his head.

"You're here to help," Merewen observed, looking up into his face.

"Well, yes," Rel said, and gave her a brief grin, barely discernible in the weak light reflected from down the tunnel. "But I hope you don't want me taking on Kessler Sonscarna and Dejain alone."

"Dejain?" Atan asked. "There was one called Zydes, I was told, but I don't remember mention of a Dejain."

"Magician. Considerable ability. Not good, finding her here."

Atan understood then that Rel had been making a joke about taking on the enemy alone. He didn't laugh, and his deep voice hadn't changed, but there was a suspicious narrowing of the eyes, and the realization was so unexpected that she did laugh.

It was a merry sound, free and unaffected. Rel was amazed that a daughter of the legendary Landises, rulers of the world's oldest kingdom and emblems of what history, song, and story claimed to be the most sophisticated court in the world, should be so ordinary of countenance — except for those distinctively shaped eyes, which had stared out of so many old portraits and histories — dressed in an old-fashioned, threadbare riding tunic and trousers. No, not ordinary. That word did not encompass that sense of fun, the quick alertness, the concern for others, or the mannerisms natural and free, not in the least court-trained.

The little one asked him questions, gazing at him with an unblinking blue stare. He answered very much at random, trying to marshal his thoughts.

Why could he not think? Perhaps it was hunger and thirst, or the residue of whatever spell had held him in Eidervaen until he'd gotten too weak to move, and then there had been the discovery of Kessler and Dejain—

"You've never heard of Eidervaen?" the little one persisted.

"The capital," Atan said. "We will be going there soon, to destroy Norsunder's spells if we can." She glanced back, tense and concerned. "How did you come to be here?"

Rel sighed as they descended the last bit and he was able to stand upright. He rubbed his neck. "In the ravine, or in the kingdom?"

"Um, both," Atan said, noticing that he spoke with a trace of accent. And she remembered his shout in that unknown language that had decoyed the Norsundrians. What had *that* been about?

"I was in Eidervaen for some time. I don't know yet how long. Caught in some kind of spell, until a man came along and gave me a thump to wake me up. Said to go south and find you, because you'd need help. I recognized your family name, of course. As for why I came to Sartor, I'm here because I wanted to see it —" He shrugged. "And I seem to have a nose for trouble. As for the ravine, I ran from some searchers. This ravine took me out of their line of sight. I was going to wait for dark before pushing farther south."

"It's good that you're here to help," the little one piped, and when he looked at her, she gave him a sunny smile and said, "I'm Merewen. Now, how much do you know of our history?"

She began talking about the old war, and about Savar and the orphans in Shendoral, as they crossed a great cavern. In the distance Rel heard singing, a waterfall of sound that tied together with echoes some of the ballad forms he'd encountered in his ramblings all over the southern hemisphere.

An inadvertent intake of breath silenced Merewen.

"I'm sorry," he said.

"You like the singing? So do I," Merewen said. "Very much. We're to hear more chamber singers later — oh! Here come our others."

Rel soon found himself surrounded by young people of various ages, including morvende, and all curious. When Atan announced that she and Merewen had just rescued him and that he was there to help, some cheered, some exclaimed, and a few eyed him speculatively.

One black-haired young fellow sidled up, and when no one's attention was on them he murmured, "Can you use a sword?"

"Yes," Rel said.

The boy seemed relieved. "We're going to have a practice after the next meal. Atan wants to try for the city soon, and I don't know what kind of defense we can count on there."

"Not much," Rel admitted. "I was in Eidervaen not long ago. Most of the people are still dazed, many still frozen, and Norsunder is patrolling it. Tight grip."

The boy nodded and ran head down the tunnel, probably to pass the word.

Atan led the rest more slowly, everyone trying to talk over the others. They emerged in a huge cave, at the center of which had been spread a nest of pillows. A shout of approval met the news that savory-smelling soup and nutcakes awaited them.

Rel hadn't had much to eat for the past couple of days, which (he decided) explained the mental fog. He found it hard to concentrate on any one person unless he was addressed directly. Mostly he ate, grateful for warmth and good food, and he enjoyed the chatter of high voices around him. It reminded him of friends far away in Mearsies Heili on the continent of Toar —

When he looked up next, it was to find himself being stared at speculatively by a self-possessed girl around Atan's age, her face framed in curly bright hair.

"Are you some kind of prince on a quest?" Her tone made the question a joke, but her eyes were too appraising for that.

"No," he said, setting his plate down. "I'm just a wanderer. Father was a shepherd, I understand, though we've never met."

"Ah." She nodded and turned away in scarcely disguised disinterest.

Rel chuckled inside and reached for another helping of nutcakes.

NINE

A tan loved the caves. She loved the people. But every day that passed increased the danger that Norsunder would find out that the enchantment was disintegrating, and come back to restore it.

Yet she still did not know how she was to destroy it, and she'd been so sure that meeting other Sartorans, especially morvende, would furnish the last clues.

After a night of restless dreams, she woke up in the small, round chamber that she'd been given. The stone was smooth, as if carved out by water millennia ago, and the morvende had made it cozy with glow globes, soft rugs woven in the colors of spring flowers, and pretty knotted hangings that reminded her of rose blossoms and violets and sweet-peas. She sat up, stretching her hand to touch one of the hangings, when she heard a clack, then the ring of steel.

Sick with dread, she scrambled into her clothes and hastened out fearfully, to discover Mendaen, Rel the newcomer, and a bunch of the others gathered on a smooth platform of stone below her cave, practicing with their swords. Lilah had joined them, working away earnestly with a smoothed stick in the shape of a sword, alongside several others her size.

It didn't take long to see that Rel was not only the tallest, he was the best. Easily. He was quick and sure, warding the others' blows, then he'd stop and explain—demonstrate—and sometimes, with his encouragement, he and his partner would move very slowly through an exchange.

Atan had never held a weapon, but she could understand the principles he was trying to demonstrate. For the first time she found herself interested in self-defense, and made her way down to the platform. There she watched from the sidelines until she was joined by Mendaen.

"He's good," Mendaen said to Atan in his low, husky voice. "He's really, *really* good."

"I see that."

They observed Rel's easy strength, Mendaen with the yearning of one who has sought mastery, knows what it is but not how to achieve it, and Atan with a mix of emotions she couldn't define, except that they were intense. If he joined them, maybe they'd have a hope of succeeding.

"M'dad used to say that the big fellows were never fast, just strong, but Rel's both strong and fast." Mendaen grinned. "Though he doesn't brag, as you can see. Opposite. He told us he's tangled with that Kessler once, in the past, and Kessler whupped him bad."

Atan was surprised by the sharpness of her disappointment. She recognized the cause: she wanted to believe he was the best. Then she steadied herself with inward laughter. Even if one person was the best in the world, he's still one person. You don't defeat Norsunder with one person, however good he is with a sword.

And if Rel himself admitted that that horrible Kessler was better... "Does that mean he thinks we ought to abandon our plans?"

"Oh no, not at all." Mendaen shook his head vehemently. "He says we can't take on any of Kessler's people by force, because they're too well-drilled, but we might be able to get in by stealth."

Atan snapped her fingers. "Irza! She got Arlas out through the drains going through the old ruins."

Mendaen dropped his gaze at the sound of her name, his mouth tight.

Atan said quickly, "I'll ask her if you'd rather." There was already enough bad feeling between the noble-born forest-dwellers and the rest.

"First snow!" The shout came from outside the

alcove.

Those practicing with sticks or real swords paused, looking across the vast cavern, to where a young morvende called.

"Come, everyone! Celebrate!"

Atan watched Rel carefully clean his sword and slide it into its sheath, aware of disappointment again. This time it was personal. She wanted to watch some more. But that, she decided, was selfish, and she certainly wasn't going to say it out loud. She fell in behind those streaming down to the lower level, where they discovered the entire cavern on the move, excited voices echoing.

The morvende were coming together for a great sing, in honor of the visitors and of First Snow.

The first snow in Sartor in over a hundred years.

The glowglobes had been clapped into darkness, and the vast cavern was lit by hundreds and hundreds of candles, each carried by a white-haired morvende. The opalescent glow was replicated in glints and gleams from the stone around and above them; the susurrus of quiet morvende voices sounded like a rushing river.

"There you are!" Lilah appeared and drew Atan to sit down next to her. "We snagged a good spot for listening. Hinder says the echoes will be best here. There he is, with his family."

Mendaen and Sana sank down on either side, Sana's face lifted, expressive of exaltation.

"How is the planning going?" Lilah asked. "I've barely seen you—those grownups keep talking to you."

"I know. It's like they're testing me about my magic knowledge and my awareness of history. But plans? I don't think they know what I am supposed to do any more than I do."

"Hmm. Well, we've been practicing with Rel."

"I saw that. He looks like he's a good teacher."

"Oh, he is! No swagger or boasting. Do you know he had an adventure with Kessler last year, and he was rescued by girls my age?" Lilah's tilted eyes widened with delight. "Girls who study magic! He says they get into lots of adventures. Oh, wouldn't it be wonderful to meet them?"

The morvende began to sing.

It was a simple song with no counter-harmonies, but the melody was so very old, reaching so far back into early memory that it caused many throats to constrict and eyes to burn. It was the song of Thanksgiving, brought apparently from another world entirely, and its melody had formed the basis for much of the world's musical patterns.

After it had been sung, the candles were set into flower-shaped holders, and food was passed from hand to hand, everyone taking a share. Lilah and Atan delighted in the soup with blossoms floating on top that were actually edible herbs, five different kinds of nut-cakes, and vegetable dishes made with savory sauces. The morvende, like their cousins the dawnsingers — did not eat meat, fish or fowl.

When at last they shared cups of spiced cider, the music began.

This time, everyone was enthralled, even those who had little taste for song. So many voices wove compli-cated harmonies, telling vivid stories through poetry.

Of course, there were songs that honored the Landis family, but also songs that celebrated others who counted their ancestry as part of their identity, and songs that praised all the branches of human endeavor, from cooking to weaving.

Weaving was a frequent element, Atan noticed. This was not surprising, as the deceptively plain tunics that the morvende all wore were woven of natural fibers in fascinating patterns. Colors were so muted they were more of a sheen, and because nothing was ever exposed to the elements, their garments were made for softness and for draping well. Youth dressed like Hin and Sin, in short tunics. Adults mostly wore them from knee to floor length.

The last song had ended, the echoes sounding like silver bells as they faded, when the people took their candles and began to vanish in many directions. The air was sweet with the scent of berry-wax and of cider. Already many of the younger children had fallen peacefully asleep, Julian among them, undisturbed by the quiet bare feet of passing morvende.

Tired as she was, Atan's mind was too busy remembering melodic diapason; music had been rare in

Delfina Valley, except for the weaving songs and some festival melodies, sung by the villagers. She tried to hum some of the morvende music in order to commit it to memory, but so much of it was polyphonic, or sung in round. Elusive.

Since the area that had been set aside for them was filling with those who wanted to sleep, she rose and wandered away so that no one would be disturbed by her not-very-inspiring hum, but when she recognized Rel's tall figure separating from some of the morvende boys, she turned her steps that way.

Rel saw her and paused.

"I wished to thank you for sharing your skills with the others," she said. "Mendaen tells me you're better than any of our group."

Rel opened his hands. "Anyone can improve. I promised them I'll do the best I can."

"It's good of you to make our cause your cause."

"Why not? I'm came south to find a way to help. Seems right now I've found one." He fingered the sword at his side, then gave a slight wince of regret. "Truth is, it makes me feel less bad about stealing this from one of your benighted city people."

"You can always take it back, if we are successful," she said. "And if we're not, it will not matter."

"True. I know the house and the street. I marked them especially."

She found that she'd led the way back up to the cozy stone alcove the morvende had given her. She sank down onto the pillows with a little sigh.

Rel hesitated, then ducked under the archway giving onto the alcove. He sat against the opposite wall. Atan observed with sleepy detachment that he seemed to fill the little space, yet she did not feel crowded. His hands automatically shifted the sword so he could sit, as if he was accustomed to wearing one.

"I'm going to have that music running through my dreams," he remarked. "I hope it will be for a long time to come."

Atan laughed in delight, surprised at the small spurt of gratification that warmed her—as if she'd had anything to do with the music. It was good that someone shared her enthusiasm. Even Lilah's attention had been wandering, Atan couldn't help notice. "You have not heard them previously, then?"

"Not the ones down here so far south. North, yes." And, at her prompting, he tried to describe the differences, though neither of them had a musical vocabulary.

But that led to geographical difference, and it seemed natural to ask, "Where have your wanderings taken you? Mendaen and Lilah said that you encountered Kessler Sonscarna in another place."

Rel's eyes narrowed. "I was his prisoner for a time. Refused to join his and Dejain's little project to murder every monarch they could find and govern by their warped notions of merit. Then we met again, not long ago." He shook his head. "One of the reasons I came this way was to seek some more training, because I didn't do very well either time. So I went to Khanerenth's military school for a season. Then I decided to come here. Explore as far in as I could."

"We've been alone a long time, you see. The rest of the kingdom is beginning to break free of the enchantment, but I don't think they're entirely free yet."

Rel clapped his hands on his knees. "I saw."

His expression hadn't changed, at least not overtly. But she noticed the subtle signs of reaction—of reluctance. "They are emerging from the magic and remembering the war," she observed.

Rel didn't deny it. "It's bad, some places," he admitted. "The grief is new for a lot of those people in your city." He raised his dark eyes to meet her gaze. "Even if you manage to axe the Norsunder magic, you're not going to have it easy. Some of those people are also desperately angry. Feel betrayed."

"By the king, my father. Yes, Tsauderei prepared me for that. I know that my poet of a father was a terrible war leader. No lack of courage, but Tsauderei told me once that in times of danger a poet-king is considered by some a luxury no one can afford." She saw Rel's slight wince, but he did not disagree. "If I do free us, that will, I hope, help in some measure. But the reactions are going to happen." She bit her lip, then said, "If you don't mind a question—"

Rel's brows rose. "No, I'm not a prince in disguise."

Atan's her face flooded with the heat of embarrassment. "I was not going to ask that."

Rel winced. "I'm sorry. I ought to have known *you* wouldn't —" He shrugged again.

Atan had a strong suspicion that she knew who had been asking such questions. "I was going to ask if, in your travels, you have met others my age who rule. Lilah hinted at something like it, earlier."

"Yes, I have," Rel said. "And they do well." He lifted one of his big, capable hands. "You also have a lot of young rulers behind you in your own ancestry. Quite a number. But then you know that — probably a whole lot more about 'em than I do." His eyes crinkled.

She said, "You want the truth? Sometimes my ancestral history feels heavier than all this stone above us." A sudden yawn pulled at her jaws, and though she suppressed it, tears burned her eyelids. She was desperately tired, but still she did not want him to go yet. He was interesting — he was from the outside world. "I have my ancestors' standards to live up to, in addition to the expectations of those gathered here." She opened her hand toward the entryway.

"I think I can imagine," Rel said. And then, as if in oblique apology, "I say that my father is a shepherd, but I don't really know. My guardian told me when I was small that he was a wanderer, and the only people I'd seen who wandered were shepherds, so that's how I understood the word. However, I do know there are no crowns buried under my straw mat." Rel's eyes narrowed again in amusement. "I'm not only free to wander, but free of anyone else's expectations. I have to add, after what I've seen, if I did find a crown under my bedroll, I'd be sorely inclined to chuck it into the nearest horse pond."

Atan shook with silent laughter. "No established royal family is likely to leave a crown lying about," she said finally, when she'd wiped her eyes. "Not unless there'd been a war like ours. I was hidden, though I always knew who I was." She considered. "Of course, if there'd been a revolution, I guess it might be different."

"A new government would make it their business to track the ousted rulers, wouldn't they? No one wants a newly grown prince boiling about his denied inheritance suddenly riding up—especially with an army at his back," Rel said wryly, with another brief grin that emphasized the deep dimples in his cheeks. "Especially these days, when so many of the formerly prominent kingdoms are in trouble."

"I believe I have some family—the Deis—and I might try to find them," Atan said. Then she added, for the first time ever, "Though I might not. I—I have heard mixed things. About them."

Rel's dark gaze altered again, now serious. "My guardian said my father was too restless to raise a son, and so he left. If I want to find him some day, I can. But from hints over the years, I gathered that both he and Raneseh, my foster-father, are actually from Everon. The Deis are known there." He hesitated before offering to ask, lest he come off as pushy or presumptuous.

"Ah, a kingdom with a history more tragic even than ours," Atan murmured.

"Yes. I mean to go there next, now that I've gotten a little more training and a little more experience. See what's what." There. That was general, not quite an offer.

She was wondering if it might sound pushy or presumptuous to ask him to look for descendants of her relations, then saw his jaw flex—and realized with an inner laugh that he too was fighting yawns as he added, "But I'll help here first, as long as I'm needed."

"As long as you're needed," Atan repeated, and the back of her neck heated. "You're dropping hints, aren't you? Not about the Deis. Or..."

Rel spread his hands. "This is your kingdom."

"That's no real answer. But what you said about the angry people. The breaking spell. The waiting is over. Should be over, is that it?"

Rel said soberly, "Is the release of the enchantment and the resumption of time working against you or for you?"

"It was standing still in Shendoral," Atan said. "But it doesn't, really?" She thought about the wisdom of listening, of planning, but her gaze was on his averted eyes, and a new idea occurred that made her prickle all over. "But that wasn't the real question. It's me. I. Is that what I'm doing? I'm waiting for someone to come along and tell me what to do?"

Rel rubbed his jaw. "You've a lot of helpers. All willing to do their bit. I'm among 'em."

"But I'm the one Tsauderei has been training for ten years to get the job done. And I do, sort of, know what must be done: I must get to that old Tower of Knowledge, the only structure that Norsunder was not able to destroy. Apparently something there will direct me. Except for being the last Landis—the key to the enchantment—this last bit has little to do with princesses and commons, but magic and..."

"Guts," Rel finished. He put up a hand, and his eyes watered.

Atan caught the yawn anyway.

"Then I guess it's time for me to stop dithering, and do it. Go to sleep," she said, hoping the words would set her course, give her courage, direct things to the right end. "I'll talk to the mages about any magic aids they might know to get me past Norsunder's searchers. And I need to talk to the forest-dwellers about ways into the city. If you'll keep drilling them so they feel ready, even if we can't fight armies?"

"That I can do." Rel got to his feet. "Sleep well."

He ducked out and moved away, his step light, for so big a person.

Atan stretched out on her pillows and closed her eyes.

"And you searched for bodies?"

"Four days," Kessler said.

"Four days!" Dejain frowned. "They were probably all killed."

"Maybe." Kessler's voice was flat. "We were snowbound for three. Fourth, we started the search, turning over rocks until we reached soil. All I wanted for evidence was one body. Nothing."

Dejain started to speak, but he lifted a hand, one of those quick, impatient gestures she remembered from the old days. "In shifting some of the bigger stones, we set off another landslide, lost two. Third badly hurt. We found all three of ours."

Dejain's impatience vanished, to be replaced by a

sense of threat. She'd been debating whether she was secure enough to label Kessler's thoroughness foolhardy. Now her perspective shifted. "I know there used to be caves full of the fish-skins. But their caves are weeks of travel west, I thought."

Kessler didn't disagree. He'd studied his maps.

"Those brats must have been removed by magic," she said. "But so many at once? It's a very rare mage that can manage that kind of transfer."

Kessler said nothing. He was obviously not going to speculate about magic.

"The ring." She frowned. "Why didn't you or Zydes take it from her when she was here?"

Kessler had had four days to consider whether or not he would report that he had grabbed the wrong child.

He owed Dejain nothing. In the disaster the year before, she had not betrayed him outright. She would not be standing there alive if she had. But in the process of doing what he had asked for in the way of magic, she'd secretly bound the spells somehow into some kind of complicated magical feint against Zydes, who was at that time commanding the occupation of Bereth Ferian. It was that feint that had unexpectedly helped shape his own defeat. He'd found out only after Zydes's fall, and by accident.

He had decided not to tell her that Yustnesveas Landis had not been to the Norsunder base. Just as he had not told her that he was — on his own, and whenever he could without being seen — studying magic.

He said, "She told us she'd lost it. Zydes did not deem it important enough to put her to the search."

"Fool," she exclaimed.

Kessler did not ask whether she meant Zydes or himself. He didn't care either way.

Dejain eyed him, as always unsettled by Kessler's flat affect, his utter lack of reaction. There was no discerning what he was thinking, much less what he wanted — that left her in the weaker position. (She tried not to think about what Detlev had learned about her own weaknesses when he'd asked outright — and she'd answered.)

Well, there was nothing for it. "If it's true she was trained by Tsauderei, it's possible that the ring was in part a transfer talisman. That would also explain how she and Irad managed to get away so easily," she added, keeping her words general. Kessler was not to know about her part of that business. "It's possible that she did manage to transfer them all to safety before the rock slide reached them. But where would they have gone? Have you sent someone to Shendoral?"

"Yes," Kessler said. "No report as yet. Probably won't be for days, unless you yourself want to track them down by magic. The snow was very heavy, unremitting for most of that three days. My guess is they're mired somewhere north of the wood."

Dejain hoped they were, but she didn't trust it. That answer was too easy. "There's the possibility that she and her brats have reached Eidervaen."

Kessler said, "I sent half my detachment to lock the city down. They'll be searching every house. But we'll need more people there if we're to guard the perimeter as well as the main city routes."

"The bindings have all disintegrated?"

"Not over the palace, I found out before I used this." He held out the contact token she had given him. "We sent a patrol in, and they have not come out. No one has come out, either ours or the civs."

"Detlev will have bound the palace even more thoroughly than the city, and the smaller the boundary, the easier it is to bind," she said, her thoughts skipping from subject to subject — from vexation to vexation.

Why didn't Detlev reappear and reestablish all his old spells? His absence was sinister — oh, everything about him was sinister. She'd had time to think about that abortive coup, and had come to the conclusion that Detlev had wanted her to see what happened to Vatiora. He didn't need to make any verbal threats. His actions were more effective than mere words would ever be, especially in a place like Norsunder, where everyone lied whenever convenient and there was no such thing as trust.

But there was expedience.

She would not contact him. Neither would she try any moves against him. The problem here was that she could not possibly recreate the powerful, lethally intricate enchantment that had once bound Sartor. She did not have nearly enough resources or capability to duplicate those spells — something she would not admit unless forced to.

Maybe she couldn't duplicate Detlev's magic, but she could try something different, beginning with some of the traps she'd already concocted for Zydes. Why not recast those spells in Eidervaen, only set the trap for the Landis brat?

Three days of snow meant winter. She loathed the idea of submitting herself to the merciless bone-chill of weather unleashed after a hundred years of binding.

There was no help for it, and she must not betray any sign of weakness.

She said, "Organize whatever and whoever you need. We'll transfer directly into the city. Prepare a welcome for the troublesome brat whenever she does show up."

TEN

Atan stared in astonishment at the woman with the tousled brown hair more or less pinned up by a writing quill stuck through it, her rumpled shroud of a robe worn out at elbows. "Erai Yanya," Atan exclaimed, then flushed when she remembered the last time she'd seen Irtur's mother had been right after her humiliating failure at Bereth Ferian's mage school. "How is Irtur?" she asked, hoping that the mage would not bring that incident up.

Erai Yanya flashed a smile. "Evend has accepted him as his heir. He's neck-deep in study. You can imagine how happy he is."

Atan could indeed. Erai Yanya's son was a few years younger than Atan—an insurmountable difference when they were small, but each time they'd met, the difference had been less obvious as they talked endlessly about their magic studies.

"I'm alone in Roth Drael now," Erai Yanya went on briskly. "Though I might take on an apprentice. But that's a topic for future discussion. Tell me about your situation now. I should add that Tsauderei is crouched over his scry stone like a vulture, watching for Detlev's return. He stresses that while that man..." Erai Yanya turned her head and made a spitting motion. "...is on our sister-world, causing trouble there—and our allies are doing their best to return the favor—this is the time for you to act."

"I know," Atan said. "But though there's a relatively short distance left to go, it's the hardest. As it is, I nearly got caught once. Poor Lilah Selenna was taken instead."

"I'm aware. Tsauderei agonized over that. But she's back, yes?"

"She is. I can introduce you," Atan said.

"Later. Tell me about the rest."

Atan did, in heartfelt words. All her fears, and failures, poured out. Erai Yanya listened with her steady kindly gaze, then gave a sniff. "It seems these children are not all joy, then. No authority."

"The mage Savar was to some extent."

Erai Yanya's brow furrowed. "He vanished. We can't trace him. I hope he's hiding. But we can't rely on him for help."

"And so, I keep wondering how to defend myself, and all those children, when light magic is useless in situations of battle and war."

Erai Yanya sniffed again, louder this time. "Even dark magic can't enable a weapon to fight on its own. Though some have tried that, and other foolishness — which we find a way to defeat. If we had the time, I could tell you stories about the extent that Zydes went to, before we succeeded in booting him out of Bereth Ferian! But that doesn't mean we are unable to do anything. It take imagination. And some work. So! Lonender and the elders are waiting for us, but I wanted to have a chance to see you first."

"I'm glad to see you," Atan exclaimed. "Thank you for coming."

Erai Yanya gave a grunt of laughter. "Wouldn't miss it."

They left Atan's little cave, and traveled down the path worn by many generations of morvende feet, to find the elders awaiting them. Atan's mind was on magical matters, but she noticed little Julian who had escaped her determined watchers in order to play about on the path.

The child dropped the pebbles she'd been building into a pyramid, and trotted contentedly behind Atan, who sent her a smile.

But that was all the attention Julian got, for as soon as the adults saw Atan, they started in with their earnest talk about spells and wards and traps and other stuff.

It looked like it was going to last a while. Julian looked at all the serious faces bent over the flat stone planning table, and then closed her eyes. She'd learned that the most of the older forest-dwellers thought she didn't understand anything she heard, especially when she played with her stick dolls or curled up with her eyes closed.

Well, sometimes she *didn't* understand them. Oh, she knew what each word meant, but not what they meant altogether.

Like Before, when she was almost four. One morning her mother suddenly pulled her hair. Julian remembered the smart, the sting of tears in her eyes, her own gasp, and her mother saying in a low voice, *Do not pick your nose. Princesses never put their hands near their faces.*

Am I a princess? Julian had asked, thinking of her cousins. Everyone called them 'Prince' or 'Princess'.

No, but one day you will be. Her mother had gripped her chin, which also hurt, and smiled and said, *You've got the eyes.*

She'd known what every single one of those words meant separately, but together they had not made sense, not until Cousin Atan came, and Julian saw her eyes. They were the same funny shape that her own were, when she peered into Irza's little mirror.

Another time, after one of the birthday parties, in those Before days. It had been a better birthday party than most, for Prince Iskandaer had not pushed her into a pond, or poked her when she was about to eat a bite, or laughed when her food splashed, making Mother angry not at him, but at her.

This time he'd bent down on hands and knees and let the little prince and princess cousins and Julian climb on his back. He made horse noises, and everyone had fun. Cousin Atan had been a very tiny baby then. Mother sat beside Aunt-the-Queen and laughed. Julian could still see their hair outlined in the window, Mother's light as a candle flame, and Aunt-the-Queen's dark, but otherwise they looked so alike, with their crinkled eyes and their happy laughs. But after, when they went away, Mother had said, *You will never have a sister to steal a throne from under you.*

Julian knew every one of those words, too, but not what they meant together.

Except for this: whenever her mother had talked about behaving like a princess, she had pinched and slapped and her voice was not kind or sweet. Julian had decided, right then, after that last birthday party, that she never wanted to be a princess.

"Here's the palace," Irza said, her hands moving across the stone table. Her voice was pretty when she wasn't talking right *at* you. When she talked *at* you, she sounded too much like Julian's mother had. When she talked to Arlas, her voice was pretty. She wasn't talking *at* Atan right now. "The drains go here, and here, and here. Now here are the grill-ways I remember..."

Julian lifted her eyelids for a longer peek. Irza was still bent over the smooth stone, sketching with chalk. Her curling pale hair was outlined in silver light from the cool white glowglobes overhead. It was the same color as her mother's hair. Irza had once said they were a kind of cousin. She'd seemed very happy about that. Julian didn't feel happy or sad, even when both Irza and Arlas both called her Cousin.

Julian looked at Atan. Butterfly wings tickled her heart. It was a good feeling. She'd had butterfly feelings when her mother had been happy with her, and when the Landis cousins were all kind.

Besides words, there were things she didn't understand, like how Atan, who had been the baby cousin at the last party in the old days Before, had come to Shendoral tall and older, and Julian was still six.

Julian had been glad inside when Hinder whispered to her, "Do you know what it means to have your cousin here? No one will try to make you be a princess."

How had he known she didn't want to be a princess? She hadn't told anyone. But maybe he knew why she refused to learn to read and to write, or to wear the pretty dresses that a proper princess would wear, even when Irza got that sour mouth like her mother had gotten, and talked *at* Julian about duty. Except Irza had never ever hurt her or slapped her. Sometimes she walked away, angry, but other times she'd smiled and said, *You're too little to worry about these things now. But I promise if you are brought to the throne, I'll be there to teach you. I will be your guardian and teacher, just like I was to my own sister. I will be a big sister to you.*

Irza hadn't figured out that Julian did not want to be a princess. How had Hinder done it? Was it because of his white hair? The white-haired people seemed to know things that others didn't know. But Atan did, too, and she didn't have white hair. Maybe it was the way they listened, with their gazes on you, not on the ceiling or the floor, or your messy clothes and hair, or someone else.

"...and that is all I remember about those drains," Irza finished.

"Thank you," Atan said. "These two accesses near the tower are probably what we need. If the grills still lift."

"Why shouldn't they?" Irza said. "The city has been magic-bound until recently, and I would be surprised if the Norsundrians would ever think of even looking at drains."

Mendaen said in his soft voice, "If we can get into them, we can cover you as far as the tower. We can use the decoy plan and leave someone at each drain access to lead the enemy off, if necessary. We can also begin raising the city if people are waking up. But we still cannot get you past all the Norsundrians riding around outside the city."

The others stilled. The new one, the big tall one called Rel, had been silent all along. Julian took a quick peek at him without turning her head. He reminded her of a walking mountain.

Then Merewen said, "Rel, you know what to do. Why do you not speak?"

Julian was surprised. She hadn't seen Merewen join the group. Her voice came from behind, which would explain how she'd arrived without Julian seeing.

Merewen also knew things, and she listened not just with her ears but with her whole body, like you were important, and your words were your words, not the words somebody else wanted you to say. Merewen gave Julian the butterfly-wing feeling inside.

Even at the very end, the last thing her mother ever said to her, she hadn't looked at Julian. Julian remembered her mother whispering with someone at the door, and then she sat down in the old window seat at their house, and she cried and laughed at the same time, and how frightening that had been! Every day had been frightening, at the end of Before.

After she finished crying and laughing, Mama turned to Julian, and though she talked right at Julian her eyes stared and stared, as though Julian were a window, and Mama gazed somewhere Julian couldn't see. *Dead! They're both dead, but maybe there's a throne to be wrested from the chaos. Come, child, we are going to ride!*

And then her fingers, hard as tree roots, yanked Julian—

Rel spoke. His voice was deep and quiet, and the terrible memories whipped away like wind through old cobwebs. Julian thought Rel sounded like a mountain as well as looked like one. "I hesitate to put myself forward. But there's a chance I might be able to trade on my past encounters with Kessler and decoy him, if we can catch him near the city gates. If he thinks I'm leading an attack, it might draw their attention long enough for your group to slip inside."

"But we haven't anyone to go on attack," Atan said.

Grandfather Lonender said, "Remember, you have magic. All Norsunder needs is to *think* they are being attacked."

"Ah. Illusion. *That*, I can help with," Erai Yanya said, smiling.

Dejain pulled her coat closer about her and retied the sash, but it made no difference. Drifts of snow swept out of the low, iron-gray sky and stung her face. Her nose and lips were nearly numb, making it almost impossible to perform magic.

Kessler had permitted his guards to build a fire here atop the sentinel station on the city gates. She bit the glove fingers, pulled her hands free, and plunged them toward the fire, as close as she could bear. The prickles of discomfort were stronger than the warmth, but she ignored them. Damn it anyway, how one needed gesture and word in order to get the human brain to compass

magic and execute it. To mumble, to make a vague
gesture, was to lose control of ingathering power. With
dark magic's lack of safeguards, that could kill you.

She bent her face down, hoping to thaw it. Through
the wavering smoke-wreathed air she studied the north.
It was very irritating that she had to stand on the city
rampart, but the magic had not worked in any of the
sheltered places she'd chosen previously. She huffed a
laugh and watched her breath fog. It was gratifying to
have discovered a weakness in Detlev's magic; the
interlocking of his spells into the great enchantment
should not have negated other magic.

But that did not help her now. She'd been forced to
come up here, where there was no lingering trace of
Detlev's spells, and where she would have an unimpeded
view of the progress of her workings; she knew she
should probably be closer to the tower, but she wanted
the proximity of the fire.

No one, save Kessler's pairs of riders, was in view.
He'd apparently established two perimeters, one outer,
patrolled by riders, and the inner one along the city walls.
It was efficient. No one was going to get past him. His
efficiency, unfortunately, increased the sense of pressure.
The weak link in this chain of defense was magical.

Rubbing her still-tingling hands, she turned her
head and glanced down into the city, sloping away to the
southeast. No one walked the streets, except warriors at
the two visible crossroads. Yellow lights glowed between
the shutters of some of the houses, but this wing of the
old palace was still dark, and Kessler couldn't patrol that.
At least, the people he'd sent in had never come out. The
ancient tower at the west end, the lower half ivy-covered,
the upper half made of bone-white stone, looked blank.
It, too, was unapproachable, lest one get bound in the
still-powerful spell whose periphery had diminished, but
whose strength within those borders had not.

She had tried to approach the tower herself, but
warning magic caused a hasty retreat, and the unsettling
awareness that Detlev's fading binding spell was, despite
its limitations, despite its diminishment, stronger than
any new one she could cast.

Well, but how long had it taken him to lay this
enchantment? Maybe weeks — months. If she had enough

time, she could layer plenty of wards over this accursed place.

She just had to lay the first one, and have it stick.

She clapped her hands, which were now warm enough. The smell of singed wool augmented the sting of heat as her clothes shifted. She stood so close to the fire she was nearly in it, but at least it had thawed her.

She straightened up, raised her hands, and performed the ward-spell she'd prepared—

Bluish lightning flared, rippled over the rooftops, bounced away from the white tower, and dispersed like a spill of milk across the sky.

She stared, aghast. *Warded!* No, it was worse than that. This ward was stronger even than a mirror ward, which was the most formidable type of ward she knew.

There was nothing for it. She tightened her coat and hood, drew her gloves back on, and fixed her attention on the wall nearest that tower. The she transferred. When the transfer-nausea faded, the cold bit into her with fangs of ice. She looked down at crystallized moss along the worn sentry path at her feet, and then up at the tower. Smooth white stone gleamed beneath ivy. She could always try to bring the thrice-damned thing down. Fire was useless against rock. Was there a loose stone somewhere? Some rubble or mortar that could be shifted?

No. She bent and picked up a pebble. Transferring something solid into the wall might at best make cracks— if she judged the distance right—but it would suffice as a test.

She performed the spell, keeping her gaze on the smooth tower wall at eye level, finished, and felt the snap of power—

The stone shattered into dust, which the wind dashed away in a blink. She bent, picked up a smaller stone, and this time attempted to transfer it inside the tower.

Magic glowed, blue and threatening. It flashed in echo far in the distance, against one of the mountains.

Her stone landed with a *thok!* at her feet.

Two ineffectual tries. The transfer, and the cold left her feeling as brittle as old leaves. With the last of her strength, she transferred back to her spot by the fire and stood there until she'd recovered, her hands out and head bowed to hide the reaction. Hide her defeat. Hide the fact that no amount of magic that she could concoct any time soon was going to make any difference to that level of power.

She closed her eyes. It wasn't just this tower. The weird, mysterious magic of whatever origin that she'd heard so much about was real, and furthermore it was free again. Free, and maybe even stronger than it had been, after the long binding.

Maybe this was why Detlev had dropped the matter into her hands. He might know that he wasn't going to prevail, so he was in effect leaving someone else in charge of a disaster. No — that was too easy. This is *Sartor*. Its loss would catch the eye of Them, in the Garden of the Twelve.

If that was so, then the logical conclusion was that Detlev expected her power to be great enough to prevail here.

Once, the idea would have pleased her. That was before she stood on this frozen rampart and nearly destroyed herself concocting spells that had about as much strength as a firefly in a rainstorm.

She had better think of something else.

She summoned one of the runners. "I am going to set wards over the roads connecting to the city. Then I will return to the Base to make more preparations. Tell Kessler he's in command here."

And she transferred out.

Lilah finished exploring a very old cave with Hinder and his friends, had a good swim at a falls, and then returned to watch Rel drilling Mendaen's group.

She sighed inwardly. She'd already decided that a few lessons with one of those swords wasn't going to make her any good at all, even with a great teacher like Rel. Nothing was going to fix the fact that she also needed years of practice. She'd have to stay out of the way.

Yet she really wanted to ask Rel to tell them more about those adventuring kids he knew. But he was so ... so ... what was he? He looked so stern. No, not stern.

Formidable. Yes, that was the word. Though from Atan's reactions the brief times Lilah saw Rel and Atan together, he couldn't be all that formidable. Atan had actually laughed, which meant he had to be making jokes, even though you sure couldn't tell from looking at him. Deon at home was like that — made her funniest cracks with a very straight face. Maybe it was just the fact that he was so tall and his face reminded her of those old stone carvings of ancient heroes.

As she stood there in doubt, Rel said, "Water break."

Sweaty forest-dwellers flopped down on their mats, slurping water from waiting bowls and jugs. Up above, Atan came out of her little stone room with the newly-arrived magician, who wore a rumpled dress and bare feet, even though her brown skin and hair made it clear she was not morvende. The mage went off in the other direction with the elders.

Lilah twitched. Everyone was busy except her, magic lessons above, and sword practice below.

No, there was little Julian, playing with her stick dolls again. Atan took her hand and Julian skipped beside Atan, dragging her ratty robes behind her. Lilah hung back. Every time she started playing with Julian, Irza turned up, crowding Lilah by blabbing on about how she was Julian's guardian during the forest days. Even though Julian didn't look particularly delighted — Lilah saw Julian looking toward Atan and Arlas more than Irza.

She turned away. Rel was alone, neatening the pile of practice sticks that the younger ones had dropped.

"Rel, do you mind a question?" she asked.

The craggy face turned. His expression didn't change, at least not overtly, but the way his dark brows twitched and his eyes crinkled that made her think he was smiling inside.

"How about we swap, one for one?" His voice was a low rumble.

"Me?" Lilah nodded, astonished. "Sure, but wouldn't it be better to ask a grownup? I don't know anything!"

Rel dropped down to sit with his back to the stone, and laid his sword beside him. "Maybe," he said.

Shadows quirked the corners of his mouth. Definitely a smile, if not very much of one. "Go ahead. You first."

"I wanted to hear more about those adventuring kids. The ones who invented the word 'kid,' which can mean a boy or a girl. *Are* they the same ones Derek told us about? You met him, right?"

Rel's face lost the hint of a smile. "We … sort of met. We were Kessler's prisoners. I do remember him. And his brother."

"Where do those kids live? What are they like?"

"They live in Mearsies Heili, which is on the continent of Toar. Some distance north, and about halfway around the world either east or west. As for what they're like..." He shrugged. "They love jokes and fun, but at the same time they're fierce in defending their little kingdom."

"Like Atan and Mendaen," Lilah said.

Rel nodded, smiling inwardly. He'd spent his time drilling these Sartoran youths until they were woozy from exhaustion. He never told them that they wouldn't be good enough, that a few days' sweating out blade drills and footwork—no matter how long or how earnestly they worked at it—was not going to prepare them to face Norsunder.

They were going to face Norsunder anyway, if his decoy plan didn't work. So he drilled them and also listened to them talk, trying to figure out how they thought. There was a lot about honor, for instance. Some of that was what he thought of as real, that is, a groping toward a greater good, but the rest of the honor-talk was the familiar, desperate not-quite-bragging that was akin to beating one's sword blade against a shield, a courage booster, a way to brace oneself to face almost certain defeat.

Then, of course, there were the one or two who had a tendency to make well-rehearsed speeches about honor and glory, as if invisible heralds were hiding behind rocks, noting them down.

Lilah was different. She really did remind him of the Mearsieans. The honor talk seemed to embarrass her. She certainly didn't add to it. Therefore, when she said apprehensively, "Your turn. You had a question?" he said honestly, "Yep. And I don't want to accidentally stumble over someone's honor without knowing it."

"Oh." Lilah breathed the word. "Go on."

"My question concerns Dorea, who told me she's a curtain runner. What's that?"

Lilah gasped, then clapped her hand over her mouth lest a snicker escape. "I *can* answer that," she whispered. "But it's only because I had to read so much Sartoran history. It's a very old fashioned custom — at least, we don't have it in Sarendan anymore. Maybe they still do in other countries. But in Eidervaen and the other big cities, only people at the highest rank issue invitations for parties and things. Everyone else either has their parlor curtains open when they want company after the late morning bells and before evening bells, or have them closed if they don't want company. Like if they're going out to visit."

"A curtain runner does what? Opens and closes the curtains?" Rel asked. "Or does it take two or three for that job?"

"No!" Lilah saw the quirk deepen around his mouth. He was making a joke! "The runner goes about whatever streets he or she is told and sees who is home and who not, and returns with the news, and then the people decide who they'll call on. I guess runners could be sent out many times in a day, no matter what the weather, and they were expected to be accurate and fast," Lilah added. "And some were good at peeking inside and seeing who was there, but they weren't supposed to be caught at it. That would be vulgar."

Rel nodded. "Now I see why Dorea mentioned it. She's got amazing endurance."

A new voice interrupted. "Anyone hungry?"

Rel and Lilah looked up. Here was Atan, alone. Lilah glanced past her and discovered little Julian sitting with Irza and her sister close on either side, like two pieces of bread outside of a piece of cheese. Julian's round face turned, her eyes wistful, then Irza whispered something, and the little girl turned back.

"I can wait," Lilah said.

Rel lifted a shoulder. "So can I. Turn anyone into a snake today?"

He said it with no change in expression, and Atan replied in her quiet, serious voice, "Rocks. Half a hundred fewer morvende, lots more rocks."

"That's where they get 'em all," Rel said, and smacked his hand against the rock he leaned against. "Did I know this one?"

"A nosy traveler," Atan said.

Lilah's mouth opened. They were joking! Just like Lilah had joked with her fellow adventurers in Sarendan! She gawked in surprise. Nobody'd *ever* gotten Atan to joke like that before!

Rel said, "We're looking as good as we can." He tipped his head. This time the chin pointed in Mendaen's direction. He was serious again.

So was Atan. "And I finished preparing my spells," she said, and though her throat hurt, she said the words, knowing that this would make them real: "After we get a good sleep, we're starting for Eidervaen."

ELEVEN

It was a nightmare.

Atan had imagined that rest, a shared meal, and a
united goal would somehow smooth all the crankiness
and fire everyone with the righteous cause. For even the
youngest understood that they would soon reunite with
any family who had survived the attack. It was certainly
that way in histories.

But they weren't united in a shared goal. First of all,
they weren't all going. Of those going, they all apparently
had ideas about what they were going to do.

To Atan's unexpressed surprise, Irza was the least
troublesome. She repeated to anyone who would listen
that she meant to get them safely inside the city — and she
repeated it to those who weren't listening. Atan heard
Lilah mutter to Hinder, "Is she looking around for a
scribe to write down all that about loyalty and sacrifice?"

Other squabbled about who was in what group,
who would lead, and how long would it take?

Rel appeared out of the bickering, fussing crowd.
He lifted his hand, smiled, and said, "We'll meet again in
the city." Then he walked away.

Atan watched him go, surprised at the sharp sense
of loss that hurt behind her ribs.

She tried to banish it by keeping busy, making
certain everyone was ready, had neatened the loaned
blankets and mats and dishes, then had thanked their
hosts. The little ones didn't argue, but needed help with

everything. The nobles balked at having to wash their dishes and put blankets through the cleaning frames, but Atan insisted by saying, "You may leave and go where you like at any time. I will not leave until this area is as tidy as it was when we first arrived."

And when that was done, and she had formally thanked their hosts, and turned to say farewell to Julian and all those under ten, Julian's sudden, shockingly wild weeping rose to a shriek that Atan had never heard from her before. "I won't stay, I won't, I won't!"

She pushed away from Coral, Hinder's mother, who had been so kind to Julian, and whom Julian had seemed to like. Atan stared in dismay, unable to move, even to speak.

Atan stared, utterly frozen. She couldn't take a six-year-old into Eidervaen, not with Norsundrians swarming everywhere!

Irza left the line and marched up to Julian. "You *said* you would stay with Coral," she said in a coaxing voice that did not quite hide her exasperation.

"I thought everybody was staying," Julian howled. "You can't leave me!"

"You are being willful and troublesome," Irza whispered, but her voice carried. She didn't care if anyone heard, because it was *true*. "I *told* you that I can't watch over you while I sacrifice myself in leading—"

Julian then put her small hands against Irza's chest and pushed. "I don't want you! I want *Cousin!*"

"I *am* you cousin," Irza stated, red in the face.

"YOU'RE NOT!" Julian shrieked, and ran to Atan. "You can't leave me, you can't!"

Atan gripped her hands tightly together. She understood that Julian was being both willful and troublesome, but was that a bad thing when you were six and you thought you were being abandoned?

Atan knew it would be completely wrong to bring a six-year-old. But wasn't she just as wrong to bring these others? Was ten really old enough to face an enemy like Norsunder?

"I *won't* stay, I *won't* stay," Julian sobbed. "Atan, you *promised...*"

Irza knelt down and took Julian's shoulders. "Behave yourself! You are acting like a brat, not like a princess," she hissed.

Julian shrieked on the word princess, her face purple.

Atan's nerves flared. She held out her hands, hoping no one else saw how they trembled, and said, "Julian, come with me. But you will have to be as a mouse when we need you to. All right?"

Julian wrenched out of Irza's grip and ran to Atan, and though she still gulped and shuddered, and her face was wet with tears and snot, she was no longer screeching.

Atan said over her head to Coral, "I'm sorry."

Hinder's mother said sadly, "The child seems to need you. And you are all in danger." Her soft words hit Atan like an invisible fist.

Atan drew in a breath. "Let's be quick."

The trip didn't take long. Julian clung tightly to Atan's hand, but when it came time to move up the last tunnel in the dark, Arlas and Irza caught up, and Arlas whispered to Julian, "We do want you, Julian. We do, it's just we didn't want you in danger, and that's where we're going."

Irza said, "That's right."

Julian gave Arlas a troubled look. "I will be quiet as a mouse." She hiccoughed, running closer to Atan, so that Atan nearly tripped on Julian's train. "But you promised, Atan. You promised."

"What did I promise?" Atan asked. "I didn't think I promised to take you into danger."

"You promised not to leave me."

Atan's throat hurt. "Julian, the worst danger will be there, where I am. I might have to ask you to hide. Can you do that, if I ask you to?"

"Not in the caves," Julian said, hiccoughing again.

"Not in the caves," Atan agreed in defeat.

"It's time for quiet," came Hinder's soft voice from the front of the line. "Take hands, for we will be walking in the dark the last little way."

Atan's fingers were tight in Julian's grip. She reached with her free hand to take Lilah's square, capable hand. Somehow she felt a little better, though she knew that nothing was better, their task was still impossible.

The darkness closed in. Atan listened to the quiet

shuffle of their feet. To distract herself, she tried counting steps until light shafted ahead, cold air rolled in, causing shivers, and they emerged from the tunnel into a wintry day.

Lilah dropped Atan's hand so that the Sartoran princess could go to the front of the group and do the magic fog spell she'd prepared. Julian trotted after, and Lilah hoped that the little one wouldn't get hurt. She didn't want anybody hurt!

Amusement spurted through her when she saw Irza poking about the entry. Did she think she was fooling anyone, pretending to fix the tie on her shoe as she scanned for some sort of sign? Lilah was sure that the morvende would be changing the tunnel access as soon as everybody was out, and she snickered under her breath.

Why would Irza want so badly to know how to get in and out anyway? She didn't seem to be interested in the caves all that much. Maybe she was one of those who liked knowing secrets just because they were secrets. Funny, how different people could be.

Different indeed. From the silver world to the gold world, Merewen thought happily as she took in the peachy-yellow early morning light. The morvende and the surface worlds were both beautiful, and so different!

Mendaen searched the horizon all the way around for warriors. His breath hurt, he was so worried. Atan was a mage, but what if Norsundrian warriors found them? He wished Rel was there to lead them. They couldn't possibly fight off Norsundrians.

He gripped his sword hilt in his sweaty fingers. *Defend Atan. Fight until I die.*

While he watched the horizon, Atan looked around at the early sunlight shafting between the big snow clouds drifting across the morning sky. The hills lay smooth and white as she and her band picked their way down a rocky ledge that the wind had swept clean. An icy breeze buffeted their faces. Here and there, low-lying tendrils of fog coalesced and drifted along the ground in puffy cotton snakes.

She breathed in the dank-stone smell of fog, sensed no wards or traps, and appreciated the subtlety of light magic, drawing moisture from the water-saturated

ground to mix in the air. Dark magic would have forced
a fog so heavy and so pervaded with magic that it would
feel unnatural, and the effects would rile the weather
patterns for weeks. Or longer.

"Try not to leave prints," Mendaen muttered to a
couple of younger forest-dwellers, who had ranged away
from the rocky trail into the thin layer of snow, glancing
around anxiously.

Atan took in the morning-lit faces, red noses, and
hunched shoulders as her band picked their way single
file, the last two using a couple of branches to walk
backward and blur their tracks. She could see in the sharp
angles of skinny shoulders, the stiff or nervous fingers,
the quick glances that everybody was aware that they
might not live to see the next dawn.

Atan bent, put one palm on the cold rock, and
jumped down to the next level. She half-lifted Julian
down, then they rounded a huge boulder and skidded to
the flat ground. Julian gave a soft laugh after skidding.
Atan was relieved to hear the sound, but then the worry
closed in the sharper because Julian was so small.

Atan looked around. The wind scoured over an
overturned wagon, one wheel spinning with lazy
slowness.

"Oh," someone said.

They surrounded the wagon, and a couple of the
smaller forest-dwellers searched around in the snow,
finding a broken basket and a bundle of cloth that had
frozen solid. Atan's stomach churned. The wagon had
been looted more than a hundred years ago, the drivers
killed and gone—but it had happened recently to the
Sartorans they would soon meet. The forest-dwellers
stared at the wagon in muted horror, the more thoughtful
turning anxious glances at the road.

Atan gently disengaged her hand from Julian's so
she could lay her hand on the wood, old and not old, but
before she took two steps, a flash of light color startled
her, and Merewen stood between her and the wagon.

Merewen did not seem to mind the cold any more
than the morvende did. She gazed up into Atan's face,
her own anxious in the strengthening sunlight, as she
said, "I—I don't know why. But I wish you wouldn't
touch that thing."

"Why not?" Atan asked.

Someone muttered about splinters, but Merewen frowned at the ground, then at the sky, and shook her head. "Fire. I saw fire, here." She touched her head. "And here, too." She laid her hand over her heart. "When you started toward it."

Atan drew in a slow breath. "Of course. I know, that is, I think I know what it means. Tsauderei has taught me about the standard dark magic wards when they want to prevent someone entering a place. There are probably fire wards on every single conveyance within half a day's travel. They do not know that we are walking."

Merewen looked troubled.

Atan lowered her voice. "I thank you for the warning, but please don't get between me and danger. Then two of us are threatened. Just shout at me. Or grab my braid or something." She tried to smile.

Merewen tried to smile back, but her round, sky-colored eyes were wide, and her forehead was puckered with concern.

Atan said to the others, "Single file! Let's go."

Wind had blown most of the snow against the east and south sides of the road bank. Ice puddles and rock-hard frozen ground curved south toward the city. Drifts of her fog began to swirl northward. Atan thought she could make out the city's towers, gray pencil marks on the white horizon.

It was her ancestral home. But not yet *her* home.

They began to walk toward those distant towers, Irza in the back looking around with a troubled, intense air, and Julian so small and so trusting.

Irza ignored the child, for now. She had greater concerns, like the future and her position in it. Her hints and questions and wanderings had produced absolutely nothing with respect to those morvende accesses. Her overt admiration of their music and weaving and other arts had not netted her any invitations to inner secrets.

She surveyed the featureless snowy countryside. The prospect for glory was nigh, and it was her duty to see that the Ianth name was among those sung at the triumph celebrations, whether they survived or not. But she wanted to survive, to *hear* it.

Atan turned to Lilah. "Rel must be well ahead. We

have a long road still before us. Let's run."

Rel urged the fresh, mettlesome young horse he'd caught wandering toward Eidervaen's south gate. He was impressed with the speed with which the morvende had produced the news that Kessler was currently south of the city on a tour of inspection.

Though the morvende weren't in any way a military culture—he hadn't seen a sword anywhere except for his stolen one and the few belonging to the forest-dwellers—they seemed to have quietly and efficiently developed a formidable defense strategy.

It made sense, he thought as he breathed in the foggy air. Fighting with long blades in uneven tunnels was a fool's game. It made better sense to strike and run, and use the dark and confusing tunnels to get away. In the big caverns, arrows would be useful. Those steady breezes from the air vents underground meant little would spoil your aim.

He'd learned that trust among new allies had to go both ways. He would give no sign that he'd noticed how the carvings on the various stones set about so decoratively around some of the tunnels varied between one dip in the bathing pools and the next. The tunnels also had different markings.

The horse shimmied sideways, then halted, flicking its tail, ears flat. Rel made out the soft thud of hoofbeats in snow.

This had to be Kessler's outer perimeter. That didn't mean he was with the riders. In fact, that seemed too great a coincidence—unless the morvende had somehow managed to guarantee it wouldn't be any coincidence, by letting Rel out the adit nearest the enemy. If so, their abilities to spy far surpassed his guesses... *Later.*

Rel stared into the thickening fog as it eddied and whorled away from the riders intersecting his path. He made out two, four, six, eight shadows, and a ninth at the lead. Despite the bitter cold, Rel's palms were damp, his armpits soggy, and he hoped the ensorcelled stick Atan had given him wouldn't fail to work because of the damp air, like tinder failing to spark.

A gust of frosty air revealed the foremost rider. His cheeks and nose were blotchy red, and fog-damp hair slung in curls across his forehead, so sharply did his head turn. Rel did not recognize Kessler until he met those blank blue eyes.

He broke the stick that Erai Yanya had given him, clamped his legs against the horse's sides, and raised his fist as if in signal. His heart lifted when he saw the ghostly forms of riders appear, helms gleaming. The illusion spell was impressive!

Time to ride.

Kessler recognized Rel and frowned in confusion. Rel was a part of another life completely. Last seen in Mearsies Heili, when he'd attempted to find out why the Mearsieans had betrayed his plans.

Then Rel shouted something in Mearsiean, wheeled his horse, and clucked for the animal to gallop. Behind him, barely visible in the fog, rode a good-sized host of helmeted and mail-clad riders.

Where had they come from? This had to be dealt with. Kessler said to his aide-de-camp, "Back to the city. Order the southern roads sealed off."

Then, whipping his tired mount into a gallop, he set off in pursuit of Rel and his ghostly entourage, the rest of his patrol riding in perfect formation at his back.

Atan and the forest-dwellers ran, slipping and falling in icy patches, while Kessler's aide galloped flat out for the city gates.

The aide reached the gates, shouting Kessler's order. Sentries on the gate shot fire arrows upward in signal. The pinpoints of flame turned the grim, cold city into an ant-swarm of activity.

The Norsundrian guards had been bored and cold. They were delighted at the prospect of action. Quickly they assembled outside the south gates, one wing to guard, and the other as reinforcement to Kessler's patrol. They rode south to the expected attack.

About the time they reached the outer perimeter and the wing commander spotted a patrol to hail for the latest report, Atan and her group reached the northwest wall of the city.

The fog was thick, and though the sun was almost as high as it was going to get on this wintry day, the sentries on the gates could see and hear nothing amiss from the mist-obscured ground. Everyone's attention was either southward or on the roads directly below the gates.

When the forest-dwellers began to make out the wall through the thinning mist, Atan waved Irza to the front to take the lead.

Irza did so, trembling with excitement. *She was now the leader!* Fear curled through the excitement: what if her memories were untrustworthy?

Then she spotted the very same juxtaposition of wall and old vine-wreathed trees that she had seen so long ago, and waved at the others. *Oh yes, glory at last!*

In silence they spread to search. It was Hinder's group who found the grate first, almost at the foot of the old mossy wall.

Mendaen, Brick, Pouldi, and Sana struggled with each corner of the grate, but they managed to shift the heavy iron. Below, in the dank-smelling darkness, water rushed and tumbled. Hinder sent a comical grimace at Atan, then lowered himself down.

Splash! Atan mouthed the words, *Thank you!* to Irza before she followed Hinder. Arlas and Irza followed, joyous, giddy with triumph. Why, this was easy!

One by one, the forest-dwellers jumped down, their feet splashing in a thin stream of rushing water below the city. Irza gestured for them to follow a little ways away, gathering on a broad flat area that (Irza explained rather self-importantly) had been a tiled terrace four thousand years before. Lilah gazed about in gratifying amazement.

"I think that tunnel takes you to the palace," Irza said. "I know that this way goes under Eidervaen, branching out—" And she rapidly named different city districts.

"Here is where I have to go on alone." Atan knelt down to address her little cousin eye to eye. "This is the most dangerous part of our plan. Julian, I don't think you should come into the tower. I don't know how many enemies I will find there, or how many will chase me. I would feel safer if you stayed with everyone else."

Julian leaned against her. "But she's going." Julian pointed at Lilah.

"I'm going to guard her back," Lilah said, also kneeling down. "And I have a way to fight if one of those nasty Norsundrians comes by. But you don't have a way to fight."

Merewen closed her eyes, then opened them. "You have to stay, little one," she said. "And be brave."

Everyone turned her way, Atan quickly, Lilah in apprehension, Irza impatient. To Irza, Merewen seemed half-mad, and certainly negligible as far as future social position was concerned.

Julian said, "Why?"

Merewen squatted beside Lilah, her thin cotton tunic fluttering around her bare legs. She seemed immune to the cold. She pointed upward. "The tower magic, it might swallow you up. I can't explain, but I can't *see* you there. It troubles me. I hope it means you're safest here. I don't know. It's just ... feelings I get here." She touched her heart. "I don't hear any words here." She touched her head, not telling them that she could sense the Loi as a kind of blue presence somewhere outside her thoughts. She suspected that the Loi were trying to send her words, but she couldn't hear them. This was not the time to explain her shortcomings and add to Atan's worries.

Irza stepped forward, hands on her hips in a way that Julian instantly recognized. "Julian may remain in my charge. Arlas and I know how to watch over her. She will be safe with us—or at least as safe as we ourselves will be."

Atan let out a cloudy breath. They were all in danger, but she knew hers was by far the worst. "Yes, that's a good idea. Julian, please stay. And—and if I'm successful, you come stay with me again, and you don't ever have to go somewhere else, unless you want. I promise."

Arlas knelt down and took Julian's hand in her cold fingers. "Stay, little cousin."

Julian sighed, too, her cloud smaller. "I'll stay." Her reward was a slight easing in Atan's troubled face.

"Let's go quickly then." Atan kissed Julian's brow, got to her feet, and walked swiftly away.

Hinder caressed Julian's cheek and followed. Lilah grinned at Julian, Merewen looked troubled, then they were gone, too.

When the sounds of their splashing diminished, Irza saw Mendaen about to speak, and forestalled him. *She* was the leader, not him. "It is time for us to split into our groups and get busy rousing Eidervaen."

She busily motioned the crowd of forest-dweller into their groups; most had already separated, for that had always been the plan. Some moved, but others gave her irritated glances and stayed right where they were. They would move when Mendaen moved.

Mendaen lifted a hand to his group and started off. He never spoke to Irza if he could avoid it, but he was annoyed at her taking it upon herself to utter a totally unnecessary order.

Irza watched in satisfaction as he and his group departed down another tunnel, their footsteps slow and tentative. He had no birth to speak of; nobles were born to lead.

"Now. You stay close by," Irza said to Julian. "You will have to run, for we must be swift. We're going this way, into the city."

Julian had been looking down the tunnels, then back up at the grating where it was light.

"Atan said to stay," she said. "I promised. I'm going to stay."

Irza firmly controlled the spurt of anger that made her hot inside. Julian was small, and getting more tiresome every day, but she might one day be a princess — Atan's heir — and she would need a guardian.

Irza had to make sure the child knew obedience, or what was the use?

She looked around. Mendaen had vanished down one of the tunnels, the sounds of splashing feet echoing back. She turned back to the child, whose solemn six-year-old face and unreadable Landis eyes stared back up in the weak light reflected from the grating.

"You must. Come. With. Us." Irza bit off each word sharply.

"No. Merewen said I could stay. I'm going to stay *here*. I promised Atan. She will come *here* for me."

Irza glared, her palm itching to slap that insolent

face. "This is *not* the time to act willful," she said. "She meant for you to stay with us, not stay in this gutter."

"No."

Irza gritted her teeth, then forced her voice to be even. Reasonable. "You promised to help. Obeying is helping." Her tone sharpened again. "Being a brat is *not* helping."

The word 'not' rang out, sending sharp echoes down the tunnels. Irza's group waited, some sidling looks in a way that irritated Irza even more.

Julian pointed back to the hole next to the wall. "I can help by being here," she said. "Nobody can put that thing back. Hinder worried. Atan worried. Everyone worried."

"That's true," Arlas whispered.

"Quiet," her sister ordered in a fierce whisper.

"So if I stay here, you can find me. But if *they* come, they will think I fell down here." Julian crossed her arms. "It's *my* plan. Hinder would listen. He'd let me stay."

Vanya said, "Leave her. At least we know where she is."

"And we're *all* in danger, wherever we are," added Dorea.

Irza hated to even listen to a mere curtain runner, but Atan had selected the teams, dividing up the nobles among all those of lesser rank. She wavered, then realized that standing about was not going to win them any glory at all.

She bent over Julian. "A princess," she whispered, "would do her duty and listen to her elders." She touched Julian's face — not in a caress but, quick and sharp, she pinched her ear. Hard.

Just like Julian's mother used to when she talked about being a princess.

Julian's jaw jutted, and her eyes narrowed.

Irza felt better. To forestall the brat's wailing again, she straightened up and turned away. Maybe it was better not to be slowed by a noxious, short-legged six-year-old. "Very well," she said. "*We* must do what we promised, at least." She turned a last glare at Julian. "As for you, *stay here*. And be quiet and careful."

She walked away, and as Julian faded from sight she faded from mind, for the familiar turnings of the tunnels harrowed Irza with memory. She motioned to Dorea and said, "You should be able to find out where we are."

"I never ran in the drains," Dorea said. "But I'll try."

Julian heard Dorea's voice echo, then all she heard were the diminishing footsteps. Let them go. She smiled. She had a job, a real one, an important one, that no one could take away or pretend was theirs. And nobody was going to pinch her ear and call her *prin-cess*.

She sat down on the old tile, swept clean by years of water, tucked her ragged hem around her feet, pulled Merewen's soft, warm yeath-coat around her, and looked up at the sky through the open hole left by the shifted grill.

As it turned out, she hadn't long to wait.

Kessler's instinct was to capture Rel and choke from him the reason he was here in this kingdom, how many he led, and where they were.

Very soon, he began to wonder if his first reaction — that this was some kind of ruse — might be true. Rel's unaccountable presence and his shouted command in the Mearsiean language was far too inexplicable, and the timing suspect. That suggested a deflection or decoy. Kessler would expect Darian Irad at the head of a mysteriously raised company, but not Rel.

He wheeled his horse out of the line and waved at them to continue their pursuit.

He rode hard back to the city. His horse had nearly foundered when he reached his reinforcements, who were advancing exactly as he'd ordered.

"I think it might be a feint," he said to the leader, and broke the would-be strike force into smaller groups, taking under his own command the greater number. Pausing only long enough to make one of the warriors exchange his fresh mount for Kessler's spent one, he rode off, leading his new search force.

Fog swallowed them, in some places so thick they were forced to a walk. Though Kessler could hear the others behind cursing and fuming, it gave him time to think.

If in fact Rel was running decoy here in the south, it meant that whoever he was protecting was probably somewhere in the north. The old magic tower lay at the west end, attached to the palace, which couldn't be patrolled. If an army was on the attack, they'd go for the gates. But if it was magic they were after, the tower would be the target.

Magic. Kessler dropped his hand to his pocket. Dejain had departed without giving him one of her transfer tokens.

He cursed, then said, "To the north side of the city. We'll have to search along the walls."

Dejain had been brooding about what she'd discovered to be true, and what not. She'd also reflected on the unlikelihood of any child being able to transfer thirty or forty people at once from under a landslide, which meant they'd been able to hide somehow. Every explanation opened disturbing possibilities.

The thought of going back to the palace walls was sickening. She loathed cold, but more than that she loved her command, and the way to keep it was to be thorough, to avoid disaster first. If defeat seemed unavoidable, she had to maneuver to make certain that Detlev could find no blame to ascribe to her, and that meant thinking ahead.

That meant she must force herself back to the hills where Kessler had last seen the children, and search for magic traces herself.

She didn't think it likely, but it was always possible that some of those old animal caves were disguised morvende tunnels. She hadn't heard of any geliaths this far east. Everyone knew that morvende after the Fall had honeycombed deep in the western mountains, but their geliaths were protected by very old magic that was far beyond her abilities to break. Anyway, if the ancient geliaths still existed, no one had reported seeing morvende popping in and out.

If a rabble of brats could find an abandoned, empty geliath, so could she.

A morning's fruitless search in the cold and

increasing fog had steadily diminished her hopes when she heard the sounds of pursuit. She transferred up to a hill at the edge of a wood in order to look, and found herself surrounded by even thicker fog.

A lone figure on horseback rode past her, followed by a thick swirl of such magic-charged mist a faint shimmer coruscated on the edges of her vision.

She tried to blink it away as the rider glanced back. An ebb in the swirling haze outlined a vaguely familiar shape. The low sun shone on black hair and a handsome profile that she'd last seen in Kessler's desert camp in '33. She frowned. That couldn't be that big one Kessler had taken prisoner from Tser Mearsies, could he? What was his name?

It didn't matter. She continued her search, until she discovered herself surrounded by Kessler's own picked guard.

"Where's the force?" the patrol captain asked Dejain. "We were ordered to pursue them."

She peered past him into the glittering vapor, and made out vague shapes.

Oh.

"There is no force," she yelled, furious. "You idiots! This magic—it's nothing but illusion! It's a ruse!"

A ruse? They whipped round and thundered back down the road.

Dejain whispered, "Landis."

Why hadn't she considered what that meant? If a real Landis heir had shown up, who knew what powers she'd been taught, or would re-emerge in her name? Trouble wasn't just possible, it was *here. Now.*

She transferred back to the base to get the last-ditch defenses she'd prepared.

TWELVE

A tan tried to console herself with observing that at least the water running along the slough was warm. Perhaps this was because of all the fires above, kindled in kitchens and on hearths as more people woke up from the enchantment each day. Either that or it was caused by some strange, mysterious old magic that she would have to learn about...

Mind. Stop wandering! Pay attention. Danger will not go away just because you want to hide.

The drain water was also clean, save for a few leaves and grass and the detritus of autumn, which meant it had to be part of the river. The walls varied in the type and size of stone used, but all of it looked very, very old.

"This way," Merewen panted, when they reached a fork.

Atan sensed a weak tug of whatever magic guided Merewen so unerringly, and changed direction to follow. Hinder and Lilah plodded grimly in her wake, Hinder gripping his bow and looking in all directions. Lilah kept her hands balled in the pockets of her black clothing. She wasn't going to tell anyone, but after she'd been so sure about "a way to defend them" to little Julian back there, she'd remembered all those plunges in into water, and had surreptitiously checked her pockets.

Sure enough, the Lure had turned to a mass of rotted leaves. Only the faintest whiff escaped the bag, meaning that the blossoms' effectiveness had completely washed out somewhere in the morvende hot baths.

All right, so she'd learned other skills. Now it was time to put them to use.

They ducked around a new waterfall coming down from a street grate, and found themselves at another crossing. Merewen frowned.

"I think we had better go alone," she said, pointing to herself and Atan.

Atan stared. Merewen's face was a pale blob in the weak light from a distant grating. "Is it the enchantment?"

Merewen turned her head from side to side as though listening for something beyond normal hearing.

An image of some kind—not her memory, it had that blue 'feel' to it which meant it was from the Loi, somehow—overlaid dream images, so bright and vivid and urgent she almost couldn't see her own bare toes on the watery stone. It was all too quick and too strange for her to make enough sense of it to explain. She could only shake her head and point, and hope that as these images were getting stronger, they might become more comprehensible.

Hinder said, "It's got to be the tower. That means the palace is up that way. Maybe Lilah and I should begin our guarding from here." He hefted his bow.

Lilah gave a lopsided smile. "How about if we each patrol back and forth? I've got my Sharadan Brothers tools. They ought to be good for something."

Atan drew in a shaky breath. "There are only two of you. And you are very dear. Maybe we should go together. Four would be better, should we encounter the enemy."

"Guarding your back actually means decoying them away from you," Lilah reminded her. "We can't do that if we're all together."

"Now." Merewen rubbed her eyes, then darted into the left fork, her bare feet smacking on the old stone. Atan cast a worried look back at the other two, then followed after.

"Let's go," Hinder said, and Lilah followed, trying to quell her churning stomach.

⊙━━▸╪━━━

After a long time of quiet, Julian heard horse hooves and voices. She stood up, hoping it was Rel.

A circle of unfamiliar men gazed down at her. They looked like those terrible riders who had chased them. That meant they were the Norsundrians.

She'd thought out a plan in case they came.

"Help?" she cried, trying to sound as babyish as she could.

They talked in low voices, then a man said, "Well, bring her up."

A man extended his hand, reaching down. Julian stood on her tiptoes. Fingers grasped her wrist and hauled her to the surface and set her down. The light seemed bright, and she blinked.

"Who are you?"

"Julian. Who are you?"

"Kessler," the man said, as someone behind laughed.

Kessler shot a glance backward, and into the instant silence, he asked Julian, "How did you get down there?"

"I fell," Julian said. "I was playing."

"Playing!" one of the men repeated, and laughed. "In the middle of a war?"

Kessler said, "I don't think she's an artifact of the war. This grate was recently moved. Look at the scrape marks." Then, back to Julian, who understood that her plan had gone awry. Her eyes stung. She'd thought it out so carefully!

"You moved that grate yourself?" Kessler asked.

Julian said stoutly, "Sure."

"Then let's see you put it back."

She knew she wouldn't be able to move it. Once again, disappointment made her eyes sting as she gazed up at Kessler, whose eyes were so much like Atan's in shape, but their color was a much lighter blue. Was he a cousin of some sort?

He looked down at the teary face with the same interest: This child had the Landis eyes, but she was too small to be Yustnesveas Landis. A sister? Cousin?

Whoever she was, he knew she was lying. Well, so was everyone else. The brat was smart enough to get an early start.

He tipped his head back and glanced skyward. To

the west stood the old tower, the one even Detlev couldn't bring down, only bind by magical wards. What had happened was clear enough; someone, probably the Landis girl, had gotten into the city via the drains. The only surprise was that they'd left this brat behind to cover for them.

"The Landis girl and her little band have not only breached the city, they're probably in or near that tower," he said to his men. They muttered, then he cut them off and pointed at the drain. "Tell Abselec to flush 'em out," he said to one of the runners, who leaped up on his horse and galloped away.

Then he turned back to Julian. She was small, but smart. "Come along," he said. "My guess is that Yustnesveas Landis won't like seeing your fingers broken one by one, will she?"

Julian's eyes welled with tears at last, not from fear, for she had scarcely comprehended his words, but from the conviction that her plan, her own plan of which she'd been so proud, had gone completely wrong. She should have stayed with the sisters, even if Irza pinched and whispered about *princesses* —

Julian gulped, and then bit her lips, struggling not to cry in front of these enemies.

Kessler laughed, and lifted her up onto his horse. "Cheer up. Nobody dies from broken fingers, and my guess is your friend will only be able to stand seeing one or two broken before she gives it up. I promise I'll let you go as soon as she does."

Julian heaved a shaky sob.

"I'll even set them for you, first," Kessler said, still smiling, for he now had the wherewithal to stop Atan — whether or not Dejain showed up with all her magic spells that, so far, did not seem to be working. "I learned how to set bones when I was your age. It happened often enough to me, and I never did have any friend to bind mine."

He mounted behind her, and they rode away straight for the city gates.

Merewen and Atan found their drain tunnel angling

upward. It became a passageway, complete with glowglobes set at intervals. The air was very still, cool but not cold.

Abruptly the passage changed to a stairway, which they ran up, both breathing hard. The came to a wooden door, pushed their way through, and found themselves standing on a carpet of midnight blue, woven with intertwined lilies. Atan smelled dust and wool. Her neckhairs prickled because the scents were so familiar, yet the place was new to her eyes.

It was her *home.*

She tried to take a step and discovered that she was trembling. Merewen glanced her way anxiously. "This way."

The pull of the magic was stronger now, for them both.

They ran down the carpeted hallway, their footsteps soundless. Atan tried to be aware of her surroundings, but only retained impressions of carved furnishings, handsome inlay, wall-sconces, and tapestries. A window cast low winter light aslant at their feet as they passed. The smell of mildew made her want to laugh because it was so... so ordinary, so unexpected, and because if she didn't laugh she might yell and scream.

They rounded a corner and jolted to a stop, face to face with four Norsundrian soldiers.

Lilah and Hinder toiled back and forth, eyeing the many dark tunnel entrances. For a while, neither spoke.

"There are way too many of these tunnels," Lilah finally pointed out.

"You didn't see which one they used?" Hinder sighed.

Lilah grimaced. "Great rear guards we turned out to be."

Hinder put his hands on his hips. "Then we lost them. I don't think we'll make amends by walking around to no purpose, unless the Norsundrians come."

"Then let's be organized. We'll choose a tunnel, explore to its end, then retreat back here. Go to the next. Keep doing it until we find their tower."

"Good idea."

The next stairway they came to, they toiled up, Lilah grumbling about how nastily her shoes squished in the moss. Hinder, barefooted, smiled inwardly.

They reached the top and discovered a latched grate that seemed to be built into a kind of well. They swung the grate down, popped their heads up—and found themselves in a little courtyard. Surrounding them were a number of Norsundrians, all watching with interest. Swords, knives, and bows pointed their way.

They looked at one another and heaved a sigh.

"So much for my good ideas," Lilah muttered. "I know..."

Hinder was astonished when she gazed around, her mouth open. "Where am I?" she said slowly, as though blind.

The enchantment! Delighted with her quick thinking, Hinder extended his hands, as though feeling along a darkened tunnel. "Where am I?" he echoed, fumbling around as if they'd just woken up from the century-long dream.

Atan and Merewen dove under a side table.

The four Norsundrians marched right past, their gazes so fixed and distant it was clear that they were enchanted. The girls could have stood right out in the open and those warriors never would have seen them.

How long had those men been marching around like that? Atan wondered. It didn't matter. The important thing was that the enchantment binding Sartor still seemed to be in force in places, but so far, at least, she and Merewen were escaping its effect.

So far.

"Up here." Merewen pointed at an archway, through which they could see a curving stair. Atan swayed, rubbing her eyes. *I'm dizzy.*

The stairway was narrow, made of a peculiar glistening white stone. It spiraled upward twice before opening into a round room jumbled with tables and rolled tapestries, and shelves and trunks. Near at hand were books spread open on a little round table with thin gilt-edged legs. The books looked very, very old. Atan bent down to look. The book was so old that the writing was vertical *Old Sartoran.*

Atan was *here.* This was the ancient tower.

What was she supposed to find? Tsauderei had felt certain that once she reached this place, she would discover the means to end the enchantment. So far, in spite of all the dangers, she'd made it. She must keep on.

She turned in a slow circle, taking in every object: the rich velvet hangings, the fine molding on the hilts of a stack of swords against a cabinet, and shelves and shelves of books and scrolls. This chamber appeared to be an archive, with most of the written records neatly stored, except for that pile over on the walnut table with the curving legs that looked like stylized animal legs. The small pile of books lay in disorder, as though hastily put down. And they did not look old, either.

She picked up the closest. The writing was small and dense, each entry topped with a date more than a century ago. This was a diary or journal. She leafed back through, until her eye was caught by the word *Dei.* She skimmed rapidly, and saw that it was an indictment of the Dei family for conspiracy —

She closed the book and laid it down, turning around with a furtive, almost guilty glance.

Merewen stood on the other side of the room, watching her.

"Is it bad for you, too?" she asked.

"Bad?" Atan didn't know how to answer, so she shrugged.

Merewen sat down, hugging her arms close. "You don't see double, like me, do you? I think you are feeling bad about the Deis, aren't you?"

Atan could not hide her surprise.

Merewen sighed and turned her head to observe the pale blue shapes crowding about, somewhat like the flickers in the water of the lakes underground, but these were made of air. Sometimes she could see through them to the solid walls and furnishings of wood and stone and fabric, but then there were brief, sparkling moments when she saw different shapes, a little like shadows except in color, and there were the hands that had shaped the stone walls, and carved the wood, and woven the fabric—memories sent by the blue ones. Many whispered.

When Atan opened the book, Merewen heard a whisper reading the entries aloud. When Atan laid the book down, the whisper went silent. Merewen was glad. She didn't like the tone or the hurtful words about the Deis, who she knew were part of her family.

As Atan stood looking sad and puzzled, Merewen moved through the crowd of blue shadows step by step, as though she were in water, until she found herself in reach of a new object made of paper with words on it, a great, beautifully bound tome. Golden clasps kept it shut. All the blue shadows gathered around.

Merewen looked up at Atan. "Touch it."

Yes. That was right. The blue hands reached, some with fingers spread, some with cupped palms, as though holding precious water. All over and around and under the book.

Atan extended a grubby hand. She saw her own dust and mud-smeared fingers and snatched them back, and tried to wipe them clean, but her clothes were also grubby and damp. She reached again and gently laid her hand on the book, the barest touch so as not to get grime on it.

Snap! With a spark of magic, more felt than seen, a glowing image of a plump, sweet-faced woman of grandmotherly age appeared between the girls.

"Lilith the Guardian," Atan whispered, wonder-struck. Tsauderei had told her about the Old Sartoran sorceress often enough, and shown her a sketch made by unknown hands, in a scroll a thousand years old. She, like the authors of Norsunder, lived beyond time.

I leave this message with the Loi, for the one who comes to break the spell, she said.

Atan glanced at Merewen's bowed head. Did she hear something different?

The binding spells are here in this book, but you must be trained in magic to perform them, lest you lose yourself between what we call the measures of time.

The woman's image faded into faint twinkles, like distant stars, and then winked out, leaving Atan staring down at the gold-clasped book.

"That's me," she said. "I am the one."

She opened the book.

Irza and her party halted in a drain when they heard scrapes and sloshes. The noise swiftly resolved into Kessler's guards marching along the main drain, one of them cursing.

Irza grinned. "This is the right one," she whispered. "I remember it, I remember it!"

"Do you know where we are?" Sana muttered next to Irza's ear.

"Oh yes, I do," Irza whispered back, full of joy. "I know *exactly* where we are. That way is Parleas Terrace, where Ianth House lies." Even whispering, her voice was full of pride. "So the Apsos is over there. And some very rough ground, where the ancient tiles are loose and upended. Step only where I step!" She raised her voice. "Oh, *Princess Yustnesveas Landis!* This way!"

Arlas laughed, then cupped her hands around her mouth. "Here, Princess Yustnesveas, over here!"

"The Landis queen! Princess, here!" Sana called in her clear, beautiful voice.

Landisss.... Landisssss.... Princessss.... The echoes spread through the drains, causing a sudden silence. Then they heard the sound of running feet. Many running feet.

Irza chortled as she led the way down the tunnels, drawing the Norsundrians out and away from the palace.

Kessler and his men clattered through the city gates to the courtyard of their command post, the horses sweaty and foam-flecked. Kessler sprang down and began issuing orders. He was still speaking as he reached up to lift Julian to the ground.

One of the garrison runners approached. "We just now nabbed a pair of children from one of the drain wells. We think they might just be locals, but—"

"Bring them here," Kessler said.

The runner took off for the other end of the palace complex, where the time spells had faded. There Hinder and Lilah had been locked up for later questioning, the

Norsundrians having fallen for Lilah's hasty ruse.

The room they were locked in had one single window, perhaps shoulder height, far too narrow for a man to get through. Two children, however, managed with a squeeze, a push, and a grunt.

They found themselves on a narrow ledge. It had been formed when the upper story was added to the ancient wall, using a different type of stone. Keeping their backs to the wall, they sidled along the ledge. Lilah tried not to look down.

Hinder had fewer problems with heights. He reached the battlements first, then pulled Lilah after him.

Inside the tower, Atan looked up from the book, her eyes burning from her repeated attempts to complete the chain of powerful spells she found there. Her mind struggled against a flowing tide of magic power; she swayed, gripped the table, and the book almost toppled. "Oh, Tsauderei," she muttered under her breath, her eyes stinging. "How I wish you were here instead..." Then she stopped. Even in her own head it sounded like accusation. Tsauderei had warned her, and taught her, and prepared her.

I am here. I *must* succeed.

Merewen steadied the book, though she, too, fought to comprehend the two worlds, one human and one not, that lapped and surged against one another but did not quite converge. The room was so crowded, she gave up trying to guess which figures belonged to which world.

"I think I need to outside," Atan whispered. "I can't do it here. I have to see the horizon, really see it, to anchor myself to the world..."

The blue figures danced about, soundlessly clapping their hands and pointing, and Merewen drew a deep breath. "Yes. Outside. It's right."

The blue figures flowed outward, receding to clear a path.

Merewen tucked the book under one arm, and Atan's unresisting hand with the other hand, and followed the beckoning blue figures toward next pair of stairs.

"Up there!" someone shouted from below.

Lilah and Hinder peeped down at the courtyard to see Kessler's runner pointing at them.

Behind, a swarm of dark clad warriors fanned out.

"They're gonna chase us," Hinder said.

"Let's run," Lilah said, pointing in the other direction. "Get as many as we can after us. Because if they chase us, they can't chase Atan."

Hinder ducked his head. "Right."

The wall was barely broad enough for them to attempt a low, loping sort of run. Hinder took the lead, running until he fetched up above an arched bridge. They stared down in surprise at all the people who had come out of their homes and shops. The people stood about in apprehensive clumps, looking around at one another. "They're just getting out of the spell," Hinder guessed.

From the other end of the great square, a lone horseman rode an archway, twin to the one Hinder and Lilah stood on.

"Rel!" Lilah exclaimed, as the Norsundrians poured into the square from a side street and once more fanned out.

Rel's head lifted. Lilah saw his deep-set eyes take in the square, the enemy, and also the bridge, with Lilah and Hinder standing on it. His hand flicked in a private salute, and she grinned and waved back.

"It's working," Hinder breathed, the rising breeze ruffling his blue-white hair. "We're keeping the enemy away from Atan."

Lilah wondered how he knew as below, Rel rode the horse in a prancing circle and began to shout, "To arms! To arms! Yustnesveas Landis has returned, and needs all of Sartor to rise!"

His words were met by stares and open mouths. People exchanged looks.

Then a woman from one of the inns took a swipe at a passing Norsundrian with a great iron skillet. The clang rang up the stone walls, the man staggered, and an eyeblink later the court was filled with shoving, struggling figures.

The battle was grand for about the space of three

breaths. Then the court filled with fast threesomes of dark-clad warriors who cut their way through the surging crowds. Lilah saw blood and heard cries of anguish, and she wailed, "Stop! Stop!"

"Come, Lilah," Hinder said sorrowfully, wondering why Lilah hadn't known what 'raising the city' meant. He pulled her arm, having no idea that the sight of fighting threw her back into memory of angry crowds the summer before, during Sarendan's revolution. "See that tree in the next square over? If we can reach that, we can get down. We'll have to hurry, for the Norsundrians will be out on our part of the wall soon."

Lilah gulped, her chest heaving on a sob.

"They're defending their city," Hinder said. "It's the only way we can get the time for Atan to do what must be done magically. Don't look, Lilah, because you can't stop it, and your pain won't help them." Hinder drew Lilah over the bridge, along another wall to where the branches of a mighty tree reached over.

Back in the great square, Rel watched the people rise against the enemy. His reaction was a combination of admiration and dismay. He'd counted on a crowd. He had not expected violence — not after a hundred years of magical sleep. But to these people it had only been days since their king was killed.

He could not stop it now. They were too angry, and more poured into the court with every breath. At least they were slowing the Norsundrians, but at what cost? He winced at the sounds of ringing swords and cries of rage and agony. He forced himself to ride on, for it was only a little ways to the house where he'd found the sword.

When he reached it, he saw that it was empty. He dismounted and laid the borrowed weapon on a windowsill, hoping it was not too late for the unknown owners.

The tired horse stood patiently, its hindquarters shivering. Rel spotted an inn yard across the street and led the mount there. A small boy peered fearfully at him from behind bales of fresh-looking hundred-year-old hay.

"Take the horse?" Rel asked. "Needs care."

The blue eyes shifted, rounded, and the boy nodded

firmly.

Rel ran back to the square just as Kessler arrived from the other end, scanned the chaotic scene, then looked up and stilled.

Rel looked up in the same direction — and made out two small figures on the top of the great white tower. They were silhouettes, but those knee-length braids had to belong to Atan.

Kessler gestured to some of his followers to come close, and he began issuing a rapid stream of orders. Rel remembered the plan: delay, deflect, decoy. He looked around, spotted a fallen blade, and grabbed it. With an inward groan, he swung his way through the Norsundrians.

Kessler looked his way and smiled.

Then Rel was too busy to think.

On the tower, Atan heard the shouts of Sartorans coming to the rescue, and clashes and clangs of steel. Every clash meant that someone was hurt or fighting for their life. Hurry! She wiped her sweaty palms down her sides and gripped the great book in both hands.

She whispered the first part of the spell over and over to herself first, knowing that it was going to tax all her ability to hold it. She lifted her gaze to the horizon, purple in the already-setting sun, and began.

The world narrowed to the sound of her voice.

Merewen kept watch beside her, surrounded by blue figures looking down, down, waving their hands downward. Merewen sensed danger, warning, threat, its cause unidentifiable until a black flowering of destructive magic smote the blue figures away like a scouring wind.

Merewen stared down at the spot where Dejain had appeared.

Rel attacked Kessler, who shouted orders over his shoulder as he met Rel with saber and knife both.

A few of the Norsundrians had begun to surround them, obviously preferring to enjoy the show and leave tangling with the hapless citizens to their fellows.

Kessler's short commands sent them scattering.

Rel fought for his life. He'd forgotten how strong Kessler was, in spite of his slight build and medium height. Kessler was not only strong, he was unnervingly fast, as only those with a long-term single-minded focus on the niceties of killing with steel can be.

Though he'd improved, Rel soon knew he was going to lose, and concentrated on not making it easy. He had no idea it was the best fight Kessler had had in a long time, one that under other circumstances would have been worth prolonging, but he had glimpsed Dejain on the edge of the observers, and he had to end it fast.

Rel's chief advantage was his strength and reach, but Kessler was faster, and he had the knife as well as his saber. *High defense, low, feint, feint.* Rel stepped to ward a blow, putting his blade at exactly the angle Kessler wanted. He caught Rel's blade between the hilts of his weapon and used his body to force Rel's arm backward and loosen his grip on the sword.

Stepping close, Kessler whipped the knife from underneath and stabbed Rel in the shoulder, not to kill, for he'd not given up on recruiting him, but to get him out of the way.

He yanked his knife free. "Come," he commanded the last man, as Rel dropped his sword and staggered. "Leave him. He's not going anywhere. Bring the brat."

The Norsundrian holding Julian by the arm half-carried, and half-dragged her after Kessler.

Rel had fallen to one knee as he fought against the shivery nausea of pain and the weird rippling shadows that threatened to overwhelm him. He had to stay awake! He staggered to his feet, blinking at Kessler's rapidly diminishing figure — and Julian being towed along behind. He bent to retrieve his sword, faltered, fighting against black waves, then drew in his breath. He was determined not to pass out.

Kessler ran across the quadrangle.

Dejain beckoned to him and held out a silver crossbow bolt. The greenish gleam of dark magic spells glimmered along its edge. "Kill her," she said, lifting her chin toward the girls on the tower. "The tall one with the book."

He took the bolt. Magic tingled under his fingers.

He wondered what ugly spell had been bound to it as he grabbed a crossbow from one of the sentries, slapped the bolt in, cranked it back, raised to aim—

And shot.

Up on the tower, the blue figures crowded around Merewen so close she could almost feel them. She could almost hear them, but her attention stayed on Atan as the princess gathered magic in a sky-wide vortex discernible only to those who had the training; it was the magic of her ancestors, of the place where she stood, of time. At a distance, both Erai Yanya and Tsauderei wove wards to protect that magic beginning to stir.

Merewen saw the woman below handed a thin thing that glowed with fiery threat to a man with a crossbow.

Between heartbeats, she stepped once, twice, until she stood between the unheeding Atan and the red-glowing bolt flying toward her, the blue hands wreathed around her, tight, tighter—

Merewen gasped at the cold prick of icy pain and recoiled not only physically, but in the realm of the spirit. She let go of her human self at last, felt mind and spirit caught by the waiting hands—

And transferred.

The metal bolt dropped with a clatter onto the tower stones at Atan's feet.

Atan glanced aside. In the briefest instant she saw the bolt, and Merewen falling away into a glittering wink of blue light that vanished. Horror and grief seized her by the heart, as deep and sharp as if the bolt had torn through her own flesh. But she had this task, and too many people's lives depended on her finishing.

Don't look. She forced herself to keep speaking without faltering, though her heart wailed in anguish.

The vortex began to turn, slow and massive, gathering power and speed, plucking at body, mind, and spirit—

Kessler said, "The little one took the bolt."

"Quick," Dejain said, handing him a second bolt. "Now. It's the only one left." It had taken her an entire night to enchant only these two.

Rel knew he was not going to make it before the rising waves of blackness overwhelmed him. But he could do one thing: free an innocent child. With the last of his strength, Rel picked up his blade and brought it hilt-down on the head of the Norsundrian holding Julian.

The stunned Norsundrian crumpled, freeing the child, who sprang straight at the enemy.

Kessler raised the crossbow —

And Julian bit him on the leg as hard as she could.

Unexpected pain flowered in his calf, causing his arm to flex the moment he triggered the release. The bolt flew harmlessly a hands-breadth over Atan's head.

Kessler looked down. "You leave her alone!" Julian shrilled.

Atan closed her eyes, mind, heart, and spirit holding the magic ... holding it ... *mind and magic and time* —

The last word —

— and *finished.*

Everyone — Norsundrians, Sartorans, morvende at a distance, Erai Yanya and Tsauderei at his scry stone — felt Detlev's enchantment snap and vanish like ash dispersing on the clean, driving winter wind.

Atan swayed on the tower roof, then sank to her knees, clutching the book tight to her chest as tears filled her eyes for Merewen.

Dejain cursed, a flow of bitter invective, and transferred back to the Base, abandoning her minions.

Kessler slung away the crossbow and laughed.

THIRTEEN

A tan bent down and studied that fallen silver bolt. She saw no blood on the thing. Yet it had been knocked down onto the roof by something, instead of sailing overhead. Merewen was not there, either fallen dead or senseless. She'd vanished.

I will not grieve until I am certain she will not come back. Atan forced herself to look out over the city whose map she'd been studying ever since she was small.

Under the low northern light, the slanted roofs gleamed cold, rank on rank of fine houses in the district called Parleas Terrace. Though it lay on the other side of the river behind the palace, the nobles had claimed it was part of the palace's district from the early days when there were three districts, and again when the city expanded to six. To the northeast the rooftops were more interesting, curled around almost like Venn knots in the Apsos, the oldest part of the city. Atan could barely make out the ordered roofs of the outer part of the city, built beyond the city walls, called 'new' in all the records, though it was several centuries old before the enchantment.

She turned. Straight east, where the river bisected at the gate, lay houses and businesses, and then south, the fourth, fifth, and sixth districts—the latter the military area. Her city. *Her* city.

Urgency displaced wonder. Tsauderei had said over and over, *If you do succeed in banishing that spell, that is when your work begins.*

She brought her gaze down to the square as the last of the magical residue glittered and winked away. People surged, startled, recoiling—shouting—as some of Norsundrians vanished by magical transfer, and those without transfer tokens began a retreat before the swelling number of confused, angry Sartorans who were no longer bound by enchantment.

Atan searched through the people—*Sartorans!*—until her gaze caught a tall, dark-haired figure who bled copiously from the shoulder. As she watched in helpless anguish, Rel struggled up from the ground, his face lifted toward the tower, and she saw his mouth move—he was trying to say something. She stepped to the very edge of the tower roof, the rising wind catching at her hair and clothes as she strained to hear. He took one step toward her, and then fell flat on his face.

Julian wailed, running to his side. Most people took no notice. They were too busy exclaiming to one another, looking around, some organizing to chase Norsundrians.

This is what Tsauderei meant, Atan thought.

Would anyone listen to her? The time had come to find out.

She looked around once more, her heart aching when she caught sight of the bolt lying there. *No blood on it, so I will not grieve*, Atan told herself, clutched the heavy book tightly to her chest, and turned to the stairwell. *But Rel...*

She wouldn't let herself finish the thought. She couldn't bear to finish the thought.

As if she could outrun the thought, she skipped down the stairs, plunked the book back on the table where she'd found it, then ran back to the stairs.

This time she did not pause to appreciate the ovals worn in the stone or the smoothness of the carved rail, polished by centuries of hands. Her breath came fast, her heart juddering counterpoint to her steps as she ran down, and then bolted for the hallway that led to the square.

She banged through the doors and began pushing through the crowd. "Pardon," she said breathlessly. "I'm Atan—that is, *Yustnesveas* Landis—"

The old-fashioned, clumsy name was difficult to get

out, rusty from disuse was her weirdly detached thought, attended by a mad hilarity. But she may as well have used her heart-name, for nobody paid the least heed. She knew her voice was not loud enough, and she couldn't catch anyone's attention as everyone around her talked more, trying to be heard by their oblivious neighbors. *I'm just another girl, awkward and dressed wrong—just as I was in Bereth Ferian...*

But she was in Sartor. Her responsibility.

She began ducking and dodging, sometimes shoving past extended arms, until she stumbled into Hinder and Lilah, who had linked arms and stood over Rel. He sat on the ground with his knees pulled up and his head resting on his knees, one hand clutching his shoulder, which bled sickeningly on both sides, a viciously deep stab wound.

"Wound," Atan said, relief welling inside her. "He's alive." Her eyes burned, and her head seemed to be floating somewhere above her, unconnected to her body. She stood blinking until she became aware of Lilah's steady gaze, and her voice repeating, "Atan? Atan? Um ... Atan?"

"I'm here." Atan looked around. "I need to get..."

What?

Lilah snorted out her breath. "I know what comes next. It was almost like this when the revolution ended. Well, not really. Except for the yelling crowds." She darted at Hinder, grabbed his arm, and pulled him close as she whispered in his ear.

"I'm louder," Hinder said to her. "Remember who called the drills in Shendoral."

"All right," Lilah said. She made a face, bent over with her hands on her knees, and Atan watched, bewildered, as Hinder put his taloned bare foot on Lilah's knee, and then, as Lilah straightened, he nimbly leaped up and settled on her shoulders, feet tucked in her armpits.

People around stared as Hinder cupped his hands around his mouth. "The queen is back!"

"Queen?" The word rippled outward, interspersed with others saying, "What was that?" and "Who's the morvende?"

Mendaen appeared and in his louder voice roared,

"The Landises are back! The princess saved us!"

"Our new queen broke the spell!" Dorea shrieked, elbowing through from another direction. "The queen is come!"

One by one people looked around, and took up the shout.

The queen is come!
The queen is come!
The queen is come!

A clear space grew around Atan, revealing more fallen people. Some were still moving, others horribly still.

"Shouldn't we carry them inside the palace?" Atan asked, pointing behind her. "Is there a healer?" As people looked at each other as if waiting for the someone to be the first to move, Atan heard whispering. "What did she say?" and "I'm not touching one of the Norsunder offal."

Atan turned in a circle, tightened her stomach, and tried to look princessy. "Find a healer! Our first duty is to the wounded." Ordering a crowd didn't work. So try individuals? "Brick! Pouldi! Can you help Rel inside?"

"Glad to!" Brick said from somewhere in the crowd, and Pouldi's genial voice followed, "Hai! Shift it, there. Make way." The two boys leaped to Rel's side. Mendaen helped as all three got Rel to his feet and began moving toward the palace.

"Some of the rooms are burned," a shrill voice cried.

"Find rooms that are not burned," Atan said. *One by one, just like building a ward*, Atan thought tiredly. "We'll use that wing of the palace, right there, for the wounded, as it's close. It's not burned—I was just in there."

Yes, people could agree to that.

"I'll help!" Sana caroled in her singer's voice. "Make way—queen's order!"

"Queen's order!"

"Queen!"

"Who?"

"Me, too! Me, too!" Voices chimed in, and as the Shendoral group began moving purposefully.

And then, finally—blessedly—"What can I do?"

People emerged out of the crowd to offer help, and Atan raised her voice firmly, "Help the wounded! Fetch bandages. Healers!"

It was a little like the magical vortex. First there was the surging chaos of the crowd, then as the forest dwellers began moving purposefully, taking up the cry Queen's orders, others joined them, or spread out to pick up others lying in the vast courtyard.

Atan saw Rel borne inside. Then Mendaen vanished with a bunch of other people, mostly men, who divided up and began moving up the streets in search of Norsundrians. They waved swords and other implements, like blacksmith tools and hoes.

That was when a woman emerged from the crowd and addressed her. "I saw you up on the rampart. Are you really the princess?" the woman asked, looking doubtfully into Atan's face. She flushed. "You have a look of the royal family. Very much. But the princess Yustnesveas is a babe in arms!"

"Gehlei, My mother's guard ran with me..." The crowd fell silent as Atan told her story. At the end, Atan's dry throat ached, her voice hoarsening. She hadn't eaten since they'd left the caves, nor had anything to drink. She was desperately thirsty and found herself repeating words without knowing what to say as people just stood there, staring. "A hundred years?"

They looked at one another in disbelief. "A hundred years?"

"More like ninety," Atan began, but her voice was going — and word serried through the crowd, a susurrus of wonder, disbelief, and a little fear.

Lilah stepped up to her side. "Hannla's going to find us some food," she stated firmly. "I think you need some supper. Maybe tell them to go home?"

Atan gazed at her, the sides of her vision glittering. "Julian! I nearly forgot. I promised her..."

Lilah looked up into her face, recognizing that lost look. She'd seen Peitar wearing that same expression, at the end of the revolution. Well, she'd been in this situation before, and Sartor might be the oldest country in the world, but those people looked a lot like ordinary people to her. "Hannla has her," Lilah assured Atan. "You need to eat."

"I can't. There's too much to be done," Atan said over the slowly rising hubbub. The silence had broken, and now it seemed that everyone wanted to be heard — to tell their story and to get justice, aid, direction. To demand the proof about the century.

There were too many wounded to be seen to, and too many people wandering around. Some were angry at having discovered their houses burned down, others having been looted.

Hinder reappeared, shoving his way unceremoniously, Sinder helping. Over his arm Hinder carried a basket of fresh food.

"It's that inn down that street," he said, pointing. "If you'll see to it they get paid, they said they'll feed all comers, until supplies run out."

"Then let us send for food for the wounded right now," Atan said as Lilah handed her a cup of water, and when that was gone in three swallows, some bread and cheese. It might be hundred-year-old bread and cheese, but to the people walking around, talking, exclaiming, exploring, it was yesterday's provender.

She scarcely got to eat half of it.

Everywhere she walked, she saw expectant faces, many wanting to tell their story of the war, others wanting decisions to be made. Decisions, revisions, compromises, most of them were increasingly painful.

The sun vanished, yet the streets were still filled with people carrying lamps, torches, candles. Atan stayed where she was, constantly surrounded, until Lilah and Hannla got the morvende to link hands in a circle around Atan, and draw her gently but inexorably inside the palace.

The moment Atan stepped inside, her thoughts flew to Rel. "He's asleep," Hannla said to Atan's worried question. "And so is Julian. I took her to my family's pleasure house. We tucked her up, and she dropped off before I could count to three."

Count to three ... sleep ... Mendaen and Sana closed the door to the wounded wing at midnight. Despite the rapping and banging, they kept it shut and guarded it.

Atan wasn't even aware. After she saw Rel resting comfortably, his shoulder bound up, she discovered her feet ached almost as badly as her head. She made it to the women's side, and there was a bed...

The second morning of her queenship, she remembered the gown that she had made so long ago, and her promise to Gehlei. She ducked out of the wounded wing and its makeshift tumble of bedding on the floor that had been looted from rooms above, and found an undisturbed antechamber not far from the wounded wing, where she hastily changed. This palace was supposed to be home, but it felt cold and strange and unwelcoming. She had no idea where anything was, and the smell of burnt wood in those enormous state chambers was horrible.

But someone had left jugs of water and a stack of basins on a table. She helped herself, and she washed as best as she could, shivering in the frigid air, then finger-combed her hair and braided it.

When she emerged wearing her new dress, yesterday's worries crowded back, Merewen foremost, Rel second, with that anxious sense of responsibility for Julian a close third. She made her way into the wounded wing, to discover that Rel was gone — he'd left with Mendaen and the others to do ... something, no one knew what.

No one knew anything. People walked about, poking, exclaiming, asking for her. Atan wanted to run and hide, but by midmorning a vast change occurred when many of the old palace servants reappeared, people who had sensibly gone to ground at the end of the war.

They took over, chasing off would-be souvenir-seekers and loungers. Those with legitimate business were told to line up in the square, where someone would take names and queries. The new queen would see people by appointment only — as always.

As always, just like normal, remember the rules. These were magical words, promising the restoration of order, and the crowds thinned rapidly. That freed Atan to walk the length of the great building that had housed her ancestors for so many centuries. She surprised little groups here and there, busy with brooms, mops, wood-working tools, needles and thread. All traces of the century-old battle were being removed from the public rooms. Only the private wing upstairs remained untouched, pending Atan's orders.

She could not yet face her parents' rooms.

When she neared the kitchen, she smelled baking

bread, a homely, simple smell, but somehow it made her throat close up with the ache of sadness. She ran along the hall until she came to the linen storage, where stacks and stacks of beautiful linens waited to be used, and she stood there with a century-old damask table cloth pressed over her face as sobs shook her.

Your work begins, Tsauderei's voice echoed. *Your work begins...* She fought the tears under control and walked out, determined to start. She'd begin with keeping promises.

She found Hannla in the wounded wing, and said, "Please take me to Julian."

Hannla smiled. "She's waiting for you."

Atan turned her head, and to her relief, found Lilah talking to Dorea.

Lilah held out a sheaf of papers. "Here's the first batch of questions. The people waiting for answers are over on that side."

She beckoned toward the courtyard.

Atan forced her aching eyes down the first page. Not a single query about magic. She looked up, "This is all complaints. About..." It seemed somehow disloyal to say *silly matters*.

"Practical stuff," Lilah stated. "It was just like that for Peitar, after we got the kingdom back for good. Peitar said that questions about their front parlor having been used as a stable by the invaders, and who was to pay for broken windows, are not small matters to them. It's the whole world to them."

"It's the resumption of order," Atan said, hauling her mind back to the paradigm shift she'd seen before. "I can't go out there yet. I need to know what I've got before I can start giving it away."

"Come to my house," Hannla said. "My family survived, and my da knows all the latest talk. Ah! Latest before the enchantment caught up with everyone."

"This way," said someone else. "If you don't want to talk to anyone yet, don't let them see you until you're ready."

That made sense.

And as Atan shuffled behind Hannla to a side street, where tiny flurries of snow drifted down, she kept reading, mentally sorting the questions and demands.

She turned often to Lilah with her own questions.

Lilah prefaced almost every remark with "Peitar says," or "When Peitar..." Atan found these comforting, as she respected Peitar, who had wrested a devastated kingdom into the beginnings of order in the months succeeding his uncle's exile.

Peitar was only four years older. If he could manage, she could manage.

When they reached Blossom Street, and Hannla ran ahead to let the family know who was coming, Atan said in a low voice, "I don't know if it's a good thing or a bad thing that we haven't seen the Ianth sisters, or any of the Parleas Terrace people."

Lilah's smile had vanished when Atan mentioned the sisters. She liked Arlas, but found Irza difficult. But this was Irza's country, not Lilah's. "I think it's more a ... a *thing*. Maybe they went home to find out who is alive, and if their houses are still there. People having been talking about burnings and nasty things like that. Some think their family is dead, when they might be hiding."

"That makes sense. So let me ask how Peitar dealt with the first and second circles—the nobles?"

Lilah remembered some of the things she'd overheard Rel telling Mendaen and the warriors in training about some of his adventures.

"In Sarendan, the nobles wanted everything to go back to the way things were. They might here, too. Because Sartor was invaded. It wasn't civil war, the way we had in Sarendan, where the nobles were the first ones who got attacked, then when my uncle took the kingdom back, it was the revolutionaries who they went after."

Atan nodded soberly.

Lilah was amazed that she seemed to be making some sort of sense. It had been easy answering questions about personal disputes or pleas. Go to the Glaziers Guild about the windows; get busy with a broom for the room full of hay and horse apples. But this here was a broader subject, touching on the matters Lilah hated thinking about.

She went on with a bit more confidence, "You know, the nobles didn't want Peitar to take away their land, or titles, or privileges. And he didn't, except for some of the privileges. I mean, they are answerable now.

I told you about that, remember, after Merewen joined us."

Atan's neck tightened at the mention of Merewen's name. There was no body, she reminded herself. Dead bodies Disappear only when someone does the Disappearance spell.

Then she reflected on how easily Peitar had been able to change some of Sarendan's rules. She suspected it was not going to be the same with Sartor; already on these sheets of paper she was seeing references to past traditions, laws, customs. *How Peitar became king is not a map for me to follow.*

Hannla's voice broke into her thoughts. "Come in, come in!" She waved from the doorway of a three story building whose light stone was covered with some kind of vine. Brightly shuttered windows were all open in spite of the cold.

Inside, Atan and Lilah found a scene akin to that at the palace — cleaning, repairing, polishing, and sewing.

Hannla turned, her curly hair bound up in a kerchief, and called, "Here, everyone, it's the new queen!"

People stopped in the middle of their tasks, brooms and dust cloths and scrub brushes in hand, and performed bows and curtseys.

A spurt of humor made Atan wish that Rel was there to see those brooms and dust cloths waving. She said awkwardly, "Please don't let me interrupt. I came to see Julian."

Julian herself appeared from a side room wherein Atan glimpsed cheerful decorations in bright greens and golds and pinks. "Atan my cousin, my real cousin!" she cried, and pointed back into the room. "We're playing a game."

Atan paused and glanced in the room, where she saw children gathered on a thick rug woven in patterns of vines. In the middle of the group lay a game board with six sides. On it was painted colorful patterns on which rested markers.

"I came to see if you are all right," Atan said to Julian. "I'm sorry I lost track of you last night."

"Hannla said you had to worry about the hurt people," Julian said. "I didn't get hurt." She added proudly, "That man was going to break my fingers, but I bit him. As hard as I could. I'm glad I bit him though it tasted like blech."

A couple of the children giggled, and a small one who couldn't have been more than three — though born nearly a century before — said, "Blech!"

"I'm glad you bit him," Atan said honestly. "Tell me what happened."

Julian did, in a jumbled fashion. Atan comprehended the gist, angry at first at the Ianths for abandoning Julian until Julian herself made it clear that she wouldn't go, that she'd had her own plan. Atan tried to imagine Irza standing there, afraid Julian would begin screaming and bring the Norsundrians. She still didn't quite understand why Julian rejected Irza's company, when she and her sister had been such dedicated caretakers, but now was not the time to get into that. If ever.

I just don't know enough about small children, she thought as she studied the child's solemn brown gaze. *But here, like with the kingdom, I had better make a start.* "Julian. We are the only ones of the family left. I'm sorry, but from what I heard last night, it seems that your mother did die somewhere outside the city, and my family is all gone as well. If you want to be my family, I will be yours."

"You mean, be a Landis?" she asked, her eyes narrowing.

Atan took her hands. "If you like."

Julian said, "I would like to be a Landis with you, because then we are really truly cousins. But I *don't* want to be a *princess*." She spat the word, then braced herself for Atan to argue.

Atan saw those thin shoulders hunch and the small mouth press into a line. "You don't have to be anything you don't want to be. I'd just like to have you as family. Really truly cousins."

Julian grinned, bouncing a little in her happiness.

Atan bent and kissed the top of her fresh-washed head. "Do you want to stay with Hannla, then? Until we can figure out how we're going to live in that big palace?"

"I want to stay here," Julian stated. "*Princesses* live in palaces."

"All right. Stay here, where it's warm and you have

friends to play with. Then—whenever you want—you can come to the palace and pick out a room for your very own, and you will not have to be a princess in it."

Julian agreed. Atan saw her run back to take up the game again. She stood in the doorway long enough to watch Julian, who seemed happy with the company of children her age.

Feeling a strong sense of relief, she went out to seek Hannla, to be told that she and Lilah had gone back to the palace to help with the wounded. "Thank you," Atan said awkwardly, as a round woman with curly hair bowed. She had to be Hannla's aunt. "I'll find some way to pay you, when things get settled."

"There is no need, your highness," Hannla's aunt said. "You restored Hannla to us. I still don't remember what happened, only that I was carrying blankets to help the people forced out of their homes by fire. Hannla's mother sent the child with me, carrying a basket of fresh buns. But then..."

She passed her hand across her face. "I found myself standing in the middle of the Grand Chandos Way, and the blankets were gone. People were wandering around, and Hannla wasn't there. I was searching, and searching, and fell asleep again, and then people were shouting in the streets, and the Norsunder warriors were riding away as fast as they could, and then Hannla came home, took the rest of our blankets, and ran out again!" She smiled happily, and went on to exclaim and wonder and guess at what had happened to them all before Atan freed them from the evil spell.

Atan made herself wait patiently until the end of this story, so much like the many she'd already heard. And was going to hear again, over and over, she suspected.

She thanked the woman again and walked out, proud of herself for finding her way back over the bridge to the square. Just like the records said, one could always orient on the white-stone tower, which nothing had been permitted to exceed in height.

She returned to the wounded wing. Here she found Rel, with one arm in a sling, helping to pass out bread to those too hurt to move. He and Mendaen were deep in talk until she walked in, then both smiled her way.

Relief blossomed inside her "How do you feel?"

"Wound's clean," he said. "Hardly feel it." He lied, hefting his basket with his good arm.

"We went to the garrison," Mendaen said soberly. "It's nearly empty. Most everyone must have been killed before the magic took hold. Rel showed the rest of us how to set up."

Atan turned Rel's way, as he said apologetically, "Only what I've seen in other places. I worked half a summer as a guard trainee, and from what I saw there and on my travels, most garrisons are pretty much alike."

Mendaen said, "A few old retired guards showed up. They're going to help us get patrols going again. In case Norsunder is around still."

Atan understood in his determination to keep working that this was Mendaen's way of dealing with the fact that both his parents, who had been part of the garrison, had been among those dead. Mendaen turned his dark gaze up to Rel before saying, "We asked him to help by leading a patrol, at least."

Rel gave his head a shake. "I've never made patrol captain anywhere. Haven't any idea how to."

"Your highness," someone said, plucking at Atan's elbow.

She became aware of a crowd of people having come up behind to listen. Foremost were some of the palace servants. Atan turned, seeing in each face the urgency of someone who had something to say, to ask, to report.

She wanted to stay, to thank Rel, to talk further, but that pressing sense of duty drew her away. *Later,* she thought. *There will always be later,* and she smiled inside.

Atan's neck ached and her feet hurt and she was thirsty again, when she found Hinder at her side. Impatience burned in her middle, but she resolutely banished it. The line of people wanting to talk seemed like it would never end, but end it must. And Hinder would not bother her with something trivial.

Hinder said, "Rel is leaving. I thought you should know."

FOURTEEN

Atan's mind blanked. Voices dwindled into the chatter of distant birds.

She scolded herself. Of course Rel would leave. He wasn't Sartoran. He had never claimed to be taking up his life in Sartor. In fact, she remembered him saying that he'd planned to travel to Everon next.

She remembered every conversation they'd had.

"I must thank him," she stated firmly. To the waiting people, she added, "Rel the Traveler was one of those who helped me end the spell. He fought off the Norsundrian leader."

As those in front turned to their neighbors to whisper, she slipped behind Hinder, who elbowed expertly through the press.

Atan's throat had tightened again. She had to thank Rel properly, in a way that showed how much she appreciated his help. It was important to make that clear, and to also make it clear he could come again to visit, that he would always, always be welcome.

What would be a way to thank him that was suitable? A gift, maybe? She liked the idea of a gift, but what? What would be important to Rel? She had absolutely nothing ... except a palace full of stuff. It was all hers, because no other Landises had appeared. She really was the last. Norsunder had been very thorough.

But not thorough enough.

She straightened her shoulders and whispered to

Hinder, "I'm going to get something."

There were all the people waiting to talk to her, but she discovered that if she moved, they had to move away. They could not keep her in one place. So she gained more confidence, saying right and left, "I will return in a moment. I have something to see to."

As soon as she reached the back hall beyond which the servants didn't let anyone penetrate, she smiled at the old fellow on guard there and ran to the tower.

When she reached the upper room, memory brought Merewen back, and the grief and worry. But she didn't pause, because *she was not going to worry*. She looked around, then caught sight of the swords in a carved wood rack near the table on which she'd found the great book.

She selected a long, well-made blade, suited to a tall person, and carried it with both hands downstairs. The sight of the sword acted strangely upon the crowd — they backed away as if she held it threateningly. That was interesting. She would have to think about why, but later, because she found Mendaen silently helping Rel shrug into a fresh sling. Mendaen looked as upset as she felt.

When Rel saw Atan, a flush of happiness warmed him, but with it came an intense awareness of the curious faces crowding in around them. His emotions were very like hers, though neither of them had the experience to observe it.

Atan fumbled for the right words, her face burning. She remembered Tsauderei saying once, after they had talked over a record about the Dei family, *If and when you find yourself the center of attention — and you will, if you are successful, you won't be able to help that, being who you are — never say too much.*

Gehlei had said, *When in doubt, good manners always work.*

She said in what she hoped was a formal tone, "You cannot leave without at least a trifling token of my ... of Sartor's ... gratitude for your help." She held out the sword, with its swept hilt, fine but not too fine, a blade both practical yet made by an artist — balanced yet it looked like something that would benefit a large man. "Here. And thank you."

She could see that the formal tone was not right, but

what was right? His expression had gone stony, making it impossible to know what he was thinking, and she found herself burbling on. "Please know that you are forever welcome to come to Sartor and find friendship waiting. And I would so like to hear about your travels, as it doesn't seem that I'm going to be doing much traveling."

Rel's left hand gripped the hilt, his face the deep red of mixed embarrassment and pleasure. Intensely self-conscious, he mumbled in Mearsiean, "I thank you —"

Atan said, meaning to be encouraging, "*Daelender*? A fine new name for the blade."

Rel was taken by surprise. Where he came from, nobody named weapons, and the words she thought a name meant *my gratitude* in Mearsiean. But she looked so pleased, her head tilted at a wistful angle, and anyway there was no chance of speaking because Mendaen and Sin and Hin and their companions sent up a great cheer, echoed by the people crowding in to see what was happening.

I've got to get away and think things through, he decided, as Atan forced a smile that felt as false as her attempt at formality. She wondered how she could possibly say farewell without sounding silly, when she became aware that the cheer had not ended — that in fact the noise outside was not a cheer, but shouting.

Was that a scream?

Atan whirled around, to discover Irza back at last. She wore a fine gown with a costly brocade over robe in the old style.

Irza stared at Atan with a mixture of urgency and a barely-acknowledged resentment. She and Arlas had arrived at their home to find it undisturbed, except for hastily set-aside things and a burned cake left in the now-cold oven. Arlas had run up to her room, found all her old toys, and sat down and cried. Irza had wandered from room to room, lighting all the lamps and candles when the sun vanished, though she did not know why.

Late at night there came a noise below and the girls had crouched in fear on the landing, regretting the lights until they saw servants enter, bearing bulky receptacles, following which their mother strode in, looking around with a frown.

Her face had changed to relief and a smile when she looked up and spied the two faces on the landing, but that after that bright moment, everything after felt like the descent of the sun.

Mother had called them into her formal receiving room, and required them to recount everything. She had stopped them frequently to correct pronunciation — *You have picked up some disgustingly low idiom and enunciation. That will change at once* — and to ask questions — *Who is this Savar? He's gone? What was his title?* — after which Arlas had asked, "What happened to you, Mother?"

"Never mind that. The past is past, and we survived, the three of us. We must not betray the memories of House Ianth by letting sentiment get in the way of service. This young queen owes you a great deal, enough I should think to gain us Second Circle or higher. You will help her understand this by reclaiming the Dei brat. With her turned out properly, when Yustnesveas Landis summons her first Star Chamber, you can claim guardianship of Julian Dei..."

Julian had refused to come to Irza, even though she'd scolded and, in fear of her mother, begged. No one at that pleasure house listened to Irza's commands to hand her over. Nobody paid Irza any attention, except to say, distinctly, "The child may stay as long as she wishes. It was the queen's order."

Irza had walked out and found...

"There is a mob about to execute someone," she said to Atan. "They will not listen to me —"

Atan pushed past and ran down the steps.

Irza led the way past the orderly line (everyone turning heads to stare at Atan as she dashed by) to the other end of the square, through an arch and into a smaller square, outside the old palace guard enclosure, which the Norsundrians had taken over. This was where Hinder and Lilah had been so briefly imprisoned.

As the two girls arrived, several people tried to drag a struggling woman toward a wall, where two men and a woman stood with bows in hand, arrows nocked.

"What are you doing here?" Atan yelled, but no one heard her above the screams of the woman and the angry shouting of the crowd.

Fury gave her energy. She murmured the spell,

aimed the ring she still wore up toward the sky, and the courtyard lit with a flash of light painful to the eyes.

Silence.

Atan turned to the leader of the mob, a stout man with a thick beard. "I am Yustnesveas Landis. What are you doing?"

"I've had Candal Mityan in my cellar since your father died, princess," the man said. "We in the House Guild—"

"That's inns, eateries, and pleasure houses," the thin woman with the bow pointed out in a self-important tone.

The man sent her a look. "We swore to close down when the city was taken. But Candal Mityan broke that ban. We burned her house just before they put the binding spell on us, when we found out she'd been collaborating with those Norsundrian soul-suckers, excuse my language—"

An old woman shrieked, "She took booty as payment! Booty they looted from the dead here in the city!"

"*Entertained* them!" yelled a burly man with bright red hair. One of his huge hands held the struggling woman by the arm. "We swore she'd die first thing we got peace, and so we mean to keep that promise!" He shook the accused woman as he spoke.

"Then we haven't peace," Atan said.

"What?" The thin woman gawked.

The bearded man flushed. "We're keeping the new peace by executing a traitor."

"Not true," the bound woman said hoarsely.

The red-haired man let go and she dropped to the ground, where she struggled to rise. It was difficult, due to her bound hands.

"Cut her free," Atan said.

No one moved.

Anger flashed through Atan, so hot and bright it made her prickle all over. "Fine, then I will do it myself, but if anyone moves before she has a chance to speak for herself, then ... then I'm going to go back to Sarendan, and you can fight among yourselves for another hundred years, and save Norsunder the trouble of destroying Sartor for good."

The crowd muttered at that, some glowering at the

lynch mob, others side-eyeing Atan skeptically.

Hinder glided round one of the adults. He pulled a stone knife from a hidden pocket in his tunic and silently cut the woman's bindings as she sobbed.

"Princess," she said, making a visible effort. "I am no traitor. I did take them in. Entertain them. The stonebacks killed my daughter the first night. She was a guard at the palace. They were taking what they wanted anyway, all my drink and food. I—I thought to turn on them, but not by fighting, but by my arts. And so I got them drunk, and talking, and bragging, and every word they said I passed on to my brother, also in the guard."

Hannla appeared at Atan's elbow, her aunt beside her. The older women looked grim, and Hannla afraid, her eyes huge.

Then an old man at the back muttered, "And made yourself rich doing it?"

"Where's this brother?" someone asked.

"She had a brother in the guard, right enough," the thin woman with the bow admitted in a grudging voice, her gaze down. "Might be dead, though."

"I don't know. He hasn't come by, so far." Candal Mityan lifted her chin. "What would he have to come back to? If Garrod Thesvar there hadn't caused my house to burn, you would have found every single thing I took in payment down in my cellar, waiting to go back to its owners. I never took one silver of blood money, not one. Go look in my cellar. See if you don't find melted metals, silver and even a little gold, for they never paid much. Mostly they just took."

Atan had been thinking rapidly.

So far she had listened to people, and the decisions, the orders, had been easy. *Settle the wounded in this room. Send guild problems to the guild houses. Find out who is willing to serve food, and we'll pay later.*

Now she had to take command in the sense of passing judgment. She had the title. And the look of her ancestors. The question was, whether or not the title and the look of a Landis were enough to mantle her with authority.

She lifted her voice. "Everybody here has discovered that some family members aren't going to come wandering back. And another thing I've learned as I listen to people is that we all know people who ought to be honored."

Except for a stirring and a few whispers, no one spoke.

Atan turned in a circle, meeting as many gazes as would meet hers. Her heartbeat drummed in her ears as she declared, "At sunset we will make the mourning circle through the boundaries of the old city, as we have done ever since Sartor was first established. Then *everyone* will go home and begin to rebuild their lives. Everyone."

A hundred people began to remonstrate, but she held up her hand.

"Tomorrow, on the third day, as is proper, I will summon a convocation of the Star Chamber. And we'll meet every day, as long as there's need. Anyone who wishes justice, speak to your guild chief or to your governor. Everyone can speak, and everyone will be heard after we make our vows, me to you, and you to me. There is to be no taking of lives, or we may as well hand the kingdom right back to Detlev. I'm sure he's waiting somewhere, hoping we get busy destroying each other and saving him the labor."

Another silence met this pronouncement, but Atan, so used to watching others for tiny clues to what they thought, saw in exchanged looks and loosened hands, and shuffled feet that though no one was particularly happy, again they were willing to have a kind of order imposed. They knew what to expect.

"Go eat dinner. Find your families. And your white robes for mourning."

The crowd dispersed. Hannla's aunt led the accused woman off to the wounded wing.

Atan ignored her quaking insides, her watery knees and dry mouth, and tried to remember what she had been doing—

"Rel is gone," Lilah said, appearing at her side. "And Irza was trying to make Julian go with her. That's why they're here." She tipped her head toward Hannla, who stood nearby, looking a little lost.

Atan swallowed painfully, aware of the sharp knife of disappointment. *Rel's only doing what he said he would.* She did not have so many friends that she could bear to lose one. This pain was worse, however, the opposite of feelings she was beginning to acknowledge. Though Lilah had been her first friend, and Hinder her favorite of the Shendoral group, it was Rel she kept thinking about most, whose conversation she remembered most.

As Atan walked slowly back to the great square and the palace entrance, she remembered what Lilah had said about her mother's diary, and the behavior of adults in love. *They think about nothing else. It turns them stupid.*

Atan wasn't full grown yet, but she knew it would happen in the next year, unless she cast that spell to delay it. She had not crossed the physical threshold between child and adult, and yet, when she thought about Rel, it was like the days when she used to fly high to the border of Sartor early on summer mornings. There she would hover and watch the sun come up, shafting golden light upon the ranks and ranks of mountains.

Before the sun actually appeared, she could feel the nascent warmth as well as see the first glimmerings of light lifting the darkness. Then the sun would come, blinding if she looked straight at it, warm and then hot on her skin.

Is that was adulthood felt like?

Now all the poems and songs made sense. That is, she'd always known what the words meant, but they'd seemed either silly or decorative. She hadn't guessed at the depth of pain when love was not returned for whatever reason. She could imagine the brilliance of that internal sun rising, if it was. That dazzle was for those who had the time for it.

And I don't.

She excused herself from Lilah, pushed past the others without hearing them, and went to retrieve her pack. As soon as she found a corner without people, she stopped and held her breath, her eyes squeezed shut. It hurt so much to think of Rel gone. How much worse could it get? Again she remembered Lilah's mother and the snow bank. It might seem romantic to those who had time for love, but to anyone else it was as Lilah had said, selfish. *I can't let it get worse,* she thought desolately. *I can't afford it now.*

If she used that spell to retard physical maturity, she could leave it that way for, say, a year, while she settled

Sartor. If Rel didn't come back, then the feelings would go away, right?

With shaking fingers, she took out that spell. Her eyes blurred with tears and she couldn't see the paper, but she scrubbed her sleeve fiercely across her face until her sight was clear. And she performed the spell.

Nothing felt different. The thought of Rel walking away toward the border hurt exactly the same.

But it will go away, she thought, and made herself walk downstairs to where she knew people were waiting for her.

Rel's thoughts paralleled Atan's as he passed the old north gate and headed up the road away from Eidervaen. He'd never felt those feelings before. He knew what they were, and where they might lead once he released the youth spell. *After I find my father*, that's what he'd promised himself when he first got the spell done on him to slow the approach of adulthood.

Now he was glad of the spell. These feelings were intense enough. He didn't want them — not for Atan, no, give her the full name, Queen Yustnesveas Landis, the only living representative of the oldest kingdom in the world. All those friendly faces — Irza at the head of them, all the rest of her nobles — would sour if they thought that Rel the Traveler had pretensions.

Someday Atan might choose to marry, at which time she would be courted by every prince in the world. That was the way things worked.

So he'd better get on with his life, be glad he was able to help, and busy himself somewhere else in the world.

When the sun crowned the highest peak in the northeast, the streets filled with people of all ages, dressed in white, or as near as they could get to white in undyed cloth, each bearing a candle.

They converged on the remains of the ancient city wall, called Grand Chandos Way, though it actually comprised a great circle. On two sides it bordered the northern and middle branches of the river, the waters of which threw back reflections of liquid light as people slowly circled behind the old tower, along the north side of the palace, and through the exclusive shop area called Aliana Circle, though it had not been a circle for centuries.

Atan peered into the faces she passed along the way, knowing that their grief was new and raw. Her vision blurred. The older folks stopped to sing ancient songs at each of the twelve stations, which were ancient symbols for the Twelve Blessings. Some of the buildings were empty and others nearly destroyed. People struggled to join the memories of a century ago with the present time.

When Atan reached the grand doors of the palace, called the dragon gateway, opposite the tower, she spotted a small blue figure gazing up at the gleaming carvings that were still grand, though smoke-blackened.

"Merewen?"

Atan stopped. Those following her wavered, whispers muting into a susurrus.

"Who is that?"

"She's blue!"

Merewen skipped lightly down the steps, blue eyes wide, hair floating behind her. She was very much alive, and Atan smiled mistily as Merewen exclaimed, "I found my people at last!"

"Yay!" Lilah yelled, as Atan exclaimed, "Come. Join us on the mourning walk, and tell me everything."

Merewen skipped. "How pretty the candles look, like a river of light. As for me, I don't have words. Yet."

"What happened on the tower?" Atan asked, glancing over her shoulder at the tower, gleaming in the moonlight.

Merewen shivered. "I was so afraid, but the blue people were around me, and when that horrid thing came at me out of the air, they *pushed*, and I, um, learned how to unbody—no, that sounds silly. How to not be human, and be a Loi instead."

"Oh," Lilah let out a long breath. "Is it as wonderful as the caves?"

"Different," Merewen said. "Words don't work. And time is different. I thought I was gone a little bit, but

I wanted to come and tell you that the Loi said that now I know how to go back and forth, I can be your Aroel."

"Good," Atan said happily. "So the Loi are form-less?"

"No. Yes. I will explain when I understand better."

Merewen shivered. "This I can tell you. Savar was killed by some Norsundrian magician. Vashee — Vorshee — Vatiora. That's it. Not that Dejain, the pretty one who was doing all the magic against us. An even worse one, they said.

"I feared so," Atan said, and added firmly, "When a new building is built, it's going to be named for him. That I promise."

Merewen smiled mistily. "That makes me happy in the middle of my sad."

The mourning circle was done.

The nobles were the first to peel off and resume the excavation of their stately homes along Parleas Terrace.

Arlas skipped along, happy to still be alive, for she was not the target of her mother's low, irritated voice. "You could not reclaim the child, I comprehend. Those pleasure house people are, of course, out for whatever they can get. I will take my place tomorrow at the convening of Star Chamber, but only long enough to make my vows and demonstrate that Ianth House is alive. We will not waste our time with the rabble that will no doubt line up to make demands that that child cannot yet give. She has an empty treasury, unless there are outland holdings, and it will take months to sort that out. But there is always spring."

There is always spring, Irza was thinking as her mother went on ahead. She and Arlas followed, hand in hand. At least they were home, and Irza was one of the Rescuers. She had been helping that new term get noised about...

Mendaen and Sana and Vanya and Pouldi accom-panied the remaining guards from a hundred years ago to their barracks, to tell them what had happened since they fell into enchantment.

Hinder and Sin vanished to report to Grandfather

Lonender.

At last Atan and Lilah were left alone.

"You might as well send me back," Lilah said. "I know what comes next, from watching Peitar. You've got to start queening, which means you'll be busy. I can't do anything about that and anyway, I want to spend New Year's with Peitar."

Atan hugged Lilah tightly, wordlessly, then said, "You were my first friend here, and one of the most loyal. Do not let this be our last time together."

Lilah shook her head, snuffling a little, then wiping her nose defiantly on her black Norsundrian jacket.

"If I may, I'd like to come talk to Peitar," Atan added. "Once things settle down."

Lilah said fervently, "I know he'd like that."

Atan did the transfer spell.

When the transfer reaction wore off, Lilah found herself in Miraleste. She ran through the quiet palace, which seemed new and modern after the one in Eidervaen. She found Peitar at his desk, as always.

When she appeared, his face eased. She said, "Sartor is free again! And I'm *starved*."

Peitar laughed and drew her to the kitchens to eat. She talked the entire way, finishing up very late that night.

"... and there was a vast big blue light, kind of. Sort of like lightning, but it didn't hurt. But it made everyone dizzy. And when we all got over being dizzy, some of the Norsunder people vanished by magic, others ran together, ready to fight as they retreated. A few of them looked around like everyone else, then ran into the crowd."

"I suspect that some of them were bound by enchantment," Peitar said.

"Anyway, they were gone, so Atan said we would do a mourning circle at sunset tonight. Just like Sartorans have done for centuries! I felt a bit like some kind of spy, being the only one not a Sartoran, for Rel was gone. But Atan seemed to like me being there, and oh, I felt like a girl in one of the old stories! Then, when we got back, Merewen was there, and Atan smiled again. I was afraid she would never smile again, and I wondered if it was being a queen that made her so solemn. Even sort of sad."

Peitar Selenna frowned a little as he gazed out the window. As usual, Lilah found it impossible to tell what her brother was thinking. Outside their cozy parlor room, snow fell with steady softness. Beyond that, Lake Tseos lay, a silvery frozen stretch. And beyond the lake, way beyond, impossible to see through the soft white fall, were the mountains that divided Sarendan from Sartor, which was now free.

"Go on," Peitar murmured.

Lilah sighed. "Then they all went home, and we were alone. And I think she wanted to explore that palace, but I got the feeling she wanted to do it by herself. Because she didn't ask me to come, like she did for the mourning circle. She asked me what I wanted, and I said if she didn't need any more help, could she send me home. Sartor has about a million years of customs and rules and stuff, and I felt like I didn't belong."

Peitar nodded. "I see. So you felt you'd shifted from help to being another problem for her to solve."

"Exactly," Lilah said, relieved her brother under-stood, and that his pensive expression — so oddly a mirror to Atan's after Rel left — had vanished. "She made me promise to come back, and wants to talk to you when she can."

"Of course she's welcome," Peitar said, still smiling. "Good job, Lilah. In fact, a great job. I could not have done half so well. Here, your dinner's gone cold. Let's get some hot chocolate, shall we?"

SARTOR'S REBIRTH

Atan walked inside the palace, *her* palace, knowing what had to come next. She would have to arrange tomorrow's coronation. It would be a slapdash affair, but that was all right. Nobody would expect the customary panoply because everything was still a mess, and her father's body had probably been Disappeared a century ago.

Holding the ceremony three days after the death of a king was custom, and Tsauderei had taught her enough about history to understand that when everyone willingly participates in custom, it means they want order.

She would have to find a crown in that storage room upstairs, if they hadn't all been looted, and she'd go inspect the Star Chamber room, which she knew the servants had been cleaning. She had no idea how badly it might have been damaged, but it was the traditional space, so they would meet there and knit order back, one person at a time, as they spoke the old vows.

Then would come all the messy stuff as life resumed.

Tonight she must contact Tsauderei and talk to him, and she would bring Gehlei back, for she'd promised her once to give her any position she wanted. Gehlei had said, *Not for me the coronets and lands, and all the elbow-wrassle of politics and precedence. And I'm too old to take up the sword once more. Make me steward of your palace, and I will make it a home again.*

All that could wait a little while yet. The first thing she had to do, while she was by herself, was to go into her parents' wing.

She took a candle and climbed alone to the area that Gehlei had described so well. She looked up at the stairwell, the light making the long shadows jump over scorched tapestries and a few shattered statues. She tried to scold herself into practicality. The violence had taken place almost a century ago, not yesterday.

She trod upward until she reached the royal wing. She laid her hands on the latches to the double doors, drew in a deep breath, and then opened them.

Horrible imaginings of blood and mayhem, or burnings or lootings, had troubled her ever since she was small. The dim light revealed the three main rooms, each opening onto the next.

She set the candle down and experimentally snapped her fingers. To her surprise, the glowglobes responded with a flood of light. Either the spells were good after a century, or they had frozen in time.

Unless someone had been here and renewed them.

The outer room was a kind of parlor, apparently undisturbed. The next was the bedroom. Again she snapped her fingers and said the word, and light glowed into being. There, just as Gehlei had described it, lay her mother's nightgown, thrown across the bed.

Grief seized Atan by the heart as horribly as if the tragedy had happened yesterday. Tears flooded her eyes as she remembered Gehlei's words... *and your mother dressed, giving orders all the while, while your father clutched his head, exclaiming in bits of unrelated poetry while he searched all through his desk, leaving everything a welter of papers. It was the last time I saw them, for I took her at her word, and scooped you up, and ran out into the rainstorm, glad of its cover...*

Atan scrubbed her wrist across her eyes. There was much to be done this night. But she had to finish this painful visit first.

She ran her hand over that nightgown, trying to imagine her mother's warmth in it. What scent had she worn? It would be something nice, like fresh flowers. Atan lifted the fine fabric and pressed it to her cheek. It smelled like dust and cotton, and a fleeting sense of autumn leaves, carried in no doubt through the windows left open these many years.

Atan laid it gently down and looked around, aware of some kind of anomaly. Everything was orderly, with no signs of looting. The wardrobe — she opened it — was still full of clothes.

She trod to the far door, the one to her father's private study. It was a beautifully appointed room, dominated by an equally tidy desk.

"...leaving everything a welter of papers..."

There was no welter of papers here. The desk was orderly, the papers stacked and aligned. By whose hand? Atan knew it could not have been her father's, for he had been so desperate that last night. Even at the best of times, he had apparently seldom been very orderly.

Someone had confined the pillaging to the west wing — someone with enough control over Norsundrians, who were not known for merciful treatment of their prey.

She looked at the desk, sickened at the thought of Detlev, for it could only be he, seated here at her father's desk, reading everything at his leisure.

She approached, her flesh unwilling, her mind clamoring. She had to know.

She looked down at the papers in their stacks. The words were difficult to make out in the light from the bedroom. She snapped her fingers and said the magic word, and the glowglobes forced back the shadows.

She turned back to the desk.

The first stack of papers appeared to be domestic lists. Another was of logistical reports for an evacuation order that apparently was never carried out. More — lists of fallen, of demands, of losses.

On the top shelf, a single paper lay, with a note in a neat, slanted hand.

She bent closer, picked it up, and discovered her full name written out.

Yustnesveas Landis ...

She dropped it as though her fingers had been stung. It had to be from a Norsundrian, for surely no one else could have been here.

Her first instinct was to carry the note straight to the fireplace and use magic to make a blaze, but she knew this was a stupid idea, that whatever the note said, it was better to know than to wonder and perhaps to be denied, through her own weakness, a clue to her enemy's thought.

She sat down at her father's desk and, without touching the paper again, read the words written there.

> *The report has just reached me that my orders*
> *have not in fact been carried out, and your*
> *governess dispatched the one who would have*
> *been your assassin —*

Coldness roughened the flesh along Atan's outer arms. This letter had been written not long after the defeat — and — she glanced down to the bottom — it was unsigned, but she knew. She *knew* it had to be from Detlev himself.

Her heartbeat drummed in her ears. She read on.

> *Though my subordinates are roaming about,*
> *gloating over their victory, your continued*
> *existence causes me to consider this exercise*
> *incomplete.*

Tension tightened the back of Atan's neck.

All right, she thought, get some control. The villain is not omniscient — or I wouldn't be here. He's assuming that I would someday reappear, and that I — or some-one — might manage to negate his spells, or else I would never see this nasty note of his. So here comes the threat, no doubt.

> *You will do well to remember that what I begin*
> *I always finish.*

She looked up. Well, that was sufficiently sinister.

The instinct to glance fearfully at shadows for lurking Norsundrians tensed her muscles, so she forced herself to get to her feet and to cross the room, and look out the broad window overlooking the river below, and on the other side, the broad boulevard of the Chandos

Way below Parleas Terrace. In the darkness, orange glowed skyward — bonfires. They were part of the celebration, for through the open window came the sounds of singing.

Facts.

Detlev was *not* here. Nor had he appeared to wrest Sartor back. She'd won. The singing swelled as people added their voices. Directly below the window, someone laughed.

Right now the city was hers. The kingdom was hers. Battered, bewildered, and a century backward, Sartor was hers. Impoverished, grief-stricken, angry, facing a winter with few resources, Sartor was hers. Its problems were hers, and its defense was hers.

Was she happy? No, her feelings were too deep for mere happiness. What she felt as she stood at the window in her parents' silent room, listening to the singing voices in the rise and fall of the melodic triplets of Sartoran music — once thought vanished from the world — and looking out at the ancient rooftops outlined by the ruddy glow of bonfires, was joy. It was a quiet joy, a determined joy, one aware of sadness.

As soon as she could, she would show Tsauderei the letter and discuss a strategy. She knew what he'd say — more important, she knew what to do. She would regard Detlev's threat as a warning.

Imagining Tsauderei's smile and his slow clap of approval, she laughed and slid the note into one of the pockets of the gown she'd sewn when she was a dreaming princess sitting in the Delfina cottage and wondering what her future would bring.

This was her life, and it was just beginning.

About the Author

Sherwood Smith studied in Europe before earning a Master's degree in history. She worked as a governess, a bartender, an electrical supply verifier, and wore various hats in the film industry before turning to teaching for twenty years. To date she's published over fifty books, one of which was an Anne Lindbergh Honor Book; she's twice been a finalist for the Mythopoeic Fantasy Award and once a Nebula finalist. Her YA fantasy novel *Crown Duel* has been in print for over twenty years.

She reviews books at Goodreads and blogs intermittently at Dreamwidth.

Find her at Patreon.

Visit her website www.sherwoodsmith.net, and sign up for her newsletter to learn about new books!

About Book View Café

Book View Café is a professional authors' publishing co-operative offering DRM-free e-books in multiple formats to readers around the world. With authors in a variety of genres including mystery, romance, fantasy, and science fiction, Book View Café has something for everyone.

Book View Café is good for readers because you can enjoy high-quality DRM-free e-books from your favorite authors at a reasonable price.

Book View Café is good for writers because 90% of the proceeds goes directly to the book's author.

Book View Café authors include New York Times and USA Today bestsellers, Nebula, Hugo, Lambda, Chanticleer, National Reader's Choice, and Philip K. Dick Award winners, World Fantasy, Kirkus, and Rita Award nominees, and winners and nominees of many other publishing awards.

BOOK VIEW CAFE

bookviewcafe.com

www.ingramcontent.com/pod-product-compliance
Lightning Source LLC
Chambersburg PA
CBHW051139030726
47504CB00004B/953